HUNT
FOR THE
FALLEN STAR

QUANTUM TREK BOOK 1

CHRISTOPHER COX

Join the Quantum Trek monthly email newsletter

Hunt for the Fallen Star

Quantum Trek Book 1

Book cover © 2024 by Christopher Cox

Line edits and proofreading by Motif Edits — www.motifedits.com.

ISBN (Hardcover): 978-1-7330186-4-7

ISBN (Paperback): 978-1-7330186-5-4

ISBN (Ebook): 978-1-7330186-6-1

To my beautiful, patient, loving, wonderful wife, Esther. For years, this book has languished, but with her support and encouragement, it's now a reality.

And also to my children, who continually want to know if I've been working on my books.

———◉———

Our dreams are limited only by our belief in what we see through eyes of faith.

Thank You

Thank you for choosing my book.

As an independently published author, you, as a reader, are vital to help me as an author.

While I enjoyed writing *Hunt for the Fallen Star*, what matters is if you are entertained with the adventure.

When you're finished (or even before the end) if you liked my book please recommend it to others. The best way you can help is through a short written review on the book's page of the site where you purchased the book, and a short post on social media. Both, or either one, would be helpful.

Most people appreciate a good book recommendation from a trusted friend. Be that trusted friend.

Once again, Thank You!

Christopher Cox

———◦———

Want a taste of what's to come in this book? Check out *Hunt for the Fallen Star* book trailers on YouTube

Contents

Chapter One

A New Pyramid

C ASEY'S LEGS FELT LIKE gelatin, straining to keep him upright. Ahead of him, his brother, James, had stopped, machete paused mid-swing, legs crouched slightly for balance as the ground shook beneath them. Between the brothers, their best friend, Heather, held her machete low while her body swayed with the ground swells.

The incessant buzzing of mosquitoes and insects was silenced by the violent and random shaking of the jungle undergrowth. Unknown objects dropped from the canopy overhead and crashed through branches before thudding into the ground. Ten seconds later the shaking subsided, and the low din of jungle buzz resumed.

Heather brushed aside a strand of brunette hair from her sweat-streaked, tanned face. "Do you think that was the mainshock?"

Casey's left hand tugged at his khaki shirt, the moisture resisting his efforts to unstick the fabric from his chest. "Maybe," he said with a wry smile. "It was the biggest of the last few days. But, if a bigger quake hits, this would just be another foreshock."

James wiped his beige, rolled-up sleeve against the dark-blond hair plastered to his forehead. "At least we're not in the concrete jungle, where walls might fall on us." He looked back at his older, and shorter, brother. "Any idea how much further? I'm guessing we're about where your LIDAR showed the pyramid."

The wide brim of Casey's jungle hat drooped, his machete hanging limp in his right hand as his left studied a small global-positioning device hanging from a lanyard. "It looks like we're about there." He wiped away a drip of sweat sneaking towards his eye and looked ahead at an apparent dead end of greenery.

Shards of filtered green light danced through rare openings in the jungle roof. The air was thick, humid, and filled with buzzing dots. The entangled jungle understory and floor layers made it almost impossible to see more than a few feet away. Small game paths randomly crisscrossed the ground and cut under foliage.

Casey shrugged. "Maybe another fifty feet. Of course, in this mess we could probably walk right past and not see it."

Raising his machete again, James hacked into the wall of green. A barrier of large leaves, choked with snake-like vines, fell beneath his cut. He and Heather stopped at the sight before them. Distracted by a squadron of mosquitoes, Casey nearly walked into Heather.

With a large grin, James shot a glance at his brother. "You gotta love GPS."

Barely visible among the jungle growth, a stony, one-hundred-foot-wide, triangular mound rose fifty feet up from the ground. Random vegetation and trees covered the pyramid-like sides and reached skyward from one-time steps eroded from centuries of weather. Wind-deposited dust, soil, and debris filled cracks and crevices, and provided locations of opportunity for intrepid plant life. The trees on the pyramid mound were not as high or thick as the surrounding jungle. The top trees were smaller, and their perch on the ancient structure gave the illusion of a small depression in the jungle expanse. Above them a tropical blue sky filled the afternoon. The threesome picked their way towards the base of the vegetation-infested ruins.

"Well, that looks like what I saw on the drone's LIDAR yesterday," said Casey.

"What do you think we'll find?" asked Heather.

James shrugged. "Who knows? Maybe nothing. That's probably why the professor wanted us to check it out first."

"Not to mention he's up to his eyeballs in the Temple of the Sun back at the dig site, trying to discover if the supposed tomb is actually an antechamber to something more," said Casey.

James pointed his machete to the left. "Let's split up for an initial assessment. I'll go left around the base. Heather, you go right. Maybe there's a base entrance, like at the sun temple. Casey, you go up and see what you can see."

Heather and James each started around the perimeter of the ancient structure. Casey looked up the green-encrusted slope, wiped a bead of sweat from his forehead, and muttered, "I'm sure it'll be just like the other side of the temple."

Slowly, Casey climbed to the top. The edges of eroded steps crumbled underfoot, and he paused to catch his breath while wondering what he was looking for. His expertise was technology and aircraft, not archaeology. Throughout his short climb, he appraised the ancient temple; was he looking for a way inside, artifacts, or signs of the ancient civilization?

After a few minutes, he reached the fairly flat, twenty-foot-square top. Crumpled remains of short walls surrounded the top, eroded columns at each corner and four-foot openings at the midpoint of each wall. Through the squat trees that tangled among the broken stones he could see the vegetation stretching down the four sides of the pyramid onto the jungle floor. The tenacious plant life, bushes, and trees grappled the cracks, desperately seeking the sparse soil deposited onto the pyramid by ancient weather.

Cautiously, he walked around the top edges. Below him, amid the trees, he saw his companions scouting the base of the pyramid. He took turns watching each one as they quickly glanced or poked into the occasional crack or crevice. Beyond the pyramid, trees filled the junglescape like swells of a multi-green ocean.

He turned his attention back to the pyramid's top. At its center, a large flat stone lay across a once-circular altar, its edges chipped and eroded. Pieces of jagged mortar clung from gaps, crumbs littering the ground. Hoping for a better view of the jungle, Casey hopped onto the altar. There was a crack, and a hand-size section split along the top-stone. Looking down, flecks of red between the cracked edges caught his eye.

Curious, Casey jumped off and tried to remove the broken section. After a few minutes of adjusting his grip, pulling, and pushing, the broken piece scraped and fell off the top. He jumped to the side when it crashed near his feet. Images of ancient characters and drawings marked the newly exposed surface of a second top-stone, this one hidden under the first, and its surface was smoother than expected, except for fresh scratches from the sliding stone.

He examined the broken edge of the top-stone that still capped the altar. It was a couple inches thick and rested on regularly spaced, small pieces of wood that suspended the flat slab above its base. The poor mortar job around the edges looked like the top-stone had been laid quickly to hide the real top.

Casey pulled a small shovel from his pack and scraped its blade around the edge, easily breaking away the old mortar. He tried to move the stubborn top slab, but it refused to budge. Remembering the scratches, he decided he needed help.

He went to the back edge of the pyramid. Below him, among the trees at the base, James was examining something hiding in the bushes. From Casey's right, Heather was converging on James's position.

Casey cupped his hands around his mouth. "Hey you guys! I think I found something."

James looked up. "What'd you find?"

"Looks like an altar, smaller than the sun temple, but there's, like, a painting under the top."

Heather cocked her head. "Don't break anything," she said as she started climbing the pyramid.

Casey's cheeks warmed, and he refrained from responding.

James looked back down into the nearby bushes. "I found something as well. Maybe an opening. Looks like it may have recently opened up. Probably from all the tremors we've been having lately."

James marked his find with a small rock mound then climbed the pyramid, joining them where Heather was already examining the portion of newly exposed altar.

"Looks like there may be petroglyphs of some sort under the slab." Heather pointed at small, regularly spaced piles of wood debris on the surface. "This is probably why the top piece broke. Looks like the wooden slats that were holding it up have disintegrated."

"I tried to move it, but it's gotta weigh at least as much as I do," said Casey.

"Guess we need to get you some more exercise," teased James.

"Very funny," replied Casey. "Although it's true I don't have the finger strength you do with rock climbing."

Heather's voice carried a slight rebuke. "We need to be careful not to damage the images anymore. Maybe we should get more of the team here."

"We're supposed to be checking this place out, to see if it's worth the team's time," replied Casey. "Without seeing what's underneath, how can we really know?"

"Casey's got a point." James shrugged. "The dig's taking all the professor's time and the team's limited resources. There're so many ruins hiding in the jungle it's impossible to begin to figure out which ones are worth checking out." He nodded reassuringly at Heather. "We'll be careful, but we need to be quick. I found something we should check out, and we're on a time crunch."

He pointed around the slab. "Spread out around the top-stone. The three of us should be able to lift this. And watch your fingers. Ready?"

The others nodded as they positioned themselves around the altar.

"On the count of three, lift and set it against the side. One. Two. Three."

They grunted, and Heather winced as the stone scraped slightly from its location. A moment later, they set one end of the slab on the ground.

Heather's eyes shot back to the newly exposed top. "Wow! That's incredible." Her wide eyes squinted. "I think we found a big piece of the puzzle."

On the left side of the exposed surface were carved images of the sun, moon, and several stars, each with ancient hieroglyphic characters nearby. Fading colors hinted that the carvings had been brightly painted in the past. To the right was a large carved circle with six smaller concentric circles inside of it. Around three of the circles were repeating images. The other three circles had differing characters. In the center, a face stuck its tongue out.

"Looks like a variation of the Mayan calendar, probably adapted for the local culture," said Heather. She studied the circular relief on the right. "But I'm not sure about the characters on the other parts. Some of them kind of look Egyptian." She shook her head. "But that can't be right. Not in Central America." She took out a small digital camera and began snapping photos.

Casey pointed to the sun, moon, and stars. "Aren't those arranged like points of an upside-down triangle?"

Near Casey, the moon image was at the bottom point. At the top left was a stylized image of the sun made in the similarity of a compass rose. On the top right, equidistant from the sun and the moon, was a cluster of seven stars. Six stars formed a hexagon around a single center star with streaks radiating upwards. More hieroglyphic-like characters were under the center star.

"Heather, are these runes?" asked James, pointing to some of the characters inside the cluster of stars.

Heather shifted her attention to the glyphs James was pointing at. She shook her head, unconvinced. "No. Runic alphabets are more from ancient Germanic languages. There have been some runestones found in North America, but I haven't heard of any in Central or South America. And those characters aren't familiar to me."

"I thought I'd seen them before..." James stopped when he noticed Casey's wide eyes.

"Aren't those like the markings on your crystal?" asked Casey.

Recognition lit James's eyes, and he nodded.

Heather's brow lifted with her unspoken question while James pulled a silver chain from inside his shirt. Hanging from the chain was a small sinewy cage that protected a crystal disc.

"Is this about your lucky charm?" asked Heather.

James pulled aside some of the sinew and freed the small circular crystal. With the crystal in his palm, he asked, "Can you see them?"

Heather leaned in closer. The crystal was opaque with silver hues that glittered in the sunlight. It was thin, about the thickness of a quarter. She shook her head. "Looks like it usually does."

James rubbed the crystal briskly for several seconds and held it out for Heather to watch. A sixteen-pointed star, which looked like a compass rose, appeared. Four large points were equally spaced around the center. Between these were four intermediate points, and shorter points radiated from between those. A couple dozen tiny, but discernible, characters appeared around the edge. Several were identical to those under the center star on the altar.

"Why didn't you show this to me before?" accused Heather.

"I have," said James, "though I probably forgot to show you the writing. And we didn't have any idea what it might have meant."

"So, what does it mean?" asked Casey.

James nodded. "That's the question. Though I'd guess the disc came from this culture."

"Just like the tribal elder told you," said Casey.

Heather examined the crystal disc in James's hand, the rune-like characters slowly fading. "I'll need to get a closer look when we're back at camp and compare it to the pictures I took. But, if it's really like what's on the stone, it's not familiar to me."

Casey's eyes shifted from the crystal to the altar top. His left brow rose. He pulled out the GPS and looked at the sun image on the stone.

Then he turned slightly to face the star cluster. "Interesting. I think it's a map. From where we are, here at the moon, the sun image is in direction of the dig site."

"So, there might still be a temple for the stars in that direction," said James, continuing Casey's thought. His voice carried an edge of excitement as his eyes tried to pierce the dense jungle growth. "Maybe one particular Temple of the Fallen Star."

"Didn't your drone scan this whole area?" Heather asked Casey.

"The information the professor discovered only indicated something in this direction. With limited flight time, I flew the drone out for a LIDAR scan this far and confirmed these ruins. There wasn't anything to point us that way."

A satisfied smile lifted his mouth as James's eyes lit up. "Now we have another lead."

"I'll take it on a flight tomorrow to see what the scan uncovers," said Casey, "but there's no time today if we're going to check out what you found."

Heather snapped a few more photos before they climbed down the pyramid to the marker James had placed.

"Careful," said James as they neared his small rock pile, "the ground started to give way when I was looking into that crack, right before Casey shouted down."

They cautiously approached the jagged, dark edges gaping at them through the undergrowth. Casey took a flashlight from his pack and pointed it into the blackness. The opening was a few feet wide and angled sharply down a fifteen-foot dirt slide. The odor of freshly exposed, moist dirt, mixed with decaying vegetation, filled the nostrils. Dirt and rocks intertwined with roots down the slide to where an opening broke under a large foundation stone.

Pointing down, James commented, "I think the recent quakes might've broken something loose down there, along the foundation, and caused the ground to sink in. I think it's probably safe enough to go down, at least with a rope to get back up."

Heather shook her head disapprovingly. "I don't. But I know better than to convince you otherwise. Just be careful."

James gave Heather a mischievous grin as he retrieved a rope from his pack. "You may want your lights, just in case there's something interesting down there for you to take photos of." He tied the rope securely to a nearby tree and carefully fed it down the dirt throat. He replaced his hat with a headlamp and slid feet first down the opening. Loose rocks and dirt cascaded below and chased after him. He quickly reached the opening in the foundation and slid through.

James's voice returned muffled from the hole, "I'm good. Give me a couple minutes to look around. Get ready in case it's worth coming down."

Heather shook her head while she and Casey put headlamps on and stuffed their jungle hats into their day packs. A minute later Casey's light illuminated James's dirt-encrusted face smiling up from the dark abyss.

"You guys gotta see this!" James said. "Heather, you'll definitely want photos."

Chapter Two

Narrow Escape

WITHIN MINUTES, HEATHER AND Casey slid down and through a broken section of the foundation wall.

Heather's light focused on the break in the foundation. "The rocks in this section look different than the rest of the wall. It may have been an entrance at one time, but it looks like it was quickly filled in for some reason."

"Yeah, and badly done," said Casey. "Must've been in a hurry to cover it up. Probably the same reason for the rush job on the altar."

"You two can debate things later," said James. "Right now, you've got to come see this."

He led them along a short passage where the walls were close enough that outstretched arms easily touched them. A half-dozen paces later they entered a square chamber, the size of a large bedroom. A blanket of dust covered the remnants of once-colorful murals on the walls to the left and in front of them. Small chunks of stone were discarded on the floor, torn from the walls as a testament to ancient vandals and robbers who had been there first to loot. Among the murals were star clusters and constellations. Another passage was centered on the right wall, but flashlights quickly revealed its abrupt end in a pile of rubble.

The walls of the room were made of upper and lower stone sections. The lower panels were about three feet wide and seven feet tall, with five panels per wall except at the two walls with passages, where two stone panels were on either side of the openings. Ancient cement filled the minuscule joints between stones. Spanning across the lower wall sections was a three-foot-high stone cap, which stretched the length of each wall. Primitive tool marks marred the walls.

"Looks like someone was trying to find something," said Casey.

James nodded as his light skimmed across the damaged wall. "Or hide something."

A blinding light instantly flashed the room. Casey jumped.

"Sorry," said Heather sheepishly as she lowered her camera and rubbed her spotted vision. "I forgot the flash was on."

James squeezed his eyes shut a few times. "A warning would've been nice."

Casey stepped towards the opposite wall and swept his light across it. Amidst the severely chipped wall and tool scars were the remnants of a fragmented and faded jungle scene. Above the trees, right of center at head level, was a star with streaks that shot out in diagonal rays into the top right corner, giving the impression of a shooting star. Hiding in the trees below the star was a chipped, deformed black jaguar, its face disproportionately larger than the body. The jungle cat's eyes stared menacingly at those in the room. Small pieces were missing from its gaping mouth, and something reflected the light as it passed over the maw.

Approaching the mural, Casey pointed his light into the jaguar's mouth. Inside was a small vertical slot, barely a half inch wide, its sides lightly chipped as if something had tried to pry at it. A vertical strip of yellow light reflected from inside the slot.

Wondering what Casey had found, James and Heather followed him across the room.

Heather bent slightly to peer inside the mouth. "How'd you see that?"

"I think it was the flash that reflected off it. But something about this section of wall seems different. It doesn't look as damaged. Almost like the same tools couldn't do much to this wall."

Casey pulled out the knife on his multi-tool and started poking in the slot. The knife tip was barely long enough to clip the edge of the object. A minute later, a gold, coin-shaped object rolled out, and Casey caught it. He turned it over in his fingers. On one side was some runic lettering, and a shooting star was engraved on the other.

"I think you hit the jackpot," said James.

"It might actually be gold," said Casey. "Definitely has a little weight to it."

Casey's attention returned to the painting remnants. In the center of the star was another slot, camouflaged among the dark flecks and chips. He shone his light inside and poked around with his knife. Then he stopped and cocked his head at James. "What was it you said the tribal elder told you? About finding the twin star?"

James thought for a moment. "His instructions were: 'The Fallen Star and the Bridge of Light need two stars. Take the star to the star in the moon. Place the star in the star and shine its light. The second star is beyond Ek Balam.' My English translation doesn't sound as good." James's eyes lit up. "Wait! Ek Balam is a black jaguar. Do you think this is it?"

Casey nodded. "The 'star in the star?' Do you think your crystal is the star he was talking about?"

James pulled the crystal disc out, released it from its protection, and flipped it over between his finger and thumb. "Maybe. What do you think we need to do with it?"

Casey pointed to the slot in the star. "We're in the moon temple. Put the star in the star."

James stepped to the wall and peered into the star in the mural. He hesitantly turned the crystal over in his right hand. "I don't know. I'd hate to lose this."

"Okay," said Casey, "then let's just go back and let the professor know."

James's eyes narrowed at his brother. He pinched the small disc and placed it into the slot. It slid back beyond his reach. Nothing happened.

"All right, you two," said Heather, shaking her head. "You're going to have to come clean about what James was told and what you guys know. But first, were you told what was supposed to happen?"

James shrugged. He pointed his flashlight into the slot to see if he could retrieve his crystal. The light splintered into the crystal, and, for an instant, the slot was brightly lit with refracted light. The wall reverberated with a muffled growl.

Heather's brow rose in concern. "I hope you didn't set off a booby trap. I'd hate to try to run out of here with a big boulder chasing after us. Or a spiked ceiling crushing down."

"No," said James, his eyes moved to the ceiling. "I think we're safe where spiked ceilings are concerned."

"And boulders rolling down seems unlikely as well," added Casey.

They stared at the wall. Nothing changed. No movement. No sound.

"You two are freaking me out," said Heather.

Casey leaned forward and pressed his ear to the wall. He didn't hear anything, but it felt different. When he pushed back from the wall, he felt a little give, almost imperceptibly. "I think it's a door. Help me push."

"Are you serious?" asked Heather. "That wall looks solid. Whoever hacked at it didn't budge it. Even if these rock sections weren't part of a wall holding up a pyramid above us, they probably weigh a ton or more."

James shrugged and joined Casey against the wall. Heather resigned herself and helped push. For a moment, nothing happened.

Then crackling, like the soft crunch of freshly fallen leaves, resounded in the half-dark. Vertical cracks sprinted up and ripped around the center of the wall, outlining the jaguar and star section. Pieces of ancient cement broke, and the joints tore open from the floor up to about seven feet on both sides of the three-foot wall section. A horizontal seam exposed itself and joined the tops of the two vertical ones. The right side, where James was pushing, moved inwards a quarter of an inch and stopped. Encouraged, they pushed harder. But the wall section refused to budge any further. They stopped after a couple of minutes to rest.

"Well, that was fun," said James. "I don't think I've done that workout before."

"Call it an exercise in futility," remarked Heather.

Casey stepped back. "Do you think it's supposed to open the other way? I mean, maybe we're pushing, but the sign says to pull."

"I didn't see any sign," said Heather. "And how are we supposed to pull when there's nothing to grab hold of?"

"Except," said James thoughtfully, and he looked into the jaguar's mouth and then the small opening in the star. He inserted the fingers of his left hand into the jaguar's mouth and his right fingers into the star, like pocket holds on a climbing wall. Crimping his fingers, he pulled out. More mortar broke away from the edges of the door frame. The right side of the wall section moved outward several inches, and pieces of broken stone exposed a rounded edge. James released his finger holds and stepped away to catch his breath.

Heather moved a step back. "I knew you had impressive rock-climbing skills, but your rock pulling is equally remarkable."

"I think it'll come out more. I just need to reposition myself." James looked at his left hand where some of the skin was roughened from the stone. "The vandals sure did a number on the jaguar's mouth. It almost looks like my fingers have been chewed on."

Heather poked her flashlight through the right edge of the stone door. About four inches from the front edge, it looked like a router had smoothly cut a beveled edge that angled back. "Looks like a small ledge, maybe a door handle on this side."

"Now that we have an idea of which way it goes," said James, "you two can try to help from the opened side."

Heather and Casey grabbed the edge to pull.

"Pull on three," said James. "One. Two. Three!"

The door resisted for a moment. Then, as if a catch had been snapped free, the door swung open to the left, and they stumbled backwards. On the backside of the door, opposite the star, James's crystal sparkled in the light beams.

"Guess the door needed some light oil," said Casey as James retrieved his crystal.

Beyond the stone door, their flashlights pierced the narrow, low-ceiling blackness and reflected off dust floating in the air. On the hinge-side of the stone door, two leaf spring-like contraptions struggled to hold the door open. Shiny flecks of metal revealed fresh breaks in the mechanism.

James's light glinted on the springs. "Well, now we know why it was so easy to open. At least, after breaking through the cement."

Casey's nose wrinkled. "Smells like it hasn't been opened in centuries."

"Probably hasn't," said Heather. "Maybe it's time we go back to camp to let the professor know."

"But do we really know it's worth checking out? Is it worth taking resources from the other dig site?" James asked. "There might be nothing back there. We're here, so we should at least see what's there. And you know the professor will want more pictures for proof."

"I'm not sure," cautioned Heather. "If those springs fail and the door closes, I don't think we can open it."

"In that case, we'll just find the emergency exit," said Casey.

"What if this is the emergency exit?" said Heather.

James waved away the warning and entered the narrow passage, followed by Casey. Heather shook her head and followed after the brothers. Twenty feet later they entered an undisturbed chamber.

On the wall across from the passage, dust-covered ceremonial staffs and spears leaned into the corners. Swords and other armaments lay on stone shelves that were built into the wall.

A long stone box lay against both left and right walls. A variety of urns sat on top of each box, some with clay lids, others open, and a few were sealed with a yellowish wax. Two levels of built-in shelves lined the right wall, each holding an assortment of daggers, knives, and ceremonial jars. A painted mural covered the left wall.

Heather's left hand stifled a gasp as her light illuminated skeletal remains on the floor near the right box. The dried skin looked like it was shrink-wrapped onto the skull and bones. Empty eye sockets stared up, and the lower jawbone hung open as if frozen in a final gasp for air. The remains of a small earthen jar lay nearby, a gray-white powder spilling out of the pieces.

Casey's flashlight hovered over the remains. "Looks like a botched robbery."

James squatted near the broken jar. "Or maybe that jar had some kind of poison or embalming stuff in it that killed this guy, and then sped up the drying process."

"That's probable." Heather nodded. "He could be the one set to guard this place. And, if those boxes are sarcophagi, he'd also be here to protect whoever might be in them. I think it's time to get some documentation and get back to camp." She brought her camera up to her face. "Picture," she warned.

For an instant, the stone chamber was brightly illuminated. A spark on the left wall caught Casey's eye. While blinking away the spots from his eyes, he aimed his light at the wall. Another camera flash, and this time Casey saw the source of the sparkle.

Similar to the painting in the previous room, the mural depicted a jungle scene. The difference was this mural was undisturbed. The treed landscape had three native homes, which resembled grass huts, in the foreground. The sun was high in the left side of the sky, and the moon was low in the center. High on the right, a stylized falling star was depicted with elongated triangles pointing outward like eight directions of a compass. Rainbow streaks stretched from the star upwards to the right corner. The twinkle of light had come from the falling star's center.

Heather and James watched Casey's light pan across the mural. Casey moved to the far end of the stone box to get a closer look. A circular crystal in the star's center refracted flecks of light around the room. Casey reached up to touch the crystal, and it moved slightly. He pinched it between his fingers and gently pulled.

"No! Wait!" shouted Heather.

The crystal popped out effortlessly. Casey was startled, partly from Heather's shout and also because he had not expected the crystal to come out. At first it felt cool in his hand, and then it quickly warmed. He held the wafer-thin, one-inch-diameter crystal up close to his face. In the wall it had looked clear, but in his hands it was more silver.

James leaned in closer. "Looks like mine. Try rubbing it."

Casey rubbed the crystal briskly for a few seconds and held it up. The added heat revealed a faint sixteen-point star. Along the edge, several faint glyphs began to slowly appear.

"Question for you two," said Heather. "How'd you figure out the rubbing thing?"

James smiled. "By accident."

"James forgot his necklace by a pool. When I found it, it was hot and I noticed some markings on it," added Casey.

"Normal body heat doesn't seem to affect it. So, after the markings faded, we tried rubbing it to see if the extra warmth had a similar effect."

"It seems this crystal is of the same material as yours," Heather said to James. She added to Casey, "But you should've left it in place until this place was categorized. We need to get a team back here to get it documented, before it gets more disturbed."

A faint rumble reverberated through the floor, walls, and ceiling. The rumble transitioned into shaking.

James's eyes darted around the room where some artifacts wobbled. "Did you set off a booby trap?"

Pocketing the crystal, Casey replied, "Feels like another tremor."

"We better take cover, in case something falls on us," Heather suggested just as the shaking stopped.

Casey grinned. "See, just another small quake. It didn't even knock over any of the jars."

"Yeah, but there've been a lot of tremors lately," said James.

A loud crack echoed from the passageway, and three flashlight beams shot towards the sound. The light pierced the short passage to the open door where the blackness of the antechamber was disappearing.

"The door's closing!" shouted Heather, and she and James sprinted down the passage.

Looking around the room, Casey stuffed a dagger into his belt and grabbed a couple spears and short swords from the wall before racing to help.

When Casey reached the closing door, James was desperately trying to push the heavy stone open. Heather had barely squeezed through, but the opening was now too tight for either brother. She desperately tried to pull the door open from her side.

Casey jabbed one spear into the narrowing gap at the top. The stone crushed to a stop against the spear shaft. Glancing at the double leaf spring mechanisms, he saw one had snapped. The other was straining under the full weight of the door, flecks of metal popping off. Casey angled one short sword in the doorway, bracing it between the wall and stone door. He slid the second spear out the opening and then he grabbed the first spear's shaft to try prying the door open. Combined with James pushing and Heather pulling, the door opened a couple more inches.

After shifting the spearhead, Casey used his feet to shove the short sword down a few inches to further wedge open the door. "Get through, James!"

Hesitant, James stopped pushing. When the door held in place, he squeezed through the opening while Heather helped him from the other side.

Heather pointed to a nearby debris pile. "Help me get some of those stones," she urged. "We need something more to jam the door open."

James grabbed a couple of the large stones and placed them in the door's opening. None were large enough to keep the door open on their own.

SNAP!

"Umph!" groaned Casey, and he fell back holding the shaft of the spear.

The obsidian spearhead fell to the floor where it shattered into volcanic confetti. The sword wedge was starting to slip from its position with the full weight of the door pressed against it. James grappled the door's edge, braced his feet against the wall, and pulled against the closing slab. The movement paused.

Casey tossed his pack through the opening and started squeezing through. He grunted when the stone shifted.

"No," wheezed James, his face dark red with the strain. His feet pushed against the wall while he struggled to force the door back.

Heather's wide eyes searched the dim room desperately. Seeing the spear on the floor, she grabbed and thrust it through the opening below Casey and James, levering the door open. The stone's movement paused momentarily, then jerked, snapped the spear shaft, and toppled Heather backwards.

"I'm through," gasped Casey as he pulled his legs clear.

James released his horizontal squat and fell onto his brother.

Another loud crack reverberated through the door slab, and the stones James had placed began to retreat from their futile efforts to hold the heavy door open. Between the doorway and massive stone door, the angled short sword cowered, bent back from the encroaching stone, and then slid back into the black passage. In a few seconds only the odd pile of small rocks next to the wall hinted at anything unusual.

James slowly stood. "You guys okay?"

"Yes, barely," breathed Casey from the floor. "I know I could lose a few pounds, but I don't need to get that skinny."

Heather punched Casey on the shoulder. "Don't do that again."

Casey rubbed his shoulder and grinned. "I think it's time to take Heather's advice and get back to camp to report our findings."

They picked up their gear and headed back to the opening. Heather quickly wormed up the hole with the aid of the rope.

"Hurry up. I feel like I'm still shaking all over," Heather called down.

Inside, dust started falling from the ceiling.

"Uh, um, I think there's another tremor," said Casey. "I know we're supposed to stop, drop, and hang on, but I'd rather be on the surface."

Rocks and debris began cascading down the hole as Casey and James scurried up. When James reached the top, a seismic ground wave knocked them off-balance, and the shaking intensified. They scooted away from the hole as the sides began to crumble and fall in. Several large rocks broke free and tumbled down the earthen mouth, only to be stuck in the throat. Dust and dirt swirled and billowed, and the hole seemed to cough with the onslaught of debris. After nearly a minute, the rumbling stopped, and the one-time hole looked more like a shallow pit.

"I don't know about you two, but I think I've had enough close calls for the day," said Casey.

James half-smiled and then laughed. "You should see your faces! You two are filthy."

One corner of Heather's mouth lifted in a smile. "But at least I don't look and smell as bad as you." Her eyes narrowed at Casey. "There's a reason you don't take things from archaeological sites." She sighed at the pyramid, frowning. "I wonder how much was damaged, and if we can get back inside. That mural was amazing. You two may not know it, but it's extremely rare to find metal swords like what we saw down there. Many people still believe ancient Americans didn't have metal swords."

"You mean like this one?" Casey grabbed a hilt protruding from his pack and pulled out the second short sword.

Heather punched him on the upper arm. "Don't you ever learn!"

"What? We're out safe."

"Barely. Especially you."

James leaned over towards his brother. "Let me see that," he said, offering his hand.

Casey handed the sword hilt to his brother. "And I grabbed one of the daggers as well." He removed the dagger from his belt and showed it to Heather.

Heather shook her head. "You two and your fascination with swords and weapons."

"As I recall from our many martial arts classes, it's not like you don't like them too," James teased.

Heather smiled sheepishly.

Casey placed the dagger into his pack and then pulled the crystal from his pocket. The waning daylight sent a rainbow through the crystal onto his hand.

James glanced at his brother. "Do you think that's the twin star?"

Casey nodded.

Heather's head cocked at the brothers. She decided to be practical instead of asking her questions. "We should head back before it gets dark. Maybe the professor can give us some insight into that crystal."

"Maybe," James said doubtfully.

Chapter Three
At Camp

T HE JUNGLE CANOPY WAS rapidly darkening in the evening twilight when they emerged into the clearing. To their right, on the east, fringes of the ancient ruins of the sun temple were swallowed by the encroaching jungle. Intrepid vegetation disguised the old Mesoamerican temple as an obscured pyramid-like rise in the jungle at the edge of a natural clearing. The archaeological camp lay ahead of them in the center of the large clearing where a variety of grasses prevailed. Sparse trees sprouted randomly throughout the field, among scattered bushes and other low-lying vegetation. A small road—used weekly for supplies and little more than a trail—was a black hole in the jungle fringe to the left. A cluster of old olive-green canvas military tents stood in the center like dark sentinels against the backdrop of a blacker rainforest.

The few dig workers and staff had already finished dinner and were about their evening tasks or relaxing from their day. Voices, muffled by canvas walls, offered snatches of conversation as the threesome passed on their way to the center of the small tent city.

The central structure was a large military tent. The flaps on three sides were rolled and tied up, which exposed the regularly spaced wooden tent poles. A green-colored mosquito net draped the sides and billowed gently while two large industrial fans near the unopened fourth wall pushed humid air throughout the tent. A dozen beat-up tables, surrounded by folding chairs, were scattered around the four central poles that supported the tent's ridge. Five of the local workers gathered around a solar battery-powered TV, watching and yelling at a soccer game. The TV's speaker crackled as an overzealous announcer described the plays in animated Spanish, punctuating passes, steals, and a missed goal.

Before entering the tent, the threesome stopped by a portable sink to wash off some of the dirt and grime. After shaking the water off their hands, they walked through the mosquito-net door flaps at one end of the tent.

From the opposite end, where the cooking and storage tent was attached to the fourth wall, a familiar voice called out in native Spanish, "At last, the adventurers return."

Pablo, a dark-skinned native and camp chef, was finishing some cleanup as he greeted the new arrivals and placed three foil-wrapped meals on the table. "There is still some dinner left for you."

Heather smiled at him and responded in native-sounding Spanish, "Thank you for saving some food for us."

Heather and the brothers took the meals and unwrapped the foil to reveal large chicken, rice, and bean burritos.

In fluent Spanish, James asked, "Did you feel the earthquake earlier?"

"It would have been impossible not to feel it, but it didn't cause any problems here. The radio said there were some damaged buildings in the city, a few deaths, and hundreds injured."

Feeling self-conscious with his broken Spanish, Casey asked Pablo if he knew where the professor was.

"Professor Anthon is in the office taking care of some business," said Pablo.

After the three latecomers had eaten several bites, Pablo looked cautiously around and motioned them closer. His voice was hushed, "You should know, bad rumors being whispered. Some of the men are scared and talking of leaving."

"What rumors?" inquired James.

"The Anaconda," came Pablo's whispered reply.

James shot a glance at Casey and Heather.

Heather's eyes widened. "Why would they even think of our site? We haven't found anything worth stealing."

"I thought they dealt in drugs and guns," said Casey, inwardly cringing at his bad Spanish.

Heather shook her head. "They'll attack anything or anyone that can make them money. Even taking tourists for ransom if they don't just kill them."

James nodded cautiously at Casey. "If it's known the dig site found anything of worth, we'd be a target."

Pablo shrugged and finished wiping a nearby table. "I'm not that worried. I grew up with much worse. Just thought you should know."

They thanked Pablo for the food and walked out into the darkness towards the professor's office, a medium-sized military tent a short walk away. Unlike the central tent, the office tent walls were down. Light split the door flaps through the insect netting.

The drone of a fan muffled a conversation inside the office. After a short pause, the door flaps opened and the silhouette of a man, backlit by the light inside the tent, stepped out. A rifle over his left shoulder and a handgun hanging on his side indicated he was one of the two night guards.

The guard startled when he saw three people emerge from the darkness. His face relaxed as recognition set in. Without a verbal acknowledgment, he simply nodded and walked off into the night.

Heather and James pushed aside the tent flaps and entered.

Casey hesitated and watched the guard stop near one of the outermost tents. *He's on edge*, he thought. His eyes squinted into the surrounding darkness. *Something doesn't feel right*. He brushed aside the uneasiness, attributing it to Pablo's words making him imagine things. He turned, pushed the flaps aside, and entered the office.

To the right, a laptop sat on a long table that served as a desk. Small stacks of paper reflected the soft glow of the computer's screen. A folding metal chair was pushed aside. At the back of the tent, a cot was set up alongside four large waterproof shipping crates. In the center, two rectangular tables stood side by side to form a larger surface. Scattered across the tables were laminated maps of the dig site, pottery pieces, and other artifacts. Various letters and numbers were written with grease pen on some of the maps, and most of the items on the table were tagged.

Professor Dwuane Anthon was leaning over the table, his focus on several pottery shards. Most of the crew referred to him simply as the Professor, as he had doctorate degrees in ancient Mesoamerican civilizations, archaeology, and anthropology. His tall frame hunched over his examination, his back towards the door. Thinning, gray-brown hair, which had been hastily combed over earlier in the day, was now doing its own thing. Anthon's obsession with the dig kept him distracted from his unkempt look, filthy khaki pants, and beige button-up shirt.

Realizing someone had walked in the tent, Anthon looked up and turned towards the new arrivals. Several days' worth of gray-white stubble sparsely populated his jawline, neck, and around the mouth. His face had started to twist in annoyance but unwound when he recognized his visitors. The mouth relaxed as he said tiredly, "It's about time you kids got back." His eyes focused on Heather. "I could've used your language skills earlier today, but I think I got things worked out. Just set me behind a little."

Casey suppressed a half-smile, thinking the professor was always behind where he thought he should be. "Pablo said the earthquake didn't do much here."

"Maybe not for him," grumbled the professor, "But it made the day at the temple site limiting. The earlier tremors scared most of the crew. Then the big one made a mess of things I had out for cataloging. With all the interruptions, I'm finally getting around to finishing."

An aftershock rattled the sparse furnishings and knocked over a couple pieces of pottery on the table. The professor muttered under his breath, "Blasted earthquakes!"

As Heather, James, and Casey walked to the table, the professor scrutinized their dirty appearance. "So, was the day worth it? Or did you just waste your time?"

Casey stared at the table. Several of the pottery pieces had identical sun, moon, and star images as they had seen earlier while exploring the newly discovered temple pyramid. He nodded at James and Heather, who also noted the similarities.

"We found the Temple of the Moon," said James.

The professor's thinning hair seemed to twitch. "And what makes you come to that conclusion?"

Heather moved to the desk and connected her camera to the laptop computer. The professor watched while she clicked through the images. Casey realized he did not know she had taken so many.

"First, the pyramid is nearly identical in size to the sun temple," stated Heather as a picture of the vegetation-covered pyramid appeared on the screen. "On the top, Casey discovered an altar that has some kind of map on it." She pointed to an altar photo. "The images are very similar to the ones on these pottery shards, as well as some of the mural paintings you discovered inside the sun temple last week. James also found an entrance that had been recently exposed. Similar images were on a mural in the antechamber. From what I could read, among the image remnants on the outside map and inside murals, it seems a lunar calendar may have been used at that location, where you believe a solar-based calendar was being used at this site."

"Why not the Temple of the Fallen Star, as those pictures might suggest?" asked the professor, pointing at the stylized pictographs of a falling star on the mural painting.

"Based on the drone's LIDAR scan and photos yesterday, we hoped that'd be the case," said Casey, "but the map on the altar appears to indicate a third temple, where the three temples are the points of a large triangle."

Casey waited a moment while Heather zoomed in on a couple images of the map and mural painting, then continued, "I'd like to take the drone up tomorrow and scan the areas where the third temple might be. If the map's correct, the Temple of the Fallen Star is east of here, equidistant from the Temples of the Sun and Moon."

Professor Anthon's head bobbed in agreement. "An excellent idea, although we don't have the manpower to explore and document either of those sites at this time. But..." He paused, and one could almost see the thinning hairs twitch as a million thoughts raced through his mind. After a moment, he added thoughtfully, "Sufficient evidence might secure more funding, more staff, and an extended dig time. And more protection."

"And there's something else we found," added Heather.

She nodded at Casey encouragingly. He felt betrayed at first, but then smiled as he pulled out the small sword he had strapped to his pack prior to the hike back.

"That's not—" Heather started but stopped when she saw the professor's intense interest in the sword.

Professor Anthon's hands shook slightly with anticipation as he took the sword and examined it for a few minutes. "Without a more detailed analysis, all I can conclude is that the sword is not of any make currently known for this civilization, or even for this part of the world. Hmmm." His eyes moved in close to the sword, and his head cocked. "And its metal doesn't look like others I've seen. Although I admit metal swords are an extreme rarity for this time period."

He mulled over a few thoughts, and then his demeanor shifted from excitement to seriousness. He returned the sword to Casey. "It's unique, but since it's not part of our current dig, and may be unrelated to this culture, you should keep it safe for now." He raised a hand to stop Heather's protest. "It may not be proper, but I'm sure Casey can keep it safe until it can be accounted for and documented. Might just be something a treasure hunter dropped. I shouldn't say this, but I've got enough to catalog without dealing with a sword that doesn't have a reasonable explanation."

"There's a crystal as well," blurted Heather.

Anthon's eyes narrowed at Heather, who smiled encouragingly at Casey. When Casey reluctantly pulled the small crystal from his pocket, the professor picked it up curiously, and took it to the magnifier light on the table.

"Geology isn't my strength," commented the professor absent-mindedly, "but it appears to be nothing more than..." His voice trailed off. After a few moments he continued, "Most interesting. I didn't see these before. It's like faded characters are appearing on the crystal."

James and Casey tried to appear surprised.

"Any idea what they might say?" asked James.

"I hate to admit it, but I am unfamiliar with these characters, what language they might be, or what they mean. I suspect it's probably a label for the crystal."

A subtle movement of the closed back door flap caught Casey's peripheral vision. Turning, he saw a brief glint replaced by a crack of darkness between the two flaps. He walked cautiously to the back of the tent and pushed gently against the canvas door. The flaps were tied shut outside the mosquito netting. He pushed against the canvas, and the flaps moved outwards a few inches.

The others had paused to watch.

"What is it?" asked James.

"I thought I saw something through the door flap, like maybe light reflecting on something. But there doesn't appear to be anything now. Maybe the fan blew the flaps."

Casey returned to the table. The professor turned somber, removing the crystal from under the magnifying light and studying it in his hand. While his face appeared occupied, his eyes shifted from the back door to Casey.

"I think we need to keep this in a safe place," he said. He nodded at Casey and added, "And I think you'll agree."

Casey bit back his objection while the professor set the small crystal among several pottery shards. Then he pretended to pick it back up, but, in its place, he picked up a small shard of pottery that he held enclosed within his hand. Professor Anthon raised a brow at Casey and gave a short nod towards the pottery shards on the desk. Casey nodded back.

The professor walked over to a small, locked chest near the desk. He opened the chest and placed the object from his hands inside, being careful not to reveal what he was holding. While James and Heather watched the professor, Casey's left hand reached among the large pottery shards, slid the crystal between two fingers, and then tucked it securely into his palm. He pocketed the crystal while the professor locked the chest.

"So, what do you think the crystal might be for?" asked Heather.

"If you're right," started the professor, "that is about there being a temple for a fallen star—and James always thought there might be something tangible to the legend he related to me—then that crystal could be some sort of key."

"What exactly is the 'fallen star?'" asked Heather. "You mentioned it before, and Casey and James both talked about it when we were at the temple site earlier. Are those photos I took of the mural referring to some meteorite that crashed in this area?"

"Actually, we don't really know. But that is the logical guess," said James. "And it might explain where the crystals came from."

"Precisely," added the professor. "The ancient indigenous people of this area likely built a temple to the fallen star, perhaps to satiate some star god from bringing destruction again. Heather, you know the people in this area are deeply religious and carry superstitions through generations. We are only scratching the surface, and it's likely, from the sword and crystal, that this civilization was more advanced than we're giving them credit for. In fact, some of our finds today indicate that later generations may have rejected some—"

Boom! Boom! Boom!

Three high-caliber gunshots ripped the night air. Instinctively, everyone dropped low. More gunshots and shouts followed, then silence. A minute later the tent flaps flew open, startling those inside.

"Professor?" inquired a thickly accented voice.

Manuel, the lead security guard, stood in the tent doorway breathing heavily, sweat dripping from his dark face. Despite the excitement, he was calm and held an old AK-47 at his side.

He glanced around and noticed the group low, near the table. "Professor? You good? Enrique thought he saw som'ting, like the Anaconda *espias*. He started shooting."

"Did you see anything?" asked Anthon.

"No'ting," said Manuel. "Though, maybe it be jaguar. Gone now. Juan *y* Pedro are looking more."

"Thank you for the update," said the professor.

"*De nada*, Professor." Manuel turned and walked back out of the tent.

"Guess security's a bit on edge with the Anaconda rumors," said James.

Dwuane Anthon looked around the tent as if he were having an internal debate. Another gunshot broke the silence.

"What were you going to say about the dig today?" pressed Heather.

"What? Oh, I think that can wait until morning. Though I daresay what was found may be connected to this fallen star and other items that seem out of place. We found another chamber inside the sun temple."

"You found another?" exclaimed James.

"Well, I didn't, but Leila did," replied the professor with a yawn, "But it's getting late, and I think it would be best to retire for the night. Be ready at first light. Casey, don't forget to get that drone of yours out and scanning as soon as possible. I've got a feeling this fallen star is more important that we realize."

Anthon's statement carried an air of finality. Heather, James, and Casey knew it would be pointless to push for more information. After leaving the office, they speculated briefly on what might have been found and how it might relate to their discovery.

The walk back to their tents was more cautious than usual, and the darkness felt more foreboding. Outside of the immediate glow of the lanterns scattered around the tents, the thick jungle surrounded the camp with a black, impenetrable wall. Under the starlight, a hazy mist settled into the rainforest canopy. With a new moon, the night would only get darker after the camp lights were turned off. The hum of a small generator was occasionally punctuated by some jungle inhabitant's growl, taunt, or cry. High-pitched buzzing accentuated the night's orchestra.

The office tent was on the east side of the camp, closest to the dig site. A dozen tents were scattered around the central tent. While most of the staff and crew thought it was safer to be closer, James and Heather had chosen to set up their tents about a hundred feet north. Heather's tent mate, Leila, was one of the few women in the camp.

Casey swatted a mosquito as they approached the two tents and wondered how long his temporary assistance would be needed. He had earned the professor's trust early on through his technical expertise and had already been asked to stay longer. He was not thrilled about the hot, humid jungle, but he felt good that his skills were of use, and sometimes, like today, there was an adventure.

James paused outside his tent and smiled at Heather. "Thanks for going with us today. I know you would've liked to have been here for whatever they found. But it was fun to have some time away, and I'm glad you convinced your uncle to let you go."

Heather grinned. "It was probably more exciting than being here. Although I probably wouldn't have almost gotten killed if I'd stayed."

"Yeah," added Casey, "I don't think the professor would've approved if we'd told him exactly what happened."

"That's for sure. But I would've gone anyway." Heather gave James a lighthearted punch to his shoulder. "I can't leave you two alone or you'll get into worse trouble."

"Hey, you like getting dirty just as much as we do," said James defensively.

Heather stifled a yawn. "You guys have a good night. I may not mind getting dirty, but I prefer to sleep without the excessive dirt. I'm getting cleaned up before I go to sleep."

Heather disappeared into her tent, and the muted voices of two women filtered through the canvas. James pulled aside his tent flap and went in. Before following his brother, Casey took a moment to look around. From Heather's tent he could hear the splashing of water in the little wash basin. A moment later the hum of the camp's generator was silenced, and most of the lights were sucked into darkness. Only a few solar-powered lights shone dimly from their perches littered throughout camp. A couple of flashlights moved like fireflies, disappearing and reappearing from behind tents. Slivers of light split a few tents. He watched a couple of dark shadows—the night guards, he guessed—walk slowly through camp.

Casey entered the tent to hear James's mumbled voice. "Don't forget to get your pack ready before going to sleep."

Casey eyed his brother, already asleep, with the mosquito net pulled around the cot. In the dark, Casey wasn't sure if his brother had even changed clothes. He followed James's suggestion and took a few minutes to check through his pack. With the excitement of the day wearing off, he changed into light shorts and a T-shirt, pulled the mosquito net around his bed, and decided to read for a minute before his eyes objected too heavily.

Chapter Four

Rude Awakening

T HE AGED MILITARY COT jostled Casey awake. His eyes opened to the coal-black tent ceiling. His breath released as the aftershock faded. A quick glance at the dimming hands of his watch revealed an early 4:37 a.m. His eyelids sunk back together, then opened when he heard a vehicle engine break from the jungle fringe.

A brilliant flash and concussive wave breached the tent flaps as an explosion rocked the old wall tent. Shouts and screams racked the air amid the intense rattling of automatic gunfire. Casey rolled off his cot, taking the mosquito netting down with him. In the darkness he heard James flop to the pallet-covered floor. Seconds later, the gunfire stopped.

The noonday brightness of spotlights momentarily pierced the door flaps and passed by. A native dialect, mixed with Spanish, broke the silence with undecipherable commands. The rapid *pop-pop-pop* of a gun followed. Then more silence.

Casey crawled to the door flaps. For a moment he watched black figures, silhouetted by the spotlights, move intentionally among the tents in the central camp.

"Good thing you didn't stay in the guest tent," whispered James as he inched beside his brother.

Casey nodded and freed himself from the netting. "We need to get out the back before they come this way," he whispered. "Hopefully Heather's taking Leila out the back as well."

More commands were shouted across the camp. A couple of four-wheel-drive trucks, with spotlights mounted on roll bars, moved between tents. The beams swept the camp like piercing eyes. A shadowed operator stood behind each light, one hand on the spotlight while the other gripped the handle of a mounted .30 caliber machine gun.

Two gunshots burst from the darkness in the east. The shadow behind one mounted gun slumped over, and the light beam shot into the night sky. More shouts and chaotic gunfire followed. The gunner on the second truck fell off. Confusion and orders erupted. A different shadow climbed up behind one of the spotlights and directed its beam towards the temple ruins.

"Time to move out," urged James.

Casey and James moved towards the back of the tent, staying low. More gunfire shredded the night air, and the whiz of bullets buzzed through their tent. Casey grabbed and slung his pack over his left shoulder. His foot kicked something. His eyes saw the outline of the short sword topple to the floor. He grabbed the sword and scrambled to the back door where he waited for his brother to grab his pack and retrieve a 9mm handgun from a small chest.

Casey hesitated near the back flaps. Something bothered him.

"What is it?" whispered James.

Casey shook his head. With the sword in his right hand, his left unzipped the back door screen. More gunfire erupted in the main camp. Using the sword tip, he slowly pushed the left flap out.

A black blade slashed through the tent flap just below the sword, and Casey jumped back as the lower half of the flap dropped. Any closer and the slice would have been through his abdomen. Another blur sliced the right door canvas and cut clean through the thick wooden door pole right in front of Casey. The raised peak of the tent's back door collapsed.

"Go to the front," said Casey as he shed his pack, ducked under the collapsed tent roof and dove through the back. A dark-clad figure, who had started towards the tent front, reversed direction. A sliver of dark metal extended from the shadow's right hand, the long blade nearly invisible in the night. The blade whipped forward and snapped at Casey like a scorpion tail. Casey jumped back and lowered the short sword enough to parry the attack with a ring of clashing blades.

Immediately the longer blade jabbed upwards. Casey stepped back, blocking the thrust, and the blades met with another shrill ring.

"What's—" started James.

Behind him, Casey heard the soft *clack-clack* as his brother pulled and released the slide action on his handgun.

Through the darkness, Heather's voice hissed, "Casey? James? What's happening out there?"

"Don't—" Casey was cut short as he dodged right and parried left. His upper left arm burned when his sword failed to fully defect the thrusting blade's bite. Around the cut his shirt began to feel wet and warm, and the fabric darkened in the starlit night.

In his peripheral vision, Casey saw James carefully maneuver under the collapsed tent end. The black-clad figure in front of Casey glanced at James, then the movement in the next tent. The shadow darted towards the central camp and disappeared in the chaos.

Two spotlights panned back across the tents. Casey ducked as he tried to determine where his attacker had fled to. More shouts followed, and two more gunshots ruptured the night. One spotlight winked out in an explosion of sparks while its operator stumbled back.

Angry shouts, punctuated by gunshots, fired off into the night.

From his vantage point, Casey watched the second spotlight swing back towards the nearby ruins. Truck high-beam headlights added illumination to the area. Rapid gunfire from camp targeted the temple ruins.

James stepped next to his brother and whispered, "We should head straight back to the jungle and figure out where the threats are before we try engaging these guys."

Casey nodded.

Heather's head poked out of the back flaps of the nearby tent. Her head cocked with an unspoken question. James began to motion instructions to her when a truck engine roared to life somewhere in camp, its gears growling with a launch into drive. Shouts rose throughout camp as the truck's headlights split the night and charged west towards the small jungle road in a desperate escape. Gunfire pursued the truck in its mad dash, and a single spotlight chased after the fleeing vehicle until it disappeared into the jungle.

Two more gunshots echoed out from the ruins, and two more screams came from intruders. Harsh, undecipherable commands were shouted out.

The sky in the east was beginning to lighten. Casey risked a glance back at the main camp. Three smaller tents near the center were flattened. One of the two trucks started to head down the jungle road while a couple of bags were tossed into the back of the second before it pulled out. Three stragglers grabbed onto the back roll bar and pulled themselves into the truck bed.

The brothers watched the two trucks vanish into the jungle, and silence returned to camp.

Heather cautiously stepped out the back of her tent wearing sleep shorts and a T-shirt. Her brunette hair, freed from its daily ponytail, brushed against her shoulders when she glanced over at the brothers.

"Whoever it was seems to be gone now," said James.

Looking back into her tent, Heather nodded.

Leila poked her head out, her braided raven hair almost glistening in the early morning twilight. Her voice was quiet and tense as she scanned the area. "Do you think they'll come back?"

James felt a pinch on his arm, and he instinctively slapped at the rogue mosquito. "Maybe. But if we don't all get changed, we'll get eaten before those guys come back."

Casey turned from the camp towards his brother. "We should go see what the damage is, and what we can do to help."

James gave a single nod.

Casey slapped a mosquito on his leg. "Just give me a second to change clothes," he said, and he squirmed under the collapsed tent flaps.

"Give us a minute and we'll join you," said Heather. She and Leila ducked into their tent.

In the tent, Casey retrieved his backpack and quickly swapped shorts for pants. He stuffed a shirt into the pack and strapped the short sword to the side before he exited the tent. A few seconds later, Heather and Leila joined the brothers, wearing khaki pants and tan button-up shirts.

Warily, they walked into the center of camp. Several staff and crew members cautiously poked their heads out from hiding places.

"Leila, you were at the dig yesterday," said Casey. "What did they find that was unusual?"

Leila's dark eyes widened. "How'd you know?"

"The professor implied as much last night."

Leila glanced around as if she was about to reveal a secret, then quietly responded, "I found a small hidden door and crawled into an undisturbed chamber. Inside I found, among other things, a couple of small gold figurines. I was going to leave them, but the professor was insistent I bring them out so he could personally analyze them. So, I made some quick documentation, took photos, and brought them back to camp. The professor made a really rough, tentative analysis. He was a bit unsettled and said they're similar to some Egyptian statues he's seen, but he thinks these were less than a thousand years old."

"That sounds cool," said Heather. "Better than almost dying."

"Yeah, but that's not the odd thing," said Leila, "The professor said they seem to be statuettes of Ra."

Heather's eyes widened. "You mean the Egyptian sun god?"

"Isn't he a little out of place here?" asked James.

"More like out of continent," said Casey as they approached the office tent. "No wonder the professor was a bit overwhelmed when we brought more unexplained discoveries."

Leila's eyes shifted to Casey with a curious look. "Yeah, and you'd probably think otherwise, but apparently Egyptian solar temples didn't usually have statues of Ra in them."

Not far away, a few men were bringing cots into the large central tent. In the brightening twilight, a couple of women and men were moving under the tent. One of the workers sat on a chair while another bandaged his arm. A couple of bodies moaned and moved slowly on cots. Outside the tent two bodies lay silent on the ground. Nearby, other workers were assisting each other with minor bandaging.

The office door flaps abruptly flew open, and the professor stormed out. He wore the same clothes as yesterday, with additional wrinkles in them. A bandage was wrapped hastily around his head, red darkening a spot on the left side. Speaking more to himself than to anyone in particular, he muttered angrily, "Those bandits took them! They have no respect for history."

"What'd they take?" asked Heather.

The professor seemed surprised to hear her voice. He turned and recognition softened his features. He sighed, "Along with some minor trinkets, they took the statuettes of Ra."

"Are you sure they were Ra?" asked Casey.

"Of course I'm sure," the professor said with an air of annoyance. "I know it doesn't make sense. There's no explanation for finding them inside a hidden chamber of a sun temple in the Americas. I expected something more native, not from the other side of the world. Leila discovered a small hidden passage soon after you left, and later found the artifacts. We brought them back yesterday afternoon and tried to keep their discovery under wraps until we could actually verify what it was we found. If this remarkable, and unlikely discovery, isn't properly cataloged, nobody will take my findings seriously."

"No wonder you wanted to keep it quiet," said Heather. "If they're authentic, they're probably worth a lot."

"Not as much as the historical significance. Which is precisely why we weren't going to talk about it." Realization lit his dark eyes. "You must've gotten Leila to tell you this. Probably just as well." He turned and stared back at the office tent. "I wanted to get more security before"—his arms motioned erratically at the tent—"before exactly what happened, happened."

"If the statuettes were really of Ra, he's definitely out of place here," said James. His voice slowed in response to his thoughts. "But, considering what we saw yesterday, I wonder if the key to understanding this is in the Temple of the Fallen Star."

"Casey!" exclaimed Heather. "What happened to your arm?"

With the adrenaline of the past several minutes, Casey had forgotten his earlier encounter. He looked down at his upper left arm where dark red had stained around a slice in the short sleeve. Scarlet had crusted a small cut in his skin. The burning he'd felt earlier returned.

"One of the thugs was trying to fillet me," said Casey. "I didn't fully parry his last thrust, but it doesn't feel too bad."

"We should still get you bandaged up," said Heather "I think Pablo has some bandages."

Heather disappeared into the large central tent. She returned a few seconds later with the camp cook.

Pablo arrived with bandages hugging his right arm and leg. He gave a small first aid kit to Heather. "Professor," he said with highly accented English, "we's still missing some men. David *y* Mateo gone. *Y* Manuel."

At that moment Manuel walked around the tent holding a hunting rifle. Sweat trickled down his face, and he wiped away a bead of moisture. "I's here."

Casey assessed the camp guard. "Were you the one shooting from the ruins?"

Heather ripped his shirt sleeve a little more and started to clean the wound. Casey grimaced when the alcohol pad wiped across and around the cut.

Manuel suppressed a grin. "*Sí*, I's gets some good cover before it get bad. I's glad they leave, though. Out of ammo." He shrugged, looked at the professor, and added, "Good morning, Señor Professor."

"I'm glad you're okay," said the professor, "but it's far from a good morning. Those thugs stole our find from yesterday."

Pablo frowned. Casey felt a bite of pain and turned to watch while Heather applied some antiseptic, two butterfly bandages, and then taped gauze over the cut.

The professor explained to the others, "Pablo was with us when Leila found and squirreled through the opening into the hidden chamber. Maybe we should've left them."

"Thank you, Heather," said Casey as she finished up. He looked at Leila, who was sitting quietly. "Did your secret chamber happen to involve a painting with a jaguar and an image of a falling star?"

Leila's jaw dropped. "How'd you—"

Flocks of tropical birds erupted in a flurry from the jungle canopy on the west side, squawking their annoyance as they flew off. The rising sun, still below the trees, brilliantly illuminated the plumage as the colorful flock rose into the air. Voices in camp fell silent, and eyes warily shifted towards the road. The camp remained still while the muffled growl from the road steadily grew louder.

Near the central tent, a voice trembled, "The Anaconda!"

The sunrise kissed the treetops when four trucks burst from the jungle road. Standing behind roll bars in the truck beds at the back of the truck cabs, men dressed in old jungle fatigues held on to mounted guns while bandanas and goggles covered their faces. Next to the machine guns, spotlights grasped the roll bars. The glass faces on two of the spotlights were shattered.

"Run!" shouted James. "Run to the ruins!"

Pablo and Manuel darted into a nearby tent as automatic weapon fire raked the camp.

Leila froze next to the professor. Casey grabbed their arms to pull their attention away, and they sprinted after James and Heather towards the ruins a hundred yards away. Gunfire pummeled the camp behind them.

With only twenty-five yards left, the professor groaned loudly and stumbled to the ground, his hand clutching his right shoulder tightly. Under his fingers, the dirty khaki shirt darkened into crimson. Breathless, he said, "I'm—hit."

Casey and Leila stooped down beside him.

"Hang on to me," said Casey as he tried to pull the professor's arm around his shoulder. "I'll get you to safety."

A short distance ahead of them, Heather looked back, paused, and started to return. James grabbed her arm while his free hand pointed first to Casey and then back to the ruins. Heather's head shook vigorously, and she ran the short distance back to her uncle.

"You—need—to go." Anthon's eyes widened with concern when they saw his niece drop to her knees next to him. "You must—go. Not—safe—except jungle."

"No," insisted Casey, "If we leave, they'll kill you."

Heather touched her uncle's arm. The muscles around Anthon's eyes quivered as he tried to stoically hide the pain. He momentarily studied his niece. His head moved slowly, and his voice labored between breaths. "If—you stay—we're all dead. Besides—I'm not dead—yet. Go! And Casey—protect— Heather."

Leila urgently pulled at Casey and Heather. "C'mon, we gotta go."

Casey's legs wobbled as he stood. Reluctantly, he and Heather darted after Leila towards the sun temple ruins. Seconds later they joined James behind several large stones that mingled among the trees clustered around the base of the pyramid like disorderly sentinels. Except for the west side, which opened to the clearing and camp, the rainforest encroached on the ancient temple and provided cover for the foursome. They looked back at the camp and felt some relief at seeing no pursuers. On the far right, a couple of the archaeological crew ran for the jungle, also seemingly unnoticed by the invaders.

The four trucks abruptly braked near the central tent. Several men jumped out of the vehicles and swarmed the nearby tents. Other than the Anaconda, there was no movement in camp. Casey watched the professor lying motionless in the tall grass.

A large, black-windowed sport utility, with a roof-mounted gun, raced from the jungle towards the camp. As it approached, the Anaconda soldiers reluctantly broke away from ransacking the tents and gathered near the trucks.

"Whose truck is that?" asked Leila.

"No idea," said James, "Probably their leader's."

The black SUV glided to a stop next to the trucks, and the soldiers' attention riveted on the newly arrived vehicle. They seemed both ready and reluctant to run.

The turret gun rotated slowly. The two passenger-side doors opened, and three men, armed with AK-47s and dressed in black camouflage, jumped out. Their callous faces looked ready to shoot first and not bother with questions ever. They fanned out into a wide semicircle around the right side of the SUV. Outside the semicircle, the other men froze.

From the rear passenger door, a man casually stepped out. Like the other three, he was dressed in black camouflage, but a black beret capped his head, and he had no guns. In the morning light, his olive-toned face shimmered slightly with moisture. He stood in arrogant confidence, his left hand resting on a thin cylinder, that looked like a woven handle hanging from his belt.

The Anaconda soldiers stood conflicted, simultaneously at attention while trying to avoid the man's gaze. The man in the beret took several steps towards the soldiers and started speaking, his left hand continuing to rest on the handle.

From their cover near the ruins, the four escapees could not hear the conversation and simply watched the leader motion to one soldier.

The unfortunate man stepped forward and walked uncertainly into the semicircle. The three armed guards ignored the man and maintained their focus on the other soldiers. Standing several feet from his leader, the chosen man was desperately explaining something. He pointed animatedly towards the pyramid, near where the group was hiding. The man in the beret calmly spoke while the other man lifted his hands up in protest.

A flash of light split the air in front of the protesting man, and he slumped lifeless to the ground. The leader's right hand released the handle. The soldiers outside the semicircle shifted uneasily.

"Did you see what happened?" whispered Leila.

Casey shook his head. "Not exactly, but he did something with the handle-thing."

"Whatever it was, it was the quickest thing I've never seen," said James.

Across the clearing, the black-bereted leader casually pointed at another soldier, a dark-skinned indigenous man, and issued an order. Even from over a hundred yards away it was clear that the soldier's face had paled with fear. The chosen man turned towards the others, pointed towards the temple, and shouted urgently. The Spanish command carried across the clearing.

"Quickly, after them. Don't let them escape. No one returns until we get the crystal."

Chapter Five
Escape into the Jungle

THE ANACONDA SOLDIERS SPRINTED towards the ruins, eager to be the first to avoid any fallout from their leader.

James fired two shots into the rush. One of the lead soldiers stumbled to the ground clutching his left thigh. A second tripped while grabbing his right shoulder. The remaining soldiers dove to the ground and fired randomly into the ruins.

"I don't think they're accepting the un-invite," said James.

Casey's head ducked low. "Yeah, it's time to leave this party. Head behind the pyramid."

James waved the others to follow as he turned and darted among the morning shadows of the trees and weathered stone. Bullets haphazardly spit random bits of dirt and rocks from the ruins they kept as obstacles between them and the soldiers.

James glanced back and fired two more rounds. Two more soldiers, who had rounded the large stones of the first hiding place, stumbled, grasping body parts. "Keep low and keep moving. That'll only slow them down a little, since they don't know how many guns we have or where we are."

A shower of automatic weapon fire peppered the ruins as the group went behind the old temple. After several seconds of intense, rapid shooting, an angry voice rose above and silenced the gunfire.

James's eyes zeroed in on his brother, and he waved his handgun towards the excavation entrance into the temple, a low opening near the base about fifty feet away. "Casey, you're better at covering tracks. Make it look like we went to the entrance, then backtrack and follow us into the jungle. Take this, just in case they catch up to you." He handed the handgun to his brother. "I'm not sure, but there's probably only ten rounds left."

Casey started to object.

James positioned the handgun's grip towards Casey. "I know you don't want to shoot anyone, but it's our lives or theirs. I can read the jungle better and find a good path. You can track me. Heather, Leila, keep close. Walk where I do, and we'll lose them in the jungle."

Casey nodded; his right hand grasped the gun. "Head east. The Temple of the Fallen Star should be that direction. Maybe we can lose the thugs and hide there and know where we are in relation to camp."

James clenched his jaw set and gave a short nod. He motioned for the women to follow and then ducked into the undergrowth.

Leila hesitated at the jungle fringe. "We're not actually going in there? Are we?"

Heather's hazel eyes smiled. "Better than sticking around here. Don't worry, James is really good in the jungle." Then she quickly vanished through the green-hued wall after James.

Shaking her head, Leila followed Heather.

Casey scrambled quickly towards the pyramid's entrance, intentionally knocking loose stones. When he neared the opening, he carefully retraced his steps to leave no evidence of the new direction. At the edge of the jungle, he obscured the groups' passing and disappeared into the underbrush. From the pyramid, voices carried through the thick vegetation.

Through the lush leaves, Casey glimpsed an Anaconda soldier cautiously picking his way around the ruins. Three more appeared a second later. The eyes of the first scanned across the ground and then followed the careless trail towards the opening. He pointed to the temple entrance and excitedly shouted to the others.

Casey quietly turned, covered some tracks, then swiftly followed a small game trail. At a convergence of multiple trails, he paused for a second to find his brother's boot scuff. Leila's boots trampled nearby while Heather's were barely discernible. Studying the surrounding trees and vegetation, he carefully bent back a branch and rigged a quick trip release. He obscured the group's passing again and a few minutes later caught up to the others who had momentarily stopped.

"What took you so long?" asked James.

Casey half-smiled. "Remember the High Uintas?"

James grinned appreciatively. "Well, hopefully it'll work as well as it did with those poachers." He motioned with his chin towards his intended direction. "We need to get moving before they catch up."

Sweat dripped along Leila's chin. "I was hoping we'd lost them," she said between breaths. "I'd never figure out where we went."

"Slowed down is the best we can hope for," said Casey. "I get the feeling that black-beret commander guy isn't one to give up or let those under him give up. Someone's bound to discover where we went."

James urgently nodded. "Best to get as much distance as we can, until we find a safe place. Remember, tread carefully, and don't break branches."

Without waiting, James continued along small game trails, dodging and ducking the undergrowth. The others followed with Casey at the end.

Heather glanced back at Casey, who was scanning the jungle and frequently looking back. He stopped at another branch, pulled it back, and rigged another release.

Leila noticed Heather's look. "What's he doing?" she asked.

"Setting snares," said Heather.

"And I thought he was just the drone pilot and computer geek."

"Actually, he also has airplane and helicopter pilot certifications."

Leila's brow rose towards Casey. "Why's he here? He could be making more money flying."

Heather shrugged and ducked under nets of branches. "Not sure. He has a hard time settling. Kind of like his brother. Honestly, though"—her voice lowered further—"their dad was killed a few years ago. It's been really hard for them." A knot formed in her throat. "And me, too. He was like a dad I never had."

Leila's whisper seemed lost in thought. "Death has a strange way of affecting us. Sometimes it takes years to rediscover who we are."

Heather swallowed a lump in her throat and turned her full attention to following James.

———◦———

An hour later Casey was once again catching up with the group after setting another snare. Over the past hour, the paths James had chosen had led them into thicker jungle. Sweat streaked faces, and hands alternated between swatting insects and sweeping aside foliage.

A noise caught Casey's attention. He paused to listen while he examined the shades of greens and browns of the jungle undergrowth. His breath released when a small animal scurried nearby. He turned back around and nearly bumped into Leila.

Ahead of the group, like a ghostly green specter rising up from the ground and obscured by vegetation, stood a twenty-foot-tall wall-like structure that extended for hundreds of feet to the left and right. Where the wall ended was swallowed up by the jungle that snuggled up close to the vertical surface. Above the wall rose a three-peaked hill, covered with trees and bushes of various shapes and sizes. Looking closer, they realized the three peaks were the top of a large pyramid; the jungle had engulfed the lower sections and held a firm stranglehold on the upper part. Trees grasped desperately to the pyramid sides and reached their branches out and up. Above the wall in front of them, multiple shorter walls rose up from each lower tier to the wide center, topped by the three peaks, the central one taller than the rest. Through the vegetation engulfing the pyramid, a small walled structure could be seen on top of the center peak.

"Wow!" said James. "That's easily a hundred feet up."

Leila stared up the pyramid. "Where did that come from?"

"There're thousands of structures hidden in the jungles," replied James. "Some are stumbled upon accidentally. Others get discovered by technology, like LIDAR. We've been heading the direction Casey indicated from camp, so this might be the Temple of the Fallen Star."

"Looks like a giant squashed the top layers in," commented Casey.

"Do we go up or around?" asked Leila.

"Other than climbing the vines and branches, does anyone see a way up?" asked James. "I'm not sure if we want to take the time to see how far these walls go. And we might gain an advantage from higher up."

"Looks like something over there," said Heather, pointing a short distance to the left where rubble littered the base of the wall.

They dodged the outreaching fingers of the rainforest undergrowth towards the rubble and found ancient stone stairs crumbling their way up to the center peak. Smaller trees, brush, and vines littered the stairway, their roots greedily reaching into cracks.

James led the group up. After several long minutes, and a few brief pauses, they reached the center summit. Ten feet back from the top edge, the remains of four, semi-collapsed walls formed the perimeter of a twenty-foot-square building. In the center of the vegetation-infested structure stood a large rectangular altar of carefully cemented stones. The group sat on the top step for minute to catch their breath.

The morning sun was above the trees; its rays pierced through the ruined walls of the building behind them and brightly illuminated the jungle canopy. Looking down, the side of the pyramid could easily be mistaken for a green-covered hillside in the tropical forest. Across the entire structure, the roots of all sizes of trees intertwined in a centuries-long battle for optimal holds on the many ledges and large steps.

The shorter peaks to the left and right were four-sided and, from the group's perspective, were set a little forward of the center peak. Short ridges below the two smaller peaks joined with the center somewhere in the obscuring vegetation. Through the trees at the base of the pyramid, the wall appeared to stretch six hundred feet where it turned and continued around the four sides of the ancient structure.

Casey's gaze shifted from the sky, to the pyramid, and then the surrounding jungle. "Incredible. Even from the air it'd be hard to guess this was a pyramid without a LIDAR scan."

James's head shook. "Probably looks like one of thousands of rolling jungle hills."

Heather studied the western view, where the jungle rose and dropped in swells like green ocean waves. Wisps of gray-black clouds were dissipating above the tree line. "Is that where we came from?"

James squinted in the direction she was pointing. "Yeah. Looks like something might be burning."

Heather turned to Casey, who had pulled a GPS from his pack, and asked, "Do you think this is—"

"Yes," came Casey's immediate reply. "I think we found the Temple of the Fallen Star. Guess I didn't need to take the drone out this morning."

"No," said his brother. "We just needed to get chased out of camp by a bunch of machine gun-wielding goons."

James turned and walked to the vine-covered entry of the stone building. He cautiously stepped through and disappeared behind the toppled wall.

"Shouldn't we keep going?" asked Leila, her breath still short. "You've got me a little curious about this fallen star thing, but, you know, this isn't the time to admire the sights."

"You'd rather keep hiking through the jungle?" asked Heather.

"Actually," said Casey, "I think this is a good place to stop."

James reappeared. "You may be surprised, but I'm ready for a break. Maybe the Anaconda thugs will just ransack the camp and leave and give up trying to chase us down. A lot of the locals aren't too fond of wandering aimlessly through unknown jungle. We can easily survive here a day or two. Longer wouldn't be hard if we can find a water source and food. Then we can send someone back to check if it's safe to return."

Casey's head shook, his mouth thinning. "I doubt those guys will stop. Not because they wouldn't want to, but because they're afraid of that guy in the beret. And they're probably not too far behind us. If we have to face them, I'd rather be rested and ready when they catch up. I didn't see how many actually followed us, but we could have an advantage here."

"I was trying to think positively," said James.

"That'd be nice," replied Heather. "But, if you didn't hear, that beret guy really wants the crystal. Those wannabe soldiers probably aren't going back until they get it."

James nodded knowingly. "Yeah, I heard that. And you're right. The question we don't know the answer to is: What crystal?" He shifted towards Casey. "The one you gave the professor?"

A tired breath escaped Heather. "I'm all for not running anymore, if we can stay alive. But we should find someplace more secure to hole up, instead of the top of this staircase."

James grinned. "Agreed. Let's move back into this ruined building to rest a bit and get some water while we weigh our options."

The group moved inside the vegetation-encrusted structure. Inside the remains of the four walls, vines and plants fought for the sparse soil on the floor and desperately grasped the walls. In the center, a four-foot-tall stone altar spanned six feet in width and stretched towards the back wall about twelve feet.

James and Casey pulled water bladders from their packs and passed them around.

After a sip of water, Leila's deep brown eyes assessed Casey. "Do you really think they're tracking us? You did a great job hiding our trail."

Casey swallowed some water he had held in his mouth. "The short answer is yes. It was a rush job. Even a novice tracker could discover our backtrack in a short time. Our best hope is they messed up the backtrack signs through carelessness. Maybe they'll waste some time inside the sun temple before realizing we're not there. After that they'll spread out along the back side of the ruins to figure out where we went into the jungle."

Leila's shoulders slumped while Casey continued.

"Once they pick up our trail, it'll be easy to follow. No ultimate-tracker-skills required. Only someone blindfolded or not paying attention would miss where we went. Hopefully the snares slow them down." Casey chewed briefly on his lower lip. "I've got an uneasy feeling. They're coming and, unless we figure something out to stop them, we'll probably be killed."

Leila's braided black hair shook with her head. "This doesn't seem like a typical Anaconda raid. Don't they just grab and go? Or at least that's what news reports imply."

"I've heard that as well," said James. "But it probably depends on what they want. Some of their reported raids and targets have been different than other gangs or cartels."

"But archaeological sites?" Heather lamented. "And don't you think it's odd they raided once and then returned almost immediately? It's not like we found much of value. And how would they have even known what we found?"

"What about the statuettes of Ra?" asked James. "Those could fetch a nice price on the black market."

"Wait," said Casey, "back up. You're right. How would they know what was even found unless someone told them? The statuettes were only found yesterday. And I showed the professor the crystal last night."

"What about a crystal?" asked Leila. "You said you found one? It must be like a diamond, or something really unusual, for that guy to threaten lives over it."

Casey, James, and Heather exchanged looks. Casey chose his words carefully. "We found a crystal, and it's probably more on the unusual side than valuable."

Leila's brow knitted. "Do you have it?"

Casey sheepishly glanced at James, then back at Leila. "We do, but we'll just keep it safe where it is. At least for now."

"Back to the question," said James. "Who would've known?"

"Maybe it was whoever was looking through the tent flaps last night," suggested Casey. "The real question is how would they know what this crystal is? But we don't have time to debate this. Right now, unwanted company is coming, and we've got to do something."

James stood. "Casey's right. Let's see what this place can do for us before they arrive. Who wants to stand watch while the others look around?"

"I'll watch," offered Heather.

"Great, there's a good spot with cover over by the stairs," said James, pointing to some piled stones. "It overlooks our trail and the climb up. If you see someone, give your bird call."

Heather nodded and concealed herself near the edge.

The brothers began assessing the collapsed structure and altar.

Casey's eyebrows rose with intrigue. "Interesting. It's a lot bigger than the altars on the other two temples. It looks more like a huge box than an altar."

Casey began walking around the extra-large altar. Multiple shades of green lichen covered the stones and infiltrated the precisely cut spaces and joints. The top slab, with its surface four feet off the floor, was a single stone nearly a foot thick. Small plants strangled several stubby protrusions that rose from its surface.

When Casey reached the farthest end of the altar, he stopped and leaned in to examine the stonework. "James, did you notice anything odd here?"

"No," said James as he and Leila joined Casey. "What is it?"

"This end is different. The long sides and other end are single stones. But there are two stone blocks here, and the gaps around the right one are bigger, almost like it's a door." Casey pulled his small trowel from his pack and quickly slid the edge around the left vertical stone.

James half-grinned.

"What're you talking about?" questioned Leila. "It's just another section of the altar, and we need a plan before the Anaconda get here."

Casey pushed in on the stone and felt a slight give.

"Did I just see that move?" asked James.

Casey nodded and continued to push. James enthusiastically joined his brother pushing against the stone.

"Guys, we're wasting our time here, and probably risking our lives as well," said Leila. Old mortar cracked, and the stone jerked inward. "Whoa! I wasn't expecting that."

The stone grated back about three feet and stopped. A musty smell exited the opening, and sunlight revealed a step-down to a small landing inside the three-foot-high doorway. On the right side of the landing, narrow stairs sharply descended along the right wall ten feet, where they U-turned to the left and continued down into a black abyss on the left wall.

A bird called out. Over the nearby forest canopy, a rainbow of birds took to the sky and joined in chorus. Casey and James tensed and looked towards the pyramid's stairs.

"Was that—" whispered Leila just as Heather slid past the collapsed walls of the ancient structure.

Heather's hushed voice was urgent. "They're at the base. I counted at least eight, including the beret. Looks like all of them have automatic or semi-auto weapons. We need a plan now. And I don't think running is a good option."

Casey smiled. "I have one."

Chapter Six
Into the Temple

"Y OU'VE GOT TO BE joking," hissed Leila.

James's voice was quiet and edged with tension. "No time for that. Casey's right. Going inside's our best option. If there were half as many, we might stand a chance out here. But we're outnumbered and out-gunned. The only real advantage we have right now is they don't know where we are."

Anxiety rose in Leila's voice. "But we'll be trapped like goldfish in there. They tracked us here; they'll easily find where we went."

"We'll have to shut the door," whispered Heather as she looked hesitantly inside the stone doorway, "and hope they don't figure out how to open it." She paused. "And hope there's another way out."

"We'll suffocate," said Leila, her voice a soft whimper of defeat.

"Maybe," said James, "but odds are higher we'll die out here. I don't think they brought AKs and SKSs for a barbecue we'd like. There's probably enough air for us to survive in there. It's not like the door was sealed airtight."

"Maybe we could just give them the crystal," suggested Heather.

"What?" exclaimed Leila, her whisper elevated.

Casey raised an eyebrow at Leila's reaction, but his head shook in disagreement at Heather. "I don't think handing the crystal over will keep them from shooting us."

"Let's see if they're even coming up," suggested Leila. "Maybe they'll just move on."

"Not likely, but okay," said James reluctantly. "It'd be good to know where they are. Casey and I will go back out to check. But we didn't do much to disguise our little hike up here. You two get inside and wait. If they're coming, we can get in and shut the door quickly."

"I'd prefer to go see," said Leila, her eyes darted apprehensively into the darkness beyond the small doorway.

"Fine," replied James. "Casey, give me the gun. You and Heather get ready to close the door. Leila, stay low and out of sight. You take the right. I'll look down the left."

Casey handed the handgun to James and entered the low doorway with Heather. Casey fumbled in his pack for a couple seconds before retrieving a flashlight and handing it to Heather. He slipped a headlamp on for himself.

Outside, James and Leila cautiously exited the ruins and moved towards the long stone stairway. James motioned to Leila to keep down and quiet as they inched towards their respective corners of the pyramid top and peered down.

Along the wall at the pyramid's base, eight figures carefully moved around assorted rainforest plants and trees, like wolves trying to locate the scent of their prey. Four went left, towards the stairs, and three scouted to the right. The man in the beret stood still, his black camouflage making him look like an eerie jungle shadow. Unlike at the camp, the man now held an assault rifle. The beret tilted upwards as he looked towards the peaks. Even from the pyramid top, the man's cold, dark eyes sent shivers up James's spine. James felt a fear enter him, like he'd been discovered and needed to run. He fought the urge and forced himself to be perfectly still. The gaze moved slowly to his right.

Leila stifled a gasp when she saw the man stare in her direction. Instantly the assault rifle lifted and quickly fired off two rounds. Dirt, rock chips, and vegetation exploded in front of Leila as she ducked and scurried from the edge.

The man shouted to the others and pointed to the top. The four nearest the stairs started to ascend. From the other direction, the three soldiers dodged through the plants as fast as they could to reach the stairs.

"Get to the door," hissed James.

Looking down the pyramid, James fired a couple shots towards the foursome starting their ascent up the crumbling stairs. Both shots missed but succeeded in causing the four to dive for cover. James smiled with satisfaction as he noted dark diagonal bruising across the face of one of the men. *Looks like a snare got him*, he thought. His eyes shifted back to the commander, whose eyes were piercing in his direction. The rifle lowered.

James instantly pushed himself back. A burst of automatic rounds fired off, and rock chips exploded where James had been a half second earlier.

Leila had joined Heather down the first flight of stairs when James ducked under the doorway. Casey was crouched on a ledge behind the heavy rock door and started pushing it closed. From the upper stairs, James joined his brother in pushing the door, and the smell of ground stone seasoned the dusty air. With bursts of adrenaline, the door quickly slid into place, punctuated with the sound of two muffled *clunks* as the door closed. Casey's light revealed a copper-colored rod that could be slid into a hole on the side wall. The edge of the hole was chipped, and the rod's end was bent. After rotating the rod, and jamming it into the hole, the brothers moved along the wall down the narrow stairs. Heather and Leila waited just below at the first U-turn of the ancient stairway. Heather's flashlight illuminated the stairs below the brothers.

James pulled a flashlight from his pack, turned it on, and illuminated the open stairwell. A flight of stairs descended the long sides to short landings at each end. "Do you guys see anything down there?"

Heather's flashlight created a beam of light through the floating dust as it pierced down into the black stairwell. "No. It goes down for a bit and seems to end. Probably a passage, but I can't see it for sure."

"Better head—" started James, but Casey hissed him quiet.

Heather and Leila froze and stared up at the brothers.

Angry voices, muffled by the thick stone walls, filtered like a low buzz through the tight gaps at the door. Heather's light shifted back to the stairs below James and Casey. Casey put his right index finger to his lips and pointed at the wall. Then he motioned for them to go down. Reluctantly, Heather and Leila started down the next flight of stairs. When the brothers reached the second flight, a rapid succession of small thumps reverberated throughout the stair shaft, sounding like a possessed woodpecker.

"What's that?" asked Leila as the brothers caught up.

"They're trying to shoot their way in," answered James.

"Keep moving down," urged Casey, "And hope this isn't a dead end...no pun intended."

The stairs descended four flights before reaching bottom, where a two-foot-wide passage opened in the wall. James strode past the others and stepped into the passageway, his light sweeping ahead.

Heather, Leila, and Casey quickly followed. The passage angled gently downward and turned right after about twenty feet. It continued descending like a long ramp before it turned right again. A longer descending straight-way, with a subsequent right turn, followed. By this time James was about fifty feet ahead as he moved confidently through the narrow passage.

"Do you think they'll get in," asked Leila as she shot furtive glances back up the passage.

"They'll probably need more than bullets," replied Casey. "The door's thick enough it'll take thousands of bullets to whittle a small opening. Then they'll still need to figure out how to open it."

Thunder boomed through the passage, and the group instinctively ducked as the ground and walls shook lightly. A second later, a blast of air pushed past them. The sound of a confined avalanche crashed through the passage, followed by muted echoes.

"What was that?" exclaimed Heather.

Casey looked back. "I'd guess it was the more-than-bullets method."

"Are they in?" asked Leila, her voice edged with panic.

Casey's headlamp refracted through wisps of dust. "The good news is I don't think so, yet. I think they just made it more difficult to get in and down. The bad news is we're not getting out that way."

"I don't think we were counting on that," said Heather.

Dust continued filtering through the passage as they descended two more straight-ways, each section longer than the previous. The last section widened to four feet as it leveled off and ended at a junction with passages to the left and right. By the time Casey, Heather, and Leila caught up, James had quickly scouted a short distance ahead in each passage and returned to the junction.

James's light motioned to the left. "There's a small cave-in a short ways down there. I couldn't see much beyond it. I didn't get very far down the right side, but it keeps going and looks like the better option."

"Then let's choose the right," said Heather as her eyes darted behind her.

Thirty seconds later, another boom thundered behind them and shook the passageway, walls, and ceiling. Dust and small debris drifted down from centuries-old resting places.

"Hopefully they don't cause a cave-in," muttered Leila.

The passage abruptly ended at a wall where it looked like the ancient builders had just decided to stop. There was no sign of any other passage.

James bit his lower lip and examined the dead end before them. "I did not expect this."

"Maybe the other passage has something you missed," said Heather. "With all the descents we've made, we're probably at, or just below, ground level by now."

"Maybe," said James, sounding a little beaten. He resumed his search of the dead end. "But it didn't look like there was any way past that cave-in. If there was, we'd have to dig through."

"Anyone else thirsty?" interrupted Casey. He cleared his throat with a quiet cough. "I just realized how dry my throat is."

"What?" asked Leila. "How could you think about stopping to drink something?"

Casey shrugged as he pulled a water bladder from his pack. "We're already stopped. Sometimes solutions show up when you shift gears. And I can't think very well when my tongue's sticking to the roof of my mouth."

Casey offered Leila the first drink. She exhaled exasperation and then gratefully took the water pack for a sip. She offered the water to Heather, who took it as she sat defeated on the ground. Leila resigned herself and sat next to Heather.

Shaking his head, James stopped his fruitless search, wiped sweat off his brow, and joined Heather and Leila on the floor. He pulled a water bladder from his own pack to drink.

Heather passed Casey's water back to him.

Staring at the dead end, Casey leaned against the left wall and sipped his water. A couple seconds later, he rotated to lean his back on the wall. Across from him, another dark stone wall stared back. Heather's flashlight illuminated scuffled dusty footprints and debris on the floor. James's headlamp shone against the lower wall Casey was staring at. Casey cocked his head. Between the two lights, odd shadows shifted across the wall. One particular shadow caught his eye. He pushed himself away and stepped towards the opposite wall.

Approaching the shadow, Casey discovered a small nondescript hole. Pieces of thin mortar had broken and fallen from the vertical opening. He pulled out the remaining pieces of ancient mortar and found the hole to be about a finger wide and two high. Above it, cracked plaster covered something. His fingers broke away the thin cement and brushed aside crusted dirt and dust. A faded four-pointed star—with four smaller points protruding from in between the main four points—appeared, along with a few character glyphs.

Leila's brown eyes watched Casey. "What is it?"

"Something that looks familiar."

Casey adjusted his headlamp down, fished the crystal out of his pocket, and rubbed it briskly. A few characters revealed themselves with the additional heat. In the light he could see a matching character along the star image on the wall.

James echoed Leila's curiosity. "What'd you find?"

"I think the crystal is a key," said Casey, and before anyone could object, he put the crystal into the hole.

"Wait!" exclaimed Leila. "That could've been the ticket for our lives."

James stood as he shook his head. "Hope you know what you're doing."

After several seconds, Heather asked, "What did you think was supposed to happen?"

Casey shrugged. "No idea. Though I was hoping for a secret passage."

"Can you get it out?" asked James.

"Let me see if I can see it," said Casey, and he adjusted the headlamp to shine into the small hole.

Light glinted off the crystal, revealing it had rolled down a small incline and gotten stuck a couple inches back. Casey attempted to retrieve it with his fingers, but it was just out of reach. He pulled a multi-tool from his pack and extended the knife. Using the flashlight beam to see inside, he tried snagging the crystal to slide it back out.

"No," groaned Casey as the crystal rolled back even further. He repositioned his headlamp, and the light beam sliced into the black hole and lit up the crystal. Brilliant colors diffracted inside the small opening. "Whoa!" he exhaled. "That's cool."

The wall began to vibrate with a low hum, and a dull resonance permeated into the floor.

"What—" started Heather, but her words fell silent when a small section of wall to the left of the hole slid back and was swallowed into darkness.

The foursome stared inside. The door had slid back and rotated to the side, revealing a short passage that emptied into an expanse of blackness. Their light beams disappeared into the void beyond.

"Good on ya," said James. "You found a way out."

"Maybe," said Heather doubtfully, "but we haven't seen what's at the other end. Looks pretty dark back there."

"Well," said Casey with a glance back along the passageway they had come down, "better check it out before we run out of other options."

"I don't think there are other options," said James.

Chapter Seven
The Fallen Star

To the right of the opening was a small slot-like hole in the wall. Casey's light reflected off something, and he bent slightly to look inside. Resting behind a small ledge of black glass, the crystal glinted back. He pocketed the crystal and turned back to see the others watching him. James nodded and motioned for Casey to lead as he looked back up the passage they had come from, listening. Casey began the short walk along the passage while the others followed. Their lights revealed an identical floor to other passages in the old temple: smooth stone, precisely cut and fit together. Dust covered everything.

Casey reached the end of the short passage and took a couple steps into a large chamber. His headlamp swept through the darkness. The passage opening appeared to enter the large room at a midpoint, walls extending right and left over a hundred feet. A four-foot-high, narrow shelf ran along the walls. He moved the light back across the room and stopped, transfixed as the beam struggled to illuminate the opposite side. At floor level, the light appeared to reach a far wall, but higher up the light reflected and refracted off a large unidentifiable surface that occupied most of the room.

"What in the world is that?" asked Heather as she stepped around Casey and joined her light with his on the shimmering mass.

Leila stood beside Casey, watching the lights.

Twenty feet in front of them, their lights danced across a massive object that appeared like black, obsidian-like glass, a wet sheen over darkness. The object appeared to be suspended off the floor nearly ten feet, with the top another twenty feet up. The black, wet shimmer stretched into the dark room.

Behind them, James exited the passage. "Well, I didn't hear anything." His voice dropped off when he noticed the object whose surface seemed to flow with their lights. His light cut across the room and stopped on the nearby ledge that ran along the right wall. A liquid lined a thin groove on the top of the narrow shelf. He dipped his left index finger into the groove and sniffed it. After wiping that finger on his pants, he took out a windproof lighter from his pocket, ignited the flame, and touched it to the shelf. A tongue of blue-orange flame licked up and raced along the ledge. In seconds, the flame whipped around the room in a smokeless, flickering light.

The increased light revealed that the massive object was balanced on three legs, which also shimmered in the light. From side to side, the object seemed to be an elongated elliptical, and a narrow end—still hidden from view—stretched into the far side of the room. The surface appeared like smooth and liquid silver, almost like mercury, but it easily adapted to the colors of the walls. While they could discern where the object stood, its translucent surface gave it an almost invisible quality.

"Wow," breathed Leila as she tucked a few errant strands of black hair behind her ear.

"Do you think—" asked James.

"That's the fallen star," said Heather.

"Well," said Casey as he turned off, removed, and pocketed his headlamp, "it's not a meteorite."

"Thank you, master of the obvious," replied Heather.

"What do you think it is?" asked Leila.

Casey started walking towards the object. "It's an alien spacecraft."

"That's ridic—" Heather broke off, realizing she did not have a better explanation.

"I don't think I would've jumped to that out-of-this-world conclusion," said James, "but, it's a possibility. I just didn't understand the elder's story that way."

"What do you mean?" asked Leila.

"Well, the story I was told by the elder was his ancestors—one of the tribes which is now gone—witnessed a star fall to the earth, and it landed in this area. So, they did what many indigenous people often do: they built a temple and incorporated it into their religious worship."

"That doesn't explain the crystal, or things like the crystal-activated doors we just entered," said Heather.

"Which is where Casey's idea of an alien landing, or maybe crash-landing, the ship here could be a reasonable explanation," said Leila. "Especially if the alien were alive and introduced some of its technology."

"Except we don't have any evidence of alien technology in the archaeological ruins," reasoned Heather.

"We don't?" questioned Casey as he neared the object. "What about the crystals you mentioned? And their markings that show up under heat? And are the dagger and sword made from alien metal? Maybe we're just not looking in the right place, or we're just seeing things as we expect to see them."

Casey walked under the object. Two of the legs were at the passage-end of the object, and a third stood near the far end. Casey stopped and studied the left leg. It stood eight feet high and descended from the object as if it were a natural appendage, with no visible attachment points or openings. Like the object itself, the leg was made of the same shimmering material. It was straight with a couple of nodules equally spaced apart that looked like possible articulation points.

Heather and James followed Casey into the room and under the object.

James paused at the right leg and narrowed his eyes at it. "Hey, Casey!"

"Yeah?"

"Do you see a narrow slit on the other leg?"

"No. Why?"

"There's one, nearly hidden, about halfway up this leg. Might be another key slot for your crystal."

"I don't see any on this leg." Casey walked over to James and peered into the obscured opening. "Maybe." He took out his crystal and placed it in the slot. It went in about two-thirds and stopped.

They waited. Nothing happened.

Casey removed his crystal and turned it over in his fingers. After a few seconds, he said to James, "Let's see yours."

"Okay." James took off his necklace, unwrapped the crystal, and handed it to Casey. "Are you sure about this? There's no coin return if it doesn't work."

"Guess we'll find out," said Casey, taking the crystal. "But the slot doesn't go in very far. I'll make sure to hold it tight."

"That's not very reassuring."

Casey pinched his right index finger and thumb on the crystal and slowly placed it into the slot. Like his crystal, it stopped about two-thirds in. Instantly, a soft blue glow emanated around the opening. Casey nearly jumped back from the unexpected light but kept himself still. A half second later, the crystal duplicated the same hue, and Casey felt his finger and thumb get hot.

"Oww!" Casey yelped, jerking out the crystal. It cooled immediately, and the blue light faded away.

"You okay?" asked James.

"Yeah. Not sure if it was a burn or a shock."

"Well, I'm glad it was you and not me."

Heather stepped back from under the object. "What'd you do now?" she accused.

A six-by-six-inch square materialized above the slot on the leg, its perimeter glowing blue. It was as if it had been hidden by a fog that had blown away. Several different-colored characters appeared on the square. One, slightly bigger than the others, glowed green.

"Well, green's usually good," said Casey, and he touched the character with his left hand, still pinching the disc with the right.

"Wait!" cautioned Heather, again too late. She exhaled loudly. "When will you learn to stop pressing buttons?"

Casey shrugged.

———◦———

At the passage entrance, Leila's curiosity got the better of her, and she started walking towards the others. Halfway to the object she froze when a section of the underbelly became outlined in blue. The outlined section lowered and extended itself to the floor, becoming a ramp to the inside. A faint, blue-tinted light lined the ramp and ascended into a black opening.

Behind her, a noise caught Leila's attention. She turned around and cocked her head, listening. A hushed echo reverberated from the passageway. She held her breath as her ears strained, and she stared back through the short passage, through the far doorway, and into the dark, main passageway. A light beam briefly sliced through the darkness.

Leila hissed to the others, "They're coming!"

"I almost forgot about them," said Heather, her voice rising in panic.

"The door!" exclaimed Casey. He sprinted to the passageway, fumbling in his pockets for the other crystal and flashlight.

James raced after his brother, his handgun out and eyes fixed on the doorway into the main passage.

Casey found the little opening and dropped his crystal behind the black glass. He turned on his flashlight and shone it on the crystal. The crystal refracted the light into the dark-colored glass, and the grating began. Outside the doorway, several light beams crisscrossed the blackened hallway while the stone door slid into place. When the door shut completely, Casey retrieved his crystal. He pulled James's crystal from his pocket and gave it to him.

James quickly stuffed the crystal into his pocket. "You know they're not going to have any problem finding us."

Casey glanced at the closed passage, his brow furrowed. "Yeah, I know. Even if there wasn't a dead end, our footprints are obvious where we went."

Chapter Eight

Into the Fallen Star

L EILA'S EYES ANXIOUSLY GLANCED back into the dark passage as she followed Casey and James to join Heather under the *Fallen Star*. She struggled to compose her voice. "Do you think they'll find a way in?"

James's brow furrowed. "How to get through will delay them a bit. And hopefully we'll find a way out before then."

"The question is how soon until they decide to just blow it open," added Casey when they reached Heather. "Because I don't think they'll wait too long. And it won't take much to rip through that door."

Heather's worry cracked her voice. "Then it's time to stop playing around and find a way out. Let's split up and check the perimeter."

"Right," said James with a nod. "Casey, you and Leila go left around the room from here. Heather and I will go right. Look for anything that might be a possible exit. Be quick!"

Fear propelled them into a half-run around the room while they searched for any escape. The firelight flickered along the four walls, but only revealed one passage: the one they came in. A half minute later, they met back near the passageway.

"I'm surprised there isn't another way out," said Heather, catching her breath. "Or any other openings. The fire proves there has to be some way for fresh air to get in, otherwise the fire, and us, would be dead."

"Maybe we need to look more carefully," suggested James. "After all, the doors getting into the temple, and then this room, weren't something any of us would've found running by on a quick check."

A dull, rapid *tump, tump, tump, tump* emanated from the passageway.

"Uh-oh," said Leila, her voice laced with fear. "I think they're trying to shoot in."

Heather looked to the brothers, her face creased. "What're we going to do?"

"I don't—" Casey's words froze as he stared at the shimmering object in the room and realized the ramp was still lowered. When he had removed the disc, the blue panel had disappeared. He wondered briefly why the ramp had not retracted. A thin line of blue light ran up each edge of the ramp, seemingly to invite him up into the dark opening above. The last couple minutes had distracted him from the *Fallen Star*. He looked at the others and gave a half-smile. "We need to hide."

"Brilliant, Sherlock," said Heather.

"Did you forget?" asked James. "Our tracks in this dust will give us away no matter where we might hide."

"And where would we even—" Heather's question dropped when she saw Casey point at the ramp. Her voice rose in disbelief. "After all we've been through in the last day, do you really think that's a good idea? Who knows how fresh that air is? And if you managed to get the ramp up, how're you going to get it down again?"

Casey smiled. "I'll find some buttons to push."

"One way to find out," said James, starting towards the ramp.

Casey darted after James, Leila and Heather following. When James and Casey reached the ramp top, a soft white light instantly filled the space.

James's voice was a soft gasp. "Casey, I think you're right. This is an alien spaceship."

At the top of the ramp, on the nearby right wall, another panel emanated a faint blue outline around a red glyph that faded in and out in the center. Casey stepped towards the panel and touched the red symbol. Behind them, the blue lights on the ramp twinkled out. The ramp silently raised and melded back into place, and the flickering glow of the firelight disappeared.

"We're going to die," whimpered Leila.

The corner of James's mouth curled into a smirk. "They need to find us first."

The interior was uniformly lit with a white light that seemed to come from everywhere, but without any visible light source. On the right wall, next to the panel, the outline of a door appeared and slid to the left, disappearing into the wall. Beyond the opening, a hallway ran to the left, towards the opposite end of the ship. Casey walked into the hall, followed by James, Heather, and Leila. They passed several outlined sections in the wall—doors—but the small, red-hued panels refused entry. The hallway ended at an outlined doorway nearly the width of the hall.

When Casey stepped near the door outline, a square, flat panel on the right wall illuminated a faint dull amber. Unlike the other panels, there were no characters, glyphs, or any obvious means of interaction. Touching it did nothing. Casey cocked his head for a moment then placed his right palm on the amber-colored panel. Beneath his hand, the panel turned blue.

Instantly, another panel appeared above the first, at eye level. The same blue hue outlined a display of black, smoky crystal. A dim red light beckoned to Casey to peer through the smoky translucence. He leaned in closer, his hand still touching the lower panel. His eyes met a red flash, and a pulse of warmth surged through his palm.

Both panels faded to black, and the outlined door disappeared into the wall, revealing a room beyond it.

Casey removed his hand, shook it briefly, and blinked away the spots in his eyesight. "Wasn't so bad that time. More like a brief touch of hot water than a burn or shock."

"Well," replied James, "you can just keep taking it for the team. How'd you know about the eye-thing?"

Casey shrugged. "I didn't. I saw a light inside that looked like a window. I tried to get a better look."

Casey stepped through the doorway and entered the long end of a large oval room about twenty feet long and sixteen wide. A soft, natural white light lit the cream-colored room. The floor was a brushed dark silver. The ceilings curved down the wall and then into the floor. Except for the doorway behind him, there was little to identify where the walls, ceiling, or floor began or ended. The effect was disconcerting. Without windows, corners, or wall edges, it was like a continuous canvas that curved and arced around the room, distorting the perception into thinking there was no wall or ceiling. Along the opposite end of the oval room, a low console-like section elegantly curved out from the wall, swept towards the middle, and then sloped back four feet to form a rounded peninsula at the center.

An aisle stretched from the doorway to the center's rounded console. Five generously sized chairs were on each side of the aisle. One chair was on each side of the extended center console, much like left and right captain's chairs. Behind the two front chairs, two rows of two chairs lined the aisles. The seats reminded Casey of luxury theater seating with oversized armrests, high backs, and wide headrests.

Casey approached the console, stopping to admire the elongated center. The smooth contours of the entire console were like a section of the wall that had been pulled out taffy-like, stretched and shaped, its curves seamlessly joined. The entire console was white and devoid of any features. He moved in front of the left captain's chair.

"Wow," breathed Heather, standing at the back of room. "My eyes are having a trip trying to focus on where the walls or ceiling are."

Leila stood next to Heather, her eyes wide as she tried to take in what they were seeing. "I never thought this could be real."

James joined his brother at the front of the room. Casey removed his backpack and placed it beside the left chair, and he gingerly sat. James also set his pack down and plopped onto the right front seat. The chairs were firm but comfortable, like sitting on leather-covered memory foam. The armrest felt softer, more like a microfiber.

James grinned at his brother, who was examining the chair. "This is probably the coolest archaeological find ever."

Casey nodded. His head dropped in closer to the center console where he discovered a small slit. He pulled out his crystal and put it in a narrow opening. A faint amber hue briefly lit the slit and then faded away. When nothing else happened, he removed his crystal and looked at his brother. "James, do you have your crystal?"

"Yeah. Why?"

Casey's right hand opened towards his brother. "It might be the key to this ship."

James's voice wavered. "Okay," he said, fishing the crystal from his pocket. "I'm not sure if this is a good idea, though." He reached over, put the crystal into the slot, and sat back in the right chair to wait.

Nothing happened. The crystal simply rested snug inside the slot, its edge exposed just enough to pinch and pull it out.

"Maybe it needs a jump start," said James.

Chapter Nine
Taking Off

T HE FLOOR SHUDDERED AS if a giant had rattled the *Fallen Star*.

"Was that an aftershock?" asked Heather.

James was looking at the room's door. "I think the Anaconda used their explosive key."

Leila's eyes widened as she looked behind her. "Do you think they'll find us in here?"

"Not likely," said James. "I think we have the only key into the ship."

"And it might be a little difficult for them to find out where we went," added Casey.

Casey reached over to take James's disc out of the slot. As he touched it, the disc warmed, and a green hue illuminated the disc momentarily. Then blue, green, red, and white lights began to circumnavigate and illuminate various displays across the entire console. Alien characters appeared on multiple previously undetected screens. The white light of the room faded to less than twilight, and a faint glow flickered from the floor and walls.

Under Casey's left hand, a dome raised from the end of the armrest. A matching one rose from the right armrest. Each looked like half of a four-inch silver ball. He allowed his left hand to rest on the smooth, cool, domed surface.

James stared at the walls. "What the—"

Leila stifled a gasp.

Every outward surface of the room—the walls, ceiling, and floor—had become like glass. The blue-orange flicker of the exterior room's firelight danced and cast shadows inside the *Fallen Star*.

"Casey," said Heather. "What'd you do this time?"

Casey let go of the disc and turned back to Heather. Everything remained as it was. "Believe it or not, I didn't push any buttons this time. I was about to take out James's crystal."

Leila walked to the front console. "Maybe the key and ship have been encoded to you. Since you're the one who first put the crystal in the ship, and then opened the door into this room, maybe you had to be the one to touch the disc when it was inserted."

Heather's hand stifled an anxious yelp. "They're here!" She frantically pointed below them.

Everyone froze. Eyes followed Heather's pointing finger. Walking underneath them were two black-haired men wearing worn and faded military jungle fatigues. Their hands casually held AK-47s while unshaven and dirty faces looked up and around. A third man came from under Casey and James and engaged in some kind of dispute with the other two. Their attention turned towards a fourth person who was pointing to the ground near the back of the ship. They continued their argument.

Leila let go of her held breath. "They can't see us."

Casey got out of his chair and watched the three men walk back to the fourth. Through the rear wall they could see the back of the exterior chamber. The fire along the wall edge illuminated three more men, similarly attired and armed. One man's arm was hastily bandaged, and red streaks crossed his face. One of the three turned and disappeared among the strewn rubble into the passageway. The four men under the

Fallen Star split up. Two walked under the ship towards the front. The other two split and headed in opposite directions around the room.

After a minute, the man returned from the passage and was followed by the man in the beret. The two still under the ship sprinted to the passage opening. One was particularly animated as he gave some kind of report, his hands gesturing at the *Fallen Star*. Their commander nodded—his mouth thin with satisfaction and eyes fixated on the *Fallen Star*—and then walked towards the ship. The two men followed. The commander walked under the ship, looked up, and seemed to relish what he was seeing. The two men who had gone separate ways around the room soon joined them.

The five men were directly beneath Casey. The commander looked up. Casey thought he could feel the penetrating, black eyes that flashed with excitement. The olive-colored skin under the beret seemed almost scaly with the flickering firelight. The man had the look of satisfied awe, like a child who'd received a Christmas present he'd known about, only to discover it was better than expected.

One of the men looked up, and Casey recognized the face. "Isn't that the guard who walked out of the professor's tent last night?"

"Maybe," replied Heather, "but I wasn't really paying attention."

"Yes, he is," confirmed James.

Heather fidgeted as she watched the men below them. "I wish we could hear what they're saying," she lamented.

"I wish they'd leave," murmured Leila.

James shook his head. "That's not likely to happen very soon."

The five men continued their discussion. The commander demanded something of the others and pointed upwards. Leila jumped as the gesture aimed right at her. One of the men pulled out a radio, shook it, and attempted to call a few times. After a brief pause, he shook his head. The commander's arms became aggressive as he spoke to the radio man, who practically jumped in a sprint out of the room. The three men nearest the passageway followed after him.

Casey's right hand rubbed the back of his neck. "Even if they think we somehow escaped the room, these guys aren't likely to leave." His left eyebrow rose at his brother. "James, any chance we could take them? There's only four left."

"There's always a chance," mulled James, "but the odds are against us. I'm not sure about that beret guy. And who knows when the others will return."

Heather's eyes looked hopeful. "Except we have the element of surprise. They might suspect we're in here, but they don't know how we got in. I don't know about Leila, but it's not just you two who can take them on."

"We could just stay here," suggested Leila. "They don't have the key, so it's unlikely they'll find us in here."

"The biggest problem is there are still four others who could return at any time," said James. "And I don't think the guy with the radio is calling for takeout."

"So, where does that leave us?" Heather asked, her eyes dropping down to watch the men below.

Casey half shrugged. "Like Leila said, right here. Until something comes up."

"Or we think of something," countered James. "On the bright side, this is our best chance for a rest. While I don't suggest napping"—he motioned to the seats—"taking a seat might help reduce some stress."

Reluctantly, Heather walked over to a chair and sat down. Leila followed but chose to remain standing.

Casey stared into the orange glow in front of him while his hands rested gently on the small domes on the armrests. The cold was gone, replaced by a warmth. The surface no longer felt hard, but comfortable, like they had been fitted to him. His eyes shifted down to his hands. The fingers were slightly absorbed into the dome's surface. The feeling was light and soothing, like grabbing a stress ball made of gelatin. There was no pressure against his hands or fingers. In front of him, and on the center console, new lights and screens illuminated.

A 3D image of the *Fallen Star* instantly floated above the center console. A virtual chamber surrounded the hovering image, the walls like a transparent barrier. Beneath the ship, 3D replicas of the four men materialized. The man in the beret had just turned and was walking back to the chamber's doorway.

"Whoa! You got a different view up," admired James. "The clarity and detail are amazing."

"Like a near-perfect virtual reality," said Casey.

A second later the image reduced in size. Wrapped around the now-smaller *Fallen Star*, a fully transparent three-peaked pyramid cross section appeared. The large room with the *Fallen Star* in it was centered with the passage leading away from the room. Outside of the large chamber, the remainder of the pyramid was mostly transparent. The other passageways wound up the interior of the pyramid to the entry stairs where piles of rubble had collapsed in from the altar entrance on top. Small images of four men were climbing the stairs and maneuvering over the rubble heaps. On top of the pyramid, two more men were waiting. The 3D image expanded off the center and covered the full console. Jungle materialized on all sides of the pyramid.

"Looks like it's scanning things," said Heather as she watched the display increase in clarity.

Casey reached towards the image of the ship. Instantly the display returned to the immediate surrounding, the *Fallen Star* in its chamber. The three men under the middle of the ship were arguing about something and pointing.

"Oh, I wish we could hear them," complained Heather. Then her hazel eyes brightened. "Maybe the ship has some audio receivers."

Suddenly one man paled. He pointed his automatic rifle at the front of the *Fallen Star* and shot several rounds.

A purple hue pulsated around the 3D image of the ship. Under Casey's left index finger, a soft purple glow light faded in and out. Instinctively, he pressed in slightly and the beating light disappeared. At the same time a purple hue fully engulfed the 3D ship.

Casey watched the 3D image as the other men under the ship paled, like they had all suddenly seen ghosts. They looked around in disbelief, their rifles lowered. As if on cue, all three sprinted towards the doorway where their commander had stopped.

One man crashed into the left rear leg of the *Fallen Star*, his AK-47 knocked from his grip when he seemed to bounce back off the leg. His hands instantly covered his face where red was flowing from his nose like he had been swatted by a baseball bat.

Heather's head cocked. "What just happened?"

"Are you referring to the guy who shot at us, or the dummy who just ran into the landing gear?" asked Casey.

"Both. Because I can't see the landing gear either."

Casey turned his head from the 3D image to look. Heather's gaze was focused towards the back of the room. The man on the ground tried to pull himself together and took a couple attempts to grab his AK-47 before he stumbled away. The other two were cowering in front of the commander, who angrily pointed in the direction of the ship.

Casey looked at where the landing gear should have been. The area was empty, as if the support leg had vanished. He glanced back at the 3D image; all three legs were clearly visible. Then his focus returned to the wall screen, where the landing legs should have been visible.

James did the same double take. "Whatever you did, I think the ship is cloaked."

Heather's lips pressed together. "The ship is what?"

"Cloaked," James repeated. He added teasingly, "Have we really been friends for all these years only for me to now discover that, while you speak several languages fluently, you're sci-fi illiterate?"

"I know what cloaking is," huffed Heather. "I just thought it was science fiction."

"It's real," said Leila. "Though Earth's technology only has crude examples of it. The basic idea is instead of a surface reflecting light, light is refracted around it, so it appears invisible. The question is, how did it happen?"

"Well, it might be useful," said James "I'm not sure how, since we're stuck in this pyramid and those guys likely know we're in here. Casey, do you know how to return to that expanded view? Where it showed the outside of the pyramid?"

Casey examined the console. "I'm not even sure how any of this is working." He stared at the floating images. Uncertain, he reached out and touched the air just outside the 3D display. Instantly the display over the main console zoomed out to the wider view, its clear image more detailed than before. A smaller 3D close-up of the *Fallen Star* still hovered over the end of the center console.

Leila and Heather crowded around as James, encouraged by what he saw Casey do, reached over to the 3D display and began touching and sliding his fingers across it. After a few attempts he could zoom in and out on parts of the pyramid's interior and exterior. He backtracked along the passage to the collapsed section he had discovered earlier. Beyond the rubble the imaged revealed a door into another room.

"There's another room!" squealed Heather with delight. She stared at the image. "No offense, Casey, but this is way better than your LIDAR."

James's eyes narrowed. "But no way out. At least not that's big enough for us."

"Casey," said Leila, "did you know your hands are glowing?"

All eyes turned towards Casey.

Casey looked down at his hands. Light from the domes shone through his fingers and hands, giving them an eerie red-orange glow. A green band surrounded the perimeter of each dome. "No, I was noticing there are a few more lights on the various console screens. Probably meters or some kind of monitoring systems. But I've no idea what anything is." He lifted his right hand from the dome. The light faded. Replacing his hand on the curved surface made the glow return. "It's kind of a strange feeling."

"What do you mean?" asked James.

"Well, it's warm. More comfortable, like holding someone's hand."

"I didn't know you'd even held a girl's hand before," teased James.

"Very funny." Casey looked back at his hands. The domes felt different, looser, like they were real orbs sunken into the armrests and suspended in hidden cradles to allow for movement. He moved his hands, and the little domes rotated, panned, or tilted with his direction.

Heather quickly grasped a nearby headrest. "Whoa, Casey, what're you doing?"

"What—?" Casey's words were lost when he saw Leila and Heather trying to maintain their balance.

He watched the smaller 3D image of the ship rocking gently back and forth in relation to the room. The three legs were gone.

"You two better sit down," said James. "Casey's driving."

Heather flopped into the seat behind James. "More like learning to fly, again."

"Even more reason to sit down and fasten your seatbelts." Casey grinned. "Maybe sometime I'll tell you about my first flight."

"Yeah, maybe I should tell Mom's side," chuckled James.

Heather felt around her seat. "Are there even seatbelts on these things?"

Leila staggered into a seat.

"Ever fly one of these in your flight training?" asked James.

Casey's eyes darted from the floating images to the viewscreens in the walls and floor. His head shook. "No. The alien spacecraft was on loan to Area 51 when it was supposed to be my turn."

"So"—James's brows rose in mock shock—"you're flying illegally, without a spaceship type-class rating or endorsement."

"Technically we're hovering, and inside, so I doubt I need a rating for it."

"Just don't hit the walls." Heather frowned, her small hands gripping the armrests. "It doesn't look like you have much room to spare."

"Good point," agreed James, his tone serious. "Maybe you should land before you crash."

Casey felt his shoulders tense and focused on his breathing. "I would if I knew how. I'm not even sure how to get the landing legs down. It looks like they've disappeared in the display."

A set of alien glyphs appeared near Casey, floating in the 3D display. Under his right index finger a blue light pulsed, synced with a fluctuating warmth.

"I've got a blue light under my finger," said Casey. "Anyone opposed to me pressing it?"

"Maybe it'll stop," suggested Heather.

Casey pressed in slightly. A blue glow highlighted the outline of the ship image. Under his finger, the blue light pulsed faster. He pressed in, and the blue glow around the 3D ship extended away from the surface and fully encased it in a blue-hued bubble. In the extended 3D view, the blue bubble pressed against the chamber's wall. He moved his hands slightly, and the ship smoothly moved right. Through the wall viewscreens, smashed stone burst into dust several yards away from the ship's hull. The floating image showed the blue bubble clipping the pyramid wall.

James's mouth curled into a mischievous smile. "Looks like we have a shield."

Casey's left eyebrow rose. "And a way out."

Heather shot Casey an incredulous look. "You're not serious, are you? If you're thinking about what I think you're thinking about, you'll destroy the pyramid. And maybe us and this ship as well."

"It'll just make it more of a ruin," said Casey. "Besides, I don't see another way out."

James's teeth clenched. "Looks like more company." He pointed at the extended display, and the image responded by popping out an enlarged view of James's target. Two large helicopters—military gunships—appeared in the distance.

"Okay." Heather's voice was resigned to the option. "Let's do it. Just try to not destroy the whole pyramid."

"You've totally freaked out those men," said Leila, who was watching the floor behind them. "Except for the guy in the beret, everyone else ran out when you crashed into the wall."

"I wouldn't call it 'crashed,'" said Casey defensively. "More like a nudge. Everyone hold on to...something. I'm about to do some more nudging."

Casey caressed his hands across the silver domes. The ship rose up and moved slowly forward. He glanced back at the floor at the man in the beret. The olive-colored face radiated rage and hate. Through the dust and firelight, the eyes under the beret darkened.

Casey's attention shifted forward as pieces of stone pulverized before the shield, and the pyramid started bulging outward. The shield several yards ahead of the ship gave them the silent view of rock smashing. The blue-hued leading edge of the bubble brightened slightly while the ship continued its push through the angled wall. Miniature images of men on top of the ancient temple scrambled for cover at the intense shaking.

Green hues and brilliant sunlight burst through the front viewscreens and then filled the command room when the ship broke through its rock prison. The ship stopped near tree level. The exterior view through the walls of the command room showcased the jungle canopy as if through clear glass. Above them, thin wisps of cirrus clouds feathered across a blue sky. The most disconcerting view was through the transparent floor.

The *Fallen Star* jumped briefly while Casey made a couple of attempts to turn it around. Through the floor's viewscreens, centuries of greenery covered a triple-peaked pyramid. In the center of the pyramid's side—below and in front of them—a gaping hole like a yawning maw threatened to collapse in on itself. A massive heap of stone and rubble had slid down the side, shearing trees and vegetation from the pyramid. Rock stragglers continued to chase the main slide down to where the rubble had buried the bottom tiers of the pyramid.

In front of them, standing on the top of the pyramid, stood the man in the beret and two of his soldiers. He aimed an AK-47 in the direction of the ship and fired several bursts, varying his aim slightly. Tiny sparks peppered the shield as bullets sprayed across it.

Heather's hands gripped her armrests tightly. "I thought we were cloaked."

"We are, or were. Maybe some dust is on the shield, showing where we are," suggested James.

The commander yanked a radio from the man on his right and shouted something into it.

Two helicopter gunships flew over the treetops towards the *Fallen Star*.

"Oh boy," said Casey, his fingers gripping the domes. "This can't be good."

The 3D display quickly changed. The ship, glowing purple with a fringe of blue, hovered outside the temple at tree height while the two gunships were rapidly approaching the ship's front. A third image formed above the extended view, an ethereal globe forming into a blue-green planet with a single, bright-green spot on its surface. Directly above the green dot, orbiting the quickly coalescing Earth image, small red dots began to appear. In rapid succession, the dots turned green.

Outside, two rockets erupted from each gunship. A second later four explosions engulfed the forward shield. The front viewscreens instantly darkened, filtering out the intense brightness. The view's clarity and brightness returned just as several more rockets raced from the gunships and exploded harmlessly against the shield. Again, the forward display filtered and dimmed the intensity, minimizing the explosive brightness.

The 3D Earth image continued to increase in details and clarity. The bright-green spot became their location in Central America. Cities, rivers, mountains, and other features filled in. The image zoomed out until the Earth became a small blue-green ball. The moon appeared. Below the planet view, the main display still showed the ship in front of the ruined pyramid. The planet image shifted position and moved to hover over the front, main console, where it expanded out to a solar system view. The marble-sized Earth centered above the console with a large brilliant sun image to the left. Other planetary marbles settled into the various orbital positions relative to the sun. Several red glyphs throbbed near the bottom of the display in front of both James and Casey.

James reached to touch the immaterial alien symbols, and the display above the center console zoomed out. The ship and pyramid centered but shrank as jungle filled all directions. Several ruins, additional pyramids, and other structures became highlighted in their now-futile attempt to hide in the jungle. The archeological dig site appeared to the left. Single red glyphs, resembling an upside down *V*, hovered over the vehicles and ant-sized people still in the camp. The same glyph appeared over the two tiny gunships in the display while new streaks raced towards the *Fallen Star*. The red characters also floated above the men on the temple and over three additional gunships that materialized on the fringes of the display.

James raised his chin slightly towards the screen. "Looks like more are coming to the party."

Casey nodded.

"Can't you just fly us away from here?" asked Leila.

A pulsing warmth touched Casey's thumbs. Looking at the controller domes, color pulsed from an opaque white to a light green, with the green centering under the thumbs. He glanced up and noticed red glyphs under the solar system had morphed into a series of green characters. A matching string of characters floated across the center console image.

Heather leaned forward. "I wonder what all that means?"

Small sparks splattered across the front viewscreens as the gunships started shooting their machine guns.

A tinge of nervousness edged Casey's voice. "I think I'm supposed to press my thumbs in, but I've no idea what'll happen."

"We've survived so far," said Leila through clenched teeth. "Do whatever it takes to get us out of here."

The three additional helicopters were now within visual sight. Multiple flashes ruptured from their sides, and a barrage of missiles raced towards the *Fallen Star*.

"Now would be a good time to go," added James, gripping his armrests.

Casey pressed his thumbs in.

Chapter Ten
First Jump

THE *FALLEN STAR* LEAPED vertically into hypersonic flight. Casey's body pressed back into his seat. His vision narrowed. Lightheadedness and nausea threatened to black out his senses. Then a warm energy pulsed through his body, heightening his senses and awareness. The tunnel vision vanished, and he felt the familiar thrill of flight.

Through the floor viewscreens, the jungle greens became a sliver between ocean blues. The once-high feathery clouds were now below, the ship's speed barely disturbing the suspended water vapor.

Casey watched with awe while the Earth shrank below them and its curvature became more apparent. The blue sky quickly faded to a black dominated by the late morning sun, and the viewscreens dimmed to filter the brightness. Away from the sun, stars became visible, first as small specks and then the Milky Way stretched out through the vastness of space. Beyond the Earth's horizon, the moon appeared suspended in blackness.

Above the center console, the *Fallen Star* image mimicked the actual flight in vivid 3D. While the ship image maintained a center position, the Earth receded below to become a blue-green dome.

A deep exhale escaped James's lungs. "We're not in the jungle anymore."

"Whoa! That was an unexpected rush," said Leila.

"Shouldn't we have blacked out?" said Heather. "I felt like I was going to, then it just stopped. Wait!" Her voice rose in slight panic. "What in the world?"

Casey turned towards Heather and realized he felt light. Something bumped his left arm, and he saw his backpack floating nearby. He let go of the controls, and his body gently lifted from the chair. Looking around, the others were already floating above their seats, awkwardly navigating weightlessness.

Heather drifted over the aisle, her nervousness replaced by a giddy smile. She pushed off Casey's headrest and coasted back through the room. "Weightlessness is way better than I ever imagined. I thought SCUBA diving would be similar, but it's definitely not the same."

James smiled at Heather's comment while he struggled to figure out the motions of being weightless. He fought to right himself when he noticed a blinking green glyph floating nearby. "Wonder what that's for?"

Casey was struggling, and failing, to seat himself again. "Touch it. I can't hog all the fun pressing the buttons. But," he cautioned as his brother reached towards the alien character, "maybe we should all get in our seats first. In case we rocket back to Earth."

The warning came too late. A brief wave of nausea returned when artificial gravity yanked their previously weightless bodies to the floor. Casey and James landed clumsily in their seats. Leila sprawled onto the aisle.

Heather had just kicked off the back wall and ended up diving into the floor. "James! A warning before turning on the gravity would've been nice." Then she started to laugh.

Leila was rubbing her back. "I didn't think it was funny."

"Not you." Heather pointed to the floor. "With the respite from gravity, I didn't notice the view."

The others took in the sight, and Leila smiled. "That's a view I never tire of."

Through the wall viewscreens, the blackness of space was speckled with stars. Below them, through the floor, the full Earth—wisps of white clouds intermixed with blues, greens, and beiges—dominated the view.

Casey motioned to the walls. "Look outside."

Heather pushed herself up from the floor. "Where are we?"

"Inside an alien spaceship, orbiting the Earth," replied James. "Maybe I should turn the gravity back off, so we can feel like we're still in space."

Heather's eyes were humorless. "Very funny. I can see the continental land masses. I meant where are we going?? And do we have the fuel to get home?"

"That would be a question for the captain," deflected James.

Casey shrugged and turned his focus forward. Since falling back into his seat, he had not touched the controls on the armrests. The 3D images of the solar system still floated across the forward console in ever-increasing detail, even while maintaining the minuscule and relative size of the planets. A thin blue line glowed just below the solar system display.

A small replica of the *Fallen Star*—enveloped by a blue-tinged, purple halo—still hovered over the center console. While the Earth image shrank, increasing numbers of colored dots orbited the planet. Most had turned green. Others were amber colored. A small number took a couple seconds before changing from red to green. As new red or white dots crested the horizon, most would become green. A small image of the moon appeared to the left of the center console.

Casey felt the others quietly waiting and realized they expected him to have the answer. His cheeks warmed, and he fidgeted in his chair. He pretended to study the dots floating above the Earth. "My guess is these little dots are satellites or other objects in orbit. The green are probably the safe ones. Maybe the others are space junk or unknown."

Heather walked a few steps to stand next to Casey. "So, where are we going, Captain?"

Casey swallowed a growing lump. His dry throat made the action difficult. He felt cornered, exposed as a fraud. His head dropped slightly. "I don't know. But the Earth is right there. So, it shouldn't be too hard to get home."

"What do you think the blue line is for?" Heather asked, pointing at the image floating over the front console.

With the motion, the image changed. The solar system was swallowed by millions of minuscule specks of light that exploded across the entire forward console and formed the shape of a spiral galaxy. While the galaxy expanded over the main console, the image of the ship above the shrinking Earth retreated into a smaller form and floated over the end of the center console. The blue line morphed into red.

"Careful," warned Casey, smiling. "She's a bit touchy."

"She?"

"The *Fallen Star*."

James stood and stared at the galaxy hovering over the center console. "Is that what I think it is?"

Leila walked to the center console. "It does look like our galaxy. But what's the bright-green spot over there?" She indicated a speck of green on the far right side of the galaxy.

Casey tilted his head. "No idea. There's nothing else marked. Maybe it's the Earth? Or"—he thought for a moment—"maybe it's where the ship came from. Without any other markings, or an English map legend, it's hard to know where we are and if that's Earth or not."

Heather stepped in front of Casey and studied the galactic image with fascination. "Did you know in Maya Quiché mythology, the Milky Way is described as a great white serpent? For the Peruvian Inca it was a heavenly river. Old Chinese, northern Siberian, Korean, and Japanese myths also describe it as a great river or Celestial Stream. Interesting how many ancient cultures regarded the Milky Way as a roadway that was built by gods to link their world to ours."

She turned her head, and her right hand tucked some brown hair behind the ear. Her left hand rested on her hip as her eyes narrowed at Casey. "Do you really think this ship came from across the galaxy?"

"Well"—Casey tried to hide a grin—"I'm pretty certain it wasn't made in China."

James took a half-step forward. The green spot was closest to him, and his hand reached out to touch the ethereal speck. The entire image instantly changed and zoomed in to a seven-planet star system.

In front of Casey, on a moon of the fourth planet, the green hue blinked. "That's certainly not Earth."

"How far away do you think that is?" James inquired.

Heather turned towards James. "The galaxy's estimated to be about a hundred thousand light-years across, with our solar system about twenty-eight thousand from the center. There are an estimated two hundred billion stars in the galaxy. I didn't see exactly where we are on the galaxy map, but, if Casey's right and that green dot is on the other side of the galaxy from us, it could be seventy thousand light-years away, or more."

"Seventy thousand light-years?" exclaimed James. "That's definitely not a Sunday afternoon drive." He stared at Heather as his right hand scratched the back of his neck. "I wonder how it got to Earth and how long it took?"

"Kind of strange," mused Casey, "that it'd come to our planet out of who knows how many billions of planets in our galaxy."

Heather reached across the console and touched the green light. The image zoomed in to a small green-and-brown moon orbiting a swirling, dark-red planet. Several alien characters floated nearby.

Leila squinted at the moon image curiously. "Do you think that's really where this ship is from?"

"Since none of us can read the language, not even Heather," Casey teased, "who knows?"

"Give me some time," Heather retorted, and she leaned closer to the image.

"I'd say that it being the ship's home planet, or home moon, is the best guess," said Casey.

Heather touched the red bar, and the galaxy image returned. Curious, she swiped the blue line towards the center console. The alien planetary system reappeared above the center console. She changed the image to a close-up of the green-brown moon. A string of green characters appeared underneath the planet.

"Hey, I've got green lights again," announced Casey.

The controls on Casey's armrests were outlined with green. He sat back in the chair and gently rested his hands on the small domes. The coolness instantly warmed, and the green light pulsed in concentric circles centering under his thumbs.

"Any idea what they mean?" asked James.

"No," replied Casey with a mild shrug. "But, it probably means things are ready to go. I think I've got the basics of flying this ship."

"I hope the basics don't end up taking us to the moon," said Heather, her voice half-teasing but edged with caution as she eyed Earth's moon through the wall viewscreens, the heavenly body suspended in the blackness of space.

Several green characters floated above the console in front of Casey.

"I'm fairly certain the ship's ready to go," said Casey. "Everyone buckle...er, sit tight, and hope we get back to Earth."

Leila's head tilted. "What do you mean by 'hope?'"

"It means I hope by pressing the lights that are now lit under my thumbs that the propulsion system will work, and I can take us back to Earth. I can steer it, but I don't know how to power things on or off, including whatever engines this ship uses."

"I've not sure about this," said Heather as she sat behind Casey. Leila took a seat across from her.

Casey half-smiled. "I'm not either. But unless you want to float around in space while we try to figure things out, and hope our oxygen doesn't run out, this may be our best option to get home. What do you think, James?"

"We're still alive, at least, I don't think I'm dead yet. I say go for it."

"Okay," relented Heather. "I don't have any better ideas. I suppose the worst thing is we land on the moon at some alien rendezvous base."

"Do you think there's a base on the moon?" asked Leila.

Heather smiled. "Don't worry. After hundreds of years on Earth, and who knows how many traveling through space, I doubt anyone is still waiting for this ship to come back."

Leila gripped the armrests of her chair. "Well, let's do it. I'm curious what kind of power this ship runs on. But I'm more concerned about its energy source, or whatever, running out before we can get back."

A knot formed in Casey's stomach. "Okay. Hold on to your seats, or something."

An uncomfortable feeling nagged at Casey. It wasn't a bad feeling, which was why he did not mention it. His stomach growled with hunger, and his mouth felt dry. He tilted his wrist to see his watch: 11:23 a.m. Before he could talk himself out of it, he pressed in gently with his thumbs while he watched the 3D images floating over the console. The galaxy view still stretched across the forward console, the alien green-brown moon hovering over the center. A smaller image of the *Fallen Star* remained hovering at a lower point over the end of the console.

At that moment, Casey realized what was bothering him.

Brilliant white streams of plasma erupted from the four claw-like extrusions around the dish at the front of the ship. The front viewscreens darkened with the brightness. The streams ripped and tore into the space in front of the ship and converged at a single, distant point. The collector glowed purple, and a single arc of white plasma burst out to join the other four. Around the convergence point, the background space and stars distorted, like the lights of oncoming traffic through a rain-drenched windshield. The front of the ship appeared to stretch into the distortion. In the side viewscreens the moon and stars blurred, stretched out behind the ship as streaks of light, and instantly disappeared. Reds, blues, whites, and other colors streaked and melded together as they rotated one direction around the ship and then spiraled into another. Ahead of the *Fallen Star*, the ribbons of plasma continued to weave and cut a distortion path through space.

Casey felt as if he were in a dream where he needed to run fast, but his legs and body refused to move. His head felt paralyzed, transfixed in place. His hands were cool now, different than the normal warmth the controls exuded, although light still pulsed through the silver domes. With great effort he turned his head enough to see James to his right and Leila behind him. They were like living statues, frozen in time and place. The seats had partially absorbed their occupants, holding them perfectly in place without a harness or seatbelt.

In the galaxy display above the console, a purple dot moved quickly from the left towards the green spot on the right. The movement was not linear, but snaked in and around stars, maneuvering slightly one direction, and then another.

A new image appeared. Unlike the others, this one completely surrounded Casey. The light rings around the controller domes changed to purple. Stars, clusters, and nebulae appeared before him and passed just as quickly over and around him. He felt as if he were the ship traveling through the stars, a feeling that was exhilarating and unnerving.

The star fields washed around Casey, and the rotating colors of light continued their twisting and spiraling around the ship. It reminded him of speeding down a water slide except when he realized he felt no effects of acceleration or turns.

It felt like the controls were coaching and guiding his hands in their movement. A soft white hue pulsated gently through the center of the purple rings. Casey felt like the ship was simultaneously giving and taking energy from him. He felt elated and free, even more than he did when flying a helicopter or a plane.

Another distortion appeared in front of the ship. It was like looking through an old, sagging window pane. A red, swirling planet filled the distorted space window. In the center, a small black spot appeared. The distortion moved quickly towards the ship, and the 3D display surrounding Casey disappeared.

When it looked like the ship would break through the space glass, the *Fallen Star* instantly decelerated. Casey felt blood drain from his head and pressure build up throughout his body. At the same time, there was a counteracting energy force.

The distortion field dissolved into clarity, and the plasma streams immediately stopped. Stars in the viewscreens solidified into points of light. Casey felt his hands release the domes, and he blacked out.

Chapter Eleven

Jump Aftermath

THE SEEMINGLY INVISIBLE RESTRAINTS were gone, and Casey's limbs felt free. He could feel that he was lying down, face up, but his eyes refused to open. Joint and muscle aches radiated their complaint when he tried to move his stiff body. His right hand brushed at his face, thinking to wipe off the residue of something, but it felt nothing. He forced his eyes to open and was momentarily confused, as if waking from a strange dream.

Stars shone brightly above him, set amidst space blacker than he remembered. The constellations were unfamiliar. Behind him felt different, and he wondered, *Am I lying down in a chair?* In response to his question, he sat up and felt a chair back rise up with him. Then disorientation hit. On the left, a moon of greens and browns floated in space while a massive red planet dominated the background. More stars and black space filled the front and back. On the right, a bright sun shone through what seemed like tinted glass. Panic momentarily gripped his throat when he saw stars also below him instead of ground. The memory of what happened flooded back when his focus shifted to the other chairs and the control console.

Nearby, James, Heather, and Leila were lying down, their chairs reclined horizontally with feet rests that had extended out. Nobody else moved except for the slow rise and fall of chests with each breath.

Casey's head was groggy as he studied the 3D galaxy view that spanned the console in front of him. He realized the positioning was different, but he could not determine exactly how much. He remembered the galaxy image had shifted while they traveled, twisting and rotating into a new position so the green spot was now before him. His eyes scanned the galactic view, but he could not remember where they had come from. A red planet and green-brown moon floated over the center console, a tiny *Fallen Star* orbiting the moon. He touched the green spot in the galaxy, and the view transformed into a seven-planet system with a red fourth planet. He touched the light-bar to revert to the galaxy view.

Casey's throat tightened, and saliva disappeared from his mouth with the taste of panic. Thoughts rushed his mind: *How many stars did Heather say there are? Two hundred billion? How am I ever going to find Earth again? Even knowing it's somewhere on the other side of the galaxy probably narrows it down to a million or so planets. Maybe only a few thousand, if I'm lucky.*

He wondered how he was going to tell the others and what he might say. He had not known what would happen and they'd known that. But it had never crossed his mind that they would end up on the other side of the galaxy. *Or did it?* He remembered the uncomfortable feeling he'd had and recalled what he'd realized after he'd pressed the thumb-lights. His mind had suspected the ship would go to the green spot—the alien moon—but he could not accept it as a real possibility. It was simply unfathomable to imagine traversing across the galaxy.

Habit forced a slow deep breath in, then a slow exhale in an attempt to relax. The clouds in his mind seemed to be lifting, and he looked around the control room again. The others were still sleeping or unconscious. He did not remember anyone reclining their seats and had not realized the seats could recline.

Casey's eyes centered on the 3D display of the moon and planet. Several objects were now being tracked as white dots around their orbits. He touched one of the dots. A separate projection jumped out that looked like the wreckage of a large satellite or small space station. He touched several other dots that revealed more wreckage or debris. One by one, the dots changed to amber. Another white dot showed up on the opposite side of the moon, but touching it revealed nothing. Casey guessed the *Fallen Star* had not identified it.

The green light was on the surface of the moon above the center display. A new image leaped out in front of Casey when he touched the green spot. A section of mountain range appeared where foothills ran right up into a cliff range. Near the cliffs, a steep rocky surface revealed sparse vegetation. Scorch marks scarred the cliffs and sides of the mountain. The remains of several buildings crumbled near the foothills, just below the cliff base. As he zoomed in and out, Casey discovered several of the scorch marks were gaping black holes.

Not far from the base of the cliffs, near the foothills, an old wreckage of a massive, elongated cigar-shaped spacecraft lay half-buried in its impact crater. Large pieces had sheared off and were scattered around the crash zone. Erosion around the impact site hinted the wreck had occurred in some forgotten past.

His eyes squeezed shut momentarily, and a large yawn broke Casey's face. From his middle, an unhappy grumble gurgled in his stomach. He rotated his wristwatch, 11:24 a.m. His brow furrowed, wondering if the watch had stopped. He watched the seconds sweep the minute hand to the 25. Another yawn distracted him. Sleep was tempting. He debated whether he should wait to eat or wake the others to share some food. He leaned his head back and closed his eyes to think. A gentle flow of warmth soothed him, and his body felt like it was slowly drifting back.

Chapter Twelve

Orbiting a Moon

G ROANS FILTERED INTO CASEY'S ears. His eyes opened, and he sat up, the seat back rising while the footrest dropped. He felt invigorated, energized. Next to him, the floating *Fallen Star* image still orbited a green-brown moon. Several hundred other objects, most displayed as amber, now orbited the 3D moon and planet. A couple of faint red dots were being tracked, circling on the opposite side of the planet.

"What galaxy did we hit?" moaned James, massaging his forehead as he sat up. "That felt like I was squished into my seat and then thrust into a gelatin mold so I couldn't move."

"It felt like I was ripped apart," muttered Heather, her voice weak, "and then sucked into some psychedelic dream." She shook her head. "Casey, whatever you did, let's not do it again."

Behind James, Leila, who was still reclined in the chair, added her displeasure. "What happened? I thought my cells were being torn out. But then I must've blacked out." She sat up and felt her seat back rise up. "Are these seats, like, auto-recliners?"

"Well, I don't know about you two"—James nodded at Casey and Heather—"but I feel like Sensei put me through the wringer."

Casey's eyebrows came together as he looked at the others. "Let me get this straight—before I try to explain what I don't know—none of you saw what happened?"

James cocked his head at his brother. "Other than some bursts of light in front of us, then black, uh, no."

Heather gave it a moment's thought. "I kind of remember going through something like a waterfall of light."

Leila's eyes fixated on the center display with the moon and nearby planet. Her brow raised. "Did we go somewhere?"

"Well, yes," said Casey. "We did go somewhere. But I'm not really sure where 'somewhere' is. Remember that green-brown moon in the galaxy map? Well, I think we somehow came across the galaxy."

Leila's forehead wrinkled further. "Are you saying we're on the other side of the galaxy?"

Casey's head involuntarily nodded while his eyes looked uncertain. "I didn't think it was possible, but, yeah, it would seem so."

"So, let's just go back," replied Heather as she rubbed her head.

Casey's hands clasped together. "I would." He paused for a couple seconds. "Except for two things. First, I don't know how the ship did what it did. I can try to do it again, even though Heather said she didn't want to do it again." The corners of his mouth rose in a weak smile. "But I really don't know how, and it'd be pushing more buttons. And that's where the second problem is more of a concern. I have no idea where in the galaxy Earth is, except it's somewhere, probably, on that far side."

Casey stood and moved towards the galaxy map that floated above the front console. "We're apparently here"—he pointed at the green speck—"but there isn't a marker for where our home is, where we just came from. All we know is it's somewhere on the opposite side."

Heather and Leila cautiously got up from their seats and walked to the center console. James remained seated, his fingers rubbing his temples.

Heather studied the galaxy map. She played with zooming in and out of different sections. After a few minutes of silence and examining various star systems on the opposite side of the galaxy map, she surrendered. "Yeah, I don't know where Earth is. Without knowing more precise coordinates, we'd probably spent a lifetime looking and never find it."

"But," started Casey, pointing to the map, "the ship kept a record of this location, so there must be a record in its data of where Earth is. If we can figure it out, we can get back. That's the challenge: how do we access it?"

Heather looked at Casey, a knowing smile lifted the corners of her mouth. "To do that we need to understand the ship's language."

Casey nodded. "It's a good thing you've got a gift with languages. I'm guessing that moon is where the ship came from, and that's why it was marked on the map."

"So," Leila said, head tilting as she glanced at Casey, "you think maybe we can get some answers down there?"

"Wait a minute. Back up," said James, his hands raised. "Casey, did you say you 'saw' what happened? And none of us did?"

Casey's cheeks flushed, and he nodded. Leila and Heather shook their heads.

"I blacked out," admitted Leila.

Curious, Heather asked, "What did you see?"

Casey described the entering and passing through the distortion, and how everyone seemed to be frozen. He related how he blacked out afterwards, woke up, checked things, and then ended up falling asleep. He did not mention the sensations he felt when touching the controls.

Leila's eyes were intensely interested. "That would've been cool to see."

"How long were we out?" asked Heather. "It doesn't seem like it took very long."

"And why didn't you black out like the rest of us?" added James.

"I'm not sure exactly," said Casey. "But I did happen to glance at my watch before, because I was hungry—which, by the way, my stomach is still growling—and I noticed it was 11:23. I didn't check the watch immediately after, but when I did, it was only 11:24. The trip was less than a minute. And it's nearly 6:00 p.m. now."

"That shouldn't be possible." Heather's face was somber. Her eyes shifted across the floating galaxy while she mentally digested Casey's words. "Even if faster-than-light speed was possible, it still shouldn't be that fast. Completely theoretical space-warp ideas would still take decades or at least years to go across the galaxy." A sigh of resignation escaped as she shifted her weight. "It's interesting we all slept so long."

"Probably because of the stress and lack of sleep last night," suggested Leila.

"And now it's past dinnertime," added James with a confirming glance at his watch. "Which is why I'm starving."

Casey pulled out a couple of granola bars from his pack along with a water bladder. "Before we get on with any major plans in figuring out how to get back to Earth, I think our primary goal should be to find more water, and hopefully some food." He broke the bars in half and passed them out. "James and I don't have much. It's even less when divided among four."

James grabbed his small day pack from the floor and pulled out a water bladder. "I totally agree. My water's getting low, as is the food. If we knew exactly how to get back to Earth, and how long, maybe we could skip getting more water and food. But without knowing that, water and food are more important."

"Yeah, if I'd known we'd be heading across the galaxy I would've put more in," said Casey. He handed the water bladder to Heather.

Heather nodded her thanks, took the water, and sipped through the bite valve. She took a second sip and passed the water to Leila. "I'm just glad you two bring your packs almost everywhere." Her hands began to free her hair from its ponytail.

After swallowing some water, Leila added, "Me too." She examined the tube of the water bladder while she took another bite of her granola bar.

"Yeah, some habits die hard," said James. "Dad—and Mom—both wanted us to always be ready to go."

"Yeah, especially Dad." A grin broke Casey's face. "But I never thought it would be to go to space."

"I'm curious," said Leila. "In the tubes of your water bladders, are those in-line filters?"

"Yeah," said James with a short nod. "Not really needed for the water that's in it right now, but just in case we have to get water from an unknown source, it's helpful to have."

"Might be good if we find water," said Leila.

"I know you guys don't understand," said Heather while she rubbed her fingers vigorously into and around her scalp, massaging hair roots and shaking her hair loose, "but it's so nice to have a break from having my hair pulled back." She sat down in the chair behind Casey, her brown hair tousled and falling on her shoulders.

The foursome savored the last few bites of granola bars and sips of water.

Casey stood, stretched his hands up, and then took a step to the center console. "After the space distortion thing"—he pointed at the image of the hovering moon—"when you guys were out, I had a look at some of the things in orbit. Just about everything is wreckage or debris. I didn't look at everything, but none of it was natural looking. There are a couple of red blips on the opposite side that aren't identified. And on the moon's surface there's only a single place identified. The images look like the place was attacked and destroyed ages ago."

Casey touched the spot on the surface, and the side of the mountain jumped out into the expanded display. The image of a destroyed facility at the base of the cliff appeared. "I think this may be where the ship came from."

Leila's dark-brown eyes lifted slightly. "Why do you think that?"

"Mostly a guess. The location was already on the galaxy map so, to me, it makes sense that if it's not a home base, then perhaps it was the last place the ship was at. Maybe we—I—somehow clicked a return-to-home or back button. I don't know. But I think that facility might be a good place to start looking for answers."

"For what, an Alien-English, English-Alien dictionary?" said Heather. "That'd be nice. Because without it I'm not sure how we'll know an answer even if it bites us."

Casey smiled. "If there is, it's probably outdated. Mostly it's a starting place. And if it is where the ship came from, maybe we can learn something."

"I agree it's a good place to start looking for water," said James. "Maybe food as well. There may not be anything edible—and we may not even know what edible looks like—but that facility was probably built near water or a water supply, and that's more critical."

Leila's attention shifted towards the map of the nearby moon and planet. "What do you think these orbiting red spots are?"

"No idea," said Casey, his head shaking slowly from side to side. "If we catch up to them, maybe the ship's sensor can see them better. But I'm not sure if we want to catch up to one."

James stood and stepped towards the console, staring intently at the ruins along the cliff edge. "Something's bothering me. Why was that facility attacked? You're right; it looks like it happened a really long time ago, which could be when this ship left. Or maybe the ship left earlier. The vegetation around the scar marks haven't grown in much. But it looks fairly barren, so maybe things don't grow very fast. The real question, is there anyone still living in the area?"

Casey nodded. "I was wondering, if this ship can travel across the galaxy in seconds, and if this civilization has had this technology for hundreds of years, why aren't they spread across the galaxy? Are they just keeping a low profile and not wanting to spook us Earthlings?"

"Maybe this was brand new technology," suggested Leila. "Maybe someone took it for a spin before it could be used."

"Interesting idea," said James, nodding. "But, if that's the case, why hasn't it been redeveloped since then?"

"Judging by the destruction," mused Heather, "maybe the research got destroyed."

"Maybe nobody really knew about the research or ship, until the facility was destroyed, and the ship lost," added Leila.

"Well, I—" An audible alert interrupted Casey, and the room's light dropped to an ominous red hue.

The forward 3D display materialized into a view of the seven planets and their star. Over the center, the display zoomed out to include the red planet, along with the *Fallen Star*, now a small blue dot, orbiting the moon on the planet-facing side. From around the red planet, six red dots of light crested the horizon. Red characters hovered near the new specks of light.

Casey moved over and touched one of the red lights. A separate image popped out of the floating display, and a glossy black ship came into view. The ship reminded Casey of a crab with its stout body, several small fin-like wings in the back and two forward-sweeping wings arcing towards each other in the front. He touched the other red spots with alien glyphs floating nearby. One was an elongated oval shape that gave the general impression of a cigar except with a round, flat, extended section that sat on the forward top section of the ship, much like the bridge of a cargo ship. Three red diagonal lightning bolts were emblazoned on the side just below the bridge. The remaining red lights were more crab ships. The ships were still just behind the planet's horizon.

Casey bit his lower lip, released it, and said, "I'm not sure how the ship can identify them behind the planet's horizon, but I think we're going to get some company if they see us."

Leila's head was shaking slightly, and her voice quivered. "They don't look friendly."

"No," agreed Casey, "those crabs don't look like they're coming to play."

"And if the red light is any indication," said James, "our ship doesn't seem to identify them as friendly."

"Wait," Heather said. "I thought we were cloaked."

"Um," said Casey, looking at the holographic image, "I think the cloak is off. There was a purple glow around the 3D ship when it was on. I didn't notice it before, but I don't think it was on when we came out the distortion. I'm not even sure if it was on when we went in."

"So..." James hesitated. "How do we get it back on?"

"Wish I knew." Casey's hands dropped onto the two dome controllers. "If I remember right, it became an option after those guys fired at us in the temple. There's probably a way to turn it on before being attacked, but I don't know where or how."

In the 3D display the red-hued ships crested the planet's horizon. A second later their direction of travel diverted from planetary orbit towards the moon. Towards *them*.

Casey fidgeted in his seat. "I think they see us."

The red glyphs morphed into new characters near each ship.

"How much time until they reach us?" asked Heather.

An eyebrow rose, and Casey shook his head at the display. "No clue. With Earth technology it'd be at least a day or so to travel from planet to moon. I've no idea how far away they actually are. With their tech, it might be a few minutes or a few hours. But"—he paused and watched the display for a few seconds—"I'm guessing maybe five minutes."

"Do we have any weapons?" asked Leila.

"Sure," said James, pulling out the 9mm handgun. "But I don't think it'll be very effective."

Chapter Thirteen

Pirate Encounter

Heather's knuckles whitened on the top of Casey's seat. "Um, maybe we should try to outrun them. Maybe that space-jump thing again?"

Casey looked around. The others' eyes were riveted on the floating display, and Leila's dark skin seemed blanched. "See if you can find anything that might be weapons related." He focused on his brother, adding, "And more effective than a handgun in space. I'll do my best to outrun them, although I'm not sure where we'll outrun them to. The space-jump thing might be an option, but, like the cloak, I'm not sure how to turn it on or where we might end up." His fingers became partially absorbed into the warm domes. "If you're not seated, better do so."

An urgent alert shifted attention to the display. The six ships had halved their distance during the short conversation. The five crab ships split apart to form a *W*-like shape with a center ship, the next two ships lower in the formation, and the two outermost ships higher up. Red highlights in the center display indicated two energy streams racing towards the *Fallen Star* from each of the crab ships. In the image, the streams looked like extraordinarily long liquid ropes reaching out to entangle their prey in a cosmic web. While the volley of ten energy web-streams converged on the *Fallen Star*, a second set was immediately released.

Red hues bristled around the console displays. A blue bar illuminated in front of Casey, and he felt a warmth under his right index finger. Glancing at the dome, a blue hue encircled the finger. Casey pressed in lightly, and a blue halo engulfed the 3D image of the *Fallen Star*.

"There's our answer to their friendliness quotient," said James. "But I don't suggest we test the shields. I think whatever's coming is a lot more than AK rounds."

"Yep." Casey nodded. He gripped the small domes in his hands and turned the *Fallen Star* away from the oncoming energy streams and ships. Adrenaline surged inside, and he whipped the ship back towards their attackers.

"Umm," said Heather, "I thought we were running away."

From the right seat, James glanced at his brother, gray-blue eyes uncertain. "Yeah, I don't think this is a good idea."

The streaks of energy sped towards the *Fallen Star*, their appearance like massive space snakes spiraling in on their prey. A virtual display instantly surrounded Casey, fully encompassing him in a 3D real-time image, much like what had happened in the space jump. His focus sharpened, breathing calmed, awareness increased, and time seemed to slow down. He saw the cigar-shaped vessel still far behind the five crab ships while they tracked towards the *Fallen Star*. The first ten energy streams were interacting and forming the tendrils of a large web. The ends closer to the *Fallen Star* eagerly reached out, wriggling into space towards their victim like a massive jellyfish.

The web ends farthest from the *Fallen Star* joined together. As the entanglement sped closer, Casey moved his hands and the ship darted up. The web matched the ship's movement and quickly closed the distance. The second salvo of light streaks were coalescing into a similar energy web, a near-identical image of the first. Casey noticed in the seemingly random twisting of two energy streams that the tendrils would briefly pull further apart. He deftly dove the ship through the opening and rolled to avoid the energy web whipping back after them.

In his peripheral vision, the 3D display showed the energy streams from the first web reversing direction and once again gaining on the *Fallen Star*. In front of him, the second web was extending its tendrils towards the arms of the first.

Heather's eyes were fixated on the unfolding action in the 3D display. "Looks like some kind of energy orb."

Casey simply nodded. The tendrils of the second web were nearly touching the ends of the first, and the *Fallen Star* was still within the enclosing boundaries of the energy orb. He raced the ship towards the relative bottom of the enclosing web. Sensing another brief opening, Casey pulled up and corkscrewed a dive to the right. They burst through the opening just when the two half-webs met in a giant energy ball. The joining released a brilliant flash inside the enclosed space. The ship's viewscreens dimmed momentarily.

"Great flying, Casey! I wonder what that would've done," said James.

"I'd guess it was some kind of immobilizing system," suggested Leila. "Maybe our attackers are just trying to keep us from running. Based on what we saw, you couldn't have outrun those energy streams. I'm not sure what made you think of that maneuver."

Casey studied the display surrounding him, watching the ships regroup.

James's hands clenched his armrests. "I wish there was something we could fight back with." His eyes scoured the walls, floor, and ceiling. "There's got to be some defenses on this ship. Whatever happened to that cloaking thing? Whoa, wait, what's this?"

Two silver domes rose up from the armrests under James's hands. An orange light laced the outer perimeters. James placed his hands on the controls, and white lights lit up under his thumbs.

"What is it?" asked Casey, his attention still on the display. "I'm a little busy."

The five crab ships were closer but had split away from the offset *W*-formation. The center ship continued its flight directly towards the *Fallen Star*. The ships on the high sides veered out and circled in a dive towards the *Fallen Star*. The two lower ships had dropped further down to sweep up from below.

James tried to explain. "Two ball thingys, like yours, just showed up on my armrests. There's an orange glow around them and lights under my thumbs."

"Well, press your thumbs in. We haven't died so far."

His teeth clenched, James pressed on the lights, and a holographic display encircled him. He moved his hands on the domes, feeling the orbs rolling in their hidden cradles, and the display panned and tilted around him. The image rotated to the rear of the ship, and he saw the energy web close in on itself. Three concentric circles briefly appeared as the center of the display passed over one of the crab ships circling in from the right.

James's back straightened. "I think we may have something." His hands spun the orbs, the display around him haphazardly flipping and twisting before he got the rings centered on the ship again.

Casey's voice tensed. "Hope that means you've got something to shoot with"—flashes of light burst from the center ship—"because we've got incoming from the front!"

Near one of the light bursts that tore through space, a smaller 3D image leaped out. Inside the image, red alien characters hovered near two torpedo-like projectiles.

James shifted the orbs to place the targeting rings over the torpedoes. "Those are tough to track," he muttered.

The center ring flashed green, and James squeezed his right index finger. Green energy burst from the top of the ship, ripping one torpedo in half. A second burst tore apart the next one.

Casey rolled the ship to the right. "Whatever you're doing, do it faster. I don't think they're happy with you 'cause we've got more torpedoes coming in from all the crab ships."

The circles repositioned themselves over the next torpedo while James maneuvered the orbs. "I think they're just a bit crabby and aren't interested in talking."

The front torpedoes vaporized in succession. He shifted the display to the lower right.

———◉———

Heather's hands gripped her armrests while her attention was divided among the different 3D displays and watching the holographic display around James. "There must be something I can do instead of just sitting here."

Under her tightened hands, small domes rose up on the armrests and orange lights circumnavigated the perimeters. Startled, she lifted her hands off and set them back down on the controls. She felt her fingers gently sink into the surface. She pressed in the amber lights under her thumbs. A 3D display engulfed her, showing her a view from the underside of the *Fallen Star*. Two crab ships were rapidly approaching from two sides. In a couple of seconds, the targeting circles closed in on two incoming torpedoes from the lower left.

"Uh-oh, something happened," James said, concerned. "I can't see the lower ships or torpedoes in the targeting view. They were just here, but now my view's restricted to the top." He quickly reoriented his targeting to the incoming torpedoes from the top right.

"I've got you covered." Heather smiled, and the two torpedoes were ripped apart in quick succession. She moved the display to find other threats.

Two more torpedoes disappeared in flashes of light under James's defense.

"Hang on," said Casey, whipping the ship into a right diving roll.

James and Heather attempted to target the torpedoes, but the rotation of the ship changed their view. The torpedoes shifted directions and self-corrected their trajectories to match the *Fallen Star*'s. The spiraling dive took the *Fallen Star* below the forward crab ship, and it dove after them. The two lower ships made half-spiral turns to end up behind the *Fallen Star*. The two higher ships adjusted their dive.

"Okay, now I'm feeling a bit upside-down," said Heather as she rotated the 3D view around her to figure out where the torpedoes and ships were.

"Get used to it. We're in space," said James, scanning for targets. "There is no 'up' or 'down.'"

Heather shot back with a half-grin. "So now you're suddenly an expert in space dogfights."

"Well, I do have more hits than you do."

"Not for long," said Heather. She whipped the display aft where four torpedoes were closing in.

While Casey continued to twist left and right, James and Heather became adept at reengaging their targeting circles when the ship's rotation lost the targeting fix. Before James could fire, the view rotated and Heather shot and took out one of the torpedoes. Her second blast blew through the next torpedo, another energy burst vaporized the remaining pieces.

"Hey," complained James when the shattered remains rotated back into view, "that was mine."

"Sorry, but you need to be faster."

James's next shot went wild as the remaining two torpedoes closed in. Heather's shot passed between them. James's hands, fingers slightly embedded into the silver domes, felt moist with sweat. His next burst missed. Before he could respond, an energy bolt from Heather sliced through one torpedo.

The final torpedo hit the shield and exploded. The rear viewscreens and targeting systems dimmed. The blue hue around the ship flickered slightly, and Casey noted several meters or gages fluctuate momentarily on the flat surface of the forward console.

"James, you let one through," accused Casey.

"You didn't fly fast enough," James retorted.

"True, I'm still figuring things out. At least the shields held."

"Yeah, but that one torpedo was worse than everything those gunships shot at us."

Casey glanced around. "Everyone okay?" Leila was still pale. "Leila, you okay?"

"Yeah, I just forgot how much I don't care for that." In response to Casey's puzzled look, Leila added, "Fast maneuvering."

Heather's targeting display zoomed in on the five crab ships which had begun to regroup. "I wonder why they haven't fired anything else at us."

"Um, a yellow light meter, with some wavy curves on it, just appeared in front of me," said James. "Kind of reminds me of an audio waveform."

"It's in front of me as well," replied Casey.

"Maybe they want to talk," said Leila.

Casey gave James a sly smile. "You're the sweet-talker, and I know you'd love to talk to them. You're promoted to communications officer. You can see what they want."

James narrowed his eyes in a friendly grimace and then touched the yellow waveform. A 3D face appeared, hovering over the center console. The man in the image looked like the leader of a biker gang. Several scars crisscrossed dark, leathery skin and intertwined with tattooed markings on the right cheek. The gaze of black eyes pierced out of their sockets. Long black hair was pulled into a knot behind the head, the excess hair hanging loose. The long crooked nose looked like it had been broken several times.

Leila stifled a gasp as the alien's guttural voice rasped, *"Sor T'Roz, Sketon d-gragon Zin."* Slightly pointed teeth brandished themselves while the alien continued its demands. *"Tem unze jiimet ga reindo u vewdes bruktem."*

Below the image, an ethereal light-bar slowly pulsed red.

Casey cocked his head at his brother. "My guess is that floating light-bar is the push-to-talk button."

The corner of James's mouth curled slyly, and he touched the floating bar. The light switched to solid green. "We're sorry for the technical difficulties you're experiencing. Unfortunately, we don't have a gravitonic spanner or Barlow lens to help calibrate your quasar drive. However, since the extended warranty on your starship has expired, we can help you find a great deal that will save you loads on future repairs." His mouth twitched in an effort to keep straight-faced, and he touched the light-bar back to red.

The furrows on the alien's forehead deepened, and its dark eyes stared in confusion. The image disappeared.

Casey's right brow lifted at his brother. "I guess he's disappointed we didn't bring a gravitonic spanner." His focus shifted back to his display. "Oh, shoot! I wasn't watching. Looks like he's upset about your extended warranty offer."

"What?" asked Heather. "Oh."

The long cigar-shaped ship loomed ominously in the front viewscreens. Over the center console, the 3D display showed the *Fallen Star*, smaller than the other ship's bridge, heading face-to-face with the cigar ship. The five crab ships were circling into a *V*-shaped formation behind the *Fallen Star*.

"Should we take out some of those crabs?" James asked Casey. "I think Heather and I can take out most of them before they know what hit 'em."

Casey's head tilted to the right. "No. We don't know what the big ship can do or what it's waiting for. Let's—" The dome was warm under his right thumb. He felt the urge to accelerate and dive away from the large ship.

Casey pressed his thumb and rotated the orbs. The *Fallen Star* dropped into an accelerated dive just as several jets of light erupted from the cigar ship. The bursts passed through where they had been a second earlier. The crab ships immediately dove after their prey and launched additional torpedoes.

"If you didn't get the message, you two can start firing now," announced Casey when the cigar ship released additional bolts of energy at them.

Two torpedoes exploded as James and Heather renewed their competition.

Behind the *Fallen Star*, the five crab ships flared out into an inverted crescent formation. One energy beam from the cigar ship collided with the top shields, and the viewscreens dimmed momentarily. Heather and James continued to eliminate torpedoes.

Casey pushed forward with his left hand while rotating the right inward. The ship inverted itself and reversed direction, facing its adversaries. The crab ships peeled away, attempting to quickly reverse course, but the *Fallen Star* passed through them faster than they could turn. The large cigar ship now loomed in front of them, the distance rapidly narrowing.

Behind them, James's energy weapon took out another torpedo. A couple of shots from Heather burned through a torpedo and sent its debris tumbling in space.

More blasts erupted from the cigar ship, tearing through space at the *Fallen Star* like claws of energy. Casey banked left, and two energy bolts raced beneath the ship. A third smashed into the front shields. The energetic impact translated into an internal shudder as the energy was absorbed and redirected. Status lights and alien characters lit up around the floating image of the *Fallen Star* over the console.

Three concentric rings appeared in front of Casey. His hands gently adjusted the control orbs until the ship's heading and tracking rings centered over the large cigar ship. From the corner of his vision, he saw a light around his right index finger, and he pressed in. The front screens dimmed with an explosion of energy that erupted from the front of the *Fallen Star*. Casey momentarily wondered if the ship was entering a space jump. Immediately the light came on again, and Casey pressed it. A second rupture of energy blasted towards the cigar ship.

The first blast pounded into the large ship's energy shield. Iridescent waves undulated outward from the impact point and rippled throughout the shield like a lightning bolt splashing into a lake of energy.

A half second later, the second blast penetrated the same point. Instead of rippling outward, the energy waves were sucked into the impact site where they disintegrated. Bright fractures of energy ricocheted throughout the shields and the cigar ship's shields dissolved into nothing.

The distance between the *Fallen Star* and the cigar ship was critically close. Casey rolled the *Fallen Star* as he pulled up, and the ship flipped over the alien ship in an inverted position. As Casey continued a tight roll over the cigar ship, the pursuing torpedoes were unable to course-correct quick enough and exploded into the unshielded large ship. Six consecutive explosions blew out its side. Once clear of the cigar ship, the *Fallen Star* straightened its course.

Rotating her weapons' view aft, Heather fired at the enemy ship. The plasma bolts shredded holes through the ship's side. Small explosions began bursting from other parts of the ship. Several poorly aimed energy beams passed harmlessly by the *Fallen Star*.

"Watch out!" shouted Leila, pointing at the floor.

Casey was already responding. Three crab ships had dropped under the larger ship and were arcing towards the underside of the *Fallen Star*. Three plasma blasts raced from the ships and ruptured against the lower shield. The *Fallen Star* shuddered again with the energetic absorption. Over the center console, a cross-sectional image of the *Fallen Star* appeared, the underside pulsing yellow. Three metered lights on the console in front of Casey were also yellow.

Heather apologized and targeted one of the crab ships. "Sorry, I should've seen those."

The center crab ship lost its midsection when plasma ripped through it. The second ship was sent spinning, crippled, into space. The third ship looked like it was heading right for Heather. Her eyes narrowed, and index fingers pressed in. Two torrents of plasma ripped through space and sliced through the approaching crab ship.

"Hey!" said James. "Leave some for me."

"Awesome shooting, Heather!" exclaimed Casey. "James, keep your eyes open. There're still two more somewh—"

The final two crab ships zipped around the front of the large ship and were right on the *Fallen Star*'s tail. Casey slid his left hand back and twisted right. The ship slipped 180 degrees, facing its two opponents while flying backwards. The light under his finger lit again, and Casey released a plasma ball from the front of the ship that ripped through one of their pursuers. The last crab ship veered away and fled.

On his right, Casey saw James center the targeting rings on the fleeing ship and hesitate.

"Let it go," said Casey.

"What if he tells his friends?"

"If he has any left, we'll take care of them. I just don't feel right about shooting someone in retreat."

"Yeah," James reluctantly agreed. "I wouldn't want to be shot at if I was running away either."

Leila's white knuckles gripped the sides of her chair. "You should've taken it out. I don't think we've seen the last of them."

The display floating around Heather rotated to view the large ship. "Maybe not," she said, "but it's the right thing to do. Besides, look."

Through the rear viewscreens, small explosions continued to consume the large ship. An eruption slashed the side of the command bridge, objects and debris poured into space. Sections of the hull broke away, and the ship's course dropped towards the moon. A large piece of the hull blew off with an explosion, its gape revealing a holding bay.

"Must be some kind of cargo or transport ship," said James.

The moon's gravity tugged at the large ship, and additional explosions sent it careening towards the moon. Casey decelerated the *Fallen Star*, and they watched the long elliptical ship fall into the atmosphere.

"Looks like they're in for a rough landing," said Casey.

"Well, I don't think we have to worry about any of them coming back for more," Heather added smugly.

"Casey, that last move was pretty smooth," said Leila.

"Yeah, how'd you figure that one out?" asked Heather.

"I remembered on Earth when the ship just instantly seemed to jump, and I guessed we could turn without making the normal arc. It worked better than I thought. Of course, sometimes it feels like the ship has a mind of its own and it's guiding me. Kind of teaching me what it can do."

"What kind of damage did we get?" asked James. "I know we had a few good beatings." His head shook. "I'm surprised the ship doesn't have some kind of auto-targeting and weapons systems. It took a bit to learn how to move and target the guns."

"Maybe it does, and we just haven't gotten past the basic interface. As for damage, the cross section indicates some possible damage on the underside." Casey pointed at the 3D display. "But I'm not sure. There are a few meters or gages of sorts. Some dropped or changed colors, which I don't think was good, but it looks like things are slowly rising back up. The ship might have some sort of self-healing."

Heather touched a few light bars in her display. "Do you think it's good enough to get us home?" The targeting system and display that surrounded her seat vanished, and the domes dissolved back into the armrests.

"Probably, but we still need to know where home is. We need to find a way to access the ship's star maps or find someone who can help us. It might be good to make a quick visual check of the ship. Not that we know how to, or if we can, make repairs." He grinned at James. "We might need that gravitonic spanner. Anyway, I think we should land on the planet, I mean moon, check things out, and, hopefully, take a break."

"I like James's earlier suggestion about looking for food and water," added Leila. "But I don't want to be stuck down there if we end up having more unpleasant company."

Casey pointed at the center console where the *Fallen Star* orbited the moon. "I think we should check out the green spot on the surface first. Maybe we can find some water and answers."

Heather pointed to a small red blip that moved quickly across the moon. "What's that?"

"Not sure," said Casey. He touched the red blip.

An image popped out to the side of the blip and revealed a streak of fire racing through the atmosphere. After several seconds the flames died out, and the wreckage of the cigar ship careened towards the green spot on the surface. A few seconds later, the red blip abruptly stopped near the green spot. In the pop-out display, an eruption of debris, dust, and smoke filled the image. Within a minute the clouds began to dissipate, and the smoldering remains of the cargo ship, smashed into a self-made crater, could be seen.

Casey winced. "Looks like the ship landed. But I doubt seat belts would've helped anyone."

"Yeah," said James. "Let's not land that way."

"Maybe we should see if anything's salvageable," suggested Leila.

"Like what?" asked James.

"Maybe food."

"I'm not sure if much survived that wreck," commented Casey. "But it looks close to the ruins at those cliffs, so it might not hurt to check. Everyone buckle up, er, get in your seats."

Heather got herself comfortable in the chair. "Would we even know what we can eat?" she wondered.

James fumbled with the control domes on the armrests as the targeting display continued to wrap around his seat like a ghostly apparition. "Hey, Heather"—he removed his hands from the domes and turned towards her—"how'd you get your targeting display to turn off?" The display around him vanished, and the domes disappeared seamlessly into the armrests. "Never mind. Now we just need to learn how to activate them when we want to."

Chapter Fourteen
Moon Landing

T HE DESCENT TO THE moon's surface took longer than their escape from Earth's atmosphere, but it was smooth and controlled. Casey took his time as he felt every movement of his hands interact with the controls while he navigated based on the 3D displays floating over the consoles.

The ship soon came within view of the surface. A mountain range dominated the horizon. The ancient ruins of a facility jutted from the base of an expansive cliff, and the squared corners of destroyed buildings dotted the rise to the cliffs. The two wrecked spacecraft lay near the foothills. Within an elongated crater, centuries of weather-deposited debris covered the twisted remains of a large cylindrical object. A couple miles away, smoke poured from gashes in the newly crashed spacecraft. Sections of the hull had been sheared off, and large tears mangled the outside as if the lunar surface had ripped through the ship's skin like the claws from a giant beast.

A winding strip of green spun out from a small valley north of the cliffs and snaked out into the lowlands before disappearing. Across the landscape, shadows stretched with the fading daylight. Forests in different hues and intensities of green spread across most of the upper regions of the mountain range, and the lengthening shadows cast new saturation levels. Below the mountains, the foothills reached out into the surrounding lowlands where dominant barren browns mixed with harsh rock outcroppings and splotches of grays and black. Small hills irregularly sprung from the brownish ground and revealed layers of reds, oranges, and yellows. Random expanses of greens sprouted up in the landscape, giving the impression of a giant alien golf course spread among the wasteland.

Further south of the mountain range, the lowlands showed geologic activity. To the southwest, rocks and minerals of reds, oranges, and browns had spewed out from small craters that were scattered haphazardly across the wilderness. Among these craters were bulged domes of sediment deposits, and steam lazily rose up from the openings of the domes' tops. To the southeast, columns of eroded, red-brown stone marched across the desolation like an ancient army frozen in time.

Casey approached the old ruins from the east as the lowering sun painted reds and oranges across the horizon. He circled the two crash sites slowly before he descended further.

Casey passed near the newer crash. "Interesting."

"What?" asked James.

"The two ships. Except for one being a much older wreck, they seem similar."

"Maybe the same people who attacked us also attacked that facility," suggested Leila.

Heather's gaze was fixated on the landscape. "I thought maybe your 'interesting' was the illusion of greenery on this moon. Looks like most of the green, at least in the lowlands, is actually from various minerals exposed to the atmosphere. Except for maybe in those mountains, there doesn't seem to be much vegetation. If may be hard to determine how old anything really is."

Casey's fingers caressed the orbs. "Now we'll see if I can actually land this ship."

"Try not to bounce down the runway like you did on your first airplane flight," teased James.

Casey watched the displays while he brought the ship down. There was a slight wobble near the ground, but it settled quickly. The others watched curiously through the bottom viewscreens at the approaching ground. Then the ship stopped, and the cabin area brightened.

"Did we land?" asked Leila.

Casey turned in his seat and announced. "Welcome to Terra Luna, or whatever the moon is actually called. Sorry about the wobble. I was trying to figure out the landing gears."

Heather's brows rose in admiration. "Still, nicely done. I didn't feel a thing, except for the wobble."

"Not bad, especially for a first-time landing of an alien spaceship," said James. He stood and walked towards the back of the room.

Heather looked out the viewscreens at the surrounding area. "I hope we don't end up dying because the atmosphere is poisonous."

James and Casey grabbed their packs. Casey paused and looked at the 3D terrain views hovering over the consoles, then followed James and Heather to the door of the boarding room. A small, green-hued screen glowed near the doorway. James touched the screen, the door slid open, and he walked into the room. The ramp-way was still sealed shut, and another green-hued panel faded in and out on the wall. James touched the small screen.

Heather panicked, "Wait! How will we know if the air's safe to breathe?"

The ramp quickly descended and extended. James stood at the top of the ramp as warm air rushed up. He inhaled deeply. Then he started coughing and choking. His hands clutched his throat desperately. He dropped to his knees and rolled onto his back, his face turning red.

Heather stepped into the room and kicked him in the thigh. "I can breathe the air, too, you know."

James smiled mischievously and sat up, rubbing his thigh. "I should've gone through on my own and closed the door behind me. By the way, the air seems fine. Maybe dry. It kind of has the salty taste of being on a beach."

"How'd you know it was safe?"

James shrugged. "I didn't. Just a guess when the lights were green. I figure they'd probably be red or something, or maybe I wouldn't have been able to open the door if the air was much different than what's in the ship."

James walked cautiously down the ramp and stepped onto the ground. His footsteps made a light crunch as they broke through a thin top layer of browns and black speckled with yellows. He looked up the ramp at Heather.

"Kind of reminds me of the cryptobiotic soils in southeastern Utah, like what we saw on that camping trip out near Dead Horse Point." He took a few more steps, looked up the ramp, and added with a sly smile, "Hopefully I don't get in trouble from a ranger or environmentalist for walking on it."

Heather and Casey walked more cautiously down the ramp. They watched James sprint thirty feet and jump. He cleared three vertical feet and landed eight feet away, stumbling in the crusty soil and rolling into a heap.

Heather's head shook. "What was that all about?"

James got up sheepishly, brushed himself off, and tried to act like the fall was planned. "Well, I was hoping to fly through the air in a giant leap for mankind. But the gravity's not much different than on Earth."

Casey stepped off the ramp and looked around. Large blackened patches littered the ground. Random strands of a yellowish grass poked up through the soil. He had landed the ship so the aft was pointed towards the mountains. The older wreck's carcass jutted out of a crater a little to the south. From their altitude, the charred remains of buildings in the foothills had appeared like jagged black rock outcroppings. Among the building debris were corroded and mangled remains of machinery, vehicles, and other mechanisms. Scorched sections on the cliffs were burned-out scars from explosions. At the base of the cliffs, through the remnants of walls, a darkening maw gaped, its ragged edges urging caution to the curious.

In the opposite direction from the cliffs, about a mile in front of the *Fallen Star*, the reddish sky of the fading day looked like ghostly fire filtering through the smoldering smoke of the massive new wreck. Longer than three ocean liners, the crashed ship's bottom was flattened into the ground and buried by its impact crater. The lower and mid-level sections were smashed into the upper levels such that the ship was only a quarter of its original height. Surprisingly, the top and bridge sections were intact, except for a side missing from the bridge.

Casey kicked the ground and stooped down to look. Small black chunks of crusted ground had broken away in powdered sections. A mild reflective quality of the powder had caught Casey's interest. The closer inspection revealed black, glass-like flecks that reminded Casey of fine obsidian knapping that he and his brother would sometimes find in backcountry hikes, the remnants of an ancient Native American's efforts in crafting an arrow or spear point.

Heather noticed Leila still at the top of the ramp, looking anxious. "Are you coming down?"

Leila nodded stiffly and walked down. When she stepped off the ramp, she glanced cautiously at the newest wrecked ship smoldering a short distance away.

Casey squinted at the still bright but fading daylight. "I want to look around, but I'm not sure how much time we have. On Earth I'd give us about three hours before dark. Here, I've no idea. We've got two choices. First, we can call it good for today, go back inside, take an accounting of what we have, and head out as soon as it's light."

"And maybe decide where to start looking," added James. "We have the ruins in the cliffs, which is probably where our best bet for water is, and the wreck from today, where we might find food. The question is whether we divide up into two teams or go all together. We'd cover more ground quickly in two groups, but it's probably safer together."

Heather nodded at James. "You two know I like a good adventure. But since we really don't know what we're getting into, I'm all for safer."

Leila tried to keep from fidgeting. "I think that safer is the better option as well."

"The other option, especially since we all had a late nap, is to take a short exploratory trip before it gets dark," Casey said. "Again, probably best to stick together. Maybe even keep one person here, to keep the lights on if needed."

"I'll stay," volunteered Leila without hesitation.

James bit his lower lip and thought for a moment. "With the fires still in the wreck, I recommend we try the ruins in the mountain first. Looks like it's less than a half mile, and, if the ground is like this all the way, we could probably get there in fifteen minutes or less."

"That doesn't sound too bad," said Heather. "Hopefully we can find some water since we're about out."

"Casey, maybe you should stay too, and try to figure more things out with the ship," offered Leila.

"That'd be a good idea, except I don't want to fiddle around with anything unless we're all inside. Just in case something happens like back on Earth. I wouldn't want to leave anyone behind and not be able to get back. Besides, I'd like to look around as well."

"Well, then, if you guys are set on going," said Leila, "and if nobody minds, I'd really prefer to stay with the ship. I tolerated the jungle, but I don't really like the idea of wandering an alien moon."

James clutched his pack strap. "Sounds good to me. We'll plan to be back in about two hours. Three at the most. Hopefully that's before dark. Don't open the ramp for anyone except us."

"Okay," started Leila, "except I don't have a clock. I left my phone back in the tent, and, well, it probably wouldn't work here anyway."

"My phone's in my pack," said Casey. "It needs to be powered on. The clock should work, but I should probably put it in airplane mode so it doesn't scan for networks. I'd hate to get overage charges from here." Casey unzipped his pack, pulled out his phone and a small plastic water bottle, and handed both to Leila. "Here. It's not much, but with some luck we'll find more water to fill the bladders with."

Leila graciously took the phone and water bottle.

James raised his brows at Casey and Heather. "You two ready?"

With affirmative nods, Casey, James, and Heather began their short trek towards the cliff ruins. As they walked away, Casey looked back at the *Fallen Star*. The mercury-like skin of the ship had adapted to the environment, refracting colors and shading around its surfaces, giving it the illusion of invisibility. Only a slight distortion—almost like a mirage—and Leila standing at the lowered ramp revealed the exact location of the ship. He made a mental note of the location in relation to the scarce landmarks, then turned his attention to the approaching cliffs.

Chapter Fifteen

Ruins

THEY WALKED THROUGH A cluster of blackened foundations, the remaining testaments of former buildings. Sand, dust, and other debris congregated around the base of crumbling walls and huddled into corners while shadows lengthened across the desolation. Short green plants huddled near large rocks and wall remnants. They passed through the deteriorated remnants and ascended into the low foothills, where small gravel and rocks littered the ground.

Casey looked back and then towards the ruins at the base of the cliff before them. "I wonder when this place was destroyed."

"Without dating it," Heather mused, "I'm guessing it's much older than it looks. It seems like a fairly arid place, and if the local sun isn't as intense as ours, then things might not deteriorate as quickly."

"My guess," said James, "is it probably happened about the same time the *Fallen Star* left, assuming the ship left from here."

They continued a short distance to the base of the cliffs where jagged edges of an old structure jutted from the rock face. Inside the ruins, a ragged cave mouth opened fifty feet wide, its top reaching the height of a second story. Charred and corroded materials were strewn about. Some items seemed to have barely aged while others were so decayed they looked like the slightest breeze could break them into dust. A light wind began to blow up the foothills.

James looked back at the lowlands, cocked his head, and squinted. "If I didn't know the ship was there, I'd never believe someone if they told me it was."

"Let's go in," said Heather with a shiver. "I'm warmed up from the short hike, but let's check out what's inside. The wind's getting a little cold out here."

"Sorry, I don't have a jacket," said Casey. "I've got a rain poncho if you need it, though."

Heather smiled at the offer. "I'm good for now, but I may take you up on the poncho for our walk back."

They cautiously stepped through the collapsed doorway and walked among the broken walls towards the jagged cave mouth at the back. Several boulders—cleaved from the cliffs overhead—cluttered the dilapidated structure. The cave opening continued back nearly a hundred feet where the darkness consumed the light amid debris piles. Casey and James retrieved their headlamps as the cave walls came together into a narrow neck of night.

Pointing to fractal-like patterns of white stringy objects on the cave walls, James commented, "Looks like some kind of fungus, which is a good sign for moisture. Just don't disturb it, though."

At the farthest point back, James's light penetrated a dark opening at ground level. Shining the light through the opening, he knelt on the rocks and studied it. "Looks like it might go somewhere." He paused. "I think I can fit through it."

Heather shook her head. "I don't think that's a good idea."

James nodded. "Probably not. But if there's water here, it's most likely somewhere in there."

"Just be careful," warned Heather. "We're a long ways from help."

James got down on his belly and pulled himself into the darkness. Casey knelt on the rock floor and watched snatches of his brother's light through the opening. After a minute, a muffled but animated voice filtered from the crawlspace.

"You guys should come through. It opens up back here. Like an old hallway."

"Here"—Casey reached into his pack—"take my backup light."

Heather put the headlamp on. Then she reached into her pocket and pulled out an elastic hair band. While Casey squirreled through the opening, Heather quickly pulled her hair into a ponytail before following.

A wide hallway opened up before the flashlights. Unlike the entry building, very little debris littered the ground, and the walls were more intact. They cautiously walked along the passage for about a minute before arriving at an intersection.

James's light probed left, right, and straight. "Which way?"

"Let's keep going straight," suggested Casey. "Should be easier to find our way back. We can try the other directions another time. But, just in case, I'll scratch an arrow pointing out on this wall."

As they continued down the passageway, their footsteps woke dust from its long slumber, and three beams of light filtered through the stirred history. A few seconds later, Heather's hand jumped to her mouth. Her light illuminated the dark skeletal remains of a humanoid. Further along the passage, a series of thick doorways hung precariously from charred hinges. Above them, pieces of wiring and a variety of utility and infrastructure parts dangled from the ceilings, their counterparts haphazardly scattered among the rubble on the floor.

A little further along the passage, two alcoves were cut into the walls. The first was prior to a series of four former doorways, and the second one was between them. Skeletal remains guarded each alcove, collapsed in on themselves from their eternal guardianship.

Beyond the doorways the passage continued onward. A short distance later, a small room opened to the left. Inside, mechanical and electronic-looking devices had clearly been blasted into fragments. The remains of screens, tables, and other items lay scattered around the room. Black scars of melted rock ripped across the walls in random and fractal patterns.

The passage continued, curved left, and ended at another doorway that had also been blown apart. Three skeletons lay crumpled in heaps near the entrance. Beyond the remains was a large room. Light beams barely illuminated the opposite walls. The dilapidated and destroyed equipment hinted that the room had once been some kind of manufacturing facility or lab. Three rows of four stone pillars, each pillar standing like an emotionless sentinel, were spaced about fifty feet from each other and the walls. Some workbenches were covered with parts of equipment and machinery that had been tossed or abandoned. Near empty workbenches, old parts and pieces had been thrown across the floor as if someone had stormed the room in a rage. Overturned tables and chairs added to the chaos, and burn marks scarred much of the room and its contents.

James's headlamp panned across the room. "Wonder what they made in here?"

Casey's eyes darted over the old parts and equipment. "There might be something useful," he said hopefully, "although it looks fairly well ransacked. Still, we should divide up and meet on the other side. It looks like there may be another opening at the far-right corner."

"Casey," cautioned Heather, "remember we're looking for food or water. If we have time later, we can see if any of the gadgets are worth taking."

Casey smiled. "You know me too well. I'll do my best to resist."

Casey walked along the left side, James along the right, and Heather went through the middle. A few minutes later they met at the opposite side and the opening Casey had seen.

Inside, a wide hall curved to the right. Walking along the passage, they became aware of a dim phosphorescence leaking into the hallway ahead of them. The hall merged into a massive cavern that was more than twice the size of the manufacturing room. The cavernous room was a rough *L*-shape with the long part stretching to the right, while the shorter, wider section, lay immediately before them. Most of the ceiling and walls were natural, although the floor had been leveled and parts of the cavern had been widened. Among the stalactites that sharply pointed down from the ceiling were streamers of faint luminescence that ran the length of the room and towards a distant glow at the right. Under the dim lighting and flashlight beams, they discovered the room had been no stranger to destruction. Derelict large machinery and mechanical equipment lay in heaps to the left, either destroyed by weapons or torn apart by looters.

Casey cocked his head to the right and pointed down the long stretch. "Is that outside light I'm seeing?"

"I think so," said Heather.

They walked the longer side to where it passed through an opened doorway that rivaled an aircraft hangar. Unlike the smaller doorways inside the facility, this one had no forced entry damage. The humongous doors were recessed into the side walls, where only small deposits of dust had managed to gather. Beyond the doorway, stalagmites groped upwards from the cave floor, and daggered stalactites bit down from the ceiling. The cave arced upwards and to the right where dim light filtered in. They traversed the cave floor and through the stone spikes that reached up to their counterparts. Before them, the cave's jaws opened into the fresh evening air.

Scattered across the rocky ground were dozens of stems that each contained three round, funnel-shaped leaves that opened towards the sky. White lily-like flowers topped a few of the stems. Hardier green and orange lichen-like organisms clung to the rocks at the edge. A chilled evening breeze billowed the brothers' clothes while they surveyed the alien moonscape. Heather remained a more respectable distance from the cliff edge.

The red planet sat low in the sky. Dark clouds were beginning to mask the stars that had just begun to show themselves in the oncoming twilight. On both sides of the cave opening, the cliff bowed outward and rose up into the mountain range. The last rays of daylight illuminated the peaks on the left. Three hundred feet below, the shallow foothills stretched out into the desertscape. These became rounded steppes, slowly climbing up into the mountainous terrain. On the far left, the strip of green darkened in the fading light. The ruins they had passed through earlier lay below them. Beyond the foothills, the old alien shipwreck lay as a monument to the ancient battle that scarred this area. A little farther out, thin wisps of smoke from the newer crash created eerie apparitions in the fading light. Somewhere between the two wrecks, the *Fallen Star* expertly blended into the landscape.

"Is that where we parked?" asked James, pointing at a dark patch.

"I think so, but I'm not sure," replied Casey. "Besides the cloak, I think the ship has some kind of adaptive skin that blends into its surroundings. Kind of like a chameleon."

"That'd explain the funky firelight trick back in the pyramid," said Heather. She stepped closer to the edge and tried to keep the wind from whipping strands of brown hair across her face. "It reminds me of some of the barren places in southern Arizona or New Mexico." She looked down and then stepped back nervously. "I didn't think we'd climbed up this high."

"Yeah, I think I got a little turned around in there," said Casey. "I was thinking the landscape looks a bit like the Painted Hills in Oregon."

"How long since we left the ship?" asked Heather.

James glanced at his watch. "Just over an hour. It's getting dark faster than on Earth. With this plant life, there should be water. But, with the fading daylight, we need to head back."

Casey turned to walk back when his right foot kicked something that skidded across the ground. His light swept the ground and stopped at a dirt-encrusted *L*-shaped object near a small boulder.

Heather stepped beside Casey. "What is it?"

Casey shrugged, bent down, and picked up the object. He brushed off the dirt and dust. The object appeared to be a foot-long handgun with two barrels. The grip dropped down about four inches, but there were no indications of a trigger mechanism. "It looks like some kind of gun."

"Be careful with it," warned James. "It probably doesn't work, but just in case. It wouldn't be the first old thing to surprise us by working."

Casey put the object in his pack. "I'll take it back to the ship to get a better look at it."

"Figures you'd find something," replied James, shaking his head.

They started back in the massive cave when Casey paused.

"What now?" asked Heather.

Casey cocked his head and closed his eyes. "I thought I heard something."

Away from the wind at the cliff edge, the stillness was almost palpable. They waited. After a minute, they heard a faint, but definite, *plop!*

"That sounds like a drip," exclaimed James.

Heather's light skimmed across the rock formations. "Where did it come from?"

The three lights scoured the dark corners and recesses of the cave. James's light panned across one corner, and the beam reflected higher on the wall for an instant. He redirected the light and walked towards an apparent black hole that reflected light. He approached the smooth black surface, and a drip from the ceiling disappeared into the mirror-like surface with a soft *plop*, and a gentle ripple fanned out. James aimed his light into the liquid. Part of the beam reflected higher up the nearby cave wall, the rest refracting into the shallow depths of a small, rocky pool about three feet long and a foot wide. He crouched down, bent his head near the liquid, and cautiously sniffed. Satisfied, he then touched the surface, examined the fluid on his fingers, then brought it closer to his nose.

"Looks like water," said James. "Doesn't have a smell, but I think I'd purify it first."

"Especially since you touched it," teased Heather.

"Hopefully the filters will work on whatever might be lurking in there," added Casey. He took off his pack and pulled out a water bladder. "There's still a bit of the Earth water left. Probably best to drink it first since we know it's safe."

Casey passed the water to Heather. She took several sips through the bite valve before returning the nearly empty bladder. James retrieved his water bladder and finished off the few remaining ounces.

The brothers unscrewed the fill caps of the bladders and took turns carefully submerging the openings into the small pool, being careful to keep the drinking ends from becoming contaminated. After packing up the water containers, they retraced their steps back to the main entrance.

Chapter Sixteen
Back to the Fallen Star

THEY WORMED FROM THE hole into rapidly fading twilight. Casey slowed momentarily to pull the rain poncho out of his pack for Heather. She thanked him and quickly pulled it over her head as they walked down the slope. Unlike the dry air earlier, the atmosphere had turned still and heavy with moisture. A layer of clouds thickened above them and cloaked the sky in a robe of grays and black. A short distance away, the massive bulk of the old spectral wreck rose up from the barren wasteland.

James led them out of the ruins, into the flatlands, and stopped. He looked from the old wreck towards the still-smoldering new crash, peered into the darkness, and took a slow step forward. He shook his head, reached up, and turned on the headlamp that was still on his forehead. The light beam swung slowly across the ground.

Before James could say anything, Casey pointed to some impressions in the crusty soil and said, "Our tracks are over there." He nodded into the darkness and added, "I think I can see some light out there, probably from the ship's ramp."

Without warning, a freezing blast of wind tore into them from the lowlands, its invisible icy tendrils reaching into and through every opening of their clothes. Heather dropped her head, clung the poncho tightly about her, and braced against the frigid air.

James ducked his head against the onslaught. "Let's get to the ship quick," he urged. "I think things are about to get worse. Casey, your eyesight's better than mine in the dark, you lead."

Casey nodded and strode into the darkening, swirling air while he shielded his eyes from the grating dust and shivered. Several seconds into the howling wind, the ship's ramp became visible beneath a shaft of light. A familiar figure stepped cautiously down the ramp.

Seeing the threesome quickly approaching, Leila walked out from under the ship and called through the windstorm, "I was hoping it was you three. Find anything?"

"A lot of nothing," admitted Heather, her voice strained over the wind. "Although we did find some water."

"There might be something worth going back for," said Casey, "But—" The gale thrust an angry swipe of dust and choked his voice.

A thunderous pounding, like the pummeling hooves of a thousand wild horses racing across the prairie, grew ominous.

"Ouch!" yelped James, grabbing his arm.

Casey looked back at his brother and saw a white-green golf ball-sized object roll across the ground. "What the— Ouch!" he yelped when something whacked his back.

The thundering gallop increased its intensity. White-green balls of ice began to hammer into crusted soil.

"Oh, hail!" yelled James. "Under the ship! Quick!"

A bright flash of lightning illuminated the thick mass of billowing clouds overhead, and the ground shuddered in response to the thunderous crack. Over the nearby foothills, an impenetrable, dark-gray curtain fell from the blackened sky and hurled hailstones mercilessly into the ground.

Leila retreated under the ship as the cascade of icy projectiles quickly approached. Casey, James, and Heather dashed the short distance while the wind angrily threw darts of soil that stung any exposed skin. Behind them the ground roiled from increasingly larger hailstones that smashed into it. They paused at the bottom of the ramp, icy clouds of breath surrounding them, and stared in mute awe at the barrage outside the perimeter of the ship. The sound was near deafening. Most of the hail was now grapefruit sized, but several basketball hailstones exploded into the ground and rolled their remains under the ship.

"Let's go inside," yelled Casey, pointing up the ramp.

They disappeared up the ramp as the dark wall encroached on the ship and began pummeling its surface. Casey shivered as he touched the ramp panel. A couple seconds later the pounding was muffled.

In the control room, a red light-bar faded in and out under the image of the ship floating over the center display. Casey touched the light, and instantly the beatings on the ship were silenced when a soft blue hue enveloped the 3D image. Around them the external viewscreens revealed only black.

Casey pulled his pack off and set it on his chair. "James, let's see what we've got left to eat and divide things up."

James shook off his pack, and the brothers rummaged for remnants of something to share as a meal. Options were meager. Finding four granola bars left, they split two and saved the last couple for the next day.

James slowly savored his few bites of granola bar. "I supposed the good news is at least we should have plenty of water." He closed his eyes briefly with another bite then continued, "I think tomorrow morning we should hit that alien cargo ship and see if it has anything useful. This hailstorm should take care of any remaining fires."

"And maybe," said Heather, "we should go back to that cliff base facility for a closer look."

Casey smiled a cheesy grin at Heather. "You know, you were right. We did land on the moon at an alien rendezvous base."

Heather landed a lighthearted punch on his shoulder. "Maybe. But I didn't say we'd have an alien rendezvous that could've gotten us killed. By the way, you're getting good at flying this ship."

Casey shrugged. "Thanks. Guess it's my knack with mechanical things, especially if they fly."

Leila popped a small sampling of granola bar into her mouth and cocked her head at Heather. "I've been dying to ask you. How'd you guys meet and get involved with the dig? You're, like, best friends, but none of you have degrees that really relate to archaeology, or the dig. I know the professor is your uncle, but you three act like you've known each other for years."

Heather smiled at the two brothers sitting in the front seats, who turned around to hear how she would answer. "We actually met at a martial arts class. Like, what? Thirteen years ago?"

James nodded and finished savoring a nibble of granola bar. "Something like that. Heather was new in the class but was already an experienced martial artist." He looked at his brother for confirmation. "I think Dad had something to do with convincing Sensei to teach her. Anyway, Sensei had us spar the last half of class, probably because we weren't being very respectful towards her. Anyway, she quickly kicked our butts a half dozen times."

"And then Casey kicked mine when Sensei switched our sparring to weapons and the shinai." replied Heather. In response to Leila's puzzled look, she added, "Shinai are bamboo swords."

James tucked his last morsel of granola bar into his mouth. "And we've been best friends ever since."

Leila's head tilted in curiosity. "So, you guys trained in karate?"

"Sensei was a grandmaster in several styles," Casey explained, "mostly Japanese but also Korean and some Chinese. His classes were like mixed martial arts of mostly karate, aikido, taekwondo, hapkido, along with a mix of Kung Fu and weapons training. The other two weren't as interested, but he trained me in kenjutsu and kendo. And I took classes in haidong gumdo from another master he knew.

"Dad started us in different martial arts classes when we were little. Somehow, he knew Sensei, and when Sensei migrated to the States about fifteen years ago, Dad convinced him to train us. Heather and her mom moved into our rural neighborhood, and Dad got her invited to the class. We trained with Sensei for about ten years, before"—a knot tightened in Casey's throat—"life took us in different directions."

"But somehow you all managed to be at the dig," said Leila.

Heather's eyes stared into an unknown horizon, and she blinked away extra moisture. "Yeah. You know I love languages, so my uncle asked me to come, more as his personal translator. He convinced me the classes I took in anthropology and ancient cultures of Central America would be helpful. So, I decided to go along. But it's actually James who started it, and I think he's the one who persuaded the professor to convince me to come."

James smiled sheepishly.

Heather continued. "James spent a couple years backpacking around Central and South America. About a year ago, he took a class from my uncle. Towards the end of the semester, he asked him some questions, which led to more discussions, which led to the expedition." She raised her brow at James. "Although I know James was a big part behind getting the dig started, I'm not sure how he got the information."

"And Casey was between jobs," added James, "so I convinced him to join us with his LIDAR equipped drone after I persuaded the professor of Casey's pilot and technological abilities, and how they'd aid us in the dig."

"I thought it was because misery loves company," said Casey.

A mischievous grin raised the corners of James's mouth. "Hey, at least you're getting an out-of-the-world adventure."

"True. But I would've said 'yes' quicker if you'd just told me we were looking for an alien spaceship."

"You know I thought it was going to be a meteorite."

"If you had told my uncle you were looking for a spaceship, he wouldn't have taken you seriously," said Heather. "Still, he was quite excited about what the dig was turning up."

Lightning brilliantly cracked across black clouds through the ceiling viewscreens. The intensity of the flash was instantly reduced through the viewscreens, and the room only briefly brightened. Several more flashes slashed silently across the boiling black clouds. The reverberations of the explosive thunder were felt as the ground below the ship shuddered. Two lightning bolts speared at each other across the darkened sky, and clouds roiled together as if they were in a celestial brawl. The lightning flashes revealed large chunks of ice deflecting off the invisible shielding. The foursome watched silently while low rumbles of thunder reverberated through the ship with each lightning strike.

James's voice almost whispered, "Kind of reminds me of that freak storm in the Sierra Nevadas."

Casey bit his lip and nodded slowly.

Heather's eyes widened. "Was that when you were struck by lightning?"

Casey nodded and stared at the light display through the ceiling.

Leila's brow creased incredulously. "Were you actually hit by lightning, or just near the strike?"

James nodded. "He was hit straight on. We were trying to take cover from a mountain storm that unexpectedly blew in. Casey had twisted his ankle and insisted Dad and I go ahead to scout out some shelter. We were about a hundred yards away when the static in the air became so palpable, I felt my hair standing on end. Dad and I both looked back at Casey and saw the strike. Not near him, but right through him."

Head shaking, James's hands instinctively rose to his ears with the memory. "The thunder was so loud, the sound wave pushed me back. The flash blinded me for a few minutes, and then it took a few more for the spots to clear up. When I got up, and my eyesight cleared, Casey was lying face down on the ground. Dad had already gotten to him. When I got to him, there was smoke wisps coming from his clothes and he was unresponsive."

"So, how badly were you hurt?" asked Leila.

Casey felt his face warm at the attention.

"I thought he was dead, or at least dying," continued James. "I was about to call for help on the radio when the craziest thing happened. Casey slowly rolled over and opened his eyes. When asked, he said he wasn't hurt, just sore all over, like he'd had too much of a workout from Sensei. Since the storm was passing quickly, and Casey seemed okay, we waited a few minutes before returning to camp. Dad then drove us down the mountain faster than I'd ever seen him go before, and we got to the little rural hospital. The doctors didn't believe he'd been struck by lightning. No identifiable burn marks on the body, just some fading redness. The only evidence the doctors found of anything abnormal was Casey's clothing had huge charred holes throughout. Like some fire moth had feasted on it."

Heather turned towards Leila. "I'd known them for a few years by then. When they got back and James told me the story, I didn't believe it. Even seeing the burned clothing was hard to believe. I jokingly told Casey he didn't get hurt because he has a way with anything that uses electricity."

Realizing she was staring at Casey, Leila averted her eyes. Her stomach growled. "On a different subject, I hope we find some food tomorrow. I'm thankful you guys had something to eat, but half of a granola bar isn't much. I think going to the cargo ship is a good idea."

Another bolt of lightning flashed across the sky. In a subdued tone, Heather added, "I hope we can find a way home."

Chapter Seventeen

Night

THREE HOURS LATER, CASEY woke from an unsettled sleep. An uneasy feeling gnawed at him. After several minutes of tossing and turning, and unable to decide if the uneasiness was good or bad, he sat up.

Before retiring for the night, they had searched the ship. Most of the previously locked rooms opened freely, and they discovered several had beds that extended from the walls. Casey had selected the one closest to the control room. He got up and walked the short distance into the control room.

Dim lights lit when he entered. He walked to the front and sat in his chair. He was surprised to still hear—feel—the rumble of the hailstorm. The view outside was still dark. The 3D image of the ship floated casually above the center console, encased in a soft blue light. He stared at the image, bothered that he could not figure out what it was that woke him. He felt he had missed something, and it was beginning to irk him that he couldn't determine what it was.

The viewscreens instantly darkened in reaction to a lightning flash.

Casey closed his eyes and settled into a deep breathing pattern and mentally reviewed the events of the last day. Escaping from the camp. Finding the ship. Escaping again. Finding themselves on the other side of the galaxy. Getting attacked by aliens and defending themselves. Casey wondered if the unsettled feeling was fear lurking inside.

He continued the events of the day: Landing on an alien moon. Exploring ruins. Wrecked spaceships. A monster hailstorm. His head felt like he was piecing together a giant puzzle without knowing the image.

His thoughts shifted to the space battle and the ships he had destroyed. A lump stuck in his throat when realization hit that he had killed aliens. It bothered him that the only alien they had even seen looked very human-like. Even though they—he—had acted in defense, he did not like the emotions that began to churn inside. He had been taught his whole life—by his father, mother, and Sensei—to respect and honor life, and that he needed to defend himself, his family, and those in his care. His eyes squeezed shut, his head shaking in defiance. It was not the defending part that bothered him, it was the killing. He never wanted to kill anyone.

He had not thought about it before. The possibility of killing someone, even in self-defense, had never really been a reality until the last day, and, since the previous morning, there just had not been much time to think. He was grateful that it was ships he had shot down and he had not seen the aliens die. A question nagged at him now: Would he actually be able to kill someone face-to-face if it came down to it?

He bit his lower lip while his mind dwelled on the thought. When he could not see the other person—like aliens in the spaceships—it was easy to disassociate the action. But what if he had actually come face-to-face with one of the Anaconda thugs? Could he have pointed a gun and pulled the trigger with the full intent to kill? James had given him the handgun, but he had not needed to shoot at any of the soldiers. Could he shoot an alien that looked human?

Behind his closed eyes, his thoughts drifted to younger years. As a child, his dad had taken him, his brother, sister, and cousin on many camping trips. Many times Heather had even joined them. His dad believed, taught, and reinforced the belief that all life was sacred, and that the taking of life should be avoided whenever possible, with the exception being in absolute necessity, such as self-defense. Even in hunting they were taught to respect and give thanks for the life given that they might live. Dad would frequently remind them that a big reason for their martial arts training was to use non-lethal means to end a potentially deadly situation.

He blinked the tears that started to form from the memories churned up from the hidden recesses of the mind. He fought the moisture back and rubbed his eyes. There was not time to reminisce on the past, to live in what was gone.

Another realization boiled up. His jaw clenched as his eyes opened. His choices and actions had brought James, Heather, and Leila across the galaxy. He'd almost killed them all at least twice. His head bobbed, and he committed to himself: he would do all he could to get them safely back to Earth.

Casey blinked his eyes open. He was laid back again in the chair, staring at a dark ceiling speckled with stars. He turned his head to the right and saw Leila standing nearby. Her black hair was let down; the gentle waves from the braiding caressed her neck and shoulders.

"I'm sorry," Leila started, "I didn't mean to wake you." She paused, studying Casey for a few seconds. "You okay?"

"Yeah. I woke up and couldn't get back to sleep, until I came out here."

"Are you worried about getting everyone home?"

Casey's gaze shifted to the front viewscreens. He felt the knot in this throat return, and he simply nodded.

"It may not mean much," said Leila, also looking out the forward viewscreens, "but considering the circumstances, I think you're doing better than can be expected." The horizon was just beginning to lighten with the heralding of a coming sunrise. "I don't know anyone else who could do as well."

"Uh, thanks, though I'm guessing you probably don't know many who have flown a spaceship and gotten themselves and others stranded on the other side of the galaxy."

Leila's mouth turned up in a half-smile, and her head tilted slightly. Her dark eyes reflected the increasing sunlight. "Just so you know, if we don't make it back, I don't think it's as bad out here as you may think. I think we'll be okay."

Casey turned to Leila, his jawline set in determination. "I'm going to do all I can to get us back to Earth."

Rays of the local star pierced across the horizon, and Leila closed her eyes momentarily. "I'm sure you will. But if we encounter other aliens, don't assume they're all trying to kill us. I'm sure there are some friendly ones who may be able to help."

Casey's right brow rose. "Might be kind of hard to know if we can't understand them."

Leila nodded. She continued to stare into the brightening horizon. "If they can build space-traveling ships, maybe they have some translator technology. And Heather's got quite the gift at picking up languages. Which reminds me, when we were going to sleep, she mentioned you found an old gun-like object. Can I see it?"

Glad for the distraction, Casey nodded, fumbled in his pack, and pulled out the dirt-encrusted gun. In the rush to return to the ship he had not realized how light it was. He handed it to Leila.

She gingerly turned the gun over and examined its handle and twin barrels. The barrels were each less than a half inch in diameter. On the left side of the grip was a small thumb rest. She brushed off the bottom of the grip and discovered a latch mechanism. After working out the dirt, she shifted the mechanism and an elongated cartridge ejected from the bottom. Stacked tightly up the cartridge were over a hundred small dart-like objects, each less than an inch in length and about an eighth-inch in diameter. She set the cartridge on the center console and looked into the opening in the handle. After a few seconds, she pushed a small button that was nestled inside. A silver cylinder, three inches long and a half inch thick, popped out.

Casey watched with interest. He picked up the cartridge and rotated it in his fingers. "Reminds me of small nails."

The cylinder moved slowly in Leila's hands. "They're probably more like darts than nails."

Casey leaned over to examine the gun in Leila's hands. "There's no ejection port, so the mini-darts must be propelled by the gun." He studied the cylinder. "My guess is it's not gas powered. Reminds me of a long AA battery. Most likely a power supply."

"So it's electrically powered?"

"Probably electromagnetic. I'd guess it's probably more like what some call a rail gun."

The gun lowered, and Leila's head cocked right. "I'm not familiar with that term."

"The projectiles, those mini-darts, would be accelerated along electromagnetic 'rails,' which are probably in the barrels, and then shot out the end at high speed."

Leila nodded at the explanation. "I didn't know that's what they were called. Do you think it works?"

"If the power supply is good, yeah. But, after who knows how long it's been in the dirt, the battery's probably dead. Still, James would point out we're here on an alien moon on the other side of the galaxy in a centuries-old spaceship. So, I wouldn't try the gun in here, just in case."

"Yeah," said James, entering the control room and startling the other two, "if you're going to test an alien weapon, please do it outside."

Chapter Eighteen
Morning on the Moon

R AYS OF THE LOCAL star pierced the front viewscreens and revealed a thick fog hugging the lowlands. Overhead the sky was reddish-blue. A short distance away, the formerly smoldering spacecraft now lay in a cold heap. Backlit by the rising star, the wreck looked like a ghost ship floating on a sea of fog. Closer to the *Fallen Star*, where the fog wasn't as thick, ice balls melted amid wisps of vapor.

"Definitely not jungle weather," said Casey.

"No." James walked towards the center console and looked towards the crash site. "But the good news is, I think we can explore that wreck today."

"And maybe we can melt some ice for water," said Casey.

An involuntary shiver shook Leila. "We should wait before trudging through the ice. Unless either of you have some winter weather gear hidden in those packs, I'm really not fond of cold."

"No," said Casey shaking his head slightly. "A rain poncho is the best I have."

"But it'll probably melt quickly now that the sun, star, local sun is rising," said James. "Still, it might be afternoon before we're not wading through ice."

Heather's voice drifted into the room. "Anyone else hungry? And thirsty?"

Casey turned back to see Heather walk into the control room. Her brown hair was tangled and matted. Like the others, her clothes were dirty and wrinkled. Evidence of dust crusted her face and arms. He smiled at her and was about to say something when she interrupted.

"Don't say it." Heather's palm rose, and her tangled hair wiggled as her head shook. "I know, I look terrible. But with all the camping and hiking we've done, it's not the first time you've seen me this way."

"I was only going to say that you look the way I feel," admitted Casey.

"As for food," said James, "we have our breakfast appetizer of a quarter granola bar each, followed by the main course of another quarter granola bar. But we should have plenty to drink."

"Let's use up the water in my pack first," said Casey. "Then I'll go fill it with ice."

Within a short time, the granola bars were divided and finished off. When the water was finished, Casey excused himself and walked to the back of the ship where he lowered the ramp.

Frigid air snaked up the ramp and into Casey's clothes, sending shivers through his body. Walking down the ramp, he wished he had more than lightweight jungle khakis. At the bottom of the ramp, a thin layer of water and mud lay under the ship. The muddy soil was reclaiming the footprints and filling them in. The remains of several hailstones, which had rolled under the edge of the ship before the shields were applied, were strewn around the mud. Hail was piled along the edge of the shields around the perimeter of the ship. Outside of the shields, the mist danced in slow motion over the frozen and soggy ground.

Casey called up into the ship. "Can somebody turn off the shielding?"

A moment later the icy wall collapsed, and ice balls rolled and sloshed. Warm, moist air, tinted with cold streaks, swept under the ship. Standing on the end of the ramp, Casey reached out and used his hands to dig a small hole in the mud. Water immediately filled the void. He removed the cap from the water bladder and placed the filling hole into the water. Icy water poured into the water container while thoughts of the night distracted Casey's mind.

"Beautiful, isn't it."

The water bladder jumped, and Casey jerked around. Heather stood behind him, her mischievous smile revealing her pleasure at startling him.

"I didn't think I could sneak up on you," said Heather.

An exhale of relief escaped Casey's lungs. "Guess I need to pay attention more." He dipped the bladder back into the water to finish filling. "And yes, it is beautiful, in a cold, deserty sort of way."

Heather crouched beside Casey. "How'd you sleep?"

"When I did, I think I slept okay. But it's been a bit stressful."

The right corner of Heather's mouth lifted teasingly. "Just 'a bit?'"

"Okay, so it's definitely more stressful than any of the pilot check rides I've ever taken."

"So, what's bothering you?"

Casey's eyes closed for a moment, then opened to look at Heather. "Besides stranding myself, brother, our best friend, and Leila on the other side of the galaxy, with no idea how to get home—oh, and just about getting everyone killed a couple of times—not much."

Heather's hazel eyes softened. "Casey, we've been friends for years, and I can tell something else is bothering you."

"*Wondering* is more like it."

"About?"

"It's more an uneasiness."

"Like we won't be able to find our way back to Earth?"

"No. I believe we'll find our way back. We came here; there must be a way back. No. There's something else. I had a similar feeling before we jumped across the galaxy and things went crazy."

Heather's brow creased. "You didn't say anything about that."

"It didn't seem important. It wasn't a feeling of doom or anything like that. Just that something doesn't feel right."

"When did the uneasiness start?"

Casey stared across the piles of hailstones and into the foggy mist. "I think it may have started after our close encounter of the aliens-trying-to-kill-us kind. But it's definitely increased since last night."

"You don't have any idea why?"

"No. More like a suspicion."

"Of what?"

"I'm not sure." Casey turned to Heather. "It's like I'm trying to describe what a five-thousand-piece puzzle looks like with only a few pieces, and no idea what the picture is supposed to be. Don't you think it's odd that we end up at this abandoned planet, er, moon only to get attacked by pirate-like aliens? Why were they here?"

"It was a bit of an inconvenience."

"And what about the one that got away? Maybe we should've killed it as well."

Heather shook her head. "No. You did the right thing. I think your dad would've been proud that you did no more killing than you needed to."

Casey's hand felt numb. He looked down and saw the bladder was full. He pulled it out of the small water hole and screwed the cap on.

"Heather, I won't admit this to my brother, and I trust you to keep it in confidence."

Heather nodded reassuringly.

"Blowing up spaceships is one thing. I don't have much of an issue with that. But I don't think I can kill someone face-to-face, especially if the person, the alien, looks human."

"Well, so far you haven't needed to. And hopefully it doesn't come to that."

"Also, before I came on the dig, I visited Mom. She asked me to promise to take care of James. And you."

A warm smile lit Heather's face. "I love your mom, she's awesome. But it's probably not easy being the oldest when you get that kind of responsibility."

"Sometimes. I wonder what Mom would say if she knew what happened and where we are."

"She'd probably say, 'Kendrick Cinaed Hawkins, you're doing better than you think you are. You've got great gifts to match the energy of your heart. Trust yourself to do the right thing.' And, she'd be happy you've kept us safe."

Casey grinned. "Yeah, she does like to use my full name to make a point. Let's hope that trend keeps going."

A shiver shook Heather, and she stood up. "For now, let's get back inside and warm up."

———— ❖ ————

A couple hours passed before most of the hail melted and the ground had sufficiently absorbed the water. Patches of ice clumps, surrounded by shallow pools, littered the drying ground. During their wait, Casey and James assessed their backpacks and topped off the water bladders with the melting ice. James checked his handgun and secured his crystal disc in its necklace. Casey found a couple of squished and forgotten protein bars at the bottom of his pack, and the decision was made to save them for later.

The curious gun Casey had found occupied some of their time. After James picked out more encrusted dirt and discovered a couple of recessed buttons, Casey decided to take the gun outside.

James's forehead furrowed as he followed Casey down the ramp. "Do you really think it might work?"

Casey shrugged. "This ship, after being in a pyramid for centuries, flew and brought us here."

"True enough."

Casey gripped the gun and pointed it at a pile of slush just beyond the ship. Without a trigger, he squeezed the handle and pushed buttons in different sequences without any success. He passed the gun to James whose experiments also failed.

Heather stepped off the ramp. "My turn."

With a doubtful shrug, James handed the gun to Heather. She gripped the handle, aimed, and squeezed. Nothing. After a few more failed attempts, she whacked the butt of the grip against the palm of her other hand, and grinned when the thumb rest emitted a faint red glow. She timidly squeezed the finger and thumb buttons simultaneously.

There was a nearly imperceptible *hiss*, and the slush pile blew apart with an explosion of ice.

James's hands flew up in surprise. "Whoa! It works."

"I barely heard it," Heather said sheepishly, "And it didn't kick at all."

"I wonder what the second barrel is for?" asked Casey, "Or does it just shoot those dart things out of each barrel?"

"I say we experiment more later," said James. "We know it works, and it could be useful. No sense wasting any more of the darts. I think it's time we check out that wreck."

Chapter Nineteen

Alien Wreck

CASEY AND JAMES GRABBED their packs from the control room and met Leila and Heather at the bottom of the ramp. Heather touched the small display on the ship's leg to close the ramp, and they headed towards the recent ship wreckage.

The air was hot, and, except for a few lingering slush piles, evidence of the night's hailstorm had vanished into the ground. The crushing hail and its subsequent melting had smoothed the soil surface, and the ground was beginning to crust over again with the increasing heat. By the time the half-mile hike was finished, sweat streaked their faces and the ground crunched underfoot. In front of them, the wrecked spacecraft loomed larger than expected.

A massive trench, abusively carved into the barren landscape, trailed the crash and severely scarred the land. Mountains of dirt, rocks, and debris were heaped around the forward sections of the wreck. Parts of the outer hull were stripped off and strewn along the trench, and the lower levels of the long ship had compacted into the middle. The upper decks had only partially collapsed, crumpled inward like an ugly accordion. Wide swaths of the ship's hull had blown out from explosions, and smoke had streaked the remaining ship's skin with grays and black.

The carcass of the spacecraft was over fifteen hundred feet long and two football fields in width. The partially intact upper levels towered a hundred feet above the trench. The bridge section sat on top, with one side blown off. Towards the bow, the three red-colored slashes on the side were halfway buried and ripped apart in the crash. Through the smashed and partially exposed hull, the large center space appeared to be an empty cargo bay.

They walked along the left side of the ship towards a gash that promised entry through the hull into a less-damaged section. Small piles of icy mud retreated into rapidly dwindling shade while daylight crossed into afternoon. Just above ground level, light pierced through a gash into an empty room whose interior walls had partially buckled. Across from the outer hull wall, a bent doorway opened into a dimly lit corridor.

"Anyone not wanting to explore a crashed alien ship with questionable structural integrity is welcome to stay out here," announced Casey while he and James studied the interior.

Heather's brow raised. "It can't be much worse than almost being buried in an ancient pyramid."

"It's probably safe enough," said Leila. "If it wasn't, it'd probably already be down."

James pulled himself up and through the slashed opening.

Heather frowned slightly while her eyes jumped across sections of the hull. "Do you think anyone survived?"

"I doubt it," replied Leila as Casey climbed in. "Unless they left in an escape ship. I doubt any living thing could've survived this impact."

James and Casey helped pull Leila and Heather up the short distance into the room. Flashlights were taken out of packs before they entered the passageway. In the corridor they headed right, towards the ship's aft, where the damage was less severe. Dying amber-hued lights cast a pale glow every fifty feet. Intermittent daylight squeezed through slivers or flooded from large slashes in the outer hull to partially illuminate the hall and exterior-facing rooms. Originally, the corridor had been about ten feet high and wide. Now every wall was bent, angled, or buckled. Breaks and tears in the left wall opened into the large cargo space where streams of light revealed emptiness.

On the right, the exterior side, they passed several doorways whose large metal, oval doors had been violently ripped from their hinges. The collapsed remains of bunks were in several rooms, their bedding trashed and scattered. They entered some of the bunk rooms to examine storage compartments that lined the outside walls, but the severe damage left them inaccessible.

In one room Heather picked up a coarse blanket and immediately dropped it, like it had burned her, and stifled a dry heave. "Ugh! It smells awful!" She stepped near a few other blankets and turned them down as well. "I was hoping for a blanket, but I don't think anyone ever cleaned those."

"Well, keep it in mind if we can't find anything cleaner," said Casey, "we can try to wash it, or at least rinse it out."

Heather shivered in disgust. "I don't think there's enough water. They'd need more than a dozen wash cycles with bleach to start to get that smell out."

The corridor continued a short distance and ended at a large oval doorway that opened into a stairwell. Like other doorways, the metal door was torn from one hinge and hung precariously from the second. Filtered light trickled into the stairwell through rips in the outer hull.

Immediately before the stairwell door, on the left wall, an oval doorway opened into a large dark room. Inside the room a pale emergency light still shed its faint glow. Flashlight beams penetrated to the opposite wall fifty feet away, where another door opened to a dark hall. The room felt like a real-life illusion, where the bow end of the floor angled up and the ceiling dropped downward. Buckled walls indicated the illusionary effect was caused by the impact. Tables and chairs had pounded against the forward end of the room, leaving a shattered, smashed, and twisted mess near a bent door. Room furnishings had also crushed into several large appliance-like machines that were embedded in the wall. The mangled machine remains invited the imagination to conjure up their former purposes. Pungent odors, contrasting sharp spices and sweet savors, filled the room.

James walked into the room. "Let's check this out first, and then the stairs. It looks like this may have been a mess hall and may be our best bet for finding something edible."

Heather's nose twitched in apprehension. "And it's definitely a mess."

They approached the forward end of the room and maneuvered through the twisted remains of tables, chairs, and machinery to the oval door that was wedged into its frame and bowed into the room it guarded.

Casey's flashlight breached the darkness through the bent door. "Looks like a bunch of packaging all over the place. Might be supplies. Maybe foodstuff."

For the next several minutes they pushed, pulled, and pried to lever open the door, but it refused to budge from the frame.

"So close," lamented James while his light swept through the gaps in the doorframe.

Heather cocked her head. "Casey?"

"What?"

"Do you have that dart-gun thing?"

The corners of Casey's mouth rose like a child's on Christmas morning. "I do." He removed his pack, unzipped the main pocket, and pulled out the gun. Holding it gingerly in his right hand, he looked at the others. "Just in case, let's go back in the hall. I'll shoot from the doorway."

After returning to the corridor, James pointed his light at the bent door while Casey aimed. Casey squeezed the gun grip and pressed the buttons. His cheeks warmed when nothing happened. He tried again, and nothing.

"Don't forget to whack it," advised Heather. "There's probably some loose connection."

Nodding, Casey slapped his left hand against the bottom of the grip, and instantly the thumb rest emitted a faint red glow. He aimed a third time and squeezed gently while pressing the two buttons. Following a soft hiss, the door blew apart with a small explosion.

"I like it." Casey grinned while he put the gun back into his pack.

"Nice!" said James. "I call next turn."

They walked to the remains of the door where pieces still clung to the hinges. A large concave section of the door lay on the floor of the inner room with a ragged hole through it. Small metal fragments littered the floor.

Surprisingly, the room was larger than the mess hall. Built-in shelving had crumpled and collapsed. Storage containers were piled haphazardly, and many were broken, their contents spilled throughout the room. Some of the packaging was torn with trails of dry and wet substances crisscrossing the room. A mix of liquids glossed the floor and reflected colorful patterns from the flashlight beams.

James carefully stepped into the room and picked up one of the broken packages. Red-brown powder fell out that he cautiously sniffed. His eyebrows rose in surprise. "Smells kind of bread-like, mixed with maybe some kind of fruit or berry."

"Just a guess," said Leila, "since that guy who called yesterday looked very human-like, I'd say this stuff's probably okay to eat. Although the taste may not be to one's liking."

Heather surveyed the room. "That's a good point. Our bodies aren't used to whatever food it is, so we'd better not eat too much."

James picked up another torn bag and smelled the opening. "If we can find something edible, we should have a bite before we head back. But we should definitely wait for a meal until we can eat without relying on flashlights." The beam of his headlamp followed his eyes around the room. "See if there are any bags we can use."

They spent the next half hour sorting through the mess to find undamaged packages while tasting the contents of a few. Heather compared alien characters on packages whose contents they liked. Most of the discovered food was powder-based. Some packages contained items that looked like dried fruit, produce, or some other kind of dehydrated food. Six small duffel-like bags were found and filled.

From the mess hall they returned to the hall and entered the stairwell. A quick view downward confirmed the lower stairs were too damaged to be passable. The upwards flights of metal stairs angled inwards, towards the center of the ship. They decided to go to the top and work their way down through the levels.

The severely damaged stairs took longer than expected to navigate. They passed five levels before they reached the highest deck. The walls in the top-level hallway were blackened from smoke. At the end of the corridor an oval doorway opened into another room. Like the other doors, the hinges were ripped off, leaving tangled metal reaching out.

A single flight of stairs went up about twenty feet to where daylight and stifling air flooded into the room beyond another doorway. The room's left wall was completely missing, along with chunks of the floor and ceiling, and exposed the room to the afternoon light and hot air. Looking outside confirmed they were in the upper bridge of the ship.

Semicircular rows of broken consoles—with regularly spaced chairs fixed to the floor—curved around the room. Smoke stains blackened the walls, ceiling, and consoles. Dim lights flickered around the command room, and several consoles still struggled with fading power. Humanoids in dark uniforms lay broken around the room, their clothing torn or charred. Several handguns and weapons were littered about the bridge. Restraint harnesses had torn through several crew members with the impact.

In the center, a large single chair sat with a commanding view of the others. Below the chair, three bodies were tossed together and broken in a single heap. Nearby, a single screen intermittently flashed. The former occupant of the station was doubled in half between the console and chair. At a neighboring console, another body, its face charred, was wrapped around a chair.

Casey pointed at the flashing screen. "Wait? What was that?" Three images flashed across the screen. "Is that our ship?"

The others came over. Between blips of darkness, three images were displayed on the screen. At the top left was an image of the *Fallen Star*, backdropped by a star field. To the right was an image of what looked like the same ship perched atop a landing pad high above a sea of buildings. Below the other two, a 3D technical drawing of the ship's exterior rotated. The edge of a fourth image was partially exposed on the right side of the screen.

Casey touched the screen, and a cliffside facility instantly replaced the technical drawing. The layout looked similar to the ruins they had walked through the previous day, except the buildings were intact and green vegetation surrounded them. The top two images remained the same. Casey continued to touch the edge of the screen while images appeared and disappeared between the flickering. Dozens of moons, planets, star systems, and star maps, each with lists of alien characters, followed.

Casey's eyes swept back and forth across the display. "Either these guys were galactic tourists, or this is some kind of database."

Leila watched intently from Casey's left. "Maybe they were trying to find the ship. This could be a record of where they've searched and information they've gathered."

On Casey's right, James shook his head. "Too bad we can't decipher the language. It might give us coordinates of where to go, if we knew how to enter them into the *Fallen Star*."

Casey paused on the image of a beautiful green-and-blue planet.

"Wow, that one almost looks like Earth," said Heather. "Except the continents are all wrong."

Casey swiped the image aside.

"Wait, go back," insisted Heather.

"What?" asked James as Casey swiped back to the previous image.

Heather's eyes shot across the screen, and she nodded. "They are the same."

Casey shook his head. "I have no idea what you're talking about."

"The characters," said Heather, pointing first to some characters in the lower right, next to the planet, and then to some characters near the image of the ship on the landing pad. "They're the same."

James shook his head. "Good eye," he complimented. "I would've never seen it with the flashing. But what do they mean?"

"That, I don't know," sighed Heather. "But since they're not on both of the ship images, maybe they're the name of the planet. Or someplace on the planet."

"Maybe the top-left image is just a screen-capture of us, and they were using it to compare to their database," suggested Casey.

He digitally flipped through more images, and more pictures of the same green-blue planet appeared in succession, followed by several of a large sprawling city. A text-based screen filled with alien characters came next.

"Hold on!" said Heather when Casey was about to swipe to the next screen. "You're getting too used to seeing the alien characters as all looking the same. Look closely. Besides just having alien characters, this page is different."

James was about to retort when Heather continued, "Besides not being a picture, James, this looks like a possible transcription, or decoding of a message."

Casey cocked his head. "How do you know that?"

Heather exhaled, as if preparing to explain some elementary principle. "Look. The characters aren't all laid out uniformly. The message looks separated, as if sections were being checked or decoded." She paused a moment while the screen went black and then reappeared. "Some characters are even emphasized, like a highlight. And this part almost looks like some kind of word dictionary." Her voice grew animated. "There are English words in there!"

"What?" said James.

Within the block of characters Heather was pointing at, a row of alien words revealed "English," "Espanol," and "Earth."

Casey's head moved slowly from side to side. "I totally missed those."

One side of James's mouth rose in a half-smile. "So does this mean someone on that planet knows about our planet?"

Leila was squinting at the screen. "Maybe. Or it might just be, as Heather said, an intercepted transmission."

James turned to Leila. "But that would still mean somebody knows about Earth."

"Which is an unsettling thought," admitted Heather, her excitement tempered. "And it begs the question: Who is the message from, who's it for, and what's it about? The ship may be part of it too. Look, the same alien characters by the ship's image in the top picture are in this message."

James was somber. "If they didn't already know, I'm guessing someone on that planet knows about Earth." He looked at the others. "Going there could be dangerous, but it might be our best option for getting home. Casey, how do we take this information back to our ship so we can go there?"

"I missed that part in spaceship training," said Casey. He bent close to the console, his head cocking slightly. "But, maybe this might work."

Casey pulled out his crystal disc and set it into a small slot on top of the console. An amber glyph overlaid the entire screen. He touched the glyph, and it dissolved into a different character surrounded by green. Casey removed the small crystal disc and put it back into his pocket.

"Did you just back stuff up to your disc?" asked James incredulously. Without waiting for an answer, he continued, "How'd you know how to do that?"

Casey shrugged his shoulders sheepishly. "Actually, I don't know if it worked. It just looked like it would. Guess we'll find out back on the *Fallen Star*."

Leila fidgeted, and nervousness tinged her voice. "What happens if we go there? To the planet, I mean."

"Well," said James, "it looks like somebody might know some English, or Spanish, and maybe how to find our way home."

The pitch of Leila's voice rose. "How can we be sure they'd be willing to help?"

Casey studied Leila; her face had paled slightly. "What about not assuming all the aliens aren't out to kill us?"

Leila looked down while her mind searched for words. "We just need to be careful. If those images are right, there'll be a lot more people to contend with in that city than we encountered yesterday."

"James's idea sounds like a good plan to me," admitted Heather. She nodded at Leila. "And, we do need to be careful. I can't think of a better plan, and it beats sitting around here waiting for someone else to find us."

"Or jumping around the galaxy getting more lost," added Casey.

James opened his mouth, stopped, and tilted his head to listen. He walked to the ripped-off side of the bridge and looked outside. "Anybody else hear that?"

Chapter Twenty
Race Back

FROM THE DISTANCE A faint, high-pitched whine grew louder. Casey joined James at the torn edge of the command bridge, overlooking a drop of over a hundred feet. The sparse landscape stretched out before them and far into the left horizon. On the right, the ancient wreck protruded from its impact crater a short distance away. Further to the right the lowlands rose into the foothills and then where the cliffs melded into the mountain range. Somewhere on the right and closer to the foothills, the *Fallen Star* expertly blended in.

"I don't see anything," said James. His eyes studied small swaths of the horizon from right to left and then spotted something in the sky. "Uh-oh. Looks like we might be getting some crabby company."

James and Casey moved back under cover while a crab ship flew high overhead. The high-pitched whine diminished as it flew towards the cliffs.

Leila tried to get a glimpse of the ship while remaining back from the edge. "Maybe they aren't the same pirates as yesterday."

James raised his brow at Leila. "Do you really think pirates are going to let us go?"

"Maybe," replied Leila, her voice lacking conviction.

Casey watched the ship disappear over the cliffs. "I'm with James. I don't think they're going to let us go. Not after what we did. And, I'm thinking our ship must be highly unusual to get their interest."

James turned away from the severed edge. "We need to get back to the *Fallen Star* as quickly as possible." He motioned around the room. "Grab the food bags and whatever weapons you can find."

Heather grabbed one bag of food. "Do you think they know where we are?" she asked as she looked for some kind of weapon among the dead bodies.

"Not yet," said Casey, pulling a short-barreled handgun from the holster of a fallen pirate, "or they would've landed already. Unless they find our tracks, which they might not see very well from the air, they won't know where to find us. Thankfully the *Fallen Star*'s adaptive skin makes it hard to see. I think they're just trying to figure out where we might be." He unlatched and removed the shoulder strap that held the gun's holster and several cartridge-like containers.

Within a minute an assortment of weapons was collected.

"I wish I could get something bigger," lamented James. He secured a holstered handgun to his waist and strapped a long rifle over his shoulder next to his food bag, "Pity we don't have the time to look."

"Or the means to carry them," said Heather. "We need the food more than lots of weapons. And we might have too much to move very quickly."

The whine grew louder.

"Speaking of moving quickly, it's time to go," said Casey. "It sounds like the ship is circling back."

The whine of the crab ship was intermittently muted between torn sections of the hull as they quickly retraced their steps through the wreck. The ship passed over three times before they returned to the room they had initially entered. James gripped the alien rifle in his left hand while the familiar 9mm was in his right. The whine became distant again.

Cautiously, James surveyed out the ripped hull. "Looks like they're heading back over the cliffs."

"How fast can we make it back to the ship?" asked Heather.

"Not fast enough," said James. He glanced from the flat terrain to the mountains. "Unloaded, we could probably run there in less than ten minutes on this terrain. Unless we drop what we came for, we're going to push at least fifteen minutes or more. That crab ship seems to be circling around every five minutes. Any ideas?"

"We could stay here until night and head back after dark," suggested Casey. "Judging from yesterday and where the sun, or star, is, we probably have a couple hours to wait. If we go, it'd be better to go while they're circling over the cliffs."

"Waiting gives them more time to find our prints. We didn't take any precautions against that," said Heather.

Leila watched the cliffs. "But it might be safer to wait. We at least have the advantage of cover here if they're not friendly."

"If they're after our ship, they probably won't kill us until they know where it is," said Casey. "Our best chance of escape is the *Fallen Star*."

"I think we should make a run for it after the ship passes again," said Heather. "It'll take a few minutes before they come back after that, and we might get lucky."

"I agree." said James, "What about you, Leila?"

The whine grew louder, and Leila quivered.

"I'll take that as an 'okay'" said James. "It's not much of a jump. The goal is to get to the ship. Follow our tracks back. First one back gets the ramp down so everyone can get up quickly."

Through the hull cracks, the crab ship came into view, and the foursome dropped back into the shadows. Before it flew off, the crab ship circled back once more over the wreck.

Heather's voice was barely a whisper. "Did they see us?"

The whine circled overhead.

Casey tried to glimpse the circling ship through the slashes in the hull. "I don't think so," he said softly. "They'd probably land if they saw us, or thought we were in here. Most likely they'll head off towards the cliffs again."

James crouched near the slash in the wall and said quietly, "When it flies towards the cliffs, I'll count to three and head out first. You guys follow, quickly. Casey, you okay going last?"

Casey nodded.

The whine circled overhead a few times and then faded away.

James watched the ship head off towards the mountains and then turned to the solemn faces near him. "It's headed back to the cliffs. Ready? One. Two. Three!"

James jumped out of the ripped section of hull and landed softly on the ground. His eyes darted around, scanning quickly for danger. Not seeing any, he started running to the *Fallen Star*, following their footprints for guidance. Heather and Leila jumped out in succession and followed after him.

When Leila started running, Casey jumped from the opening. An unexpected tug on his pack pulled him off-balance, and he stumbled on landing. His heart raced as he looked back at the opening and saw nothing. From the corner of his vision, he noticed a piece of fabric torn from the top of his pack. Shaking his head at his carelessness, he darted after the others.

Several minutes later, Casey was gaining on Leila and Heather when he passed the three-quarter point. James was running almost a hundred yards in front. A shiver rattled Casey's spine as the high-pitched whine unexpectedly came up behind him. A second later the crab ship passed overhead at less than fifty feet altitude. Ahead of him, bursts of adrenaline launched the others into a sprint.

The ship flew ahead of James and circled into a quick landing with its crab-like claws pointing towards the runners. James skidded to a stop, trying to determine how much farther the *Fallen Star* was while the ship hovered and landed to face him.

Swirls of dust wrapped around an unseen object a couple hundred feet beyond the crab ship. Heather and Leila stopped beside James. Weapons swiveled to point at the ship. Casey slowed to a walk while he watched, his lungs glad for the reprieve.

The crab ship sat on three extended skids facing the humans, its claw-like extrusions ominously pointed forward. Dust billowed under the ship while the engines continued running on low power. A hatch opened on the side, and four men—dressed in armor-like vests, leg and arm guards, and helmets with darkened visors—jumped out. They immediately pointed short assault rifle-like weapons at the group. They walked several yards towards James and stopped.

"This is going to be awkward," said James as he weighed who to point his weapons at.

The lead man shouted angrily, pointing and waving his weapon at James. "*B'uki osa shiata ni okunay!*"

"I think he wants us to put our weapons down," said Leila.

James clenched his jaw. "I was guessing as much."

"James," said Heather, "I don't think we have much of a choice. The odds are high all of us will get hurt, or killed, if we don't act peacefully."

"*B'uki osa shiata ni okunay!*" came the command with greater urgency.

When the humans did not drop their weapons, the lead soldier pointed his short rifle into the air and shot off a rapid volley of multiple projectiles.

"Okay!" said James. His hands opened slightly, fingers falling away from the triggers. "We're putting them down." He looked at Leila and Heather. "Put them down slowly." He let the 9mm drop to the ground and pulled the shoulder strap of the rifle over his head, lowering it to the ground beside the handgun.

Heather followed, setting her gun down slowly and raising her hands.

The commanding soldier motioned to the handgun holstered on James's side. James dropped it next to the others. He then raised his hands with palms out.

"It's better to be alive," Leila said, placing her gun on the ground. "There is a way out of this."

Casey walked up slowly behind his friends. The handgun he had taken from the pirate ship was held out to his side, his fingers off the grip. He dropped the gun on the ground and slowly raised his hands.

The four captors stood with their weapons ready, aimed at the humans, and waited.

A ramp lowered from the hatchway the four soldiers had jumped from, and a middle-aged man walked out. Unlike the others, he wore a black leather-looking jacket over a black shirt and maroon pants. Gold insignia adorned the shirt collar. His black hair was cropped short. A few scars near his dark eyes accented his olive-colored face. The man walked behind the four guards, his cold eyes scrutinizing the humans. Instantly, his eyes softened, and the center of his eyebrows raised.

"Ot'sano!" squealed Leila. She lost composure and ran to the man.

The man's face was cautious and then smiled with surprised joy. "K'reina!"

The four guards looked uncertain as Leila ran towards the man, but his response caused them to let her pass. The man's arms opened and pulled Leila into a warm embrace. The guards continued to point their weapons uncertainly at the other humans while he and Leila held each other for a minute.

The man's large hands gently took her shoulders and held her back to look into her eyes. Tears had filled Leila's eyes and streaked down her cheeks. The smile on the man's face grew larger, and he pulled her back into another embrace.

"Okay," James said, his hands still held up, "I am so confused. Do we need to hug that guy or something? Because I'm not sure how I feel about hugging alien pirates."

Casey slowly walked up behind Heather. "Did I miss something?"

"No," Heather said, shaking her head. "I'm as confused as you two."

"So...maybe this is a good thing?" suggested Casey.

Leila and the man were talking softly. The few words that filtered across the short distance were in an alien language. She seemed to be explaining something and pointed a few times at Heather, James, and Casey. The man's brow furrowed, and his smile turned down. He shook his head in his reply to Leila.

"Not looking good," said James.

A wireless communicator squawked, and the man and the four guards listened. The man's face turned serious. He spoke urgently to Leila and motioned for her to go up the ramp into the crab ship. He issued orders to the guards. Leila started to object, but the man was insistent. He quickly returned to his ship with Leila reluctantly following. As they reached the hatchway, Leila paused. She asked the man something and he pointed to the guards with his reply. He touched her arm while his head tilted inside. Her mouth started to open, then closed, and she walked inside.

"Definitely not a good sign," replied Casey.

"*Anato, osa mono ni okunay!*" commanded the lead guard, pointing his weapons at the packs and bags.

"Okay," said James, and he slowly started to remove his pack and bandolier. "We'll put our packs and stuff down."

Casey pulled the shoulder strap and holster over his head and dropped it. He started to remove his pack when a twin-barreled object caught his attention through the large tear in the top. "I've got an idea," he whispered as he removed the pack. "Just be ready to jump aside."

"Don't do anything foolish," said Heather.

Chapter Twenty-One
Rival Pirate Clans

B EFORE CASEY'S PACK TOUCHED the dirt, another high-pitched whine raced in from behind. A dozen plasma bursts tore into the ground and ripped through the four guards. More bursts raked across the terrain as a second crab ship raced overhead. Several shots shook the ship on the ground, scarring its sides while the ramp retracted. James, Heather, and Casey dropped and scanned the area for the new threat. In front of them, the first ship's engines increased in volume, and the ship jumped into a vertical climb. The new ship, with three red slashes emblazoned across its hull, whipped overhead and released another volley of energy bursts at the ascending ship.

"Grab your stuff!" shouted Casey as he followed his own advice.

James's hands swept down, and he grabbed the stuff he had dropped. "And get to our ship!"

Adrenaline kicked in, and they sprinted towards the hidden *Fallen Star.*

The red-slashed ship circled and seemed uncertain whether to pursue the first ship in its ascent or the humans running on the ground. The whine of its engines briefly intensified, and then it shifted its pursuit towards the first craft. Plasma bolts raked across the sky. Within seconds both crab ships disappeared into the higher atmosphere.

The *Fallen Star*'s ramp lowered, and James stopped at the bottom to watch for pursuers while the other two went up.

Heather, short on breath, darted up the ramp. "How'd you...lower the ramp?"

Casey followed after Heather. "I didn't."

James sprinted up and closed the ramp while Casey raced to the control room, shed his pack, and jumped into his chair. Heather plunged into the chair opposite him. The entire control room lit up with late afternoon daylight as the ceiling, walls, and floor became clear as windows. Casey's hands were on the controller domes and the 3D ship image began hovering over the ship console.

James entered the control room. "I think that ramp has a sensor or something, 'cause I didn't lower it." He stopped short of the second lead chair. "Wait a minute! That's where I was sitting."

Heather shot him a coy smile. "It's my turn to ride shotgun."

James was about to say something, thought better of it, and sat behind Heather.

The domes seemed to mesh around Casey's fingers in a light warmth. The 3D display over the front console pinpointed their location on the surface, the atmosphere above them, and a dozen red dots actively engaged at the edge of space. Casey's right hand released its dome and pulled out the crystal disc from his pocket. He placed it in the slot on the center console, and a list of alien words floated above.

"Maybe we could just stay here until they leave," suggested Heather. "Except for Leila, I don't think anyone even knows the ship is here."

"Somebody's bound to come back looking for us," said Casey. "If we do stay, we need to find a better hiding place. That last crab ship might have seen us disappear."

Casey touched one of the ethereal words, and the image of the cliff base appeared. He pushed it aside with his hand, and another image came up.

"I think our best chance of leaving without anyone noticing is while those red dots are dancing around," said James, pointing at the display.

Heather's voice cracked. "What about Leila?"

"I-I don't know," admitted Casey, motioning through images floating above the center console.

"Seems like she knew the guy," said James. "Although he did look a lot older. And she didn't object to getting into that crab ship."

"True enough," said Heather, a hoarse edge to her voice.

"There's the city," said Casey when cityscape images swept across in 3D. "I believe that's the planet and corresponding system chart."

A floating image of the star system leaped out to the side. Another image popped open next to the star chart, and hundreds of star systems flashed by.

Heather felt a lump in her throat, and she swallowed. "Let's take a look at those other ships first," she said, pointing at the red dots in the space. "Maybe we can somehow contact Leila. Just make sure the cloak is on first."

"I'm not sure that's a good idea," said Casey, "Don't get me wrong. I don't want to leave her, unless she wants to stay. But it did look like it was her choice to go."

"Put the cloak on and let's take a quick look," insisted Heather. "Keep the ship ready to make the jump."

"Okay," Casey relented, "but remember, I'm still learning how to operate this ship. And I'm not sure when it'll be ready to jump to wherever it is we're going."

James's voice was doubtful. "Heather, are you sure?"

Heather swallowed again and nodded.

Blue-and-purple lights lit on the right controller dome. Pressing the lights, Casey engaged the cloak and shield. Then he guided the ship into a high hover. A moment later they were soaring into orbit. Two large cigar ships emerged into view, and streaks of light ripped across the black background of space. The 3D displays confirmed what they were seeing: several crab ships circling and maneuvering in a vacuum-based dogfight. Plasma blasts were exchanged, and ships rocked with the impact. As if by an unknown agreement, the cargo ships kept a respectable distance from each other and the dogfight.

"Any idea which ship Leila's on?" asked Heather.

Casey scanned the 3D display and viewscreens. "Except for the red slashes on some of them, I can't tell them apart."

The *Fallen Star* cautiously neared the battle scene.

"Looks like we haven't been detected yet," said James. "But, still, no sense getting too close."

Red warning indicators flashed, and the displays showed a crab ship approaching fast from the right. Several torpedoes chased after the ship while it attempted to outrun and dodge their advance. Casey quickly reacted and dove the *Fallen Star* out of the way. In an effort to evade the torpedoes, the pilot of the crab ship also turned. In the same direction as the *Fallen Star*.

Casey ducked the *Fallen Star* left as the crab ship and torpedoes narrowly passed, except for one. The last torpedo, trailing behind the others, adjusted its trajectory to match its elusive target, and clipped the *Fallen Star*'s aft shielding in a harmless explosion. The rear viewscreens dimmed momentarily.

"That was close," said Casey, releasing a held breath.

Suddenly the battle array in the 3D display changed. As if on cue, crab ships on both sides disengaged from their fight and regrouped. Warning lights lit up around the command room, and the display indicated all the ships had redirected flight paths towards the *Fallen Star*'s location.

"Uh-oh," said Casey. "That explosion must've gotten everyone's attention."

Heather's voice wavered, its pitch increasing. "Did we lose our cloak and shields?"

Casey's head shook. "No. Looks like we still have full cloak and shields up. I think they suspect where we are. I might be able to just duck us away."

The crab ships on each side formed mirror-image *W*-formations and launched several plasma-like streams. Four massive energy webs rapidly formed and raced towards the *Fallen Star*'s assumed trajectory. Each web targeted different coordinates so together they effectively covered a broad swath of space to more likely snag an unseen prize.

"Better hightail it out of here," said James. "I'm counting at least four of those webs. I doubt a cloak and shield will hide us. And I don't think we can take on that many ships, even if we get past those cosmic webs."

Heather's knuckles whitened on the chair's armrests. "I-I'm with James. Casey, get us out of here."

Casey was about to touch the floating display screen when a galaxy view overlaid the forward viewscreens. A green dot highlighted a point among a wide cluster of stars, and a star system map leaped out of the galaxy plane from another point in the same sector. Casey's right brow rose, and he looked from the system map to the star map floating nearby. Matching alien characters hovered below both maps, and a warm green hue pulsed gently under his thumbs.

"Hang on to your chairs!" said Casey, and he engaged the ship's space fold.

Additional volleys of light streams were released from the ships in the *W*-formations. The first two energy webs converged on the *Fallen Star*'s location when brilliant white energy blasted from the front of the *Fallen Star* and ripped into space. Around the collector dish, charged particles turned purple, and a single arc of plasma exploded out to join the convergence point in front of the ship. From the perspective inside the ship, the energy webs slowed almost to a standstill. The blurred edges of energy first sharpened into crisp lines and then distorted before disappearing. The red planet, nearby moon, array of crab ships, and everything in view blurred, stretched, and disappeared in the wake of the space fold.

Chapter Twenty-Two

A Welcome

B ILLIONS OF COLORS WHIPPED across the crystal-clear viewscreens so fast the unaided eye could perceive only white light. Ahead of the *Fallen Star*, energy streamed towards the forward distortion point. In the corner of his right eye, Casey saw Heather seemingly frozen in place. He felt a pulsing warmth beneath his hands. In the galaxy display he watched their short travel path. Unlike before, they remained in the same small sector of the galaxy. The glass-like distortion field appeared in the front viewscreens, and Casey felt blood drain from his head as the ship passed through the field and instantly decelerated. The nausea that threatened blackout was immediately replaced by a wave of warm, invigorating energy that flowed throughout his body. Through the viewscreens, the stars regained focus, and a green-blue planet floated before them in space.

Casey blinked, and his lungs released a deep breath. He still felt a little nauseous, but the warm pulse washing through his body dissipated the feeling. Suddenly he remembered one of the things that had nagged him that morning. *Footprints*, he thought. When he'd arrived back at the *Fallen Star* the night before with James and Heather, he had seen two sets of footprints in the direction of the crash site. One came from the crash site, and the second returned. *Or maybe*, he wondered, recalling Leila's surprising reaction, *it was someone going to and returning from the crash*. He'd meant to ask Leila about the footprints, but the unexpected hailstorm had distracted him. By morning, the prints had been erased by the storm.

In the forward viewscreens, the green-blue planet was starting to look the size of a beach ball. The approaching planet refocused Casey's attention. The space jump had felt quicker, but he had not checked his watch. Other than the brief wave of nausea, he did not feel exhausted like the first jump. He glanced at Heather and then back at James. Both were reclined in their seats, unconscious.

A couple seconds later, Heather stirred. She sat up, the seat back following her. Her eyes narrowed on Casey. "How long was I out this time?"

"Not long. Maybe a minute? Did you remember anything of the jump?"

Heather turned to eye the planet and rubbed her head. "Nothing more than the instant flood of lights and colors swirling over and around the viewscreens. Almost like a psychedelic waterfall. I couldn't turn my head to look away before everything became a blur. Then I was out and waking up." Her eyes closed, and fingers pressed against her forehead. "I really don't like that, although it doesn't seem as bad as the first time."

James sat up and rubbed his temples.

Heather eyed Casey. "Was it the same for you?"

"I think it was easier. I didn't black out this time. Though I did remember something from last night."

"What?" asked James.

Flashing red lights illuminated around the room. In every viewscreen, red hues instantly surrounded several distant objects like the 'screens had augmented reality. The 3D display over the forward console highlighted the same objects in red while they rapidly approached the *Fallen Star*. Around the floating 3D image of the planet, numerous orbiting objects were changing from red to green highlights.

Heather touched some of the approaching red holographic images over the center console. Side images expanded to show a variety of spacecraft. "Looks like a couple dozen ships coming our way."

"Great," said James sarcastically. "Another party. The more the merrier."

"And," said Heather, pointing to an undulating sine wave, "I'm guessing someone is trying to communicate with us. It looks like an audio signal. Shall I see who it is?"

Casey paused for a second. "Yes, but stand by with the weapons."

"Okay," said James hesitantly. He began looking around his chair, trying to remember how the holographic weapons station was activated.

Heather touched the floating sine wave, and the upper body of a man appeared. The realism of the 3D image was still unnerving. The man had dark, tightly cut hair and piercing brown eyes. He appeared to be in his thirties, but small creases around the eyes and forehead indicated he might be older. An athletic body fit neatly in a crisp navy blue uniform. Several colored insignia adorned his upper left chest, and flashes of silver adorned the lapels of his collarless shirt. He seemed briefly surprised to see who he was talking to, but quickly regained a more diplomatic composure. His commanding voice was tainted with threat.

"Ano alkayid Hajun min 'miraturiot Sokari. Laquad dak'hala alfad' alsiyadu aghayr mashri lak bielmurrawri. Ad'kur nawayek."

"Oh, great," muttered James, "someone else who didn't get the English memo."

Casey tried to keep from smiling. "Or maybe they just want to talk to us about the warranty on their spaceship."

The man stopped talking. His jaw set and he nodded to his left. The audio silenced, and the man motioned and spoke to someone out of view. His chest rose as if he were about to issue an impatient command, then the tenseness of his face released, like he was being told something he wanted to hear. Finally, after a single nod of acknowledgment, he turned to face the occupants of the *Fallen Star*. His tone was more welcoming when he spoke. "Welcome to El'Tagath."

Casey, Heather, and James nearly fell off their seats in surprise.

"I am Chief Commander Hagon Intor of the Alphanaiyus fleet of the Mysian Imperial Service."

Heather's jaw dropped in surprise. "You speak English!"

The man smiled knowingly. "No, I do not. But you hear your own language through our translator."

"Wow, that's an impressive translator," said James. "Especially since we didn't even know anyone even knew about English on this side of the galaxy."

"Can you help us find the way back to our planet, Earth?" pressed Heather.

The man paused a moment as if comprehending what was said. "There may be some record of your planet, but I do not know of it. And, if it is, as you claim, on the other side of the galaxy, then no person we know of has ever been there. I'm unaware of any single jump gates that go beyond a thousand light-years." His eyes studied James, Casey, and Heather with measured curiosity. "How long did it take you to travel across the galaxy?"

Casey decided to think of an excuse for the space travel. "Commander Hagon, our ship may have fallen through some kind of wormhole. And we're trying to find our way back."

Hagon paused, his eyes narrowing slightly. He motioned with his hand, and the audio muted while he spoke to someone off-screen. Then he nodded, and the audio returned before he spoke. "We would be honored to escort you to the Mysian imperial city on El'Tagath. The uniqueness of this situation has interested His Majesty, the Emperor Altor El'Kanah. You have been invited to a most singular honor of dining with His Majesty. You may rest from your travels and enjoy the hospitality of the emperor while we try to answer any questions you may have and discover how you might return to your home planet."

Heather nodded and glanced back at James, who shrugged his shoulders and returned a quick nod. She looked at Casey and said, "We're good with it. What do you think?"

Casey nodded and spoke to the hologram. "Commander Hagon, I am Casey Hawkins, captain of the *Fallen Star*. We are honored to accept your offer, and the hospitality of your emperor."

Hagon tipped his head forward in a small, respectful bow, a pleased smile struggling to move his mouth. "For your safety, follow us as we escort you to the capital spaceport."

The 3D image disappeared.

James raised an eyebrow at his brother. "'Captain?'"

Casey shrugged. "Seemed more impressive than telling him I'm the guy who's just learning to fly this thing. Besides, the pilot of an aircraft is often called a captain. Don't worry, we'll think of a different title for you. Heather would probably be a better communications officer, since she's not likely to try to sell extended warranties."

"Just not second mate."

The center ship—a lean, efficient-looking spacecraft that reminded Casey of a long, three-edged broadhead arrowhead—initiated a turn towards the planet. Casey maneuvered the *Fallen Star* to follow Hagon's ship and watched warily while two dozen smaller spacecraft spread out along the left, right, top, and bottom as escorts. The forward 3D display indicated hundreds of objects orbiting the planet. Among the satellites were spacecraft of varying sizes and several large space stations. The display also tracked dozens of objects flying in and out of the atmosphere.

Heather stared intently at the approaching planet. "He seems friendly enough."

"Yeah," said Casey, his voice cracking with uncertainty "But don't let your guard down. Something doesn't feel right."

"Agreed," James added. "He wasn't telling us everything."

Chapter Twenty-Three
El'Tagath

E L'TAGATH QUICKLY FILLED THE front viewscreens, and even from a distance the array of spacecraft was impressive. Several ships maneuvered around a spaceport while Hagon led the escort into orbit. A reflection in the top viewscreens caught Casey's attention. He looked up and saw a ship so massive that it would have dwarfed the pirate cargo ship. Several spacecraft of similar design to Hagon's were in the distant horizon. Hagon's ship began descending into the atmosphere.

"Wow," breathed James while Casey followed the descent. "I had no idea spaceships could come in such wide variety. I mean, sci-fi movies show this stuff, but this is...real."

Beneath them, the terrain became more discernible. Expansive mountain ranges, with peaks extending high into the atmosphere, burst through feathery clouds. Far to the right, the glistening surface of a large body of water sparkled at the horizon's edge. Through the floor viewscreens, towering structures and buildings popped up through the clouds. As their approach brought them lower, the surface became covered with extensive cities and urban networks, one flowing seamlessly into the next. Greenery adorned the tops of many buildings: terraced gardens, forests of small trees, even streams and waterfalls.

Their descent stopped at an altitude over the highest structures. Below them, the vegetation became sparse among a sprawling cityscape. The buildings were densely packed, and rivers of diverse air traffic moved passengers and cargo at altitudes in differing directions. Air transports landed or took off from the tops of buildings, docking ports, or pads jutting from the sides of structures.

A wide expanse of flat surface came into view. Four pair-sets of runways were separated by scores of round pads and surrounded by dozens of buildings. Spacecraft of all sizes sat on the landing pads while larger ships were parked next to terminal-like buildings. The regular aerial traffic of the city was routed around the spaceport, and the spaceport ships took off and landed from multiple directions. Still flying higher than the normal air traffic, Hagon proceeded straight overtop the spaceport while Casey, keeping a wary eye on the other ships, followed.

"Um," started Heather, "looks like another communication is coming in."

Casey gave a short nod while his eyes fixed ahead. Heather touched the screen, and only audio came through.

"Escorted guest vessel, you are cleared to land on platform Zigna. Acknowledge."

Without hesitation, Casey responded, "Guest vessel cleared to land on Zigna." After a pause, he added, "Can you tell me where that is?"

"Follow and land next to your escort," came the blunt reply.

From their altitude, Casey could not identify any markings to differentiate the runways or landing pads. He did not want to admit it, but he was glad he could just follow Hagon. Knots tightened in his stomach when they flew over several layers of fencing, walls, and checkpoints at the end of the spaceport and descended into a secure section. Gun turrets were mounted on towers at regular intervals, and dozens of smaller, arrowhead-shaped ships lined an inner landing zone.

Amber lights chased themselves around two empty landing pads in the center of the landing zone. Another ten pads were vacant nearby. Hagon's ship flew a half-circle before descending vertically to land on one of the pads. Three ground transport crafts emerged from a nearby building and drove towards the landing pad.

"Feels like we're landing in a prison," said Casey. He mimicked the other ship's maneuver and circled the *Fallen Star* around to land on the next pad.

"It's just a secured area for VIPs," said Heather. "Which is better for us since this ship seems to be one-of-a-kind and we need it to get back home."

Casey chewed his inner cheek for a moment. "Yes, I know. But it's for that reason I'm concerned about landing. I just hope it's as easy to leave as it is to land."

"Let's just keep our eyes open and not talk too much," said James. "Until we know who to trust. This may be our best hope to get back to Earth, but we don't know anything about these people or what they might want from us."

"Okay, hang onto your seats," said Casey.

The ship settled softly on its pad.

The three ground transports, which looked like stretched minivans, hovered towards the two spaceships. From around the corner of another building, two armored mini-tank vehicles, each with quad-barreled turrets on top, hovered out.

The three transports stopped fifty feet from the landing pads. Doors slid open on the first and third transports, and six guards, dressed in gray-green uniforms and face-covering helmets, stepped out. They quickly fanned out into two columns from the center vehicle and stood at attention, each guard holding some kind of mini-rifle. The middle transport's door slid open to reveal an off-white interior.

A ramp descended from Hagon's ship, and four blue-uniformed men marched down, followed by Hagon. At the bottom of the ramp, Hagon, flanked by his four guards, confidently walked over to the *Fallen Star* and waited.

"Guess it's our turn," said Casey.

"Should we take anything with us?" asked James, his hand fidgeting with his pack.

"We can probably leave our packs," said Casey. "I don't think we'll need them, and they're more secure to leave here."

"Just keep your crystal secured," said James. He checked the small crystal in its binding on his necklace, then pulled a small pouch out of his pack to toss to his brother. "Casey, you might want this."

Casey removed a necklace similar to his brother's from the pouch.

"It's my backup. My experience is crystals are easily forgotten about and lost in pockets," said James. "Don't ask me how I know. Just trust me, it's safer to keep it around the neck."

"Thanks," said Casey. He removed his crystal from the slot on the console and secured it in the small braided cage on the necklace.

"I don't think you should take any of the weapons," said Heather.

James was holding an alien handgun. "I want to, but you're right." He put the gun into his pack. "No sense making it look like we're dangerous."

They went to the aft room, lowered the ramp, and descended into warm and mildly humid air. Hagon and his four guards stood near the bottom of the ramp, waiting. Beyond them, the two columns of soldiers lined the path from the *Fallen Star* to the ground transport.

Casey felt Hagon's eyes scan him, James, and Heather. A look of disgust briefly crossed the dark eyes. Uncertain, Casey hesitated before stepping off the ramp. He looked at James and Heather and then realized how dirty and unkempt they appeared.

"*El'Tagath mar'ahlbaan*," said Hagon. He pressed his right fist over his heart with a slight bow.

"I guess there's no translator," commented Casey, returning the gesture.

Hagon held his hand out, palm towards Casey, in a stopping gesture. He pointed to his own ears and then to Casey's. He turned and spoke a command to a nearby guard. The guard motioned to the two closest soldiers. The two soldiers let their mini-rifles hang at their sides by shoulder straps and stepped forward. They turned sharply and walked in perfect cadence towards Casey. Stopping short of the ramp, one soldier pulled a small metallic container from a utility pouch on his belt.

Casey felt his muscles tense and willed himself to relax. He knew they had let their guns down to indicate they were not a threat. But he was not sure about the container. The guard not holding the container slowly touched his own ears and then pointed to Casey's. Casey nodded hesitantly, not sure what was going to happen. The man cautiously stepped closer and slowly reached his hands out to touch Casey's ears. It was odd to feel the fingers of a uniformed stranger massaging the lower halves of his ears and earlobes.

The man's eyes focused on something within Casey's ears. With a curt nod, the man dropped his hands and stepped back. He turned stiffly towards Hagon and nodded. Hagon returned the acknowledgment.

The second soldier came forward and opened the container. Inside was a small silver panel and a black box. With one hand he lifted the lid of the black box and revealed a dozen minuscule, dot-like objects lying on top of a black velvet-like fabric. The first soldier removed one dot and held it carefully. Casey watched as it seemed to vanish against the man's fingers. The soldier carefully placed the dot on the inside of the antitragus of Casey's right ear. He then repeated the process on the left ear. The soldier motioned his right index finger across the silver panel and said, in a strongly accented voice, "English."

"Ow!" said Casey, flinching at an unexpected sharp sting in his ears. Just as quick, the pain was gone. "That was odd."

Hagon stepped towards Casey and smiled. "*I regret I did not explain this before we landed. And my apologies for any pain you may have experienced. Most people do not feel anything when they receive translators.*"

Casey's jaw dropped. "That's amazing! I can understand you!"

Hagon returned a thin smile.

"Casey, are you saying you can understand his language with those ear-thingys?" asked Heather.

Turning to Heather, Casey replied, "I heard him speak English."

"*Not exactly,*" replied Hagon. "*You heard my words translated into your English.*"

"What did he say?" asked Heather.

"Apparently these ear things act as translators in that they allow you to hear another language as if you're hearing your own. Hagon hears English translated into his own language, and I understand him as if he were speaking English," said Casey. "The technician must've coded my translators to default to English."

Hagon nodded. *"That is more correct. Without the eeritium translator neither of us would understand the other, short of personal knowledge of the other's language. If your companions would like, they may also receive eeritiums. They are perfectly safe and can be removed if desired."*

"I'm sure they'd appreciate them," said Casey.

"What?" guessed James. "Get earrings?"

"Hagon says they're safe and can be removed. They're attached just on the inside of the ear, just out of the ear canal. I've understood everything he's said. If you want, he'll give you some. Unlike my experience, it's not supposed to hurt."

"I'd rather learn the language than rely on some computer to translate it," lamented Heather. "But since I don't have time for it, I'm in."

"If I don't have to learn the language, I'll take 'em," said James. Heather rolled her eyes at him.

Within a minute, the two soldiers had painlessly attached the eeritiums inside James and Heather's ears and returned to their lines.

James rubbed the inside of his ears. "That wasn't bad at all. And I can't even feel them."

Hagon lifted his right hand towards the transport waiting at the end of the columns of soldiers. "The transport is waiting for us. I have informed the emperor of your arrival, and he is most interested in meeting you. But first"—his eyes scanned his guests—"I am certain you would like to get cleaned up. The palace attendants should have rooms ready for you when we arrive."

"Thank you, Commander Hagon," replied Casey with a small, respectful nod. "Your offer is most appreciated."

Hagon returned a curt nod before leading the way towards the middle transport van. Casey glanced back at the *Fallen Star* while he, James, and Heather followed. The ramp quickly retreated and was absorbed back into the ship's underside.

Hagon entered the open door of the transport, turned left, and sat down in one of three overstuffed back seats. An eggshell-colored suede-like material covered a bench seat that wrapped the sides and front of the cabin and trimmed the wall posts. The front and back walls were solid, but the sides and top were like one-way glass, allowing occupants to see out but shielding the interior from prying eyes. Heather, James, and Casey sat on the bench opposite the door.

Through the transport's windows, the *Fallen Star* stood at the far end of the columns of imperial soldiers. Casey's fingers curled when the soldiers started moving towards the ship. He nearly stood, but then the ship's skin shimmered and the entire *Fallen Star* disappeared. The guards stopped their advance, and several reached out blindly, looking like amateur mimes, trying to find the unseen surface. Casey sat back, his hands relaxed, and he smiled, imagining what must be going through the soldier's heads.

Outside, several of the nearby arrowhead ships lifted into a high hover. The middle transport rose and accelerated into a vertical climb, turning away from the spaceport. The arrowhead ships escorted the transport while it continued its flight at a leisurely pace through the cityscape.

Heather diverted her attention from the windows. "Commander Hagon, my curiosity is getting the better of me. How is it that your translators know English?"

Hagon's dark eyes studied Heather's. "I do not know the actual answer. I am personally unaware of your planet or your language.

But when your ship approached El'Tagath, it scanned many of our satellites and orbiting stations at an extraordinary rate, triggering numerous alarms. My ship was dispatched, and it is a good thing too. Those with less experience might have been less willing to talk. My guess, to answer your question, is it would seem that in the scanning process, a number of communication protocols and standards were exchanged. English must have been among those protocols."

James shot Heather a questioning brow. "How'd the ship know English?"

Hagon's head tilted in interest. "Perhaps your maintenance crew keeps it up. Or it was included by the builder."

Casey's brow furrowed slightly, and his head darted to the side as if to tell James, *Don't say anything else.*

James nodded.

"How quickly can your translator system learn a new language?" asked Heather.

A smile broke Hagon's diplomacy. "I do not know the details, but the eeritiums learn a new language when the protocols are set. And it learns and adapts as it monitors native speakers."

"That'd sure be nice to have back home," said Casey. "Easier than the online translations and apps."

"Maybe for the lazy," said Heather with a mock huff. "I think it's fun to actually learn a new language, and speak it, instead of some AI giving you its interpretation."

The transport and its escorts entered a jungle of tall buildings. The mixed-material structures reached into the atmosphere. Hanging gardens draped off extended platforms and decks while rooftop vegetation hung down like green headdresses. The transport rose higher and merged into a flow of traffic. Nearby air vehicles automatically moved out of the way, allowing the transport and its escorts to pass. On several buildings, water cascaded over terraces and into blue pools on lower decks.

James turned around in his seat to look out and down from his window. "How high are these buildings? I'm not sure if I can see the ground."

Hagon's attention remained on the other three in the transport. "Some are as tall as mountains. Much of the city has been built on itself over the centuries. Rather than spread into all the natural spaces of the planet, most of the population has been gathered into the cities."

"So"—Heather's gaze darted across the immense cityscape—"how many people live here?"

Hagon sank back comfortably into his chair. "There are about ten billion on this planet. This city alone has about one billion living within its boundaries."

"I'm feeling claustrophobic just thinking about that many people," said Casey.

"Unless you're unfortunate to visit the bottomlands or underground, it does not feel that way," said Hagon. "On the contrary, it is very open. The worst is probably the air traffic when a vehicle's air guard is not working."

James's attention veered from side to side. "How far are we going?"

"Not far," said Hagon. "We just passed the outer perimeter checkpoints. We will be at the imperial palace in moments."

Chapter Twenty-Four
Mysian Palace

T HE CITYSCAPE WAS REPLACED with orchards, extensive gardens, and expansive fields. Ahead of the transport, three tiers of fortified walls surrounded a large plateau. The first tier enclosed the wide base of the plateau like an armored moat. The transport slowed as it crossed over the lowest tier and flew over clusters of buildings that dotted the green between the two lower tiers. Passing over the second tier, the top tier of fortifications stood before them like an imposing sentinel. Multiple structures topped the hundred-foot-high armored wall. The transport ships slowed as they flew through a massive three-hundred-foot-wide stone archway and into a courtyard the size of several football fields. The two escort ships remained in a high hover while the transport settled gently down and glided towards a multi-level palatial building in the center.

Heather looked up at the clear blue-hued sky. "Why didn't we just fly over?" she inquired.

"The automated defense systems would have ripped us from the sky," said Hagon. "All authorized craft enter through the gateway. Only the emperor's ship is permitted to pass directly over."

Casey's insides squirmed at the fortified walls that surrounded them. Nearby, James fidgeted, his eyes shifting across the walls and parapets. Casey noticed Heather had an expectant look on her face, as if to ask him a question. He simply returned a weak smile and stared out the windows.

The transport shuttle drifted softly to land in front of sweeping marbled steps. The eight steps topped at a wide colonnade of white granite-like pillars sparkling with silver flecks. Spaced between each column, sentinels in crimson uniforms held halberd-like weapons. Their shirts were fitted and layered at the front like a martial arts uniform, baggy pants tucked neatly into black boots. A contingent of twenty guards—uniformed in nearly identical red shirts, black oversized-pants, and glossy-back helmets with crystal face shields—cascaded down both sides of the steps.

Hagon's dark-gray eyes narrowed in seriousness at his guests. "I do not know your customs, but before we exit, I must inform you of vitally important etiquette. The emperor is anxious to meet you prior to dinner. Currently he is in the midst of imperial affairs, but we are given permission to enter the imperial chamber when you are ready. When you are introduced to the emperor, you must bow. It is a sign of respect and honor. Failure to do so will not win you any friends. And do not address His Majesty until he has first spoken to you. Dinner, which will be later this evening, will be formal. But first, you must get cleaned up. I would be severely reprimanded if I brought you before His Majesty in your current state."

Casey nodded.

Heather's mouth grinned like a child's on Christmas morning. "Getting cleaned up would be absolutely fantastic."

The door of the transport opened; Hagon exited, followed by the others. They walked up the steps, between the two columns of guards, and passed through the colonnade where muted reflections greeted them on the pillars. At the end of the colonnade, two high, jewel-decorated doors swung inward at their approach. Along the path, the red sentinels stood perfectly still; only the movement of their eyes betrayed their interest in the visitors. Besides their halberd-like weapon, each was also armed with long-barreled handguns that hung from their belts.

After passing through the jeweled doors, Hagon led the small group down a wide hall while their feet clapped mutedly against the reflective red-marbled floor. The hall reached an intersection where six guards and three female attendants stood waiting. The guards, dressed like the red-uniformed sentinels minus the halberds, stiffened to attention and touched clenched fists to their chests when Hagon approached.

The attendants wore black dress slacks and silver-gray, long-sleeved blouses. Each had brown hair pulled back into a tight bun, and their light-brown faces were expressionless. The green eyes of the woman on the right starkly contrasted with the brown eyes of her two companions. The eyes sparked of intense curiosity and betrayed the feigned look of disinterest on her face. The women bowed towards Hagon.

Hagon turned to his guests. "Meet back here in an hour. That should be enough time to freshen up your appearance. Madame Zaeha"—the center attendant bowed again—"and two of her attendants will show you to guest quarters where you can get cleaned up. They will also provide clean clothing for you. As I mentioned, His Majesty is currently attending to urgent imperial business. Your initial meeting will be short. Dinner will be later. The palace attendants will help you with whatever needs you may have. Now, I am late for some business that I must address."

The three attendants bowed politely. Hagon quickly pivoted to his left and briskly walked away.

"Well, that was abrupt," said Casey.

Madame Zaeha's nose crinkled as her eyes scoured over Heather, Casey, and James. Her voice was expressionless when she spoke. "Please, follow us to your quarters." She turned to walk down the right adjoining hall.

The attendant on the left immediately turned and walked after Zaeha.

The green eyes of the third attendant squinted curiously at the three strangers. After a moment she said quietly, "It would not be wise to keep Hagon or the emperor waiting."

Casey, Heather, and James followed after the first two attendants while the third hung back with them, and the six guards marched in cadence behind them.

They navigated several hallways before stopping, and each attendant positioned herself in front of a different door. Zaeha motioned James into the room she stood by, directed Heather into the next, then Casey to the door by the green-eyed attendant.

The attendant bowed as Casey entered the doorway. When he stepped inside, he noticed two guards positioning themselves outside of each door, and the attendants followed their assignees into the rooms. He felt his cheeks warm when his attendant followed him.

The room turned out to be a suite. They entered an entry, or waiting area, sparsely decorated with two cushioned chairs. A hallway from the entry passed two doorless openings on the left and ended at a third doorway. The woman showed Casey into the first of the small rooms where steam vapors rose off a large bath that occupied the center of the floor like an inground hot tub. On the right wall, another doorway opened directly into the next room.

The attendant's eyes measured Casey's when she spoke. "I will remain in the main room if you need anything. After you have bathed—there is body and hair cleanser in that dispenser—you may go into the next room to get dressed." She pointed to the open doorway on the right. "You may select from any of the clothing in that room. Should you not find anything that fits, or which is to your liking, let me know and I will find alternatives for you. You may leave your clothing on the floor, and it will be washed and returned to you later this evening."

Casey glanced around the room. "Looks great. Thank you. Um, that bath looks awesome." His eyes stopped shifting, fixating on the attendant's. "Um, I— My name's Casey."

The woman's cheeks flushed, and she gave a small bow. "I am called Kathera."

Casey looked around as he stepped into the bathroom, noticing the doorless entryway. The warm, moist air added to his flushed cheeks. "Um, Kathera, two questions: How do I dry off after the bath? And, are there doors?"

A pink hue briefly flushed Kathera's light-brown complexion. "I am so sorry. I did not realize you are unfamiliar with how things work here. For the door, just move your hand across this panel, either inside or outside, to activate it." She demonstrated on an outside portion of the door frame, and an opaque glass door silently slid from the wall to fill the empty doorway. She moved her hand again, and the door opened. "The dryer is on the other side of the bath."

Casey's mind conjured up several ideas of what the dryer was but decided not to ask any further questions. He nodded a small bow towards Kathera. "Thank you again, Kathera."

The corners of Kathera's mouth lifted into a barely perceptible smile as she returned the bow and retreated to the entry room.

Casey moved his hand across the door jamb where Kathera had demonstrated. The opaque door slid silently across the opening, and steam began to build on the door panel. He quickly shed his dirty clothes, leaving only his necklace and watch on, and stepped down into the hot water. The dirt, sweat, and grime from the last couple days seemed to peel off, and he soaked in the water for a few minutes. He moved over to the silver dispenser Kathera had indicated. Not seeing any kind of dispensing mechanism, he placed a hand under the opening. A clear liquid foamed onto his hand, and his nose filled with the aroma of fruit blossoms.

After washing, Casey soaked for several more minutes before he got out and walked towards the dryer side where he saw a plush red towel folded on a shelf. He smiled and walked to the towel, wondering why Kathera had not just called the dryer a towel. Before he reached the towel, a warm air current swept up from the floor and twisted around him. The air flow started evaporating the excess moisture from his body. He grabbed the towel to speed up the drying process and walked over to the doorway into the adjoining room.

The door opened, steam drifting in. Dozens of shirts and pants, in various colors, hung along the opposite wall, and a mirror covered another wall. Casey looked at several shirts and instantly dismissed them. A few others he held up in front of the mirror. Other than a few which were slightly smaller or larger, the clothes were all close to Casey's size. He wondered if someone had somehow guessed what size he wore, and if that was why he was assigned to the room. Feeling a little overwhelmed with the choices, he decided to stick with a more familiar look and chose khaki-colored dress slacks and a soft, white buttoned shirt made of a cotton-like material.

Kathera's voice came down the hall. "Are you ready? We will need to be going soon."

Casey was looking through footwear. "Yes, just need some shoes." He grabbed some loafer-style brown shoes and slipped his feet into them. The fit was not perfect, but close enough to be comfortable. He walked to the door, moved his right hand over the door frame, and the door slid back into the wall.

Kathera stood in the entry room. Her fingers stopped fidgeting when Casey stepped into the hall. Despite her attempt to remain emotionless, her eyes sparkled with approval at the change. "It is time to rejoin with Commander Hagon and your companions."

Chapter Twenty-Five
Meeting the Emperor

C ASEY FOLLOWED KATHERA INTO the hall where they joined James, Heather, and their attendants. The six guards still stood motionless, two at each door. Cleaned and dressed up in dark blue slacks and a complementary blue shirt, James looked like he would be at home on a magazine cover. Heather wore black slacks and a *V*-necked tunic with three-quarter-length open sleeves. A white-blue flame swept around the waist of the tunic and dissolved into black as it reached up into the neck and shoulders.

The attendants and guards escorted the three guests back to where they were to meet Hagon, who appeared a minute later. Hagon nodded a stiff approval, pivoted, and then led them to the end of the main hall—a wall of polished black. Two red-clad sentinels stood on each side, their halberds held in stiff attention. The center of the wall parted and revealed a large room behind it. Casey, Heather, and James followed Hagon into the room while the attendants and guards remained in the hall.

Six white pillars, each spaced about twenty feet apart, lined each side of a center walkway. The pillars were inlaid with ornate gold-and-silver designs and accented with clear and colored stones. The right and left walls, set back twenty feet from the pillars, were equally decorated. The elaborate marble floor, highlighted with red hues and flecks of gold, was strangely quiet to their footsteps. At the opposite end of the room, two half-circle tables opened to the center. An opening between the two tables at one end allowed access inside the circle and to a three-tiered dais that rose above the other side.

A large throne sat in the center of the dais's top level. Two thrones were on the second tier, one on each side of the higher chair. The two sides of the lowest tier swept out from the dais like wings. Six large chairs sat behind long tables on each wing, and intricate carvings covered the panels on the table fronts. Nine of the lower-dais chairs were occupied. Behind the two table arcs on the floor sat twenty individuals and four empty chairs.

Commander Hagon led the group through the opening of the three-part circle and stopped short of the dais.

The man on the center, and highest, throne was unmistakably the emperor. Even without a crown, he emanated power, authority, and charisma. His short dark hair was neatly cut. Despite smooth and unwrinkled facial features, the lightly tanned face had the chiseled look of experience and confidence. Sky-blue eyes held a penetrating gaze as they watched Hagon and his guests approach. A gold falcon-like amulet hung from an elaborately woven gold necklace. The falcon's wings stretched upwards to hold a red circle outlined in gold above its head.

The emperor wore a crisp, long-sleeved uniform of dark blue trimmed with silver and gold medals. The uniform was fitted precisely to accent the emperor's physique without being tight. Dress slacks matched the uniform top in color, and two gold stripes ran down the outside legs to where they met with shiny black footwear. His hands relaxed on the armrests. A wide cobalt-colored band with a clear center stone adorned his left ring finger. On his right ring finger, he wore a dark-red-and-gold-colored band that pressed a blood-red stone between its ends.

An elegant woman sat on the emperor's left. Her dark complexion was framed by black hair that caressed her neck and draped below her shoulders. Gold and silver strands were randomly intertwined into the hair like accented extensions. A golden headdress sat on her head, its top sparkling with clear and red jewels. The sides of the headdress were four layers of thin, golden, wing-shaped plates that swept downward and covered the sides of her head. Red crystal pendants hung from her ears. A cap-sleeved, calf-length black dress, made of a glistening scale-like material, accentuated the woman's fitness. Gold-laced sandals and small toe rings graced her small feet. She wore several rings on each hand, and a small falcon-like bird hung from a thick necklace of blue and red jewels that swept around her long neck.

Her dark eyes danced with amusement as she watched the group enter. While exceptionally beautiful, her gaze reminded Casey of a cat about to toy with a mouse.

On the emperor's right sat a man who seemed out of place next to the regal-looking couple. He wore a pure-white shirt that crossed his chest in a fashion similar to a martial arts uniform, except the material appeared light and silky. A white sash, trimmed with platinum, wrapped the waist and was tied on his left. Fitted trousers of identical material covered his legs and dropped down to simple white shoes. Dark-blond hair dropped to mid-neck around a face of light-colored skin with cinnamon contours. Like the emperor, the facial features seemed to belie the man's age and experience. His hands were relaxed in front of the abdomen, fingertips together, while his black eyes studied Casey, James, and Heather.

The occupants of the lower dais wore dark-blue uniforms decorated with various medals and insignia. Four were female, but their tightly pulled-back hair and expressions matched the seriousness of the others. The twenty individuals on the lowest level wore varied uniforms or formal attire. Their appearance was more varied than a United Nations council meeting with skin tones ranging from pale white to black. While most appeared human-like, several had body shapes and features that were unusual.

Hagon led the group to the bottom of the dais where he stopped and bowed deeply. His guests followed the cue and bowed.

The emperor slowly nodded and then spoke, his voice vibrant and surprisingly pleasant. "Welcome back, Commander Hagon. I am pleased you have brought us guests from the Earth planet. Which one is their captain?"

Hagon raised himself from the deep bow, and his right hand swept towards Casey. "High Emperor Altor El'Kanah, I am pleased to present to you Captain Casey Hawkins."

The emperor stood. From his peripheral vision, Casey noticed a few uncertain glances in his direction as El'Kanah stepped down the dais and approached Casey. Casey glanced at Hagon and saw a smile tug at his mouth. Casey bowed his head slightly towards the emperor and was surprised when El'Kanah extended his right hand to him. Uncertain, Casey raised his hand to accept the gesture.

El'Kanah gripped Casey's hand firmly while his left hand came up and rested on Casey's right shoulder. Strength and assurance surged through Casey as the emperor peered into his eyes and said warmly, "I welcome you, Captain Casey Hawkins, to our home world, El'Tagath, and to the imperial city Lysias. Your visit is most unexpected but welcomed." El'Kanah looked past Casey. "Please introduce me to your companions?"

Casey raised his left brow at Hagon who simply nodded encouragement. Emboldened, Casey responded, "Thank you, Your Majesty, for your gracious and generous welcome. My companions and crew are my brother, James, and our best friend, Heather."

The emperor extended his hand in turn to James and Heather and looked genuinely pleased. He leaned slightly towards Casey, "I would enjoy more of a visit with you. However, as you can see, we are in the midst of an imperial council and do not have time for such pleasantries at the moment. But I wanted to meet you as soon as it was possible. I look forward to dinner with you and your companions later this evening. Although I regret that visit will also be short due to untimely imperial matters."

Emperor Altor smiled at Heather, eliciting a blush. "I trust the palace attendants are treating you well."

Heather's head dropped in a polite bow as her cheeks further brightened. "They are. Thank you, Your Majesty."

El'Kanah nodded and returned to the dais and his chair. Before sitting, he looked again at the three guests. "Commander Hagon will escort you to your rooms, and then return as he is needed to conclude some council business before we can move on to more pleasant evening activities."

Hagon bowed to the emperor, took a step back, turned, and walked back to the large door. Casey, James, and Heather bowed and followed Hagon out of the imperial council room and back into the hall.

When they exited the throne room, Casey noticed the attendants and extra guards were gone. The four sentinels stood silently along the sides of the room's entrance.

When the doors closed, James asked Hagon, "Was one of the empty chairs yours?"

"Yes, I sit with the high council," said Hagon. "I had just arrived back in El'Tagath space when we were alerted of the presence of your ship. I was tasked to take command of the ships that intercepted you in orbit."

Hagon led them down a hallway while he continued to explain. "The woman next to His Majesty is the Empress Eranya. She is considered the most beautiful woman in the empire. Although"—he looked directly at James—"you would be wise to not stare at her."

James pretended to be interested in the walls.

"Who's on the other throne?" asked Heather.

"That is the emperor's most trusted counselor and advisor, Kishon. Like myself, he also recently returned."

A minute later Hagon stopped in the hallway near three doors. "These are your quarters, the same ones you were in earlier. The attendants will be here to escort you to the dining hall in about two hours. As you heard, I still have council business to attend to. I hope to be at dinner, but if I am not, remember you are in the presence of the galaxy's most powerful emperor. Although there is less protocol than in the council chamber, it is still best to not speak unless spoken to. What you are wearing is acceptable. However, wearing something nicer would present a better image. If you choose to change your attire, you will find additional options in your closets."

Hagon turned to walk away, paused, and looked back. "You are guests here, but outside those you have met today, you are strangers, and it would be unwise to roam outside of your chambers without an official escort."

Hagon made an abrupt about-face and quickly left the three standing alone in the hall.

James walked over to the door of his room. He raised his hand near the edge, and the door slid into the wall. "Well, if we have a couple hours, I'm going to take a short nap. That bed felt fantastic."

Heather nodded. "I'm too hungry to sleep, but lying down is tempting. That bed sure was comfortable when I tried it out earlier. If the attendant wasn't there, I probably would've slept too long." She glanced at Casey and James as she opened her door. "See you two in a couple hours. Don't sleep too long. We don't want to be late. We need to keep up the good impression, 'cause we need their help to get back home."

Casey entered his suite and walked down the hall and through the last door. A large bed occupied the center of the wall on the right. Spacious windows overlooked an expansive garden surrounded by high walls. An open space separated the bed from a small desk and two cushy armchairs on the left side. He laid down on the bed, and his body felt light and relaxed. His eyes closed and wanted to sleep, but his mind would not quiet down.

After a few minutes, Casey sat on the bed's edge while he considered his options. The open space in the room was inviting him to meditate when a thought registered. He realized he did not know how long an hour was on El'Tagath. He got up and went into the changing room. The same clothing was still hanging in the room along with a few new options. Remembering his own clothes, he looked into the bathroom and saw that his dirty clothes were gone. He turned his attention back to the clothing and decided to find something a ship captain might wear to a formal dinner.

Chapter Twenty-Six

Legend of the Fallen Star

C ASEY'S EYELIDS FLEW OPEN. Something like a bird call filtered through a partially open window on his left. A bed was across the room, and he momentarily wondered why he was not in the bed. The bird-like song called to him, and the events of the last couple days rushed back. He remembered choosing the chair because he thought he would not fall asleep. He stood, his mind still fuzzy from sleep. Outside, the gardens were fading with the early evening.

A lilting voice, reminiscent of the bird call, called from the entry room. "Good evening, sir!"

Casey whipped around and saw a new palace attendant at the end of the hallway bowing at him.

Compared to Kathera and the other attendants, the young woman's mouth was less trained in restraint, and it continued failing in its attempts to not smile. "I am Amnah. Kathera is helping Heather and asked me to check in on you. I see you are ready for dinner, which is good because it is time to go."

Casey nodded an acknowledgment and walked towards the entry. While Amnah was dressed like the other attendants, she reminded him of a teenager working her first job. She led Casey through the main door where they joined the others in the hall.

Casey barely recognized Heather standing next to Kathera. A multi-hued turquoise evening gown caressed Heather's body and dropped below her knees. The effect of greens and blues blending into and out of folds and pleats, combined with flowing sleeves, created a remarkable water-like effect that cascaded over her. Her brunette hair had gentle waves set with pearled pins, and the dress accented her hazel eyes.

James was fumbling with the last couple of black buttons of a pressed, white, high-collared shirt while simultaneously trying to tuck it into fitted black dress slacks. A few lines, evidence of recent sleep, still creased his face, and his hair had been hastily brushed. A male in a simple dark-blue uniform stood next to him.

Amnah animatedly introduced the man to Casey. "This is my brother, Amnor. He just finished his shift with the palace guard. I told him what I was doing, and Madame Zaeha consented when he asked to help."

Amnor's nod was military stiff. "A good evening to you, sir. If I can be of assistance, please let me know."

"Thank you, Amnor," said Casey with a small head bow. His gaze shifted to Heather, and his head shook slightly in disbelief. "Heather, you look stunning."

The corners of Heather's mouth dimpled in a smile, and she attempted a curtsy. "Thank you. You look pretty good yourself."

Casey's cheeks warmed. "Thanks." He then nodded politely. "Kathera, it's good to see you again."

Kathera blushed at the acknowledgment while Amnah failed to hide another smile.

Amnor, who seemed oblivious to any emotion, simply said, "It is time to go."

Kathera led the group down several corridors. She approached an archway where four palace guards stood by a wide, obsidian-colored wall. On their approach, the wall split apart as the two black glass doors silently slid into the walls. Wondrous and curious smells filled and teased their senses when they walked in, while stomach growls reminded them of how long it had been since a real meal had been eaten.

Three long tables, arranged in an open horseshoe, wrapped around the room. The open end of the horseshoe faced the entryway. Sentinels lined the walls like living statues. The wall decor was rich with golds and reds. Twelve high-backed chairs sat behind each side table. Most of the chairs were occupied. Behind the far table were eleven chairs, the tallest of which sat in the middle. The five center chairs were unoccupied.

Kathera led the group to three empty chairs on the left side, nearest the head table. She directed Casey to sit closest to the head table, followed by Heather and James.

Kathera leaned between Casey and Heather and spoke in a hushed voice. "We, or other attendants, will return when dinner is completed." Then she, Amnor, and Amnah retreated to the wall.

Casey felt like a fish out of water. He was not sure what he had expected, although there were fewer at dinner than he had imagined. Dinner attendees—dressed in uniforms or formal attire—were engaged in quiet conversations around the room. Several glanced towards the three new arrivals.

A minute later, Hagon entered the room. He nodded approval at Casey and then proceeded to an empty chair at the head of the opposite table.

The buzz of conversations silenced as chairs began to slide out and dinner guests stood. Uncertain of what to do Casey, Heather, and James followed suit.

The obsidian doors opened, and the emperor and his wife entered. The emperor wore the same uniform as earlier. Much of the empress's accessories were the same, although her clothes had changed to a red long-sleeved dress that sparkled like embers while she glided through the dining hall. All dinner guests bowed while the emperor and empress walked behind the head table and took their seats. After they were seated, the guests once again sat down.

Immediately, a dozen attendants started bringing in trays of food, serving Emperor Altor and his wife first. After the emperor took his first bite, the attendants took the dishes to the dinner guests. Some trays were left on the tables for guests to serve themselves while servers regularly offered food from others. The smells seemed aromatically familiar, but the preparation was not.

Aside from the hushed inquiries from attendants and servers, and the responses of guests, there was little conversation. After several minutes the emperor motioned his server away.

While chewing something sweet, whose texture reminded Casey of a yam, he felt like he was being watched. Glancing up, he noticed the emperor studying him.

With a smile, El'Kanah spoke, his voice authoritative but inviting. "Captain Casey Hawkins, thank you for joining us this evening. I trust you and your crew are enjoying your meal."

Casey gulped down the bite. "Yes, your Majesty. It is a remarkable feast, and your hospitality is most gracious."

"Earlier Commander Hagon told me of the unusual ship you have, and how you and your crew appeared suddenly near El'Tagath without triggering any of the outer system sensors. If we had known to expect you, we could have better welcomed your arrival."

The emperor's smile turned to Heather. "The commander mentioned you come from a planet called Earth. He has done a preliminary search of our star system maps and reported that we have no record of it. However, we have little reliable information about star systems outside of this quadrant of the galaxy, so if your planet is on the other side, we would not know where to look."

El'Kanah's gaze returned to Casey. "Captain Casey, Hagon said you traveled across the galaxy in a remarkably short time. Through a wormhole, I believe is what Hagon mentioned. You must be an accomplished pilot to navigate through the great unknown hazards of wormholes. I am intrigued to hear your account of the voyage. I am also curious, how long have you been piloting the ship?"

Casey swallowed the bite of food that was sitting in his mouth. He quickly sipped from the clear liquid in his glass—a mildly sweet drink with hints of citrus—to clear his throat while he internally debated how to best summarize the past couple days to an emperor. "Your Majesty, although I have piloted many vessels, I have only been captain of the *Fallen Star* for a short time. My companions and I were escaping from a band of murderers and thieves when we discovered the ship among some ancient ruins on our home world and we used it to get away. In the process, I—" Casey hesitated, an uncertainty brewing an internal debate, below his consciousness, on how much to tell. Part of him felt like he could trust the emperor and needed to tell him everything, while a deeper awareness was warning against it. "I unwittingly transported us across the galaxy without"—again he paused, searching for words—"ascertaining how to make the return trip."

"So," the emperor asked casually, "was it a wormhole or the ship that brought you here?"

Casey's face reddened, and his head shook involuntarily. "No, Your Majesty. I mean, it seemed like what a wormhole would be." Casey decided to shift from the space travel to where they had gone. "We first went to an abandoned base on the moon of a red planet. Pirates attacked us there, but we were able to escape. We retrieved information that hinted we might find someone here who could help us return to Earth."

The emperor's gaze shifted to Hagon, whose brows had lifted in surprise and interest. Hagon nodded at El'Kanah.

The emperor's left brow rose towards Casey. "I had understood you made a single trip, but you describe two. How long did those voyages take?"

Casey's throat felt dry, and he swallowed before answering. "I don't know the exact time." He paused, uncertain, the internal debate still raging inside. Part of him wanted to hide, but he wanted to tell the emperor everything. He wondered what a safe answer would be and tried to guess how long it would take their ships to travel through space. Then he remembered Hagon had implied their ships could not travel the same way. He bit his lower lip, again wondering how much to reveal, without lying, while he tried to guess how long they might believe wormhole travel would take to cross the galaxy, and then how long it might take to travel from the red planet. "As far as I could tell, the wormhole trip across the galaxy, and then our journey here, each took less than a day."

Emperor Altor smiled warmly and leaned back in his chair. "And you said you found the ship in some ancient ruins? Do you happen to know how long it was there? And do your people travel through space as quickly in their newer ships?"

Casey considered his response. "The *Fallen Star* is the only ship we know of that can travel through space like we did. As far as we know, the ship was buried in the pyramid for several hundred of our years. The language and symbols in the ship are alien to us. And we didn't even know it would do anything."

El'Kanah's left hand rose in invitation to Hagon. "Commander Hagon, there is an old tale, one that most consider a fable, that many centuries ago a most remarkable and legendary ship was rumored to exist. It was a ship with capabilities eons beyond anything our civilizations had at that time, and even far beyond our current technologies. It is my understanding you are somewhat of an expert on this legend. Would you briefly tell our guests what has now become little more than a myth and children's fairy tale?"

Hagon bowed his head slowly, and his eyes swept the room. Quiet chatter had been silenced by the emperor's comments and curiosity had stopped all eating while every eye now turned towards the commander. After a moment, Hagon's focus narrowed on the three guests sitting across from him. "As His Majesty stated, many centuries ago a fabled ship was rumored to exist. Some claimed to have seen it, but there were few confirmed sightings. Those who had seen it, saw it land atop some of the highest of the now-oldest structures of the city. But it was difficult to see and seemed to disappear as quickly as it was observed. Its owner and pilot was the famed inventor, Mantas Satomi, who"—he motioned around the room—"as many of you know, was also a merchant, noble, and recluse who founded the Twin Star Corporation and created hundreds of new technologies that ushered in the current millennia of space travel. From his research and breakthroughs in quantum technology he invented the jump gates that significantly reduced space travel time and increased safety between entry and exit points. But there were rumors that Satomi's ship could fold and jump through space without gates."

Hagon paused a moment and gazed around the room. Even the servers and attendants were caught up in Hagon's story.

"Some tales claim the ship traveled the unfathomable distances of space much as if stepping from one room into another," he continued. "Nobody knew where Satomi would go when he left with the ship. It left quickly and without a trace. Over several decades there were attempts to track and trace the ship, but all failed. The ship itself was difficult to see as it would bend and distort light, and it was apparently invisible to all known sensing and detection technologies. Only a couple of images of any clarity were taken.

"After years of increasing success with jump gates, rumors increased about Satomi's ship. Some, like our beloved empire, saw the prospects of Satomi's ship as furthering peace in the galaxy. Others, like the treacherous Rayneiri Imperium, with their increasing development of weapons, spacecraft, and technology, wanted his ship as a strategic advantage. According to legend, and after decades of attempts, the traitorous Rayneiri managed to discover Satomi's secret base and plotted with a pirate clan to ambush and steal the ship. When the ambush occurred, Satomi fled with his ship and disappeared, never to be heard from or seen again.

"Most assumed he and his ship were lost in space. As for his research and base, depending on the story, either Satomi self-destructed his facility along with all of his research, or the pirates rampaged through his base, destroying everything. In any case, without the ship or any records of its development, there was no proof of its existence. Even Satomi's secret research facility became legend as its location was never ascertained. In most children's stories, the ship is called *Shaina*

Ariana, which is said to either mean 'beautiful silver' or 'lightning star.' It is my opinion"—Hagon gestured around the room—"as wondrous and unbelievable as it may be to our many distinguished guests here tonight, that you, Captain Casey"—Hagon's eyes pierced Casey's as he spoke his next words—"have found the fabled *Shaina Ariana.*"

Silence permeated the room. Casey felt warmth radiating from his cheeks throughout his face, and he fought the urge to hide from all the eyes that now stared at him.

Hagon's voice became more serious. "Most in this company know what I am about to tell you, but I feel it is important for you and your companions to also know. A little more than thirty of our years ago, the Rayneiri funded a rebellion among our empire in an attempt to destabilize our peace and thwart an attempted peace accord between the nations. Our emperor"—Hagon gave a small bow towards El'Kanah—"was instrumental in restoring peace and unity in our empire. It has been my life's goal to protect and preserve the peace and prosperity that Emperor El'Kanah has fostered. You should know that some of the urgent business I had this afternoon was with regards to increasing threats against our peace from the Rayneiri, and how I may be of better service to His Majesty and our empire."

Around the room, the hush of whispered words picked up as many nodded their agreement.

The emperor casually stood, and the room became silent. El'Kanah's smile at Casey was genuine. "Your arrival, Captain Casey, is fortunate. As Commander Hagon related, over the last few years the Rayneiri threat has once again risen, as a legendary dragon from its slumber, and again threatens the peace, prosperity, and stability of our empire, as well as the collective and peaceable nations in this part of the galaxy. I am certain we can interpret the meaning of the characters in your ship, and, perhaps, aid you in returning to your home world. In exchange, we—I—would be most appreciative if you could help us further peace. We believe the *Shaina Ariana*'s main purpose was for peace. You would be doing us and the galaxy a great service in return for our meager assistance."

Casey shifted in his chair, his face flustered at the attention. He wiped his sweaty hands on a large napkin while his eyes dropped to the food on the table. A moment later he looked back up and met the gaze of El'Kanah. "As advocates for peace, it would certainly be something for us to consider."

The corners of El'Kanah's mouth gently rose as he acknowledged Casey's response. The emperor raised his left hand. One of two servers standing behind him moved forward and offered El'Kanah something from a tray. The emperor nodded. The attendant retreated behind a curtain while the second attendant whisked away the dinner plate and utensils. A few seconds later, the first attendant returned with a plate of a creamy dark-brown substance topped with bright-red berry-like fruit. Once the emperor had begun eating of the new dish, the servers began offering all the guests options from new trays.

After finishing a few more bites, the emperor set down his fork-like utensil and looked at Casey. "Captain Casey, something you mentioned earlier intrigues me, about having piloted many vessels. Do you have military training?"

Casey shook his head. "No, Your Majesty. Flying has always been natural for me."

James snorted in some food, and Casey added, "Except for the first couple attempts at landing. Mechanical things, especially flying, almost feel like an extension of my body."

The emperor nodded knowingly, and he set his utensil down on the table. "As I mentioned in our brief meeting earlier, I have some pressing imperial matters to finish. I regret that I cannot remain at dinner with you and your companions this evening. However, I would like to continue our conversation tomorrow." Casey nodded, and the emperor continued, "A final question for tonight, though, more a personal curiosity of our differing cultures: Do you have any royal blood in you?"

Casey's brow furrowed at the unusual question, and he shook his head again. "No, Your Majesty. On our world there are some countries that have royalty, but my native country does not. James and my parents were descendants of immigrants. As far as my siblings and I know, we're not descended from royalty."

El'Kanah's head cocked to the side, looking uncertain, but he nodded at Casey's response. His chair moved back as he stood and took a step to leave. Four sentinels emerged from dark recesses in the walls and quickly moved to escort the emperor. Everyone in the room quickly stood. The emperor raised his hand. "Please, enjoy your meal. There is no need to rush."

El'Kanah and his wife, escorted by the sentinels, walked around the table and into the center of the room. The emperor paused in front of Casey, James, and Heather. "I hope you find your rooms comfortable and our welcome acceptable."

Casey, James, and Heather bowed politely while Casey responded, "Thank you, Your Majesty. We are most appreciative of your hospitality."

After the emperor and his wife exited the dining hall, everyone sat back down, and the low buzz of conversations again filled the room. A server offered Casey, James, and Heather samplings from a tray of what looked like an assortment of creamy desserts. Casey opted for a red pastry-like dessert topped with a small purple fruit that looked similar to a blueberry.

While another server offered small dessert samples to James and Heather, Hagon rose from his place and walked over to Casey. Casey started to stand but Hagon motioned him to remain seated.

"Captain Casey, I regret that I, too, am unable to remain with you any further this evening. With the Rayneiri's increasing threats to our peace, there are some unexpected events I must attend to. I will be available later in the morning. As for tonight, the attendants will escort you back to your rooms when you are finished. The morning meal will be informal, without the emperor or myself. While it seems unlikely that we have star maps of where your planet is, your ship most likely has travel logs. Some of the most skilled star navigators are here on El'Tagath, and I am certain we can help you retrieve star logs that will aid your return to your Earth planet. It is my hope we can begin searching for answers tomorrow."

"Thank you, Commander Hagon," replied Casey.

"Yes, thank you," added Heather enthusiastically.

Hagon turned and left the room.

"You okay, Casey?" asked James.

"Yes, why?"

"Well, you don't usually talk that much. I wanted to jump in and add some things but didn't think I should with Hagon's warning about not talking to the emperor unless spoken to."

Casey shrugged. "Yeah, well, you do talk to people easier than I do. It's kind of strange, but since meeting El'Kanah earlier, it felt easy to talk to him. It was almost like we were the only ones in the room, that I had known him my whole life. I fought the urge to say more, to tell him everything, but I remembered there were others in the room and I didn't want them to know. Hopefully I didn't say anything that I shouldn't have."

"No, I think you did well. Like I said, I wanted to add more, and would have if he'd asked me."

Over the next several minutes, dinner guests began getting up and leaving the room. Casey and Heather slowly ate a few more bites. James stuffed one last bite of a caramel-like dessert into his mouth and subsequently stifled a yawn.

"Don't do that," said Heather, and she tried to stop a yawn. "Anyone know what time it is?"

Casey looked at his watch. "Looks like it's about midnight our time. No wonder we're beat."

When they stood up, Amnah and Kathera emerged from a small doorway at the side of the room. Without a word, the two attendants led the threesome out of the dining hall, back through the corridors, and to their guest quarters.

Chapter Twenty-Seven
Into the Garden

K ATHERA'S HEAD DROPPED IN a courtesy bow. "Madame Zaeha has assigned us to assist you tomorrow. Amnah and I will return in the morning."

"Thank you, Kathera," said Casey.

Heather's hand covered an involuntary yawn. "Yes, thank you both. Good night to all of you."

Heather waved her hand across the door frame, and the deep mahogany-colored door slid into the wall. She stepped inside, the door closing behind her.

James opened his door. "It's been a long day. I could probably sleep for twelve hours straight."

"Sir, if that is what you need," said Kathera, "that would be about the time we will be back to take you to the morning meal."

James raised an eyebrow. "Really? That'd be great." He stepped into the entry of his suite. "Thanks again. You guys have a great night." The door closed.

Kathera's head tilted slightly at Casey when he stepped to his door, as if she was weighing what to say. "Should you be unable to sleep, the gardens are beautiful at night. Both moons will be up. Continue down this hall and turn right at the next crossing. That hall ends at the garden entrance. Other than the garden and your rooms, it would be unwise to wander anywhere else."

Casey's smile was tired. "That sounds tempting, but I think I'll easily sleep all night. Thank you, Kathera and Amnah, you've been very helpful." He opened the door and glanced back. "Before you go, I have a question that you might be able to answer."

Kathera's head dropped in acknowledgment and Casey continued, "Why did the emperor ask me if I had royal blood? Is that something he usually asks?"

Kathera's brow knitted in thought. "In my experience, I have never heard him ask it before. But there are dozens of attendants and there are frequent diplomatic guests, so I don't know. As for the question itself"—her hands motioned at Casey's clothing—"it was probably because of what you chose to wear. It is an unusual choice for non-military or non-royalty." Then, uncertain if she might have said something wrong, she quickly added, "At least for our culture."

Casey flushed and scratched behind his ear. "Oh, yeah, well I thought it looked like something a captain of a starship might wear."

Kathera's mouth rose in a bemused half-smile. "If there is nothing else..." She paused, her eyes momentarily looking away before she continued, "I sometimes have difficulty sleeping in a new place." She retrieved a small, glossy black stone from her pocket and handed it to Casey. "This has helped me to sleep better. May you have a peaceful night."

Casey's left brow rose as he received the glass-like stone in his hand, doubtful that it would do anything. "Thank you. You too."

The two attendants bowed and walked down the hall.

Casey entered his room, the door closing behind him. He walked into the second room off the hall, where the clothing was, and stared at himself in the mirrored wall. His attire was more formal than he was used to, but it did remind him of a space captain. Burgundy stripes edged the legs of black, fitted dress pants. A matching burgundy, collarless shirt clasped up the right side, with gold-and-black trim lining the edge of the fabric. His cheeks still felt warm from Kathera's comment, and he wondered if he should have worn something else.

He walked back to the bedroom. On the armchair, his own clothes were clean and laid out. The windows were darkened, as if a transparency had been turned off, and he realized the window he had left open had been shut. His eyes suddenly felt very heavy, as if given permission to admit exhaustion. He set the small stone on his bed and got ready for sleep.

Casey opened his eyes to darkness. Something was warm and hard in his hand. Then he remembered the small stone when he had fallen asleep. Initially it appeared black, but as he studied it, he observed a mix of smoky black, grays, and browns. He looked at his watch. It was just past six a.m. *Probably a bit after midnight here*, he thought. He closed his eyes again, but his mind shifted into high gear. After several minutes, he got up. Immediately a muted amber light illuminated around the base of the walls, just enough to see but not enough to wake someone up. He walked to the blackened window. Reaching to the window, the surface became transparent.

Outside, the gardens were bathed in moonlight. On the left, a full moon was rising above the walls of the palace. Double shadows indicated another light source above. Casey bent down to look up and saw three-quarters of a second moon, slightly smaller than the rising one. Intrigued, he decided to get his clothes on and take a walk.

The door slid open silently to a dimly lit corridor. Casey walked in the direction Kathera had indicated to find the gardens. The exterior door opened, and a warm, gentle breeze swam past him.

He walked along a smooth path into the gardens. Intermittent, soft amber lights lined the edge of the walkway. Various plants were silhouetted in unexpected double shadows. From over the far wall, the glow of the city lights radiated into the atmosphere. As he walked, unfamiliar fragrances from the garden flora graced the soft air. Nearby water trickled unseen through some part of the garden.

The path wound through trees, bushes, and vegetation and came to a footbridge. He walked up the gentle arch and looked down into the small stream. The water itself appeared still, black, and speckled with stars and the bright overhead moon. The other moon was still too low for him to see its reflection. His eyes turned heavenward, and he was reminded of how far from home he was. It had only been a couple of days, but it felt so long ago. He closed his eyes and inhaled deeply, savoring the air in his lungs. As he slowly exhaled, tension and stress began to lessen. He stared up at the stars and inhaled deeply again, listening to the faint trickle of water.

His eyes closed, and the corners of his lips lifted into a satisfied smile. *Tomorrow*, he thought. *Tomorrow we could be going home.* The mere thought seemed to loosen the bands of stress.

A barely discernible hum caught his attention. His eyes opened; his head cocked in concentration. He jumped when a hand gripped his shoulder and an urgent voice hissed in his ear, "You're in great danger here!"

Chapter Twenty-Eight

Secrets in the Night

S EVERAL SMALL STONES SCRAMBLED over the bridge and plunked into the calm water as Casey's reflexes whipped him around. His breath caught at the sight of a black-cloaked figure, its arm still outstretched to where it had just been touching his shoulder.

"Impressive reflexes," replied a hushed, now-familiar voice, "but you shouldn't have been caught off guard."

Beneath the oversized hood and double shadows of the moons, Kathera's face looked pale gray.

"Good grief, lady, you scared me," he whispered. "Wait, what'd you mean I'm in danger? What about James and Heather?"

"Hagon is certain your ship is the legendary *Shaina Ariana*!"

"So? He said as much at dinner."

Kathera's jaw stiffened in aggravation under the dark hood. "What do you mean 'so?' You don't know Hagon. He will take it from you."

"If he gets us back home, I'll give it to him."

Kathera clenched back an outburst. "You can't—" Then her eyes lit with understanding. "You don't know him or the emperor. You completely fell for their act." Her shoulders slumped. "You're not the first, nor the last. I used to believe their lies." Her eyes narrowed slightly while she studied Casey's and saw uncertainty reflected in them. "You don't know what really happened, do you?"

Casey's reply was edged with concern. "From your face, I'm guessing I don't. And I'm not even sure what you're talking about."

"Follow me; it isn't safe here. Don't worry," she added to head off a protest. "We're not leaving the gardens. Just be quiet until I tell you otherwise."

Casey nodded, and Kathera held up her left wrist to look at something. When a dim red light appeared, she led Casey to a secluded section of the garden and sat down behind some bushes. Casey followed silently and sat down on the short, soft mossy grass. The nearby bushes effectively concealed them. For a moment Casey was reminded of a fort he and some friends had made behind some bushes in fourth grade. Nearby the stream babbled. Casey rubbed his ears in an attempt to silence a faint hum that he seemed to feel more than hear.

Kathera watched Casey curiously. "You must be hearing this." She retrieved a small black box from her cloak, and Casey felt the hum increase. "It intercepts and scrambles the transmissions sent from our translators. Everything we say could be recorded, and most translators act as personal locators. This device provides some privacy to our conversation, but only for a short time. Interesting you hear it. I've heard a few people can hear a hum, but I don't, and I've never known anyone who could."

"It's not bad. More like some faint, background static that's only really noticeable when there's quiet. So, what were you talking about back on the bridge?"

Kathera leaned in close to Casey. "In the dining hall, I heard Hagon relate the half-truth about the emperor being a hero and uniting the empire against the Rayneiri after a rebellion, and how the *Shaina Ariana* can be an instrument for establishing peace."

Casey nodded.

"That's their version, but it's not the full truth. The part about the ship being a myth is true. All anyone knows about the *Shaina Ariana* is it's a legend. As Hagon said, it and its inventor disappeared centuries ago, supposedly after some pirates attacked the hidden base. Whether the Rayneiri funded the pirates I don't know, though I suspect that part is false."

Her eyes darted to the bushes and back to Casey. "To understand more of what's happening, you need a short history lesson. Forty years ago, Emperor Eirikir Valdr inherited the empire when his father passed away. Valdr was the oldest of three brothers. Under his rule the prosperity of his father's reign increased, and after ten years he orchestrated a peace accord between the two largest empires, the Mysian—this one—and the Rayneiri. As part of the new alliance and peace, there would be a future marriage between the Mysian and Rayneiri imperial families.

"Soon after the peace accord, Valdr's wife was killed. A few months later, while gone on a diplomatic mission, Valdr's convoy was attacked, and all ships destroyed. Acting as interim emperor, Kahari, the second brother, ordered an imperial council. He could not become emperor until Valdr's death had been validated and the imperial time of mourning had passed. The council was an initial part of the process. When the council began, there was an attack that killed most of the council members. Kahari, his wife, and their children were all assassinated. Altor, the third and youngest brother, arrived late to the council and, with his personal guards, killed the assassins. He then claimed the right to the throne, became the new emperor, and took on the name El'Kanah. Because evidence pointed to the Rayneiri in the assassinations, as well as in orchestrating the attack on Valdr's convoy and the death of his wife, Altor terminated the peace accord.

"Since then, Altor has persuaded other interstellar and system nations to join him in his ambition to terminate the Rayneiri threat and reunite all nations under one rule. That's the official story. You may have guessed that Hagon is his chief military commander. But his right hand is Counselor Kishon Kummon. Kishon is the chief of the secret police and, we believe, an assassin with rare abilities."

Kathera stopped for a moment and glanced around cautiously. Satisfied no one was listening in, she went on. "It's true the Rayneiri were, and are, developing advanced weapons and ships. So are the Mysians, and the Mysian's closest allies, the Sokari. If the *Shaina Ariana* myths are true, the ship is far more advanced than anything any system, nation, or empire has ever developed, or which could hope to be created."

Casey cocked his head and raised his right eyebrow. "How is that, especially if that was hundreds of years ago?"

Kathera smiled knowingly. "You may be talented with flying, but it's obvious you and your friends, and I presume all of your people, are very inexperienced and limited in space travel. I don't understand the technology, but I can tell you that over a thousand years ago our space travel was limited compared to today. You probably know that nothing is known to travel faster than light."

"That's what they say."

"Here's a bit more history for you," added Kathera. "Over six thousand years ago our civilizations—the Mysian, Sokari, Rayneiri, and a number of others—fled from a single system whose star threatened their survival. The ability to travel faster than the speed of light, in bubbles that warped space, had recently been developed. That development allowed for thirteen transport and colonizer ships to leave the system for distant stars before their home world was potentially destroyed. But travel was still slow. Even with the warp development, faster-than-light travel still took decades for the ships to travel to the nearest habitable star systems. And intergalactic travel was new and dangerous. One ship was lost. The twelve others barely made it to their destinations. For over a thousand years it was about survival as the new colonies tried to adapt and tame their new planets."

Kathera paused and scanned the nearby vegetation again. "There were basically minimal or no technological advances for that time. Space travel was almost nonexistent, although most colonies managed to maintain contact through the quantira communicators. As the new civilizations survived and grew, it took thousands of years before there was much improvement in space travel. Some civilizations progressed more quickly, like the Mysian and Rayneiri. The evolving warp travel was sufficient and allowed for most of the civilizations to reconnect. In over five thousand years following the Great Escape, warp travel only managed to increase about ten times. That may sound like a lot, but it's not when compared to the size of the galaxy. Instead of it taking ten years to travel one hundred light-years, that distance would take about a year. But to travel across the galaxy would still take more than one thousand years."

Casey's eyebrows rose in surprise.

Kathera nodded. "Around a thousand years ago, an unknown inventor, Mantas Satomi, appeared before the technology council of the nations and demonstrated what he called jump gates. Unlike the quantira system, the quantum technology of the jump gates could transport energy and mass. However, while quantira communication is nearly instantaneous across space, travel through jump gates is not. After a gate is constructed at each end, and depending on the distance, a ship can be transported between that expanse of space in hours to several days. At distances of one hundred light-years or less, the space jump reliability was nearly perfect. Reliability decreases the further apart jump gates are, so most jumps were kept to less than the hundred light-years, and ships traveling further just use multiple gates. Satomi founded the Twin Star Corporation to further research, develop, and license the use of jump gate technology. Since then, jump gate efficiency has increased and ships safely travel thousands of light-years through multi-jumps."

Casey started to raise his hand and stopped himself. "The history lesson is interesting. But what does this have to do with the *Fallen Star*?"

Kathera looked annoyed, as if the answer should have been obvious to a child. She kept her volume in check, inhaled, and continued, "Jump technology requires enormous energy, more than our largest ships can generate. And despite being fast travel, it takes time for the jump energy to charge. It's not like ships can just go through a jump gate whenever they want to. And both entry and exit gates are needed for reliable transport. To build a gate at the far end, the materials are either transported by ship using warp drives or a remote operation is sent through a gate to a non-gate space to build the gate. These remote operations are extremely risky and usually fail. I've heard rumors that a portable gate is being developed, but it can only be used on the largest of ships. And without an exit gate, jumping to non-gated space is extremely unreliable, especially when jumping more than five light-years."

Kathera's eyes narrowed to see if he was understanding. "Anyway, your ship, the *Shaina Ariana*, is the only ship known to exist that can perform these space jumps without any gates. And it's smaller than most interstellar ships."

The gravity of the situation hit Casey. "And now the emperor and Hagon, and everyone else at dinner, know we managed to make two space jumps within a very short time."

"Much faster than anyone even thought was possible, and with a smaller ship than ever imagined as even being feasible. At our progress, it would probably be another hundred years or more before reliable, portable jump drives are developed for our largest space carriers. To shrink that technology to the size of your ship might be several hundred or a thousand years or more. And even then, the actual jump would likely require an exit gate and still take days or weeks, and you told them your ship made two jumps each in less than a day."

"Minutes," said Casey absentmindedly, then realized what he said.

Kathera's eyebrows shot up in surprise at his slip. Her head moved slowly from side to side. "Don't worry, I won't tell. But imagine what someone with the ambition to expand an empire could do with your ship?"

Casey swallowed.

"And," pressed Kathera, "imagine what they could do if they could replicate the technology and install it on other spacecraft."

"The balance of power would be forever shifted," said Casey. His eyes closed briefly. "And their version of peace forced on others."

Kathera nodded, satisfied Casey was beginning to understand.

"What about the assassination of the former emperor?" asked Casey. "Seems like you know more than you're letting on."

"It was a coup disguised to look like an assassination by the Rayneiri."

Casey's eyes narrowed suspiciously. "You seem a little young if this coup happened thirty years ago. Are you sure you have the right information?"

"History changes based on who is in power. I was born a few years before the coup, and my mother was killed several months before it happened. My father served Emperor Valdr as a captain of the emperor's personal guard, and then became chief captain under El'Kanah. He frequently told me the story of the assassination and how the emperor prevented civil war and brought peace to our empire. I believed the story about the Rayneiri assassination until about five years ago, when my father revealed the truth to me in a letter.

"My father believed all of the old civilizations should be reunited into one, with the Mysians leading the way. Altor was a very charismatic commander in the military forces and had convinced many that only reuniting the civilizations under Mysian rule would restore peace and lasting prosperity. Although most did not know his true plan, he needed a few to help him execute it. My father, despite being in the emperor's personal guard, was one who was persuaded he was doing what was good for the empire and for all the nations. After Altor became emperor, my father was promoted to chief captain of the emperor's guard, and my family received great privileges with his appointment, including my opportunity for diplomat training to become a palace attendant."

Kathera looked at her wrist where the dim red light continued to glow. "Five years ago, there was a diplomatic meeting of several of the civilizations at one of the border systems. Since palace attendants are trained in foreign diplomacy, I was invited to go. There was an attack by a Rayneiri scout ship. It had attempted to crash into the secure facility, supposedly to kill the diplomatic representatives. The ship was shot down, but it crashed into the building where my father was housed. I was returning from an assignment when the crash happened. I found my father barely alive in the rubble. He told me, 'I hoped you'd find me. Please forgive me for all the lies. I've wanted to tell you the truth many times but was afraid. I was wrong.' When he said his last words, he pressed a folded handwritten letter into my hand.

"It's rare for anyone to write much by hand anymore, and often it's to keep something hidden from the virtual spies. So, I hid it away in my clothes. Hagon arrive shortly after my father died and asked if he was dead. When I told him he was, Hagon responded, 'Good. It is best to die with honor,' and then walked away. After my father died, the palace guard searched our house, claiming to be looking for anything that belonged to the palace guard. They never took anything. I was permitted to stay on as an attendant in the palace."

"What did the letter say?" asked Casey quietly.

Kathera's face stiffened, and she blinked away moisture. "Besides what I already said, it told me how my father supported Altor in the coup and positioned himself to betray Valdr and Kahari to be assassinated. He wrote how he'd kept the secret for more than twenty-five years. But he was becoming increasingly uneasy and suspicious, and wanted to tell me the truth. He had recently discovered that Altor and Hagon had orchestrated my mother's death, making it look like the Rayneiri had been the cause of it, in order to sway my father's loyalty. He feared for his life and mentioned how the few others he'd known who were involved with the coup had died over recent years. He wasn't sure how many were left, besides himself, who knew the truth. He wrote how there were rumblings of dissatisfaction among the people and that something, he didn't know what, would need to happen to sway to people back towards Altor's side."

Kathera stopped.

Casey asked, "He didn't say what that thing would be?"

Kathera shook her head. "I believe it was the attack that ended up killing my father. I think it was another fake assassination attempt with the real goal to kill my father, so he'd no longer pose a potential threat. After the attack, Altor managed to rally the people's trust and gained their support while he stoked fears of another Rayneiri threat."

"So, you believe Hagon was behind the attack?"

"I don't think he personally did it. That's not his style. Most likely he hired someone to arrange it so the Rayneiri could be framed."

"Did the letter say anything else?"

Kathera's eyes scanned the bushes while her voice lowered. "Yes, but most of the details and other information aren't important right now. But he did mention that Kahari's oldest son had escaped the assassination with the help of a gifted palace guard. Unfortunately, he didn't know where they had gone, and said an assassin had been sent after them. Because he never heard any updates, he assumed the son was still alive. He said if the heir could be found, there might be a chance to restore peace."

Casey felt like his head was spinning. "You're talking treason, assassinations, murder, and a possible civil war—maybe a galactic war. I'm not sure what you want from me, and I'm not sure what I could even do to help." His eyes closed briefly while his fingers massaged his brow. "I don't know what to believe or who to believe. It might be better to just forget what I've heard, go back to Earth, and claim ignorance of anything outside the Earth's atmosphere. I'm not sure if you're asking this, but there's no way I can stop a civil, let alone a galactic, war."

Kathera's head shook in exasperation. "Aren't you even hearing what I'm telling you? You aren't going anywhere. The only reason you and your friends are still alive is because Altor and Hagon need you.

They tried earlier tonight, but they weren't able to get into the *Shaina Ariana*. Once they get in and can operate it, you, your brother, and your friend are as good as dead. And one or two of you may be killed before then as 'persuasion.'"

Casey's eyes shut for a moment. "Okay, let's say you're right. How are we supposed to get back to the *Fallen Star*? Not to mention leave without setting off every alarm. And then how am I supposed to take us home without knowing where home is? Do you have a plan?"

Kathera's shoulders slumped under the cloak. "I know someone in the palace guard who could possibly help. But it may take a bit to organize something. I'd guess Hagon will want to go inside the ship tomorrow. Maybe even the emperor as well. You need to keep them from going in. You need some excuse while you, James, and Heather need to go inside first. Then leave. Use the ship's fabled cloaking and avoid being tracked."

Casey shook his head in stubborn refusal. "I'm not sure what excuse would be believable." He felt his cheeks warm. "And, I'm actually still learning what the ship can do and how to do it, so I'm not sure if I could get the cloak on. Then there's the problem of where to go. I promised I'd get us home safely, but I'm not sure how to do that without Hagon's help."

A deep breath slowly exhaled from Kathera. "You're still not getting it. Think about this. The emperor knows you are from a planet on the other side of the galaxy, and nobody there even knows where you are, or if you're even alive. There is nothing stopping his spies from simply removing you, except for your ability to get in and use the *Shaina Ariana*. You need to leave this planet as quickly as you can. Maybe I can get something arranged before morning."

Defiance lit in Casey's eyes. "Why are you telling me this? And why should I believe you?"

"Because"—she hesitated—"I like... You treated me like an equal. I feel, and believe, you can be trusted. Your mind is more open than most, and willing to at least consider possibilities, even truths, which are outside your own perception. And, I believe you have a gift."

"Being taken on a mind-blowing trip across the galaxy probably does wonders to opening the mind. I've no idea what you mean by 'gift,' because so far, my gift has been to get us in deeper trouble."

"You must know or have heard of people with extraordinary abilities, even some which may seem like a superpower. Gifts can be simple sounding, like an ability to grow anything. And there are exceptional gifts based in one or more elemental domains. Maybe you've heard fantastical accounts, like miraculous healing or someone walking on water. Everyone has at least one gift, even if it's minor. However, because harnessing internal and external gifts requires difficult and disciplined training, the vast majority of people never excel in their gifts, and many never even realize they have a gift. The ease and convenience of technology just makes it easier for people to not develop their gifts. One of El'Kanah's gifts is the power of persuasion and coercion, which is particularly effective if he has made a physical connection with you."

Casey swallowed.

"And Kishon," a shudder shook under Kathera's cloak, "sometimes I think he knows what's about to happen, like he's a Guai Jai master who knows all your moves before you do. I'm not sure which gifts you might have." Kathera flicked her wrist; the light was fading in and out. "I believe there's a reason you're here. But, right now, our time is almost up. Before we go, I have something that may help you with your ship."

She handed him a small metallic-black, circular container, about the size of a quarter.

Casey opened the container. Sitting on top of a blue gel-like substance were two clear button-sized disks. "I think I already have these."

Kathera smiled with a head shake. "I don't think so. You were given audio translators, which you need to remember can also track your location if you're not careful. These are for your eyes and will act like visual interpreters. They can be a bit disorienting at first, until you get used to them. Underneath is some eye balm if you need it. They're designed to be worn for long periods of time."

"Kind of like contacts, like Mom wears," said Casey. "It always made me cringe when I saw her put them in."

"I don't know what 'contacts' are, but if they help you see better then, yes, these are like that, except these translate alien words into your native language. They do need to link to a translator service, at least to start with, and whenever they need to download a new language. You should put them in as soon as you can so you can start getting used to them."

Casey closed the lid and stuffed it into his pocket. "I'll try putting them in back in the room."

Kathera nodded and looked around for anyone who may have been watching them. "I'm not sure how the service knows your language so well."

"Hagon thinks our ship uploaded a bunch of language information to the system when we approached this planet."

Kathera moved back towards the path they had been on earlier. "Could be." Her head motioned for Casey to follow. "We really need to get going now. The scrambler time is about ended; any longer may generate an alert for someone to check on you."

Chapter Twenty-Nine

More Trouble

THEY WALKED BACK TO the building's door, and it opened at their approach. Casey stopped at the door while Kathera stepped inside.

Kathera's head tilted when she turned to Casey. "Come on," she urged. "It's clear."

"It may be clear," whispered Casey, tingles prickled his spine, "but something doesn't feel right." His eyes scanned the dimly lit hallway. Nothing looked any different than when he had left.

Kathera stiffened, her eyes scanning her surroundings. "It looks normal."

A shiver ran up Casey's spine. "Yeah, but something is wrong."

Her eyes narrowed at Casey. "Then we need to hurry and get you back to your ship as quick as possible."

"Let's get James and Heather."

Kathera nodded and led the way back to the rooms. She opened Heather's door to blackness and went inside. Casey stepped out of the hallway, just inside the door, and waited.

Kathera returned alone. Her hushed voice was strained. "Heather's not here."

Casey's jaw tightened, and his head barely nodded. "We'll find her. James might have an idea where she went."

They moved silently to the next door, James's quarters. Kathera stepped up to the door and started to raise her hand when Casey whispered urgently, "Something's wrong."

Kathera backed away from the door. "Then we need to—" Her voice cut off when the door slid open.

Light flooded out of the room into the hallway, and four large, backlit soldiers filled the doorway. Each held a long halberd, blue arcs flashing around the blades. Behind the four royal guards, eight similar figures surrounded two people kneeling on the floor with their hands on their heads. One of the kneeling figures turned to the door.

"Run!" yelled Heather.

Casey stepped back, almost tripping over his feet when the four guards poured out of the room. Kathera grabbed his shirt to pull him after her.

"There he is!" a gruff voice shouted. "Get him!"

Casey surprised Kathera when he lunged forward, breaking loose from her grip on his shirt, and rushed the guards. In the flurry, Casey's fist flew under the chin of the closest guard and smashed it upwards. The guard's head jerked back, and he fell unconscious against the wall. Casey blocked a halberd that arced in from the left and counterstruck with a front kick. The guard tripped and fell backwards to the ground.

A third guard's face snapped to the side when Casey's foot whipped across his face in an outside crescent kick. Knocked off-balance, the guard released his halberd and stumbled sideways. Casey caught the falling halberd and swept it towards the fourth guard.

The guard stepped back, uncertain, his halberd lowered while glancing at his downed comrades. Casey's halberd tapped aside the opposing tip and whipped back into the guard's armored abdomen. Blue arcs jumped from the blade tip and ripped through the armor.

The confused guard shrieked in brief agony, his body doubled over in shock, and then dropped unconscious to the marble floor.

Inside the room the other eight sentinels began to reorganize. One called for backup and nodded in response while he and three others kept the blue-flickering halberd blades fixed on James and Heather. The remaining four moved cautiously towards the doorway, wary of becoming the next one to encounter Casey.

James's voice called out, "Remember the Tetons."

Casey paused. He half-stepped towards the door when Kathera interrupted his thoughts by yanking his arm. "We're outnumbered and can do nothing if we stay."

Casey faltered for another half second, mentally wrestling himself with his options. The halberd was ready, raised slightly towards the doorway. He could not bear the thought of abandoning James and Heather. His brother's words rang in his ears. Nearby, two guards were stirring on the floor. One was beginning to stand. The four from inside the room neared the door. His halberd shifted up. *Kathera's right*, he thought. He turned and raced after her as she darted down the hall.

The harsh voice echoed from inside the room. "After them!"

Casey slid briefly on the floor when Kathera sidestepped unexpectedly into a small hall on the right. Several blasts of plasma burst open the wall as they ducked in from the main corridor. The commanding voice reverberated down the halls. "Alive! You imbeciles, they need to be alive!"

The small hallway darkened, and their pace slowed. Casey barely saw Kathera turn left at an intersection and plunge into darkness.

"It'd be nice to have some light," huffed Casey.

"Not every passage has security systems, and they'd know exactly where we are if we turn on lights. Hopefully they'll assume we'll stick to the more lighted corridors."

"But they should know it's easier to hide in the dark. Especially if they can track us through the ear things. We can move faster if we can see."

"Only if you don't know where you're going. Besides, all the main exits will be on lock-down now with additional guards. Especially after what you did, which was unexpected and impressive."

Kathera continued her slow pace through the dark. Her voice was tipped with concern. "I'd be surprised if they haven't called out the Night Watch by now." She stopped at a section of black wall and pulled out the scrambling device. When it started glowing a dim red, she moved her fingers along the wall.

"Didn't we just encounter some of them?"

"Not the palace guards. They say a Night Watch never loses its prey. But they'd probably never admit it if it happened." Kathera was still feeling around a section of wall.

"So we stopped to make it easier?"

In the near-dark, Casey saw a sly smile on Kathera's face. A small panel popped open near the base of the wall. She quickly crawled in. "Be quick," she hissed, "or we'll get caught."

Casey rolled through the opening and into a narrow passage. Kathera removed a small vial from her cloak and sprayed something into the air behind them in the dark hallway. After she reattached the panel, she took out a two-inch-long device that was as narrow as a pen. Holding up the small cylinder, a faint amber-white glow emitted from its end, and she headed parallel to the main hall, walking a short distance to where the narrow passage ended. She knelt on the floor and removed a floor panel that exposed a handle. She pulled the handle, and a small trapdoor silently lifted to reveal a ladder that dropped into an abyss.

"You go first," insisted Kathera.

Casey thought it was better not to argue. As he started to lower himself into the opening, Kathera walked back the short distance and spritzed her vial a couple more times before returning to the trapdoor. When Casey's foot touched the second rung, a wave of uneasiness swelled inside him. The feeling began building and threatened to become a fear-filled anxiety. He stopped and slowed his breath to focus his thoughts. He glanced downwards into the darkness and shook his head. Then he stared back along the small passage, through the amber-hued blackness, and past Kathera. His eyes narrowed in concentration. It was more than a gut feeling; it was like the air had turned cold and thick, as if an unseen vapor was filling the passage.

Kathera's eyes widened, her voice barely audible. "What is it?"

"I think something's behind us," he whispered.

Fear creased Kathera's face. She shot the thin light behind her where the beam intensified and filled the passageway. Nothing. The light dimmed, and her eyes questioned Casey.

"Don't you feel it?" asked Casey, staring at the opposite end of the narrow passage.

Kathera's whisper hesitated. "No. Probably just your nerves."

Casey shook his head. The blackness of the right wall disappeared as a light moved along the outside hallway. Two silhouettes materialized in the passageway where Casey and Kathera had been moments earlier. The shadows were large, tail-less, dog-shaped creatures with elongated heads pulled back from a wide nose. Powerful legs moved their muscular bodies with cat-like ease. Casey's breath stuck in his dry throat, and he thought for sure the wall had opened and they would be discovered. He raised his brow at Kathera and nodded towards the wall.

Kathera turned and froze while she watched the outside light, and her light faded to almost nothing. She motioned to Casey to stay quiet and breathed out a low response, "Night Watch!"

A second later the light source casting the shadows bobbed from behind the Night Watch as six guards followed the tracking creatures. The two Night Watch continued along the hall and then stopped where the panel was. Their heads swayed side to side, uncertain and confused, and the two creatures slumped to the floor as if they wanted a nap. Sharp motions from the guards showed their displeasure with the creatures for stopping. The guards spoke to each other as arms motioned and hands pointed at the two animals lying on the ground. One guard acted out his displeasure and kicked the nearest Night Watch.

The creature startled from its sleepy daze and snapped at the leg so quickly a blink would have missed it. The Night Watch's mouth attached to the leg, but the guard's scream was inaudible through the wall. Another guard stepped forward, and, after giving a command, the animal released its hold and its victim rolled to the floor holding his leg. After another minute two guards coaxed the Night Watch into continuing their pursuit. A couple of light beams randomly swept across the transparent wall and illuminated Kathera and Casey in the small passage. The beams moved back and continued after the Night Watch down the hall.

Casey released his breath and watched Kathera. She remained motionless until the guards had faded into the darkness.

"It's a seeing wall," Kathera said quietly. "The material transfers light from the other side, allowing us to see out but they can't see in. To them it looks just like any other wall."

"I thought you said the Night Watch never lose their prey? Did that stuff you sprayed do something to them?"

The corners of Kathera's lips lifted. "They would never admit the Night Watch aren't perfect hunters. The spray acts like a temporary sedative as their noses are highly sensitive. It's virtually undetectable, and essentially harmless. Mostly a mix of pheromones that cause temporary forgetfulness, relaxation, and even a desire to sleep. And it covers our scent. For us it doesn't do much, except in larger doses. Now we need to get going. It won't take long for someone to figure out we disappeared somewhere in that hall. It looked like a couple of them already suspect that."

Casey nodded and continued down the ladder. Kathera followed after she secured the floor panel.

Kathera's penlight shifted to a dim white-blue hue while they descended the ladder. The faint light barely illuminated their immediate area and the walls of the shaft around them.

Casey toyed with the idea of dropping the halberd as it was awkward to hold while descending a ladder. After what he thought was at least two hundred rungs, his feet touched the floor. A few seconds later, Kathera joined him in a small alcove attached to a passage.

Kathera peeked into the passage and surveyed each direction, pausing to listen. Satisfied, she motioned for Casey to follow her, and she cautiously moved to the left.

While they walked, Casey noted the walls and ceilings were unlike the main palace corridors and seemed to be hewn out of the rock.

"Where are we in relation to the palace?" asked Casey.

"The lowest palace levels. The palace you saw was built on the old palace. We're below that. Not many know of these levels."

"How'd you know about them?"

"Remember, my father was captain of the palace guard. He was privy to a lot of secrets. I secretly followed him one day when he came down here." She thought quietly about her statement for a few seconds while they walked. "Or, at least I thought it was in secret. Maybe he intentionally made sure I knew about them, but he didn't want to take me down here personally."

"Where are we going?"

"We need to get back to your ship."

Casey slowed. "Not without my brother and Heather."

Kathera turned, and her eyes pierced into Casey's. "Don't you realize they're going to be kept alive to lure you back?" She paused at his determination. "Remember, the only reason any of you are still alive is because Altor can't get into the ship, let alone discover her secrets. Since you're the pilot, they'll be most interested in getting you. And the others will be bait."

Casey halted.

Kathera stared at him defiantly. "We can escape now, or you can risk getting caught and give Altor the most valuable and advanced spacecraft ever known in the galaxy, and virtually guarantee his victory in a galactic war."

Casey narrowed his eyes, his right hand tightening around the halberd's shaft. "I won't leave without at least trying to rescue them. I'd appreciate your help. But with or without it, I need to do what I can."

Kathera's face softened, the corners of her lips lifting in a small smile. "I knew you were worthy of trust. I was hoping you wouldn't give up on them." She shook her head. "Even if it's foolish to think you could rescue them on your own." She considered a thought and nodded. "The good news is we might free them before Hagon expects a rescue. I have only one request for helping you."

"What is that?"

"Take me to the Rayneiri Empire. By now, the entire palace will know I've helped you escape and I'm as much a fugitive as you."

"The Rayneiri?"

"They're not as bad as Altor and Hagon make them out to be. I wouldn't trust anyone with the *Shaina Ariana*, but generally the Rayneiri Empire is about as good as they come."

Casey pondered the idea for a moment. "Okay, let's do it."

Kathera nodded and continued down the passage to an intersection. She turned left. "We'll need to find out where they're taking your friends. Although, I've got a good idea where to start."

Chapter Thirty
Escape from the Palace

C OOL AIR WHISPERED AROUND Kathera and Casey while they carefully maneuvered through a narrow service tunnel between walls. Pipes and conduit snaked across the ceiling and walls. About every fifty feet they slowed to pass by a two-foot-square air register at floor level.

A few minutes earlier, Kathera had located the service entrance to the old ventilation system, a place, she said, she'd frequently explored when she was younger. Casey had left the halberd hidden near the opening. She told Casey the tunnel passed several rooms that had all been converted into a temporary detainment center, and she suspected the guards would take James and Heather there to avoid any official record.

After several minutes of crawling and listening to silence, the faint, muffled sounds of a conversation filtered in. One voice was clearly agitated. As they neared the next vent, the words became clearer, and the voice revealed itself as Hagon's.

They paused while Hagon continued, "I told you. We should have just taken them when they arrived. But you insisted they be treated well. For the sake of what? An ill-conceived plan. Now the pilot and the key to the ship have disappeared and you think this new plan will work? Add to that, one of the palace attendants has turned traitor."

"If it weren't for your impatience and failure to trust in my plan, we wouldn't be having this inconvenience." While smooth and inviting, the unfamiliar voice also sent shivers down Casey's back. "Still, it is only a minor setback for His Majesty and may work to our advantage."

"If it doesn't, you'll probably lose your head. How exactly will this work to our advantage, Kishon? You think I acted hastily? If I hadn't done what I did all of them would have escaped with that traitorous attendant. Suspicions are rising. Amnor reported that several times. What exactly are your plans to assassinate the Rayneiri imperial family? Some foolish dream? And we get nothing if you fail. But the *Shaina Ariana* is still in our possession. It's more than a prize, especially if your plans fail."

"Their so-called captain will return and attempt a rescue. It's his nature. Should your men fail, we'll proceed with the modified termination plans. Just make sure you do your part as your emperor has requested."

"I'm still not convinced," responded Hagon. "The *Ariana* is too valuable to risk. It is an unexpected military advantage that we need to grasp while it is within our reach. We cannot allow a chance of it falling into our enemy's hands. Even with your abilities it's an unacceptably high risk."

The conversation began to fade, as if its participants were walking away.

"Of course, Commander Hagon," said Kishon, "the *Shaina Ariana* is indeed a valuable prize. But simply capturing it will not bring the Rayneiri to their knees—to unite with our empire—without great losses and taking much longer. Would it not be far better to unite the galaxy under the emperor's rule and obtain the *Shaina Ariana* in a more efficient way? Think about how much more you will be rewarded. Do not allow your men to kill our guests; it could make their captain less cooperative."

Hagon's voice faded in the distance. "I know how to persuade cooperation."

The voices disappeared. Kathera's face was pale in the dim light. Casey was about to ask if she was okay when she ducked under some pipes and continued along the utility passage. A few minutes later they knelt at a vent looking out from under a table into a room filled with displays and consoles. Three hallways could be seen at the far end, and four guards sat around the consoles less than fifteen feet away. With the air moving across them and into the room, Casey was thankful he did not smell as bad as he had the previous day.

Kathera stared at the monitors and then pointed to one near the center. Casey could barely make out the familiar images of his brother and Heather sitting on chairs in an otherwise empty room.

Kathera whispered some instructions in Casey's ear. He nodded, and she pulled the vial from her cloak. He held his breath while she started generously spritzing the air. The odorless mist quickly filtered into the room. Several seconds later the guards' heads bobbed. The closest one nodded his head and was out as soon as his eyes closed. The other three struggled to keep their eyes open. Within seconds all four guards were slumped in the chairs.

Kathera quickly detached the vent and pulled herself through the opening. Casey followed, still holding his breath.

Kathera smiled at Casey. "You can breathe now."

Casey exhaled. "I thought that only worked on the Night Watch."

Kathera examined one of the slumped guards. "I only used a light mist for the Watch. It does work best and longer on them since they rely on their sense of smell. Other lifeforms require more spray and it's only effective in the first few seconds, before it dissipates too much. If you feel a little disoriented, it's probably the spray."

"How long does the effect last?"

"Maybe five minutes, if we're lucky." Kathera scanned the consoles to get oriented with the controls and displays.

"Should we tie them up? Put 'em in a cell?"

Kathera shook her head. "Might take too long to get all of them. Better to use the time to free your friends and escape. We can take the weapons and shoot them if they cause problems." Her head lifted from examining a display, and she pointed to the center passage. "Looks like your companions are down the middle hall. You go get them and I'll get their doors unlocked."

Casey raced down the center corridor while Kathera remained at the consoles. Several doors lined each side of the hallway with small windows peering inside. The first few rooms were empty. He found James and Heather sitting in a room halfway down the hall. When the detainment room's door slid open, Heather and James looked up, their hands shackled to the chairs behind them.

Casey walked in. "Surprised?"

James grinned slyly. "Surprised it took so long."

"What do you mean?" said Casey defiantly as he moved to the chairs. "This was way faster than the kidnapper incident in the Tetons."

"Yeah, but we didn't find out anything," replied James. "They just brought us here a little bit ago and said they'd be back."

"It's probably best not to hang around. Kathera gave me some background." Casey examined the shackles. "And we overheard some things on the way down here. Enough to know we need to leave. So that makes up for what you didn't find out." He turned to face the doorway and called out, "Kathera, can you do something about their shackles?"

Heather's eyes widened, "Kathera?"

"Just a minute," responded Kathera. "That should do it."

The shackles opened. James and Heather quickly ripped them off.

"Let's go," urged Casey as he led them out. "We don't have much time."

"Grab some weapons," said Kathera. "These guys will be waking up any minute and I'd prefer not to kill someone if I don't have to. Makes it too obvious what happened. We need to go down to the forgotten levels, where your eeritiums can't be tracked."

"What about being able to understand you? Don't the translators need to communicate with some central system?" asked Casey as they took guns from the guards.

"After activation and initial contact, they work well enough on their own for all the common languages, including English now. They just won't sync any learned changes or get updates."

She pointed at the opened vent. "Casey, lead the way back to where we came in. I'll close this up."

Casey ducked into the opening.

"Wouldn't it be faster another way?" asked Heather, crouching through the square vent and following after Casey.

"Yes," said Kathera, "but we're more likely to encounter resistance once the guards wake up and discover you're missing. The eeritiums aren't effectively tracked at this level, which is why the detainment block was built down here. But, while we might be able to take on some guards, an encounter would confirm our location."

"Maybe we should get rid of them this time," suggested James as he climbed into the ventilation tunnel. "Remember what happened when we let that pirate ship go."

Kathera closed up the vent.

"Yeah." Casey cringed like his mouth had a bad taste in it. "But I don't feel right about it. They'll get in enough trouble as is. And Dad's words to never take life unnecessarily are stuck in my head."

"You two keep quiet and move it!" Kathera hissed.

Casey sheepishly focused ahead while he led the small group through the narrow tunnel and back to a hole in the wall of the old utility room. He retrieved the halberd from its dark corner and cautiously examined the dimly lit hallway while he waited for the others.

When Kathera exited the opening, she resumed the lead into the corridor. They walked a short distance before she ducked into another narrow side passage. A small amount of light scraped by the passage entrance, only dimly lighting the new hall. Obscured within a shadowed sliver of the right wall, Kathera reached her fingers into a short slot and pushed a slender section of wall back into a room the size of a small office. She motioned the others to follow her inside. When everyone was in, she closed the wall-door, and the sparse light disappeared. From Kathera's hand, a dim blue-white light illuminated the room in a cool glow. A few feet away, nestled against the back wall, a ladder ran through floor and ceiling grates.

Kathera lifted the floor grate and paused before she stepped down to the ladder. "Last one through, close the grate quietly," she whispered.

Without a word, the others followed Kathera down the ladder. Behind Casey, James took a last look around the darkening room, stepped down the ladder, and carefully pulled the grate shut.

Chapter Thirty-One
Forgotten Level

T HEY DESCENDED FOR SEVERAL minutes, passed through two similar rooms, and paused only to open and shut grates. Dust and grime increasingly crusted each lower rung, creating rough handholds. At the third room, the ladder ended. The door was old and unforgiving, and the others had to help Kathera pull it open. The short passage beyond ended at a sealed wall. Rubble and trash from earlier decades littered the ground and piled against the walls.

James was about to comment when Kathera strode to the left wall, carefully moved a darkened piece of scrap metal aside, and crawled through a hole. Heather turned to Casey, her eyes wide and brow rose in question. Casey shrugged his shoulders and ducked into the rubble burrow. Heather and James followed.

When they exited the short tunnel, Kathera's light was bathing a four-lane-wide tunnel with white light. Dirt and debris were scattered across the remnants of the floor.

Kathera's eyes narrowed at James. "Did you replace the cover?"

James nodded while he looked around at what seemed like an abandoned subway.

Kathera led them to a rubbish pile where she removed a few larger pieces of debris. She then pulled aside a dirty fabric cover to reveal a small four-seat, open-top vehicle that had the vague shape of a wheel-less, compact sport utility vehicle.

"Get in," said Kathera. Tossing the cover into the back seat, she climbed over the door and into the driver's seat.

Casey jumped into the passenger's seat, his attention fixated on the controls in front of Kathera.

"Good thing there aren't more of us, or we'd have to get cozy," said James as he pushed aside the cover to sit in the back with Heather.

Behind the console, Kathera's right hand gripped a joystick while her left rested on a horizontal rod between the two front seats. Her penlight dimmed to barely candle-bright while a soft hum purred through the vehicle. She gently raised the rod, and the vehicle smoothly lifted into a hover. As a pair of small wings folded out from the sides, a heads-up display appeared on the front windshield, revealing the tunnel and obstacles in front of them as if they were in full daylight. Using the joystick, she maneuvered into the center of the tunnel and started accelerating.

"What is this place?" asked Heather. "Isn't it guarded?"

Kathera focused on the front display. "Very few know about, or even remember, these old transport tunnels. They're centuries old and supposedly filled in. The few remaining entrances are well concealed and kept secret."

"How'd you find out about them?" asked James.

A mischievous grin broke Kathera's face. "When I was a child, I was exploring the upper levels, which was never allowed, so I had to do it without getting caught. One day I was about to be discovered when I ducked into a dark space and found the ladder room. A few visits there eventually led me down here." She shook her head at the memory. "I used to get in trouble for getting home late."

"Where'd you get this vehicle?" asked Casey, watching Kathera deftly fly through the dark tunnel and dodging debris piles, relying solely on the display in front of her.

"I found it and fixed it up over the years. I'm not sure how old it is, but down here things don't really age much. Cool and dry in this part. It does have lights, but I prefer to fly without them. Watch the screen; you might see some of the creatures down here."

Several times during the flight, dark, animal-like objects scurried to cover as the vehicle approached. Occasionally pairs of eyes reflected the night-vision illumination, and their dark shapes were the playthings of the imagination. They passed through multiple intersections, visible only on the display, and turned twice. After several minutes, Kathera slowed down. Then she stopped the craft and docked it gently into an alcove. Kathera's little light grew a little brighter.

Casey was about to grab the halberd from the vehicle when Kathera shook her head.

"With the guns we retrieved, you should just leave that here," she said.

Casey's hand retreated from the halberd. After they exited the vehicle, Kathera replaced the cover and used a few large pieces of debris to conceal it as another worthless pile. She walked a short distance along the tunnel, her blue light illuminating the wall. A black wall patch swallowed the light, and Kathera followed it into a short hallway. Passing through another black hole in the wall, Kathera's dim light barely illuminated the rungs of a ladder.

"Let me guess," said Casey as he climbed up after Kathera, "ladders are less detectable."

"And virtually no maintenance," she added.

They climbed for several minutes before the ladder ended at an access hatch. Kathera twisted a handle and lifted the hatch into a trash-filled room. Once they were all inside, she secured the hatch, which blended into the floor. She rearranged the rubbish to further conceal their entrance.

Kathera scanned the nearby hallway and warned, "Do not tell or reveal to anyone the location of this lower ladder."

Heather shook her head. "Don't worry about that. I couldn't tell anyone where we are right now."

The corners of Kathera's mouth lifted. "Those I meet with in the city don't know about the lowest tunnels. They think I use other passage networks."

Kathera led them along a few more corridors, up a dilapidated stairwell, and then, after a short walk along a utilitarian hall, she entered another room where they climbed another ladder up a utility shaft. Nearly thirty minutes later, and after shifting to different access passages and shafts, they emerged through a trapdoor into a brightly lit and very tidy storage room. Neatly organized shelves, filled with various boxes and containers, lined the walls. A single door was in one wall. After they were all in the room, Kathera lowered the trapdoor, and it seemed to disappear into the tile-like floor.

Casey blinked several times at the brightness. He expected Kathera to open another hidden doorway, but she walked to the door, touched a small display pad, and waited.

Less than a minute later the door opened; a familiar figure walked in and shut the door behind him.

"Greetings, Kathera, I didn't expect you so soon," said Amnor. He examined the other three and nodded agreeably. "I see you were able to bring our friends."

Chapter Thirty-Two
Amnor's Place

CASEY'S HAND DROPPED TO the handgun tucked in his belt. "Kathera, didn't we hear that this guy revealed stuff to Hagon? Can we trust him?"

Amnor's mouth thinned into a smile, and he nodded slowly at Casey. "You must be very resourceful to have freed your friends and gotten here so quickly. When I heard the *Ariana* crew was captured, I thought Kathera would come to me for help. Though I'm not surprised she jumped in without consulting me."

Kathera ignored Amnor's comment. "Casey, Amnor has gained the trust of Hagon and others in command through his position in the palace guard. He reports some information to maintain that trust, and he provides us with more information."

"A double agent," said James.

"If that is what you call it, then yes," replied Amnor. "I work two roles."

"How do we know who you're loyal to?" asked Casey.

Amnor's mouth formed a knowing half-smile. "Well, I am here and Hagon is not. The palace guard are still looking for you within the palace grounds. And as long as you stay in this room, the location beacons on your eeritiums won't be picked up."

"What about the assassination plot?" asked Casey.

"What plot is that?"

"The one to kill the Rayneiri imperial family."

Amnor's mouth turned down. "There have been many attempts. I can say there is definitely one in motion at this time. When it happens, Emperor El'Kanah and Hagon plan to take advantage of the destabilization of that empire to strike. Their problem has been getting someone close enough to the Rayneiri imperial family without raising suspicions. However, Hagon recently employed Sokari assassins, some with unique skills. Kathera may recall hearing about them from childhood tales. They're often referred to as skinwalkers."

Kathera swallowed a gasp. Casey raised his left brow curiously at her and then looked back at Amnor, who was slowly nodding at Kathera's reaction.

"Wait," said Heather. "Are you referring to legends of people who can take on the form of animals?"

"No," said Amnor. "Shapeshifting, that is, taking on a completely different physical form, is not possible, at least as far as we know, although there are plenty of myths and legends. 'Skinwalker' is a term for certain members of the Sokari race. Over the millennia environmental conditions on their homeworld have caused the Sokari to evolve. Some have used that evolution and trained their bodies, muscles, and soft tissues to be more elastic and pliable to the point where they can take on the appearance of another person. Basically, they can shape their bodies in a limited extent to look like someone else, as long as that person has a similar skeletal structure. They can't suddenly grow hair. They can increase or decrease their height by a small amount. I've heard it is quite unsettling to see their skin shift. Many Sokari even have the ability to adjust the pigmentation of their skin, much like certain animals can camouflage in their environment."

Kathera's lips curled. "They're mostly skilled mercenaries whose loyalties are to themselves and whoever pays them."

"Given their fabled reputation," continued Amnor, "they wouldn't hesitate to assassinate the Rayneiri imperial family, or any other target. As I mentioned, the challenge has always been getting close enough to strike. But I won't reveal any more than this to you: one of the Sokari seems to have gotten around this setback." He paused, deep in thought. "If I could, I'd warn the Rayneiri myself and provide information on how to detect the Sokari. But I have no way to give them a message safely and securely. And it would be hazardous to entrust the information to anyone else."

"Casey said he'd take me to the Rayneiri, maybe you could come as well," suggested Kathera. "But that'd expose your role in opposing the emperor."

Amnor nodded, acknowledging the suggestion. "Going may be best for me. I have suspicions that I've been exposed, and I've had to be much more careful in how I do things. My knowledge may be of help to the Rayneiri."

Kathera nodded and turned to Casey, who glanced at James and Heather.

"This is the first I've heard about going to the Rayneiri," said James, his head cocked slightly to the right.

"Same here," said Heather. "But if that's where we need to go, it might be good to have someone from the inside confirm an assassination plot."

James grinned. "Yeah, I don't think the Rayneiri emperor's going to believe us if we tell him there's an assassin on the loose and bound on killing him and his family."

"Probably not," said Casey. "But we still need to get our ship."

"Yes," said Amnor. "But before we get your ship, we need to fix your eeritiums before we're all caught. I have several sets that mask their identities and effectively secure their locations. Like the access tunnels below, this room is shielded so your interpreters aren't giving you away right now."

Amnor walked along some shelves to the left and pulled two small containers out from a box. Over the next few minutes, he replaced James, Heather, and Casey's ear interpreters with new ones from one of the containers. Like the first time, Casey was the only one who experienced a brief pinch when the interpreters were attached.

Casey eyed Kathera. "What about yours?"

Kathera's mouth thinned, the corners turned up in a sly smile. "Mine are back on my bed. The ones I have on aren't trackable. If the imperial guards hadn't seen me helping you last night, I probably wouldn't be on the run."

Amnor frowned. "The security monitors detected you with Casey when you reentered the building last night. While you may not have been counted a traitor, you certainly would've been called in for interrogation today."

"What about the old ear-thingys?" asked James.

Amnor placed the last set of eeritiums into the second container. "I think we'll send them on a long journey in the opposite direction."

"As for a journey, what about finding a way back to Earth?" asked Heather.

"I'm afraid I don't know," said Casey.

"If your ship has been there, it has logged the star maps," said Amnor. "My guess is you just haven't been able to access it. I may be able to help with that."

Kathera's smile encouraged Casey.

"We can drop you and Amnor off with the Rayneiri so you can warn them," said Casey, "then we'll be on our way back home. If a war is about to break out, I don't want anything to do with it. And I want to be on the other side of the galaxy if it does happen."

Kathera's smile dropped. "I was hoping you'd help us. It's more than just Amnor and me trying to restore peace to our systems."

"I'm not a warrior." Casey shook his head. "That's more James's thing. I'm not even a leader. James is better at that. And I don't know even know who the 'us' is you're talking about."

"After what I saw you do to those four palace guards last night, I'd say you're more of a warrior than most of them," said Kathera.

"It was impressive," agreed James. "I saw it from the room. Even though we've been training together in martial arts for most of our lives, I didn't know you could do that."

Casey felt like he was getting back into a corner. "Blowing up spaceships is one thing. But I haven't, and don't think I could, kill someone."

"That would be ideal," said Kathera. "To not kill anyone."

"Except maybe those who need to be," added Amnor.

"Casey," said James, "you don't need to make a choice right now. We still need to get our ship and take Kathera and Amnor to the Rayneiri. Then, if we think it's worth it, maybe we could take Heather home and come back to help."

"And leave me out?" protested Heather. "If you two stick around, I'll be here as well. We've been to two alien planets now and been almost killed how many times? Yeah, going home would be nice, but it'd be boring without you guys. We might have a chance to make a difference. Besides your mom would never believe me if I tried to explain what happened to you."

Kathera stifled a yawn in the cloak she was still wearing. "Sorry about that. I think my body just realized it hasn't slept all night."

Amnor nodded his head. "A brief rest would be in order. Casey, I'm sure the Rayneiri would welcome you and your companions should you choose to help. But my recommendation is for you to return home after dropping Kathera and me off. You are right. This is not your battle, nor is it your war. You have your lives to live on your own world."

Casey felt like the burden of decision was lifted from him.

"I'll send these old interpreters on their way," Amnor continued, "which should buy you some time. I'll return in three hours. I'm not on shift for three days, so my absence won't be noticed very soon. While I'm gone, you're all welcome to rest wherever you are comfortable."

Chapter Thirty-Three
Interrupted

THREE HOURS LATER CASEY woke up on the couch in the main room of Amnor's apartment. His nose twitched at a sweet spice that reminded him of cinnamon. Sitting up, he saw Kathera in the nearby kitchen space removing a plate of light and flaky rolls from a cabinet in the wall. He got up and walked to a large window where he craned his neck to see the neighboring buildings, all nearly identical and utilitarian, tower overhead. Bridges disguised as gardens joined them at several levels. He walked over to a small table by the kitchen. "Something smells good."

"It's probably the taka rolls," said Kathera. She motioned to some green-skinned fruit sitting in a bowl on the table. "Try some havala. In case you're wondering, just bite into it. The skin can be a little tart, but it's quite good combined with the juicy sweet insides."

Casey picked up one of the palm-sized fruits. The skin reminded him of a lime-green avocado, only soft like a peach. He bit through the soft skin and exposed a juicy pink inside. The piece in his mouth had the tart taste of citrus combined with a sweet orange-mango inside. While the bite melted in his mouth, he watched the airborne traffic maneuver through the skyways between buildings at various altitudes. Rather than traffic moving in different directions at the same altitude, each direction had traffic flying at different levels.

Heather walked in, her nose leading. "Did someone cook cinnamon rolls?"

Kathera's head tilted curiously. "I've no idea what 'cinnamon' is, but you're probably referring to the taka rolls. They're a lightly sweetened bread with a few spices."

"Sounds great to me," said James, closing in on the counter where Kathera had spread out the food. He rubbed his eyes and covered a yawn. "I need something to wake me up."

Amnor walked through a nearby door. "There's some good news. The decoy with the interpreters has attracted some attention. Several patrols are tracking them away from the city. I have also arranged with some of my contacts a way to get to your ship. But we will need to leave quickly as the window of access is very narrow."

James's eyes closed, the corners of his mouth curling up as he savored a bite of the sweet roll. "How narrow is that?"

"We need to be at the rendezvous point at the spaceport in an hour. If we miss it, my contact will just leave, and we'll have to try for another day."

Casey dropped a large pit from the havala onto a plate while the last bite melted into his taste buds. He eyed another fruit. "And how long does it take to get there?"

"Thirty minutes to a secured parking location," replied Amnor, "then it could take up to another thirty minutes to walk to the meeting point."

Casey picked out another fruit. "Good thing we don't have much to pack. Better grab what we have and get moving."

———◆———

A minute later they had grabbed their handguns, hidden them in their clothes, and had walked down a corridor to the parking pods. When Amnor touched a panel, the pods rotated past them. The pod that stopped was a five-person craft that reminded Casey of a mini-van: two seats in the back, two in the middle, and a single in the front for the driver. James and Heather moved into the back seat while Kathera and Casey sat in the middle seats.

The pods rotated for several seconds before Amnor's vehicle stopped to face an opening into the lower levels of air traffic. He touched a few controls, and the air carrier automatically maneuvered out of the landing dock and into the closest air traffic. Across the windowed surfaces of the buildings, lights of varying colors and intensities flashed alien characters and displayed short video clips, advertising a variety of products and services. A 3D ad came to life when they approached one building. The advertisement seemed to be for the latest sporty air carriers, some with sweeping canopies and others with open tops. Out of curiosity, Casey compared Amnor's craft to the other flying vehicles. Amnor's seemed average when compared to most of the same class of air vehicle, although its red color was more faded.

Amnor's craft shifted momentarily out of its directional air lane, maneuvered to a higher air traffic flow, and merged into faster directional traffic lanes that were above most of the buildings. Casey expected Amnor to be piloting the craft but, while several controls were within reach, he simply watched while the aircraft flew itself.

Casey shook his head in amazement. The modes of travel and technology he had witnessed in the last couple days were far beyond anything he had thought possible. What surprised him most was how used the majority of the vehicles looked, even though it was all new to him. Even the buildings varied in size, shape, and age. Behind them, Amnor's building blended with its neighbors, which appeared to be older but still respectable.

Looking across the cityscape, Casey realized the tunnels they had used to escape the palace had gone out a different direction from the air path Hagon had flown them in on. When Casey asked Amnor about it, Amnor explained they were flying into the main city from an adjoining sub-city. The only distinction Casey could see between the city and sub-city were the size of buildings, but even height was difficult to determine in many cases because of the geography. Squinting, the blurred cityscape looked like a hilly terrain, since many of the buildings were garnished in greenery. After a minute of flying the buildings became taller and newer looking. Light from the local sun reflected in pools on the tops of some buildings, reflecting like small mirrors. A waterfall on one building looked like liquid silver pouring down its side. On other structures, lush greenery cascaded from high-level gardens down to decks or bridges. Locals could be seen walking amid the hanging gardens.

Several hundred feet below them, gray-black streets between the buildings became increasingly obscured by a thick fog or mist. Through the fog, ground vehicles scurried along the streets like confused insects, all trying to get somewhere fast but not making much progress. Elevated above the fog, elongated train-like carriers loaded and unloaded passengers at designated platforms.

"When I was really young, there wasn't as much ruin and decay," said Kathera. "It used to be considered the jewel of the empire."

"Looks better than most places on our planet," said James. "How long ago was that?"

"Over forty years ago. I shared the story with Casey last night. The short of it is Altor El'Kanah instigated a coup that killed his brothers but made it look like the Rayneiri assassinated them. He then claimed the throne."

Amnor touched a screen, his right hand casually gripping a joystick-like control. The air carrier turned right, flew a short distance, and then turned left. He glanced at some advertising displays.

"Still, it looks better than many cities on our planet," said James as his face returned to the window. "You'll need to share what you told Casey with us sometime."

"It may look good, but you can only see the better of the bad from up here. Be glad we're not on the ground level, or worse, below the old city."

The air carrier turned right again.

"You mean where we were last night?" asked Heather.

"No, I'm talking about the old—"

Kathera was cut off when Amnor swerved the air carrier sharply to the left. The ship quickly accelerated.

"Hey, careful with the sudden moves," said James, his hands gripping the seat in front of him. "We don't have any seatbelts back here."

"My apologies," said Amnor. The aircraft dropped suddenly into a short right dive and zipped right again. "It was hard to tell earlier, but we definitely have someone interested in us."

Kathera anxiously looked out the back window. "Which one?"

"A dull black ship on the higher skyway," said Casey, his attention fixated on the higher traffic flow.

Amnor's eyebrows rose in surprise. "Yes, that's the one. How'd you know?"

"It seems like most of the air traffic is autonomously controlled. That particular black ship has been flying a little differently. Not as precise in flying and maintaining aircraft spacing like the others, and it seemed to be trying to follow us from a distance."

"You have a good eye. We'll need to do something to lose it before we get to the spaceport or we'll miss our meeting point."

A feeling of apprehension gripped Casey's chest. "Turn around, now!"

Amnor glanced back at Casey questioningly. He looked forward just in time to see three black ships drop down in front of them from between two buildings. One ship remained in front while the other two dropped back to flank Amnor's vehicle. Amnor pulled up into a higher skyway, whipping to the side as the higher black ship dropped down through opposing traffic in an attempt to box them in. Amnor side-slipped down to a lower air level and into traffic going the opposite direction. The approaching air vehicles scattered and instantly slowed as automated systems maintained control and distances. Casey was surprised no wrecks happened.

Amnor began an accelerated climb, but his air vehicle struggled to maintain the ascent and slowed. Behind them, the four black ships were quickly closing the air space.

An explosion ripped apart the air in front of Amnor's windshield, and the vehicle shook with the concussive wave. Amnor dropped the aircraft into a rapid descent, diving and rotating through several lanes of skyway.

Kathera gripped tightly to her seat. "It's a good thing those other vehicles have working awareness and avoidance systems."

"And it's a good thing I disabled ours or we would've been shut down," said Amnor as he continued a twisted turn around a building and pulled into air traffic.

"Maybe that's not a good thing," groaned Heather, her white knuckles grasping her seat.

James struggled to keep from rocking and sliding into Heather or the wall with each abrupt turn. "It makes me miss seatbelts."

Multiple red flashes ripped the air around them. On the right, a passing sky car erupted into flames when a plasma burst tore through its fuselage and plunged it into an uncontrolled spin. The sky car grazed the side of a nearby building before it disintegrated in an explosion against a terraced garden.

Two black crafts narrowed their distance behind Amnor's ship while the other two remained on a higher skyway. Amnor again dropped into a lower skyway of opposing-flow traffic. Vehicles instantly stopped or swerved to avoid collisions. He continued through the traffic, swerving to break up groups of air carriers and make it more difficult for pursuers to track them closely.

Amnor veered towards another cluster of aircraft when a blast blew apart the forward ship. Two more ships were knocked out of the group and directly into Amnor's path. Debris showered over and bounced off Amnor's air car. He banked hard to the left as a large chunk of fiery remains spun past them. The black ship immediately behind Amnor's was caught unaware, and the burning wreckage ripped through it like a giant can opener. An explosion of metallic confetti rained down into the streets far below.

The second ship pulled up to avoid the explosion, but fiery shrapnel shredded its underside as it flew over. Small fires licked its sides, and the flight stabilizing system failed. In less than a second, the ship careened into the side of a building.

Instantly automated collision avoidance systems directed air traffic to halt or ascend to higher skyways. Amnor plunged his aircraft into a steep dive, pressing everyone against their seat backs, and he rolled around two more lanes of skyway in his descent towards the streets below. The remaining two black air ships dove after their prey. Ahead of them, the ground fog filled the windscreen, and Amnor pulled his ship level, skimming above several ground vehicles.

Flying near ground level shattered the illusion of the city's uniform- and clean-looking streets. Amidst the gray fog and mists, scattered trash spilled from smaller side streets and alleys. Below them, jockeying ground vehicles slowed or stopped when the low-flying air ships buzzed overhead. Shadows of pedestrians were briefly glimpsed ducking into doorways or crouching for cover.

Amnor shifted right and left, and two ground cars erupted as energy blasts blew them apart. The explosions were close enough that the temperature of the cabin interior rose momentarily when Amnor's ship raced by.

James watched the pursuing ships dive after them like raptors. "Do we have anything to shoot back with? Other than the little handguns we took from the guards?"

"Weapons on aircraft are illegal." Kathera grimaced during another sharp left bank.

"Just a guess," suggested Heather, "but isn't helping prisoners escape also illegal?"

Casey gripped the edges of his seat. "It's probably illegal to have a gun as well."

"True enough," said Amnor through clenched teeth. He shot a glance behind him at the pursuing air cars. "I modified this craft for speed, not weapons. Much easier to avoid detection."

Two explosions erupted on the left, and Amnor abruptly swerved right when another ground car blew apart. Debris spewed into his air vehicle, tearing through the right side, cracking the windscreen, and shattering the back window. Amnor fought to stabilize his aircraft as it rocked side to side. Red lights flashed across the control panel.

"Hold on!" shouted Amnor. "It's going to be tight!"

The cracked windscreen instantly spider-webbed in all directions. The clear material imploded into the vehicle, showering its occupants. The ship jerked at Amnor's struggle to regain control. Wind rushed into the cabin and was sucked right out the back. Lungs struggled to breathe, and eyes watered as the wind rushed through.

James looked back and, through wet eyes, squinted up at the attacking ships. He pulled out the gun he had taken earlier. "Better than doing nothing," he said, and he fired blasts of brilliant plasma at their pursuers.

Heather joined him with her handgun. Most shots streaked through the air without hitting any meaningful target. Several bursts glanced harmlessly off the skin of the enemy ships. Amnor weaved through the ground level streets, skimming just over most of the ground traffic while he fought to maintain flight control.

"These aren't any good against whatever armor those guys have," shouted James over the rush of the wind.

Casey leaned in to Kathera. "Can we remove and overload the power supply of a gun to create an explosion?"

Kathera shook her head. "There's a built-in overload safety. The power supplies are only active when they're loaded."

"James, I need your sharpshooting skills," shouted Casey.

"Yeah? Tell Amnor to stop swerving. I can't hit the broadside of a barn with his driving."

The two black ships dropped behind them—one slightly higher and behind the other—and began closing the distance.

"What am I shooting?" James called back as another of his shots glanced off the closest pursuer.

"This!"

James saw the gun in Casey's hand and nodded. Casey reached out the broken side window and threw the gun at their pursuers. Instinctively James aimed and fired off a burst of three shots while he tracked his target.

The first shot completely missed the gun flying through the air. The handgun hit the lower ship's windscreen and deflected upwards as the second plasma bolt glanced harmlessly off the windscreen, exactly where the gun had hit a split second before. The gun spun through the air just above the lower vehicle when the third shot ripped through the gun's power cartridge, and the weapon exploded in a brilliant flash.

The unexpected intense blast of light, combined with light reflecting off the wisps of fog below, disoriented the drivers of both black vehicles. Confused, the lower pilot dipped his ship's left side too low, clipping the top of a ground vehicle and flipping the air car into a short-lived cartwheel before it smashed into another ground transport. The higher pilot pulled up to avoid the disaster and then dropped back in pursuit, releasing two volleys of plasma energy.

One plasma bolt ripped into the corner of a building like a vicious lightning strike. The next struck the front of Amnor's air car. The ship wrenched violently to the right. Amnor futilely fought the controls as the ship veered sharply towards an open-air marketplace.

Wisps of fog snaked across the market where hundreds of people filled the street and loitered around vendor stalls, tents, and makeshift shelters. The voices of hagglers were silenced by the whine of the mortally wounded ship diving towards them. At the sight of the smoking air car, along with a black vehicle in pursuit, the people scurried into hiding.

Red lights surged on the console in front of Amnor, and the ship lurched uncontrollably. Sparks spat from the surrounding panels, and smoke filled the cabin as the rush of air excited the sparks into flames. Amnor wrestled the controls and slid the ship's belly into the cleared promenade. Flames leaped in rage from the front of the wrecked ship. Above the wreck, the black ship slowed, circled once, paused for a moment, then zipped away.

Casey shook his head and coughed as coarse smoke scratched his throat. Next to him, Kathera was unresponsive, her head leaning against a shattered window. Behind him, James coughed.

"You guys okay?" Casey asked.

"Yeah." James coughed again. "You two?"

Smoke began to cloud Casey's airway. "Bruised, but I'm good. Kathera's out. Looks like Amnor as well. The fire's getting big. You two get out and I'll work on getting Kathera out. Both of us will need to get Amnor."

Heather kicked out remnants of the window, and then she and James began working their way out of the mangled sides.

Casey's eyes squinted through tears while smoke burned his vision. In front of him, Amnor was slumped behind the controls as flames danced along the front console. Beside Casey, Kathera was still unresponsive, and a trickle of blood dripped from her hairline. The door's panel was cracked, and the door bowed outward in its frame.

From his seat, he lifted his legs and slammed both feet against the door. The damaged frame released its hold, and the bent door clunked to the ground. He coughed and twisted towards Kathera, grabbed her right arm, and pulled it over his shoulder. The smoke began to choke him. He felt his oxygen-depleted muscles weakening while he struggled to lift and pull her off the seat. She was lighter than he expected, but the smoke sucked his energy and made him stumble with her through the broken doorway. Several yards from the crash, the cleaner air was reinvigorating, and he set her down near a food stall. Heather dashed over to him as Kathera coughed and peeked through partially opened lids.

"Good to see you're still with us," coughed Casey. "I've gotta go and help James with Amnor."

On the opposite side of the wreck, James had failed to open Amnor's door and was clearing out broken windscreen when Casey arrived. Across the console, black smoke billowed out of larger, hotter flames that no longer danced but gyrated angrily.

James covered a cough. "The door won't budge! We gotta pull him through the window. And he's got a restraint on that I can't release."

Casey nodded and sprinted to the doorway he had opened earlier and went inside the cab. He did not remember when Amnor had put a restraint harness on, and it took him a couple seconds to find the release latch. His eyes watered heavily, and he looked from Amnor to the back door. "James, come to the side door!"

James squinted through the smoke-filled car and nodded at his brother before he darted around. With the restraints released, Casey grabbed Amnor's arms and pulled him to the side of the front seat. A moment later, James took over the arms and Casey grabbed Amnor's legs to clear the front seat. Flames fully engulfed the front of the wreck, and the intense heat began to sear their faces. They half-stumbled carrying Amnor and set him on the ground next to Kathera. The fire rapidly engulfed the vehicle remains and sent thick, black smoke signals into the air.

Amnor's head moved slowly, his eyes struggling to open. "You should leave me," he groaned. "I'm not sure if I'll make it and I'll just slow you down."

James hacked out some smoke from his lungs while he knelt beside Amnor to assess his injuries. "I don't see much in the way of external injury. Doesn't mean nothing's broken or damaged inside. Judging from the fact the rest of us are mostly okay, and you actually had a restraint on, I'd say you probably got bruised ribs when you got knocked unconscious."

Kathera stood precariously and pressed her hands to the sides of her head. "We can't leave you now that Hagon's men know you're helping us."

"But," Amnor protested when James and Casey hefted him up, "I'll slow you down. I can tell them you threatened me under duress."

"Maybe, but Kathera's right," said Casey. "We're not leaving you here. Can you walk at all?"

Struggling, Amnor's left arm held James's shoulder while he shakily stood. "Breathing's a bit hard, but I think I can walk."

Sirens echoed through the buildings, their voices wailing louder with each second.

"Good, 'cause time's up," urged James. "We need to leave now, before the party crashers arrive."

Chapter Thirty-Four

Going Down

C ASEY'S RIGHT BROW RAISED at Amnor. "Where to?"

Amnor's head moved from side to side, his eyes struggling to find a familiar landmark. "I'm not sure. I'm more familiar with the skyways as I've never had a reason to be much on ground level."

"How far to the spaceport?" asked Heather.

"By air, we were about five minutes from the meeting point, before our delay." Amnor let go of James, wobbling momentarily while he regained his own balance. "On foot, we're probably more than an hour away. My contact will be long gone before we get there, if I can figure out where we need to go."

Kathera's eyes narrowed as they pierced through the wisps of fog pouring from the nearby alleyways. She took a few uncertain steps towards a narrow, black alley between abandoned market stalls. She stopped, looked at the others, and motioned her head forward. "Then it's time for plan B. This way."

The other members of the group began moving towards Kathera, when her focus shifted up to the skyways with widened eyes. "*Run!*" she shouted, and she darted towards the alley.

Trusting her orders, Heather, James, and Amnor stumbled into a sprint after Kathera as she slipped into the narrow alley. Casey chanced a glance over his shoulder.

Two hundred feet up, a black ship cautiously poked its nose out from between two buildings.

What's he waiting for? Casey wondered.

The sirens wailed loudly from the left, and six sky cars plummeted down to the emptied plaza. Two were yellow-orange, elongated box-shaped vehicles. Automated nozzles emerged from the front and rotated spray foam over the burning wreck, and long mechanical arms worked through the wreckage. A white air car with triple blue chevrons marking its side and three dark-blue, van-shaped air vehicles hovered fifty feet above the ground. The van-shaped air cars spread out and began circling the plaza in a search pattern. One moved towards the plaza end where the alley merged between the buildings.

Casey disappeared into the deep, foggy shadows of the alley as an amplified voice chased after him.

"Stop or you will be under arrest! It is unlawful to leave the scene of an accident."

Casey sprinted after the others for another three hundred feet into the alley before he risked another backwards glance. Through the fog he saw a blue air car drop its hover to fifty feet. Too big to enter the alley, the ship turned ninety degrees, and a side door flipped open. Three armored soldiers jumped out. Before touching ground, a blast of air shot down from behind them, softening their landing. They quickly surveyed the marketplace plaza and then ran into the alley after Casey.

Casey's adrenaline kicked in. "We're going to have company!"

James glanced back. "I don't suppose we have diplomatic immunity."

"Don't count on it," huffed Casey. "At least we've got a hundred yards on them."

Shells of corroded vehicles and garbage piles increased the deeper they ran into the alley, and their pace slowed to navigate trash heaps. Thousands of feet above them, the buildings crowded the air and permitted only a sliver of blue sky through. Only a fraction of that light penetrated the persistent fog that snaked through the alley. Small critters scampered over and through the debris-filled passage and thickening haze.

The amplified voice reverberated through the alley, its echoes seeming to come from all around. "You are commanded to stop, or we will use force to detain you."

"I think force was always their plan to detain us," said James as they rounded another burned-out chassis.

Lungs burning from exhaustion, Casey looked back through the haze, hoping for a respite. Through the mist he saw the three soldiers jump over rubbish heaps, jets of air aiding their pursuit. They launched over a large trash pile and, while airborne, shot at the group.

"Watch out!" shouted Casey.

Kathera, Heather, and Amnor passed behind another wreckage while James and Casey dodged to the side. Several blue blasts erupted a hole from the trash heap, and burning debris toppled to the ground.

They continued deeper into the alley. Their pace slowed when the thickening haze choked out the light, dropping visibility to a few feet, and the waste piles became more numerous. Two more energy blasts ripped into trash heaps.

Casey glanced back again and shook his head. The pursuers had vanished in the thick foggy darkness. *Good thing we've got some cover*, he thought. Looking forward again he realized James was gone. Disoriented, he stopped and looked around. He took another step and panic gripped his throat. He jumped when a hand grabbed his shoulder and yanked him to the side.

"Quick! Get in before they get too close," hissed Kathera.

Casey stumbled into the black entryway. Kathera closed the door and rotated a locking mechanism. Two dim ceiling lights illuminated grimy walls and trash-covered floors. The others stood waiting at the mouth of a staircase that dropped into an abyss.

Kathera darted to the stairs. "That lock will only hold if they don't use anything more than hands to open it."

"Were we seen?" asked Amnor.

"Not sure," replied Kathera over her shoulder. "The fog's getting really thick. I almost missed Casey. Hopefully their sensors were too confused to follow us."

Kathera led them down a flight of stairs before they were encased in night. She took out her small penlight; an amber-white glow revealed the steps while they descended two more levels. They followed the short hall to an intersection. Kathera held her light out and examined the left, right, and forward passages. Satisfied, she headed into the murky left hall.

Heavy breathing and faint echoes of foot treads rippled into the darkness as they continued down the hall to a *T*-junction. Kathera turned right, and the passage ended with two large door-like panels on the right wall. Next to the doors was a small hand-sized pad.

Kathera touched the pad a couple of times, and it glowed a sickly green. Then she unexpectedly turned around to the opposite wall and pushed in a two-foot-high panel that blended into the wall. She ducked inside, glanced around, and motioned the others to enter.

An explosion reverberated through the halls, and the clanking of metal echoed its complaints.

James glanced back. "Sounds like they didn't opt for hands to open the door."

Heather ducked through the short opening. Amnor followed, cautiously stooping and shifting his weight while the muscles in his face tensed with pain. James and Casey quickly passed through. After Casey entered, Kathera pushed the panel back in place and touched a nearby pad. The pad shifted from sickly green to a faded-rose color and then winked out.

Kathera's light illuminated a room, barely eight feet square. An access shaft surrounded by guard railing took up the back half of the room, and a metal staircase spiraled downward into darkness. Heather's face was pale as she stood next to the stairwell, like she was ready to lose the contents of her stomach.

Casey stepped closer to ask if she was feeling well, and the putrid stench of rot and sewage assailed his senses. His insides lurched.

"Follow quickly," whispered Kathera as she lifted a bar. "It won't take long for them to track us and access that panel." When the others hesitated, she added, "Get used to it. The smell will get worse before it gets better. Try to breathe more through your mouth and not the nose."

Kathera started down the stairs, Amnor following.

Heather started to descend. "Can't you lock the door?" she asked.

"The best I could," replied Kathera. "But it won't take much to break through."

"Best to get as much distance as possible," added Amnor.

"At least it's not a ladder," said Casey.

The descent dropped down several levels, passing through similar small access rooms. Kathera's promise was kept: the smell intensified.

"When we get through this," said James, "I'm going to have to gargle a whole bottle of mouthwash just to get the odor out of my mouth."

"Are we headed into the sewers?" asked Casey.

"Worse," said Kathera, her voice strained.

Amnor nodded in the dim light as they descended. "The city has various wastewater systems, but many of the oldest parts empty into the lower tunnels of the old city. And it's not just sewage, but any and all refuse that gets dumped and deposited."

"Most of it's illegal," said Kathera. "But well-placed payments get things overlooked."

"I'm not sure I should ask," said Heather, "but how do you know about this? Like, how to even get down here."

"I've been underground before and was shown safe signs to look for if I needed to find a way down."

"What about you, Amnor?" asked James.

Amnor shook his head. "I've heard rumors about these tunnels, but never knew how to find any of them."

The stairs ended. Garbage littered the ground. Trickles of water seeped through deteriorating walls. Mold freely grew on the moist walls and debris, adding its pungency to the air. In front of them an oval, rust-colored door stood out against a gray-black wall. The door appeared to be some kind of metal and was the only visible exit option. Five heavy hinges lined the left side. Three newer-looking dead bolts could be seen securing the door to the wall on the right. An old circular handle was in the door on the side with the dead bolts.

Kathera grabbed the door handle and quickly twisted it in a series of left and right turns. With the final turn, the dead bolts moved away from the wall and into the door.

Kathera cautioned the others. "Brace yourselves. The first rush of air is the worst. The air gets better once we're further in." She pulled the handle back, and the heavy, thick door slowly swung open.

When the door cracked open, an almost visible wall of odor rushed through the opening like a specter being released. Amnor turned to the side, lost the contents of his stomach, and heaved a couple more times. Heather also turned away, but successfully fought back the compelling urge to copy Amnor. A dry heave lurched James.

Heeding Kathera's earlier caution, Casey held his breath when the door opened. At the sight of Amnor, he pinched his nose when the odorous vapors reached into his nostrils. He watched Kathera slowly, cautiously, release her breath, her face a shade of pale green in the light. He slowly released his breath.

Plasma bursts blew apart debris at the bottom of the stairs. More rubbish exploded. The sound of boots echoed down the stairs.

"Stop!" blared a voice from a couple flights up. "Or you will be permanently detained."

"Time to go," prompted Kathera, jumping through the open door.

Amnor and Heather swiftly followed, trying hard to limit the inhaling of the foul air. James and Casey darted to the doorway. Footfalls raced down the stairs while several plasma blasts burst into more rubbish piles and burned into the walls. The brothers rushed to the doorway, grabbed the handle on the back side of the door, and pulled it shut. The heavy door slammed back into place and Kathera twisted the handle. Amnor jammed a metal rod he had retrieved from a nearby junk pile into the door frame, next to one of the dead bolts.

In the faint light, they backed away slowly, watching nervously while the handle tried to twist one way and then another. Heather, James, and Kathera held their handguns out, ready for the door to open. The twisting stopped.

"James," whispered Casey, pointing to the ground near where he was standing.

Casey stooped down and picked up a couple of broken metal rods, similar to what Amnor had used to jam the dead bolt on the door. James nodded, and Casey tossed one to him. James caught it with his left hand while the right kept his gun fixed on the door. Gun-less, Casey grabbed a second rod. James waited on the right while Casey situated himself on the left near the dead bolts.

The door handle twisted and shook a few times, but the jammed rod refused to allow the door to open. Several blasts reverberated through the door and its frame in an attempt to punch through. Angry, indecipherable shouts were interspersed among a barrage of more plasma and projectile weapon fire.

"Guess we're not going back that way," said James grimly.

Chapter Thirty-Five

Into the Underground

FOR SEVERAL MINUTES, THE heavy door groaned and popped as weapon fire pounded it. The smell of burning refuse and hot metal filtered through the stench of the underground air, and warmth radiated through the door. Then there was silence.

"Did they give up already?" asked Casey, anxiously shifting the two rods in his hands.

Amnor stepped to the door and placed his hands on its surface. His eyes narrowed at the metal. "Not likely," he said with a slow head shake. "But they probably realized their current efforts aren't doing anything to this door. I'm guessing they're going to get something more substantial to break through."

Kathera turned to face the passage. "We only have a few minutes lead then, assuming they have something in their vehicles." She stepped into the cross passage and looked back at the others. "Best to get moving."

Kathera studied the left and right side passageways, both of which were wide enough for ten people to walk abreast and still have room. Sickly orange-yellow lights flickered from the ceiling every couple hundred feet and added an unnatural color to the uneasiness. Old, worn-out pipes and conduits of all sizes ran along the ceilings and walls. The ground sloped from the walls to the center where burnt-rust-colored water trickled. Trash and refuse were strewn about, and piles of waste littered the spaces between the walls and pipes. Kathera's head cocked and then nodded as if she remembered something. She started walking down the left passage.

"What is this place?" asked Heather, her nose and lungs still coming to grips with the air. "Some kind of open sewer?"

"This is part of the old city. Ignored and forgotten, though mostly forgotten, except by those few who frequent the area," replied Kathera. "Some of these pipes are old sewer lines. Others for power, water, or other infrastructure. Officially these were abandoned after the last disaster, but there are plenty of newer lines that empty illegally into them. The smell will improve as we move on. I've been told the exiles pump fresh air down, and that causes the smell to get worse at all the access points, which also works as a deterrent. If you're wondering, we're about three hundred feet below the main surface."

"Whoa," said Casey, "I didn't think we'd come down that far."

"Neither did I," added Heather. "Though I suppose going downstairs is faster than ladders, especially when you're being chased."

"There are some old transport tunnels"—Kathera pointed upwards—"about a hundred feet higher up."

"I thought those were part of the old city," said James.

"I guess I should clarify," said Kathera, picking her way between piles and several large puddles. "There are actually two old cities. About seven hundred years ago, a meteorite struck the sea and caused a wall of water to rush in on the first old city. All but the highest buildings, and those on higher ground, like the palace, were inundated by water. Within a hundred years a new city was built over the old. That's the one with the transport tunnels."

"Doesn't sound like the smart thing to do, building over the scene of destruction," said Casey.

"They determined the likelihood of another meteorite-induced destruction was extremely small," said Kathera.

"What happened to that city?" asked Heather.

"Well, roughly three hundred years ago, a surprise eruption from one of the closer volcanic islands—which wasn't supposed to be active—caused the side of the island's mountain to collapse into the water. A massive wave rushed inland and inundated the city. Again, it wasn't high enough to get the palace grounds, but everything along the coast was destroyed or severely damaged. More than a million people died, and at least that many were missing. The current city was then built on that old one."

James cocked his head in bewilderment. "So, after two devastating destructions, why rebuild here, again?"

"Because it's considered the best place on this planet. Rich, natural resources are nearby. Lots of fresh water. The year-round weather is constant. Technology, engineering, and building construction all improved, along with better early warning systems. Though they say another monster wave is unlikely, the city has a combination of outer defenses to diffuse and block waves, and most of the buildings are constructed to withstand large waves. The buildings also have automated protections to seal off sections. You may have noticed the main tunnels, tube-ways, and other systems that interconnect with neighboring buildings—many of those can seal off in the event of a disaster."

Kathera jumped over a puddle. "Those, along with some other innovations, act together to increase the city's overall structural strength and integrity. And they disperse and absorb energy more quickly."

James, who was bringing up the rear, yelped when three fur-covered creatures, the size of small bobcats, leaped out of two black cracks in the wall and walloped him to the ground. After thousands of hours of martial arts training, his body instinctively reacted. One hand broke his fall while his body twisted to redirect the energy flow. One creature was tossed across the passage, and the other two lost their grip. In the next second James was back on his feet.

At the sound of his brother's yelp, Casey wheeled around to see the victim of James's toss tumble towards him. The scraggly creature rolled to all four feet and saw Casey. It reared back on its hind legs, bared long, uneven teeth, and let out a chortled hiss. In the next instant its lifeless body was flying back across the passage where it collapsed in a heap against the wall. Casey repositioned his metal bar to whack the next creature that got too close.

The other two creatures stopped, snarling but less certain of their prey. Their noses turned up, and sharp teeth drooled a frothy foam in their hesitation. The pause cost them. Casey's rod pounced forward and broke the back of one, and James's rod smacked the other's head.

Heather came behind Casey, a moment too late to render any assistance. Amnor and Kathera turned in time to see the two creatures fall lifeless to the ground.

Casey nodded at his brother. "You okay?"

"Yeah," replied James. "But," he added with a sly smile, "I could've taken them."

"Sure you could," Casey said. "But I can't let you have all the fun." His tone turned serious. "How'd we miss them? Looks like they were waiting in ambush."

"We're not on Earth, and we're out of our normal element. Not to mention those things probably have some natural advantages in this darkness."

Heather turned to Kathera. "What are those things?"

The creatures were slumped in small furry heaps. Their heads were elongated, opossum-like, ending in a dirty, pointed nose with star-like feelers. Several pointed teeth still snarled in lifeless grimaces. Small black eyes were set back in dark sockets. The fur was short and matted, varying in color from muddy brown to mottled gray and burnt auburn.

Kathera's eyebrows rose in admiration. "You have great reflexes to hit a kraz."

Heather stepped near James and assessed the small tears in his shirt. "Doesn't look like they bit you. Maybe some scratches, but I can't tell for sure."

"If that's the case, you should be okay after any scratches or cuts are cleaned," said Kathera. "They're not the cleanest of creatures, especially down here. But their bites are usually necrotizing, as their saliva is mildly poisonous."

While Kathera talked, James squinted his eyes to focus on a spot farther along the passage, where two silver dots reflected light. He nodded down the passage. "Looks like there may be more of them."

Kathera glanced in the direction James indicated. "Probably. I've heard they hunt in packs. James, are you good to go? We're not far from the spaceport."

James nodded while he examined where the kraz tore his shirt. "Is there anything else we should be on guard for?"

"I don't think there's much." Kathera started walking down the passage again. "Although I'm not really sure. There are some underground animals that have adapted to the tunnels over the centuries. And there are the exiles, some of whom are descendants of survivors of the old cities."

"You mean some human mutants?" asked Heather.

Kathera chuckled. "No. Not really, though some have adaptations, like hearing or sight better suited for low-light conditions. Most of the exiles are people who escaped the city, for one reason or another, usually to evade the reach of law enforcement. Should you encounter any of the non-human races—you may have seen some in the council—they'll be far more different-looking than any of the exiles. Mostly the exiles look normal."

Casey's eyes darted along the walls, searching for hiding places. "How do they survive down here?"

"They have their own city, if you want to call it that. I've heard they have water reservoirs, places to grow food, and they're not opposed to harvesting things from on top if the need is there," said Kathera. She stopped at a conduit intersection where some old graffiti-like markings faded into the wall. Her light grew brighter while she examined the markings for a few seconds. "Less than fifteen minutes and we should be under the spaceport. And from this direction we should be coming in under the military side." She turned and continued down the passageway.

Casey squinted down the passage ahead. Where the darkness swallowed the edge of light, a pair of silver dots reflected the light and scurried away. Casey shuddered. "It feels like we're being watched."

Kathera stopped, turned around, and cocked her head at Casey. "What do you think is watching us?"

"It's a figure of speech," explained Casey. "Meaning I think my imagination is playing with me."

Kathera nodded and continued leading the group along the passage. "We say basically the same thing. However, you may be actually sensing something down here, besides the apparent lone kraz ahead."

"How is it you know where to go?" asked James. "I haven't seen much of those old markings on the walls."

"As I've mentioned before, I've been down here a few times, though it's been a few years since my last visit. Besides the markings, like you saw, there are some coded clues as well. It's a system used by the exiles and shared with a few others by those who left the underground."

They passed through an intersection and continued straight. The next passage narrowed, and colored mineral deposits stained the walls. At the next intersections Kathera turned right and then left. Ahead of them rocks and debris filled the tunnel. Kathera's pace quickened and then stopped at the filled tunnel. Her head shook while she took in the completely obstructed passage. Her words were barely audible, and her voice drooped with discouragement. "So, close."

"How close?" asked Heather.

"Only a couple of sections, maybe five minutes."

James stepped up to the rubble. "Can we dig through it?"

Amnor shook his head at the rubble, and his hands rose in emphasis. "It'd take too long, and it likely fills the passage for some distance."

"But," said Casey, "I'm guessing there's another way."

Kathera nodded slowly. "There are a couple more. The next option will take more time to navigate..." Her voice trailed off.

"And?" probed James.

"And it skirts the edge of the exiles' city."

"And that's bad?" asked Heather.

"Only if they don't know you're coming, or they don't want you to be there. I don't have any connections with them. All that I know about them, including their signs in the passages, was taught to me by non-exiles. We'll go back a few intersections, where there's another passage." She paused and stared into the dark tunnel. "But it's vital we stay as quiet as possible. The exiles don't know we're here. And, if they did, they probably wouldn't appreciate us leading imperial law down to one of the entrances."

Kathera led them back a couple of intersections, turned right, and continued straight for several minutes. She passed through two more intersections before she slowed and stopped. Her hopeful expression was replaced with a frown.

Rock, dirt, and debris filled the passageway ahead. Unlike the previous obstruction, the trails left by rolling rocks had not begun to be covered by dust.

Casey watched while Kathera's light desperately shot into dark corners, cracks, and recesses. "I take it this isn't good," he said.

Chapter Thirty-Six
Backtrack

KATHERA WAS SILENT WHILE her penlight probed into dark spots, and she climbed part of the debris pile.

"When a woman doesn't answer right away, it's usually a bad sign," whispered Amnor to Casey.

"What's that supposed to mean?" said Heather.

Amnor's palms rose defensively. "Just that if things are good, women usually answer right away. If they have to think about it, they're either trying to think of way to not hurt your feelings, or things are so bad there's nothing left to say."

"Guys'll do that too," said James.

"Yeah," said Amnor, "but men are usually more direct in their answers."

"Will you be quiet?" hissed Kathera as she slid down the rockslide.

There was instant silence.

Kathera continued, her voice low, "This collapse is recent. I was hoping we could dig through. But I can't find anything to indicate how far we'd need to dig. It may only be a short distance or go on until the next section."

"So, what're our options now?" asked Casey.

Kathera's head raised, and her eyes closed momentarily. "The safest would be to backtrack to the underground entrance we came in, and then continue in the opposite direction for a couple sections. As long as the markings are still visible, I can take us the long way to another access into the spaceport." Her head lowered, and her left fingertips rubbed around her temple. "The problem is that access is not only farther away, but it goes to the public section of the spaceport, not the imperial side, which isn't where your ship is. So we'd still need to find a way to the government side."

Casey took a half-step towards Kathera, uncertain what he could say to counter the anxiety building in her. "You've gotten us this far, which we couldn't have done without you. Are there any other options?"

"Besides going back and trying from the surface side," added James.

Kathera's eyes closed again. After a slow inhale and exhale, she said, "It'd be risky, and dangerous."

"Couldn't be much worse than going back to the surface with the law waiting for us," said James.

"And," said Kathera, "I've never heard of it attempted."

Casey's brows furrowed. "What exactly is the option?"

"There are tunnels all over and under this place. I've heard there are lower passageways, but they go under or through exile territory. Something like an old transport tunnel that goes to the far end, the imperial side, of the spaceport."

"I think we should take the safer route," said Heather, anxiety adding a pitch of her voice. "We've already lost time and probably our connection with Amnor's contact. It sounds like the longer route will get us to the spaceport, if we avoid getting caught. We can figure out how to get to our ship once we know how things stand. Or maybe we can find an alternate route and try another time."

"Might be more of a challenge trying to get from the public side to the imperial side," said Amnor. "Especially considering all the excitement we've stirred up. Going farther down is preferable and could save a lot of time, particularly if it gets us to the imperial side."

"If I misread some marking, we might get lost and die in the deep underground," said Kathera. "Or end up as food for the kraz or something else. Or we might just get killed by the exiles since they're not expecting us. At least by staying out of their domain we're less likely to have any unpleasant encounters with them. Returning to the surface side may be the better option. There are ways to reduce detection on the surface, and I have contacts who can help. Maybe Amnor's contact would be willing to try again. It'll definitely take longer, but Heather's right that it's probably the safer option."

James faced his brother. "Captain, looks like this is your decision. I'm with Amnor and think we should try to cut some time off by going through the exile's territory. None of us wants to stay in these tunnels any longer than necessary. And I'm not keen on going through the public section of a spaceport."

The corners of Casey's mouth drooped. "You know I don't like to make decisions. I like the shorter, probably more direct route. But there's a lot of uncertainty. Seems like the exiles are a big unknown and probably best to avoid. Maybe we can get some help getting through the spaceport. I want the odds to favor all of us getting out of here and off this planet, so I think the safer option is the best. Kathera, which way do we go?"

James's mouth thinned, but he nodded. Next to him, Heather breathed a sigh of relief.

Kathera pointed back the way they'd come. "I haven't seen any markings for a surface exit, so we'll just backtrack to where we came in and then head the other direction. There should be a surface exit within a section or two."

Kathera started heading back along the passageways. When they turned into one of the earlier passages, Casey thought he saw a faint glow, dim at the distant end of the passage. Although it seemed far away, Casey knew darkness played tricks with depth perception. Something odd about the glow caused Casey to stop. Behind him, James stopped.

Kathera turned to look back when the sound of the group's footfalls changed. Seeing that Casey had stopped, she paused. Uncertain what was happening, Heather and Amnor also paused.

Casey pointed further down the passage. Kathera followed Casey's gaze and shook her head. "What is it?"

Casey squinted. "I thought I saw a light ahead, and some movement. But whatever it was, it's gone now."

The uneasiness bit into Casey like a cold chill. It had only been a blur, easily dismissed as fatigued eyesight. But he was certain something had crossed through a light speck, before it was smudged out. A shiver raced up his spine. *Something's not right*, he thought.

"I don't see anything," said Kathera, starting forward, "but let's be extra cautious. Unless we want to try our hand with the exiles, we need to keep going. I didn't mention this, but the exiles do have the occasional patrols out."

Amnor started after Kathera. Heather looked at the brothers at the end of the short line. James's body swayed forward, wanting to continue, but his feet remained planted while he watched his brother. Casey was still, his eyes still fixated on the point beyond the reach of their lights. Heather took a couple steps while she turned, and then stifled a cry of pain as she stumbled to the ground. Immediately Kathera's light shot to Heather, where she was partially crumpled on the ground. A small, guilty hole darkened the passage floor near

Heather where she rubbed her right ankle. Casey and James squatted down by her.

"Are you okay?" asked James.

Heather gave a soft laugh. "Aside from feeling a little dumb, I'm okay. My ankle twisted in that hole. Guess I'm getting a little tired."

"Maybe we should take a minute to rest while we're still in somewhat familiar territory," suggested Amnor.

Heather's tongue smacked lightly. "Wish we had some water."

Silent nods showed their mutual agreement.

Instantly, James was on his feet, and his eyes scanned the passage ahead. "What was that?" he whispered. His left fingers flexed around the metal bar while his right gripped the handgun.

"What?" asked Amnor.

"Shhh!" hissed Kathera as she strained her ears. "I heard something too."

Breathing stopped. Ears focused. Kathera took a cautious step down the passage. She held her light high, and a high-intensity spot shot down the tunnel. The edge of the light was lost in the distant darkness.

Every hair on Casey's body pricked. A multitude of clicking, muffled at first, began to build in his ears. He stood, eyes narrowing. "Something's coming."

There was a tremor in Heather's voice. "Kathera, what's that clicking sound?"

"I...I don't know," replied Kathera, her voice etched with fear. "I don't know much of what lives down here, and I've never heard anything like that." She took another step, trying to see better.

In the distance, at the edge of the light, the ground seemed to move with shiny black splinters that flooded the passage floor. The glimmering black objects quickly rushed towards the group, and the clicking intensified.

"What are—" started James.

"*Run!*" shouted Kathera. She reversed course and sprinted through the group in the direction they had just come from. "Quick! Follow me."

Casey's hand was instantly down and grasping Heather's to help her up. Amnor ran after Kathera. Heather's grip tightened on Casey's as her limp began to speed up. Behind them, James followed while dividing his attention between their flight and pursuers. Kathera's light was bright enough that it illuminated both the passage in front and behind the group. Chasing after them, the black objects roiled across the passage floor like angry black water, which was quickly gaining ground.

But it wasn't liquid. The light revealed an army of thousands of large beetle-like creatures armored in shiny, jet-black exoskeletons. Each stood several inches high and gnashed large pincers that protruded from elongated heads. The fluid-like movement of the horde continued to gain on the fleeing group.

Casey risked a backwards glance and saw James pause for a couple seconds, a gun in one hand and metal bar in the other. A hundred feet ahead of the rushing horde were a dozen faster beetles sprinting towards James, their pincers snapping together in eager anticipation. Their excitement was short-lived when several plasma bursts bolted through the air and burned through six exoskeletons, leaving behind charred remains. Seven beetles reached James, and his bar quickly knocked the heads off four and launched the bodies of the remaining three vanguard back into the oncoming rush. He then sprinted after the others.

Behind them, the advancing horde rapidly overtook the fallen beetles, and its forward progression paused only a fraction of a second while the remains were devoured.

Beside him, Casey realized Heather was moving easier and faster, though he could not tell if it was because the pain had subsided, or if the threat of the beetle army provided motivation. Ahead of them, Amnor and Kathera waited at an intersection.

When they reached Kathera, she urgently motioned Casey and Heather to continue through. With the light illuminating the passage for another hundred feet, Casey and Heather ran on. When James reached the intersection a couple seconds later, he, Kathera, and Amnor raced after Casey and Heather.

Ahead of them the passage began curving to the left. Casey and Heather approached the point where Kathera's light was effectively cut short by the curved walls. He rounded the bend with Heather close behind him, and several shadows materialized from the walls. One of the silhouettes pointed something at Casey, and a brilliant white-blue burst of light bolted through the air a second later. Flinging up his arms, Casey had only thought about shading his eyes when searing pain ripped into him.

His insides felt like they were shattering from the heat, and his eyesight fogged like the tunnel had filled with smoke. He felt stuck in slow motion as he stumbled backwards and slumped to the ground. A hard, cool surface slapped his back. Next to him Heather screamed something, but his ears throbbed, and the world was silent. His eyesight darkened, but the tunnel felt brighter. Murky silhouettes gathered around him and Heather in apparent confusion. A half second later, he dimly saw Kathera, Amnor, and James round the bend. One of the dark, blurred shadows lifted a long object and then lowered it.

The silence lessened, and Casey deciphered a gruff question, "Kathera? Is that you?"

While Casey's sight faded to black, his consciousness slipping away, he heard Kathera's response, "Anderik?"

Chapter Thirty-Seven

Recovery

THE POUNDING IN CASEY'S head reverberated in sync with his heartbeat. Except for the throbbing, he didn't feel anything. *Am I on my back?* Even his thoughts felt unsure, like all his senses were frozen, stuck in a fuzzy feedback loop. The smells of the underground were gone, replaced by fresher air that was tainted with smoke. Something seemed to be in his mouth, but his tongue refused to move, and he could not taste anything. He was not sure if his eyes were closed or if it was pitch black. Everything felt still, except the drum of his heart and synchronized head throb told him he was not in a timeless void. He tried to center himself for deep breathing and meditation, but felt lost, unable to feel his diaphragm, stomach, or lungs move with any air flow. The pounding in his head demanded attention. He tried to detach himself from the throb when a *thump-thump* started in his ears.

Slowly, the fuzzy head fog lifted, and the throb dropped into his chest where he could now feel a burning sensation when his lungs inhaled and exhaled. The ribs in his chest felt like he had been kicked by a horse. He realized his eyes were gripped shut, like some external force had pulled the eyelids closed. Instantly his nose was assaulted with pungent body odors, and he wished for his previous ignorant state.

Sounds? Casey thought. The thumping in his ears was subsiding, and he was sure he heard what sounded like whispering underwater.

He focused his mind on the sounds, but pain thwarted his efforts while his senses restarted. It felt like every muscle had been ripped off the bones. Moisture pooled in the corners of his eyes. He wanted to cry out, but his tongue was stuck in a dry mouth.

Silence returned, and time had no meaning. Seconds or days could have passed, and they would have felt the same. Numbness replaced the pain, and his regular feeling returned. He could feel that he was on his back, lying on a firm foam-like surface. Light began to filter through his eyelids. After an unknown time, the whispering returned, and shadows moved across the filtered light.

"Are you sure he's okay?"

The feminine voice sounded familiar, although Casey could not place it.

A deeper, unfamiliar voice responded. "Miraculously, yes."

The first voice continued, a hopeful gleam in its question. "How long is he going to be out?"

"Lady," the deep voice said, "I don't know. I didn't know anyone could survive a plasma bolt to the chest, especially at point-blank range. If I hadn't seen it myself, I wouldn't believe it. He should be dead. And have a hole burned through his chest. But if Dr. Phaelun says he will recover, I can't argue with that."

Casey tried to force his eyelids open, to blink. A momentary flash of light caused his eyes to squeeze tight in response. He held the eyelids shut, feeling their sensation, and then slowly focused on opening them. The muted light blurred momentarily, and then the eyes involuntarily shut again.

"He's waking up!" exclaimed the first voice.

Casey's eyes refused to open, fearful of the bright light, so his focus shifted to the sounds. The words seemed to be confined to a small space, and he guessed he was in a room. Through the eyelids, a single light source mocked his attempts to see. He turned his head slightly, away from the light, and painful muscles screamed through his neck and down the spine. His tongue broke loose as saliva returned to his mouth.

Casey croaked out, "Am I dead?"

"Not yet you're not," the gruff voice said in amazement. Casey thought it sounded like the person's head was shaking. "Though you probably wish you were."

"Being dead," said Casey, his eyes tightly closed, "would probably feel better."

"But I'm glad you're not," said the female voice.

With great effort, Casey pried his eyelids open, and they blinked several times in response. A hand squeezed his. His vision cleared; Heather was standing by him. Worry lines that had creased her forehead were beginning to soften. He tried to squeeze her hand in reply, to let her know he was okay, but only his fingers twitched.

A broad-shouldered man stepped near, and his dark eyes, shadowed in the room's scarce light, examined Casey. His head shook in disbelief while his deep voice said, "You are one lucky man."

Casey squinted as he tried to focus on the man. "I'm still not seeing very well. What happened?"

"You shouldn't be seeing at all, or even be alive, that's what happened," the man said incredulously. "Though I should probably apologize for what happened. Most unexpected visitors are unwelcome. And many are shot on sight, particularly if there's suspicion they may have any imperial connections."

Casey's muscles tightened.

"All of your friends are okay," the man added reassuringly. "Good thing Kathera stepped in view when she did or someone else might've been shot."

"Kathera?" asked Casey.

A blur detached itself from the wall and walked over to Casey. As it approached it coalesced into Kathera.

"I am so sorry, Casey," lamented Kathera. "If I'd been in front this may not have happened. But I've never been in these sections before, and that horde freaked me out. Though if it wasn't for those creatures, I may not have found the courage to go down that passage."

Casey blinked several times. His tear-moistened eyes were processing images more clearly. Another blur stepped from the nearby blackness, and he recognized his brother.

"Good thing you decided to stick around," said James. "I doubt any of us could fly the ship as well as you do. So, we kind of need you to help get us home."

Casey tried to smile. "Is that all you care about?"

"That, and... I'm not sure what I'd tell Mom. I don't think she'd believe me if I told her you'd been killed by a plasma bolt on the other side of the galaxy while we were escaping from an emperor set on conquering all the known civilizations."

The deep-voiced man stepped closer and bent down to study Casey's face and clothing. "Allow me to better explain. While we do shoot unwelcome visitors, we also try to make sure who it is before we shoot, just to be sure we don't kill one of our own. Your running around that bend surprised our scouting party. We were just getting back from checking out an earlier sentry report of suspicious activity. Sometimes we get runaways making their way down here. Most of the time its imperial troops trying to locate our city."

A younger man approached the crowded bedside. He fidgeted, and his eyes, relieved but uncertain, refused to look at Casey when he spoke. "I'm sorry I shot you. As Anderik said, we just got back when you came running like a mad man. With the warnings Anderik told us about unexpected activity, I thought we were being attacked and reacted."

"And thankfully," continued Kathera, "I came around the corner and my uncle recognized me."

"It's actually a good thing you showed up when you did," said Anderik. "In a way, we kind of owe you."

"For what?" asked Casey. "Shooting me?"

Anderik's head shook. "No. If it wasn't for you coming, and Kathera's subsequent warning, we would have lost a lot more people to that horde."

"When Kathera and Anderik got over their surprise," said James, "she told him about those beetle things. You should've seen how quickly they called for backup, and then those beetle things arrived. It was not a pretty sight, and it wasn't going well until the backup arrived. There were just too many to shoot, and those creatures were pushing forward like an unstoppable wave. Two of Anderik's men were overrun while we retreated down the passage.

"The backup brought flame-thrower devices that torched hundreds of those piranha-like critters at a time. Be glad you were unconscious for that smell! After the main threat was taken care of, they dispatched scouting parties to find the creatures that had escaped, and to check on some remote sentries who hadn't reported in."

"Apparently, every five to seven years or so those creatures increase in number enough to create these large army-like hordes," said Kathera. "It'd been more than seven years since the last attack. When the scouting parties returned, they informed us the outer perimeter sentries were apparently caught off guard and couldn't get off a warning to the city before they were overrun. If we hadn't been there to give Anderik the warning, hundreds of exiles could've been killed."

Casey rolled his body to the side, and his jaw clenched when a painful jolt shot up back. "How long have I been here?"

"Now there's another crazy thing." Anderik's head shook again. "Not only did you survive a plasma bolt at extreme close range, you haven't had any recovery time. And now you're already wanting to go!"

"It's been less than an hour since the attack," said Heather.

"Feels like days," said Casey.

"Well, I suggest you rest," said Anderik. "I have some work to do. New sentries need to be sent to the outer perimeters and replace the temporary ones left by the scouting parties. Heather can help you with whatever you need. Kathera, James, and Amnor, I can still use your help. Casey, I'll check back later."

Anderik headed out of the room, followed by the younger exile.

"Well, bro," started James, "when the doc said you weren't going to get worse, she also said you'd probably be out for a couple days. As you heard, Anderik needs some help." James moved towards the open doorway, stopped, and turned back to his brother. "I'm glad you're still with us."

James and Kathera walked out the doorway after Anderik. Amnor materialized from the shadows on the wall and followed the others.

Heather gingerly let go of Casey's hand. "I'll get you some water and maybe something to eat."

"Water would be great. My tongue keeps sticking. I don't think I'm up to food yet."

Heather left, and the room was quiet. With his eyesight cleared, Casey took a look around. From the orange-yellow light source that hung from the ceiling he could see that the small room contained the bed he was on and a chair. The cement-like walls were all bare, and there was only a single door. He could hear some distant talking, echoing softly through the hallways.

Casey closed his eyes. What seemed a moment later, someone squeezed his hand. His eyes opened to see Heather looking down at him. Her concerned brow lines melted back into relief.

"How long have you been here?" Casey asked.

"Less than a minute. I wasn't sure if you were out or not."

Heather offered him a cup of water. His arm moved his hand, but the fingers failed to fully grip the cup. Heather tipped the cup to his mouth, and he sipped. Immediately Casey's tongue felt normal and free.

"I'm curious," said Casey after a few sips, "was the plasma gun set on stun or something?"

The corners of Heather's mouth frowned. "I wish that were the case. It'd explain some things. But those guns don't have a stun setting."

She cocked her head to the side while she tried to figure out how to say something. "Casey...you really shouldn't be alive. Anderik wasn't kidding or just trying to make you feel good. You were hit point-blank by a very high-powered plasma burst. Which I know doesn't mean much to us. But you remember those pirates who got blown apart on that first planet—or moon—we visited?"

Casey nodded. It was an image he was not going to forget.

"The plasma blast from the particular rifle that shot you was similar in power to those. You should have a charred hole through your chest and torso instead of just burned clothing."

It took a moment for her words to sink in. "Must've been a different weapon. Or maybe it had a malfunction."

Heather shook her head again. "That was something they considered after you were discovered to be alive. They were worried maybe the gun was malfunctioning or not powering up as well. But then they realized it had been used against the beetles with devastation. They tested it again, and there wasn't much left of those targets."

Casey was trying to mentally digest what he was being told.

"Back in the passage, Anderik insisted we leave your body because he thought you were dead, and we needed to leave quickly, before the horde arrived. He didn't believe me when I told him you were alive, especially since your shirt was burned and smoking."

"Guess it was more of a shock to them," Casey joked.

Heather gave him a courtesy smile, then added in a quiet voice, "Casey, what happened to you is so unlikely that nobody here has ever seen it before. At first Anderik thought you must've had some kind of portable shielding. Apparently, he's the only one who has even heard of the possibility of someone surviving a plasma bolt to the chest and said it may be a unique gift."

Heather's hazel eyes watched Casey slowly move. "How do you really feel?" she asked.

"It was a lot worse earlier, before I opened my eyes. I'm aching and can hardly move without something hurting, like sore muscles a day after an intense workout. But if it really was a plasma burst, I guess it's a miracle I'm alive. It's interesting that Anderik mentioned a 'gift.' Kathera used that word before as well, although I think she was referring to some of the premonitions or intuition that I sometimes get." He paused, then added, "And sometimes ignore. I wonder why I didn't get one before running into the blast?"

"Maybe you were too preoccupied to notice it," suggested Heather. "You were helping me, and we did have an army of flesh-eating beetles chasing after us."

"True."

"And I don't think you ignore things as much as you think. I think you probably subconsciously use your intuition, gut reaction, feelings—whatever you want to call it—to prepare yourself, and then you do what you feel is right."

"Could be. But I should be more cautious before I get someone killed. And I hope I'm not running out of lives. As for a 'gift' for surviving plasma bursts, I really don't want to put that to the test again."

Heather lifted a plate with a small loaf of bread and a sliced brown root. "I brought some food as well. Interested?"

Casey slowly shook his head. "My insides don't feel ready for anything, although the water's good."

Heather moved to help him drink, but he shook his head. "I think I can probably do it myself now. Just need to sit up."

When Casey sat up, a lightweight blanket fell off his chest into a pile on his lap. Charred fabric, the remains of his shirt, hung around his torso in tattered strips and broke apart when he moved. Under the blackened strips, shades of purple, blue, and black were quickly fading into his skin while the memory of the lightning strike years ago burned in his mind.

Heather offered the metal cup to Casey. "You okay?"

He took the cup and slowly sipped. His eyes closed, relishing the cool water against his parched throat. "Who's Anderik?"

"You probably got this much: he's Kathera's uncle. And, as it happens, Amnor's uncle as well, although their relationship isn't warm. From what I understood, after Kathera's father was killed several years ago, Anderik disappeared. Kathera didn't know what happened to him, and assumed he'd been secretly assassinated. Turns out he did escape an assassination attempt and came down here, where he became the leader of the exiles after a few years."

Casey listened while Heather related to him the little bit she had learned about the exile community. He was surprised there were more than ten thousand living in the old city, spread across different underground levels. She explained that many of the exiles frequently went to the surface, usually in disguise to avoid patrols, and seldom higher than ground level. She also told him there were large rooms with underground farms and water reservoirs.

"What about those beetle things?"

"Nobody knows much about them. They're a carnivorous insect and their population goes through busts and booms. Most of the time the bugs just eat other subterranean creatures. Apparently they can go weeks, or maybe even months, without eating. Every several years or so they become so numerous they raid where they can. There have been times when a beetle horde has devoured hundreds of exiles before the onslaught is turned back.

"As you heard, it's been over seven years since the last attack. The slight advance notice the exiles got today was just enough to mobilize reinforcements before the horde found the city. What we didn't know was the horde wasn't just in the one passage, but flooding through multiple tunnels. The exiles knew that from past experiences and were able to get the other passageways protected. Anderik estimates the horde was probably over a half-million, spread over several passageways and levels. His people didn't get all of them—they never do—but they got a lot. Had they not gotten the heads-up, the horde could have eaten over a thousand of the exiles if they had broken into the various living areas."

"Sounds like it was good we came." Casey slowly reclined back onto the bed. "On a different subject, do we know anything about the *Fallen Star*?"

"Anderik had heard some rumors of the ship but dismissed them. With our arrival, he got some reports in. Nobody has seen the ship, but it was confirmed that imperial guards are guarding a vacant landing pad. They also seem to be relaxing their searches a bit. Anderik thinks they might believe we didn't survive the underground. Some of the horde cleanup crew found imperial shielding, armor, and weapons near an underground entrance. The guess is several soldiers got swept up and killed by the horde. It sounds like they came in the same way we did, but the room was sealed off from the outside. Probably to keep the beetles from getting out."

"So we're not going out the way we came in."

"Not unless we want to dig out. But the good news is the passage through the exile's city to the imperial side of the space port is available."

"That's great. We should be going then."

Heather's head tilted. "I don't think that's a good idea for you. Anderik said if you actually survived, you'd probably need a month or more to recover."

Casey rotated his body and swung his legs over the edge of the bed.

"Of course," continued Heather, "you do seem to be healing more quickly. But I don't think you should push yourself."

Casey felt a little light-headed. "Can I get some more water?" he asked, holding out the empty cup.

Heather filled the cup, and Casey took a minute to savor the water while it trickled down his throat.

"Maybe you should lay back down," suggested Heather. "You look a bit pale."

Casey nodded. He slowly laid back down and closed his eyes.

"I'll be back in a few minutes with more water," said Heather.

"Thank you."

———•———

When Heather returned, Casey had not moved. His chest moved up and down in peaceful slumber. She smiled and gently pulled the light blanket back over him and left the room.

Chapter Thirty-Eight

Emergency

"**F**OR THE TENTH TIME, I'm feeling great."

Casey's patience was being tested with the continual interrogation about how well he felt. Other than charred shirt remnants clinging to his torso, and cheeks warmed from his insistence, he felt normal.

James, Kathera, and Anderik stood around his bed while the doctor finished her examination. Amnor stood several feet away, seemingly preoccupied with something in his hands. Heather appeared in the doorway and braced herself against the frame.

Dr. Phaelun, a middle-aged woman with gray-blonde hair and medium build, was on the left of Casey's bed. She tucked varied electronic and mechanical devices into a beat-up, black leather bag. "I can't find anything wrong with him." She shrugged. "Except that he says a few muscles are sore. And he needs a new shirt."

Anderik's forehead creased. "Dr. Phaelun, are you sure? You know he was struck in the chest by a plasma rifle just hours ago. You saw him when we brought him in."

The doctor closed up her bag, and her observant eyes pierced into Anderik's. "I know that only because I personally saw it. But it might as well have been a kid's robus gun because there's nothing indicating any external or internal injury, except for the burned clothing. From what I can tell, he's in excellent condition."

Kathera lifted a hand to her mouth to conceal her smile at the woman's comment.

Heather entered the room. "Good morning. At least, I guess it's morning. You okay, Casey?"

Dr. Phaelun's brown eyes turned to Heather and quickly assessed her. "Rest certainly helped you. Looks like your ankle is better. Your friend here is quite the healer. You probably remember I saw him when you brought him in. I didn't tell you this at that time, but when I heard what happened I thought he wouldn't survive the hour. Now?" She shook her head. "Except for his shirt, I'd never believe he'd been shot in the chest by a plasma bolt, not to mention by a high-power attack rifle at extreme close range. And the security recordings confirm it was a full-power, direct hit."

Heather's head bowed graciously. "Thank you for checking on him."

Dr. Phaelun nodded, lifted her bag, and walked to the door. She paused at the doorframe and turned momentarily to face Anderik. "I have others to check on, from the horde attack. If you happen to need me, call."

Anderik nodded, and the doctor hurried on her way.

Heather walked to the bed and noticed the bruising on Casey's chest and torso were gone. "How long have you been up?"

Anderik answered. "Since well before breakfast. About four hours." Anderik motioned to a dark-haired exile in the room. "Ja'ara found him wandering with the blanket wrapped around him and brought him back here. After Casey's breakfast, the doctor finally had time to come check on him."

"Four hours!" Heather shot an accusing glance at James. "So after I helped you guys for a couple hours, I slept for nearly ten hours straight! And nobody bothered to wake me?"

"We tried." James shrugged. "But you were really out, so we let you sleep."

"Before the doctor came," said Kathera, "we were talking with Anderik about options for returning to the ship. He thinks we should wait a few days, mostly to let things settle down above. James wants to go tomorrow morning, to give Casey another day." Her right hand motioned at Casey. "But Casey wants to go now."

"I keep telling you," Casey insisted, "I'm good to go."

Heather studied Kathera and asked, "What do you think?"

The focus of Kathera's eyes shifted around the room. "If Casey's ready to go, maybe we should. But it'd probably be better to wait until tomorrow, just to be certain."

"My surface sources say the palace guard and military are stepping down their search," said Anderik. "Security is still high, but it's widely believed that non-exiles can't last more than a day in the underground. I think Casey needs more time to heal. It's hard to believe he's as well as he claims, even if the doc verified it. Besides, it'll also take at least a day to work out a suitable plan to get you to your ship."

"Amnor, what do you think?" asked Heather.

Amnor shrugged. "The biggest hurry is to warn the Rayneiri about the assassination plot. If it weren't for that, some recovery time would be good for all of us."

"Heather"—Casey's right brow rose at his friend—"what do you think?"

Heather bit her bottom lip lightly before she answered. "I think another day, maybe two, would be beneficial. From what everyone has said, and what I saw, you shouldn't be alive." A quick shiver raced up her back. "We have no idea if there are any side-effects."

Casey's hope surrendered. "Okay. So the crew thinks the captain isn't fit for command. Then let's plan on leaving tomorrow, but on one condition. Let's get our supplies together today, as soon as possible, so we're not delayed tomorrow."

James smiled and nodded once. "Agreed. What about you, Heather?"

Heather hesitated, and her eyes seemed unfocused, like she was lost in a memory. A shudder shook her shoulders, and her face paled.

"Heather? You okay?" Casey asked.

Heather forced a smile. "I'm good. Just thinking you probably need more rest to get fully recovered. But Amnor's right, even if he hasn't told us much about the assassination plot."

"It's safer the fewer who know," said Amnor.

Heather nodded. "Anderik, from what Amnor's said, the assassin is already among the Rayneiri and it's a matter of days before the plan is executed."

Amnor's mouth was a grim line. "That is correct. Simply put, the plot is to kill the Rayneiri emperor and his family. The assassination will happen within the walls of the palace, and it's expected to happen within five days from now."

"Five days?" exclaimed Anderik. "There's no way you can get to the Rayneiri in five days. The normal transports and jump gates would take you at least fifteen. Probably more like twenty, or more, if you get held up at checkpoints without the right documentation. You'd be better off trying to get a secure quantira interlink to warn them."

Amnor shook his head and frowned. "We could, but it'd be intercepted. And there's no guarantee the message would get delivered.

The other factor is an invasion planned for less than a month after the assassination. The plan being to strike while the Rayneiri are still squabbling over who should rule and before whoever takes over can consolidate power."

Anderik's left hand stroked his chin. "My surface contacts have recently reported the arrival of several battle carriers. Those usually only come for military drills, or"—he glanced at Amnor—"a military operation." He turned to James and Casey, shaking his head as if he'd caught two boys in a lie. "Are you claiming your ship can take you to the Rayneiri in five days?"

Casey shifted on the bed and nodded. "I'm not sure exactly how long it will take, but based on our previous jumps through space, it will be less than five days."

Anderik's eyes widened in disbelief.

James snorted. "Don't be so modest, Casey. You told us we came across the galaxy in a matter of minutes. Five days'll give us plenty of time, provided we can get the ship."

The jaws of Amnor, Anderik, and Ja'ara dropped at James's statement. James's cheeks reddened, realizing he'd probably said too much.

"From what I've heard," said Amnor, "the supposed capability of the ship was closer to what Casey stated. But, if what James said is accurate, it's a good thing you didn't let the emperor know the truth."

"Well, if that is truly the case," said Anderik, "you could easily wait a day or two before leaving and still have time to get your warning to the Rayneiri."

Casey's jaw set in determination. He exhaled and forced himself to relax. "I really don't think we should be delaying. Besides, the sooner we can get to the Rayneiri, the sooner we can devise a plan to find and capture the assassin."

"Fine," said Anderik, ceding the discussion. "Ja'ara will get you a shirt and some supplies. Not that you need much. He'll make sure your weapons are in order, and you can take some food and water for your journey, just in case it takes longer than you say. I'll consult with some of my officers about how we might get you to your ship on such short notice."

Within an hour, Ja'ara had helped gather supplies into small packs and provided weapons to the group. He explained that most exiles carried guns everywhere because the dangers of the underground could be surprising and unforgiving. James had strapped a short-barreled plasma rifle to his pack. Both brothers had the metal pipes they'd found earlier secured to the packs.

Ja'ara then led Casey, James, and Heather on a short tour among some of the nearby passages and large connecting rooms. He related that the city, as the exiles referred to it, was a complex network built among the old foundations and tunnels of the ancient cities. Newer tunnels and rooms were excavated over the many subsequent centuries.

Casey was admiring an extensive water storage system when he felt cold, like the warmth had drained from his face.

"You okay?" asked James, his voice etched with concern.

"Yeah," he said, his voice quiet but urgent, "but we need to find the others and leave, now."

"Are you...?" James stopped when he saw the seriousness in Casey's face. "Okay, let's go."

While they walked briskly back, Heather asked, "What is it?"

Uncertain how to explain the feeling, Casey simply shook his head. "I don't know. It feels like something's coming. We can't wait until tomorrow to leave."

When they arrived at the large commons, Kathera was sitting at a table with her uncle discussing something. Her brows rose. "I thought you'd be gone for another hour or two. Anderik's scouts haven't returned or reported in yet."

"Casey had a feeling we should leave now," said Heather. "We came back to get you and Amnor and go."

Kathera's chin dropped slightly, like words had frozen in her mouth. After a few seconds her brow smoothed, and she nodded.

Anderik opened his mouth, then shut it before saying anything. His head simply shook in reluctant disagreement as he exhaled. "There's a big problem with you leaving now. And that is we don't have any plans worked out. The scouts haven't returned yet, but I expect them within an hour. The earlier report stated the landing space was still very heavily guarded. Without a halfway decent plan, there's no way you'll get close to your ship."

"Anderik, please," said Casey, "contact any of your perimeter watches for a report."

For a second time, Anderik's mouth started to open before he simply nodded. He walked off while Casey continued, "Kathera, get Amnor and your stuff. Heather, get yours. James and I have ours, so we'll wait here for you. Get back here as soon as possible."

"Amnor's in the recreation room," said Kathera, then she and Heather darted off.

The brothers were waiting only a few minutes before Heather, Kathera, and Amnor returned, each with a small pack. Amnor also carried a plasma rifle.

A second later Anderik abruptly entered the commons, the lines on his forehead deeply furrowed, his breath short. In addition to his sidearm, a short-barreled rifle was slung across his back next to a pack and a short tube wrapped in black cloth.

"What's wrong?" asked Kathera.

"I contacted the outer perimeter guards," said Anderik between breaths. "North, east, and south all checked in without problems." He paused, uncertain if he was overreacting. "But, no response from the west."

"How often do they check in?" asked Casey.

"They're supposed to call in at each sentry change, about every six hours. In between those times, there usually isn't a set contact time. Mostly because there's rarely a problem."

"How long since the last change?" probed Casey.

"Only about five hours, which normally isn't a concern except someone should have responded."

Heather felt goosebumps on her arms. "That doesn't sound good."

"How far out are the outer perimeter sentries?" asked James.

"About ten sections out," said Anderik. "Nearly an hour's walk."

"And the inner perimeter watches?" asked Casey.

Anderik released a sigh of relief. "They all checked in."

"That's good, right?" asked Heather.

Anderik nodded. "It's good because they're five sections out, or about thirty minutes away. If anything is coming in, they haven't made it to—"

The lighting blacked out and left them in near total darkness. A few emergency lights—strategically located around the commons and nearby passageways—flickered on in a dim amber glow.

"Great," muttered Anderik.

"This happens a lot, right?" asked Kathera.

"More than we want. Usually briefly every month or two. We get a more extended outage a couple times a year. Sometimes it's caused by old equipment failure, sometimes it's the cause of an underground creature's terminal curiosity."

Heather shivered. "All the lighting made me forget how dark it is down here, until now."

James's hand was resting instinctively on the handgun strapped to his side. "How long until the power comes back on?"

"Depends on the problem and who's around to fix it," said Anderik. "Typically, it'll take up to an hour for normal lights to be restored. You may have your packs, but we still don't know how you're getting to your ship. And we're still waiting on the latest report."

From the south end of the commons, near the relaxation and recreation rooms, bright flashes scorched the near darkness. Screams shattered the darkness and were immediately silenced.

"Take cover!" shouted Anderik, diving to one side.

Brilliant flashes of red and green erupted from unseen assailants and burned through the air.

Heather lunged behind James and Casey, and they dropped behind crudely made furniture. Amid the various hues of plasma bursts, projectile fire added its percussive pops to the air, the echoes coming from all directions. More screams. In the dim light, shadows spilled in and out of the various passageways that intersected the commons area.

Handguns were out, but it was nearly impossible to distinguish friend from foe when neither could be clearly seen.

Casey tensed, his focus narrowed on a west-side opening. Next to him, Heather's eyes followed his gaze. Her throat tightened and body went rigid when an unmistakable shadow of a large dog-like creature was illuminated by flashes.

Casey mouthed to Heather, *Night Watch.* He grabbed her hand and squeezed some warmth into it. She nodded.

"Anderik," said Casey, "we need to go!"

Anderik frowned, and nodded once. Gripping the short-barreled rifle in his hands, he motioned to the east. Amid flashes of plasma erupting around the room, he sprinted towards the center passage on the east wall—a wide corridor with two rows of columns marching back into the darkness—while the others raced after him.

Chapter Thirty-Nine
Night Watch

After clearing the passage opening, Anderik motioned for them to hide behind the columns that supported the wide, arched ceiling. Behind them, smoke and dust mixed into a chaos of plasma bursts and projectiles that created a spectral fireworks show in the intermittent darkness of the commons area. On their left, five faint red orbs floated through the haze like ghostly eyeballs. Two explosions erupted behind the orbs and momentarily illuminated five trackless mini-tanks hovering into the room. Smaller than four-wheelers, several plates on their fronts angled away from an assortment of short gun barrels that rotated and pivoted.

The orbs floated purposefully into the room, their multiple red scanning beams betrayed by heavy dust. The front orb rocked in the air when it was pummeled by automatic weapon fire. A small turret on one mini-tank rotated and returned fire on the orb's attacker. Plasma bolts flared around two other orbs, and instantly three drone tanks zeroed in on the source and silenced the assault. A rocket smashed into the third orb and sent it crashing into the wall where an explosion shattered the floating sphere into shrapnel. Two tanks terminated the orb's assassin just as quickly. From the south end, seven more mini-tanks hovered over the debris as they trespassed into the common area.

The four remaining orbs and twelve drone tanks spread out across the spacious commons. While three orbs spread out, the last positioned itself in the center where its red beams scanned across the entire room. The beams crossed over the east opening with its columns, and then immediately returned to fixate on the columns. Three of the mini-tanks hovered towards the designated area.

Heather was watching the drones when a hand grabbed her arm and yanked her behind the column. The chunk of the column where she had been was disintegrated by a small explosion. Two more explosions rattled nearby columns. A fourth burst into a wall. Handguns and small rifles were out and returned fire on the small tank vehicles. Small-arms projectiles deflected off the armor, and plasma bursts dissipated in flickering arcs against energy shielding.

Shifting targets, Anderik's short rifle knocked the center orb from the air, plunging it to the floor in a wild spin.

James had holstered his handgun and was firing his plasma rifle at the mechanized hover craft. "What are those things?" he shouted over the noise.

"Imperial sentries," said Amnor. "They can be automated or controlled remotely. These look like they're governed in smaller clusters. Imperial forces are nearby because the signals can't penetrate this deep."

From the right, projectiles and plasma fired on the sentries. The mini-tanks rotated their attention to the new threat. Several sentries remained along the south side, while the remaining orbs floated around the room. From the west-side main passage, five more sentries appeared.

"Anderik," urged Casey, "it's best we don't stick around to find out what the sentries want from us."

Anderik glanced behind him, further back into the east passage. Turning to the others, he quickly gave instructions. "In case you lose me, run straight down this passage to the next city section. The passage narrows in a short distance. Keep straight until the passage ends. Take the left and go to the next intersection. That's below where you were last night. Go right and then the next left. That'll wind around to the spaceport access, which is a pipe going straight up. There's a ladder inside."

Anderik sped down the passageway and disappeared into the dark. The others were about to follow when a barrage of plasma fire blasted in from the south end of the commons, chasing after Anderik and forcing the others to keep cover.

"Not good," said James.

The three sentries formed a row and moved towards the columns, while three more sentries hovered across the commons room.

"On three, let's go before we lose our chance," said Casey.

James immediately started counting, "One. Two. Three!"

Kathera jumped from behind her column and sprinted down the passage with James, Casey, Heather, and Amnor close behind. A storm of plasma and projectile fire chased after them, ripping and tearing into columns, walls, floor, and ceiling. In less than a hundred feet the walls closed in to a thirty-foot-wide passage. They continued running.

Ahead of them a smoky haze filled an intersection, where wisps of light seemed to float around like ghostly apparitions. Flashes diffused through the dust and smoke. Three shadowed figures crossed the passage intersection. One collapsed when an orange bolt slashed through it. At the intersection, a body was sprawled on the floor, slivers of smoke rising from underneath the unmoving form. Other bodies lay twisted and littered the floor in both directions.

Kathera slowed briefly, surveyed the wider cross passage, and continued across with the others close behind. "One more...block east...then a left turn...to the north...then...next intersection," she recited between breaths. She examined the tunnel on the other side of the intersection where the amber emergency lights of the exiles' city ended and the passage narrowed by half. She spoke over her shoulder. "Get out your lights. It's going to get dark."

Before any acknowledgment, Kathera dashed into the passage. The others ran after her into the prevailing darkness. She slowed momentarily, swung her pack around, and pulled out a narrow circular band with a small crystal attached. She slipped it around her head and positioned the crystal over her forehead. A soft tap later and a light shot forward. Other headlamps were pulled out while they continued down the passage. Behind them, the reverberating sounds of the battle faded. With handguns and short-barreled rifles held ready, intermittent jogging—underscored with heavy breathing—replaced their sprint from the underground city.

Bringing up the rear, Casey paused momentarily, turned, and studied the dark passage they had just come from. James glanced back and slowed. Casey shook his head with a shrug, and they resumed their previous pace.

Several minutes passed before they reached the next intersection and turned north. Footfalls and breathing were the only sounds. By the next turning point, their pace had slowed to a walk. They turned right, and a short distance later entered the left passage. The wide passage curved to the right.

Heather's eyes strained into the darkness beyond the reach of the lights. "I wonder where Anderik is?"

"He's definitely faster than I thought," said Amnor from his position near Kathera at the front.

A minute later, Kathera, Amnor, and Heather were a couple hundred feet ahead when Casey had slowed, stopped, and whipped around. Startled by his brother's about-face, James was about to ask a question when he saw the focused intensity of Casey's gaze into the blackness. Instantly James butted the short-barreled rifle to his shoulder and joined his brother to face the blackness. The light from Casey's headlamp increased its intensity while James scrutinized the tunnel.

After several seconds, Casey glanced back again. The lights from the rest of the group glowed in the tunnel more than a hundred yards away. Heather's hand was frozen mid-stroke in brushing aside some hair. Casey's head shot back to the tunnel they had come from.

Kathera's voice trailed back. "Casey, James, what is it?"

Two large, ominous, dog-like shapes breached the limits of Casey's light. Four more, moving in pairs, followed. Armor plates covered their bodies and heads. Seeing their prey ahead of them in the tunnel, the creatures lowered their heads and pointed their noses, as if preparing battering rams, ready to run down their target.

"Night Watch," hissed Casey.

Brilliant bursts of plasma erupted from James's rifle. Casey's handgun added its response with several rounds. Multiple plasma bursts struck the two lead Night Watch. The energy arcs from James's rifle sparked around the beasts and dissipated into the ground. The handgun landed a few rounds into the lead Night Watch, but armor plates deflected the projectiles. The Night Watch slowed, moving in trained precision, as they closed the distance.

Casey shifted his aim towards a smaller target, the exposed face of a lead creature. A couple rounds later the beast's gait faltered when a projectile pierced through the opening.

Seeing the falter, James dropped his short rifle—letting it hang from the shoulder straps—and drew his handgun like a gunslinger. He fired three rounds in rapid succession at the same lead creature. The creature's movement stuttered, faltered, and then it stumbled to its knees as the rounds pierced its left eye. The dark beast toppled to its side, jerked its legs momentarily, and then became still.

Sensing a threat, the five Night Watch slowed further and varied their movement from one side of the tunnel to the other. James and Casey fired off several more rounds, and the second lead beast fell motionless to the ground. The remaining four continued closing the gap.

Behind them, Casey could hear the faint footfalls of the others running to them.

Twenty feet away from the brothers, the two front Night Watch leaped in unison. Casey ducked forward, under, and to the left of the black beast that had jumped for his head. James's movement mirrored his brother, diving forward, under, and to the right of the Night Watch that aimed for him. Claws snatched at empty space as the animals flew over.

Expecting to grapple their prey to the ground, the Night Watch misjudged their jumps and fumbled their landings. The two creatures quickly recovered their footing and pivoted back to face their adversaries. The rear two Night Watch paused, as if waiting for the two leads to position themselves.

After ducking to the sides, Casey and James spun into the center of the tunnel to stand back-to-back. Casey stared at the two Night Watch who had jumped over them and now separated the brothers from the rest of the group. James faced the other two.

A hundred feet beyond the Night Watch, Casey saw Amnor and Kathera join Heather. Their weapons were ready, but they were uncertain about shooting. He tried to track his gun on the beasts, his right index finger itching to pull the trigger, but with the beasts' erratic side-to-side movement and his friends behind them, he hesitated. He also knew if he focused too much on one beast the other might attack. Behind him James fired off a couple of test shots. James faced a similar challenge, trying to anticipate the random movements without focusing too much on one beast. Too much attention on a single Night Watch could give the other the opening to attack.

Chapter Forty
Night Blade

T HE NIGHT WATCH MOVED closer to James. Uncertain how many rounds he had left, he chose one eye to target. Several yards behind the creatures, orange-and-yellow flames flared along the length of a black sword. The two animals whipped around, and the flaming blade rushed them. The flaming sword slashed through the face of one beast, and it reared back, screeching in pain. The jaws of the second creature snapped air as the flames swooped low.

Still in the shadows, the sword's master dove between the two beasts, slashing upwards through the second beast's armor like a hot knife through butter. The animal howled as the blade seared armor into its flesh. The injured creatures lost their coordinated attack and furiously lunged and lashed at their adversary. In the headlamp beam, the attacker emerged from a roll between the Night Watch, and James saw the determined face of Anderik as he jumped to his feet.

In front of Casey, the two Night Watch shifted erratically, glancing from him to their comrades in their face-off with the swordsman. Casey desperately wanted to turn around and watch the flaming sword take on the dark creatures, but he knew the two beasts watching him were waiting for a lapse in attention. He shifted slightly backwards and to his right. In his right peripheral vision, he saw Anderik spring to his feet with the agility of a seasoned martial artist—comfortably wielding the sword like an extension of his body—and slowly back towards the brothers. A dark blur leaped from Casey's left, and he braced for impact. But the Night Watch jumped effortlessly over the brothers. James fired off two rounds that deflected off the creature's lower armor before it landed behind Anderik.

The shots came as a late warning. Anderik's focus was on the two injured Night Watch who were cautiously approaching him, and the beast's jump caught him off guard. He whipped around to face the new threat, and a Night Watch from behind him, still bleeding from its side wound, pounced. Realizing the ploy, Anderik sidestepped the pouncing beast and sliced the flaming blade up into its under armor. Flailing claws hooked Anderik's shoulder and knocked him backwards, towards the Night Watch. He whipped the sword around, and the blade flared through the armor. The creature howled madly and flailed its right forepaw. The crooked claws raked Anderik's right shoulder and sent him sprawling across the ground. The torn shoulder and impact on the ground knocked the sword from Anderik's grip, and it flew from his hand.

After James had shot at the leaping Night Watch, Casey's attention refocused on the Night Watch eying him. He tried to pin the handgun's sights on the creature's face, but its erratic movement made him hesitate, fearing he would hit Heather, Kathera, or Amnor if he missed. The Night Watch continued to shift its attention between Casey and what was happening with its comrades.

Metal rang out on Casey's left and scraped across the stone floor for a short distance. Out of the corner of his left eye, he saw a black, slightly curved, katana-like sword rocking slowly on the ground less than two yards away. The Night Watch's head lowered, and its eyes narrowed at the sword suspiciously.

Casey spun left while dropping to his knees. His left hand snatched the blade's handle as he finished the rotation. Instinctively he arced the blade into a high block as he refaced his foe, his right hand raising the handgun. The sword severed the beast's extended claws less than a foot from his chest, and it stumbled into a heap on the stumps of its forelegs. Only a few feet away, the dark creature snarled jagged teeth at Casey, and its red eyes narrowed to slits at the black blade between it and its prey. He fired off a half dozen rounds into the creature's exposed face before the gun stopped. The beast rocked its head back with the first couple rounds, twitched, and shuddered with the remaining shots. After a couple seconds it collapsed into a silent mound. From farther down the passage, he saw the others beginning to run towards him.

Casey leaped to his feet and faced his brother in time to see the Night Watch that had jumped over them collapse under a barrage of projectile rounds fired into its head. Near the fallen beast, Anderik lay sprawled on the floor, his face ghostly white.

James shifted his aim to the remaining two Night Watch, who reluctantly retreated a few paces. He fired one round before his handgun quit. He tossed the gun to the side and brought up the short rifle. "If you're done playing," he shouted to Casey, "I could use some help here!" Plasma bursts fizzled and dissipated harmlessly around the two Night Watch. His left hand reached behind him and retrieved the metal pipe from its straps.

Realizing the threat had diminished, the creatures reversed direction and stalked towards Anderik.

Casey dropped his gun and sprinted past James, his hands easily finding familiar places on the sword's handle while he closed the short distance to Anderik.

The two Night Watch snarled, bared their teeth, and bobbed their heads at the oncoming rush. One beast lunged at Casey while the second, still bleeding from its underside injuries, angled towards Anderik.

Casey sidestepped left and whipped the sword down through a curved low block to deflect the creature's paw. Targeting the second Night Watch, he lunged forward and thrust the blade into its neck. The beast jerked free of the blade's bite, stared at Casey, took a couple steps forward, then crashed lifeless next to Anderik.

Behind Casey, the remaining Night Watch yelped when James's pipe cracked against the joint above its good forepaw in a defensive parry. It limped backwards several paces, glancing at its dead comrades. Plasma bursts furiously erupted around the beast and projectiles deflected off its armor. Turning back into the passage, it disappeared into the darkness.

Amnor ran after the Night Watch, firing into the black passage. "We need to kill it before it escapes!"

"Amnor!" shouted Kathera. "It's too late. Let it go. We've got more urgent matters."

Heather stopped by James. "Maybe it won't make it."

"Maybe," said James, "but those things can sure take a beating."

Kathera ran to her uncle, who had rotated painfully to his right side. Red liquid stained his drab clothing and seeped onto the floor. Kneeling beside him, she choked back tears as her voice cracked. "We need to get you help."

A weak smile broke Anderik's whitening face. "Help you can't give. You have very little time. Even if that Night Watch doesn't return, the handlers and others will be here soon."

Casey dropped to one knee next to Anderik, grabbed his left arm, and started to help lift him. "Then all of us need to be going."

Anderik resisted, pulling back weakly with his arm. "Not me. I never planned to go with you. My place is here."

James's head shook with insistence. "Casey's right. We can't just leave you here."

Anderik wheezed. "If it's my time, I am ready."

Kathera's jaw stiffened, and she fought against quivering lips and wet eyes.

Anderik looked at his niece. "Go. Don't worry about me. I have a few tricks left." His fingers fumbled with a small gray cylindrical device he retrieved from a hidden pocket in his pants. "I'll do what I can to delay them. Your task is to save our people. Your father believed you could help bring peace to the empires." He hesitated, his eyes shifting to Casey, James, and Heather. "And maybe even to this part of the galaxy."

A knot in Kathera's throat held her response silent.

Anderik raised his brows at Casey. "You are full of surprises. I haven't seen anyone wield a Night Blade that easily since my master."

Heat flushed across Casey's cheeks.

Anderik continued between labored breaths. "Since it will better serve you than me, I will give it to you. Let me hold it one last time."

Casey gingerly presented the hilt end to Anderik and noticed the elegant blade was covered with micro curves, giving it the appearance of tiny ebony scales. He bowed respectfully out of habit.

Anderik gripped the handle, and the blade's orange-yellow flames flared momentarily. He then grasped Casey's right hand with his left and pressed the sword's handle into Casey's palm.

Anderik's voice strained. "Casey, this Night Blade belongs to you now. With training, its blade and flames will be yours to use to protect." He let go of the sword's handle, and a white-blue flame danced up and around the black blade as Casey's hand tightened around the grip. Anderik's brow rose, his head cocked into a question, but only a single word escaped with his breath, "Interesting."

The flames instantly vanished, and Casey lowered the sword. "Are the flames plasma based?"

Anderik smiled weakly. "There isn't time for technical lessons, but here is a short answer and a lesson. The Night Blade's energy is not the same as plasma weapons. Depending on the user and the flames, the blade can cut through many things, including most armor. There are lesser flames and those which require higher levels of mastery before the blade will emit them. Unfortunately, I neither have the time nor the mastery to teach you. Hopefully you will have the opportunity in the future, as this sword has an honorable legacy."

Anderik paused, turned his head to listen, then looked back at Casey. "A final lesson, as most are unfamiliar with the very basics of a Night Blade. Anyone can be taught to extend the blade to its default length, or retract it, with this concealed switch. However, with discipline you can learn to shorten, or lengthen, to a limited extent, the blade. The flames are called forth by the blade's owner, usually beginning with the lower energy levels after considerable training. Its sheath and my bag are back in the passage a short distance. There are extra handgun loads in my pack. And then you all need to leave quickly. The Watch handlers are coming, and likely with imperial reinforcements."

At Anderik's direction, James sprinted down the passage to the edge of the light and found a small shoulder satchel and belt with a one-inch metal disk hanging from it. Urgent sounds reverberated from farther back in the passage.

Kathera shook her head in defiance at Anderik's insistence to leave him.

"Kathera." Anderik's voice strained, and he winced. "This isn't the time for your mother's stubbornness. Besides there isn't room for anyone to carry me up the shaft; it's barely big enough to climb up."

James returned, handed the belt with its disk to Casey, and tossed the pack over his left shoulder next to his own pack.

Casey strapped the belt around his waist. "We can't just leave you, especially if there's a chance for you to survive."

"There's a chance"—Anderik's mouth pinched momentarily—"but not where you're going. Trust me. You have only a minute or so before they arrive. Retract the sword, stick its end against the metal, and let it hang by your side."

Resigned, Kathera and Casey stood.

Casey touched the switch. In a fraction of a second, the micro scales of the black blade melted into the handle. He touched the now bladeless end of the handle against the disk, and a magnetic-like tug gently pulled the handle from his grip. He let go, and the handle swung down, suspended by the disk.

Anderik's voice strained. "Amnor, family is more than duty. Take care of Kathera."

"Thank you for your help," said Amnor as he turned away.

Kathera's head dropped. "I don't want to leave you. But I'll honor your request and wish you the best fortune that can be had."

Anderik's eyes closed, and he nodded.

Turning away from her uncle, Kathera said, "Let's go. The exit is just around the next intersection."

Casey and James retrieved their tossed handguns and followed the others down the passage. Less than a minute later they were all standing inside a small alcove. An oval door was opened and revealed a ladder stretching up into a rusted pipe, barely a yard in diameter.

"What? Another ladder!" James said in mock surprise. "With all the technology you guys have you'd think we'd get to use an elevator at least once."

"Sometimes old tech is more reliable," said Kathera, stepping into the pipe and climbing up.

Amnor, Heather, and James followed. Casey stepped into the shaft and paused. A gentle draft of fresh, cool air flowed downwards, its taste refreshing compared to much of the underground.

Casey inhaled gratefully and grabbed the rungs. The ladder and pipe shook violently as an explosion resounded from the passage behind him. For a few moments the air flow shifted, flowing upwards through the shaft. Casey caught his breath as the stagnant air surged passed him.

Casey pulled the door shut and began to climb. "What was that?"

Above him, Kathera choked out a reply, "Remember the cylinder Anderik took out? That's what that was."

Chapter Forty-One
Going Up

THE CRYSTAL HEADLAMPS PENETRATED the blackness above, revealing more darkness. Hands and feet moved in laborious monotony, and the combined breathing of five climbers, amplified in the narrow shaft, was like a continuous crashing of ocean waves. Time on the ladder compounded the eternal night of the underground with fatigued muscles and joints. After a while even resting was tedious. Unable to sit or lie down, the climbers would lean back against the shaft wall to rest their arms, but leg muscles would begin to cramp if a rest became too long.

With the closure of the bottom door, the refreshing draft had subsided to a trickle of air. As they climbed higher, the air felt less repressive, lighter, and fresher. Lungs welcomed the change with deeper breaths.

After what felt like an hour of climbing, Kathera reached a small manhole-like cover that appeared to be sealed and cankered with rust. She examined the cover and pushed up on a small lever. Instead of an eighteen-inch manhole, a three-foot section with squared corners hinged up silently, belying the apparent corrosion. She cautiously poked her head up, then heaved herself over the top rung and collapsed onto the floor of a dark room. A few minutes later Amnor, Heather, and James joined her on the cement, rubbing arms, hands, and legs while they sipped from water containers taken from their packs.

Casey climbed onto the floor and closed the access cover. From the top, the panel blended into the irregular cement. He joined the others sitting on the floor. After sipping some water, he took a few bites from a dried fruit-like substance. Like the other unfamiliar food, he could only identify the taste as being like a sweet fruit or berry. During the break, shadows danced up and down along the walls as light beams shifted. A single door crusted into one wall.

"This place looks forgotten," said Heather. "Too much dust and debris to be used much."

Kathera nodded and swallowed a bite of food. "Anderik said this used to be a smuggling point in and out of the spaceport, but it hasn't been used in years. Too much security now. But since it hasn't been used for so long, Anderik thought it might be safe enough for us to use to get closer to your ship."

"So, where are we exactly?" asked James while he emptied Anderik's pack and divided up the few food rations, water, and projectile loads.

"Exactly? I don't know, but we're somewhere below the military end of the spaceport. We're still about a hundred feet below the surface. The remnants of the first city are below us, and this is part of the tunnels and substructures of the second city's spaceport."

"You'd think they'd be more careful on the military side of the port," said Heather.

"Except it wasn't originally for military. The port expanded and this end was claimed for military use. Mostly old passages were sealed off or forgotten about."

Casey capped his water and put it in his pack. "We should get moving and see what's up with our ship."

Kathera closed her pack, slipped it over her shoulder, and walked over to the closed door. She touched a small dark panel on the right side. When it failed to respond, she touched it again, and it remained dark. She examined the sides of the panel.

"Maybe we need to try Casey's Night Blade and just cut through the door," suggested James.

Kathera shot James an annoyed glance. Her fingers located a small gap—a crumbled section of wall—under the panel. She looked inside and grinned. After fishing a short flat object from her right pocket, she fiddled with it for a moment inside the gap, grasped the door's handle, and slid the door to the side.

Their lights spilled into a dark hallway where more dust and debris covered the floor. A rubble pile filled part of the hall on the right. Kathera led the group to the left.

"Kathera," asked Heather curiously, "can you do that trick on all doors?"

"Only if I can access behind the panel and the door isn't locked," said Kathera. "It's not so easy when it's locked."

James whispered to Casey, only half-attempting to keep the comment between them, "Wouldn't she be surprised if it hadn't worked."

"Then we'd have resorted to the more primitive means you suggested," retorted Kathera.

The headlamps chased shadows while they continued along the hall. Occasional drips plunked into small puddles or plinked against metallic debris. Sections of walls looked like they were melting in extra-slow motion as decades' worth of water damage slowly seeped through. They frequently stepped around or through piles of clutter and debris. They crossed an intersection where rubble filled the cross passage. A short distance later the hallway ended at a stairwell.

"This is it," said Kathera, peering up into the darkness.

"Does this go to the spaceport?" asked Casey.

Kathera shook her head. "Not exactly. From what Anderik told me it'll dead-end about halfway up, where it was sealed when the spaceport was constructed. There'll be a concealed access panel that'll enter the utility tunnels. From there we can find our way to your ship."

Four flights up, the stairs ended at a landing. The first step of the next flight of stairs poked from beneath a barrier of cement filling the stairwell. A large rusted metallic slab was attached to the landing's wall where a door had once been. Ominous signs of welding covered the entire perimeter, giving it the look of an ugly, but effective, patch job. Kathera examined the welded edges.

"I thought it was supposed to be a concealed door," said James.

"Maybe Anderik meant 'sealed' door," replied Casey.

Kathera shook her head. "I don't think this is what Anderik expected. Looks like the access panel was discovered and permanently sealed." She turned to James with a sly smile. "Now is when the primitive approach is needed." James grinned while Kathera added to Casey, "If you can get that flaming blade working, it could probably cut through the door."

The others stepped back as Casey gripped the handle of the Night Blade and pulled. Instantly the disk released its hold. He brought the handle into a middle guard position and touched the switch. In less than a second the micro scales assembled into a twenty-eight-inch blade edge. He raised the blade to the door, a knot of uncertainty gripping his throat tightly when he realized he did not know how to turn on the flames.

Casey inhaled, held his breath for a few seconds, exhaled, and placed the tip of the blade against the metallic slab. A shimmering blue field sparked around the sword's edges, and the black blade became a pulsating blue stream of fire. He cautiously pushed the tip into the center of the slab, and, with little effort, the blade melted through. Around the sword, the slab glowed yellow to red, and drips of molten metal oozed, leaving behind uneven trails as it cooled and solidified.

Casey focused on cutting to filter out the putrid odor of burning metals that assaulted his nostrils. He brought the blade straight down a couple of feet, almost to the bottom of the slab. There was more resistance to melting when the blade neared the welded joint. He twisted the blade to the left and around in a big oval, up to about four feet where he joined the initial cut. The blade pulled out easily, and the flames extinguished when he stepped back to admire the roughhewn oval. His self-satisfied smile was cut short as he watched the cooling metal rejoin and seal just seconds after the blade passed through. Within a few moments the metal slab had resealed and transformed the cut into a poor-looking weld job.

"Well," said James, "that was cool, until the part when it didn't pop out like I thought it would."

"I didn't expect that either," said Kathera.

Amnor's brow furrowed. "I'm surprised self-healing metal would be used down here."

"That's a thing?" exclaimed James.

"Based on what we saw," said Heather, "I'm not sure Casey can cut it fast enough for us to break through before it reseals."

"Well, let's—" Kathera was cut short when the blue flames of the Night Blade flared back up and Casey stepped to the wall, next to the metal slab.

Instead of placing the blade into the metal, Casey stuck it through the concrete-like wall on the right side. A foul mix of rotten eggs, tar, and burnt stone pummeled his nose, and heat from the lava-like cut in the wall slightly curled the hairs on his forearms. Moisture retreated and escaped from his face, and he unconsciously licked his drying lips. The blade did not move as quickly through the thicker wall, and once again he moved the flaming sword around in a large oval. When the cut returned to the top, meeting the original point, the sliced section of wall dropped slightly. When he removed the blade, the flames extinguished. The blade disappeared into the handle, and Casey re-sheathed it on its disk.

"Not what I was thinking," said Kathera, "but that should work."

The cut in the wall did not cool as fast as the metal. Cautiously, they pushed in the new cement door. It scraped and resisted for several inches before the top fell through. Then the entire slab crashed to the floor on the other side. The burned edges of the foot-thick wall looked like gray obsidian.

"Just a note of precaution," said Amnor when Kathera was about to enter the opening. "While most of the tunnels this low are not frequently used by the military, they are monitored for unusual activity."

Kathera nodded and stepped over the rough threshold, followed by the others.

The corridor stretched ahead for a short distance before ending at a T-junction. Shafts of headlights pierced through the dust, still tinged with smoke, that hung in the air.

Approaching the T-junction, Casey motioned towards a couple of narrow red beams of light that shifted and swept through the dust from the right-side passage. "What is that?" he whispered.

A dull black orb the size of a volleyball floated into the T-junction from the right. Several red beams traced out from a crystalline eye in its center and methodically scoured the passage before it.

Chapter Forty-Two

In the Spaceport

B EFORE THE BEAMS SHIFTED left, Kathera fired twice at the orb. The first shattered the orb's eye-like sensor. Sparks spat from the floating sphere as the second shot jabbed through its center. The red beams flickered, died, and the orb dropped to the floor.

"We definitely need to keep her around," said James with a big grin.

Kathera kept her eyes ahead, trying not to smile. "Keep your guns ready. Shoot anything that moves. Watch out for any other sensors. Turn your lights down so we don't give ourselves away too easily. According to Anderik, these are mostly just utility access tunnels. And we're not far to your ship."

Again, Kathera led the small group. They turned right at the *T*-junction, passing the unresponsive orb on the ground. Seconds later James sent a plasma blast down the tunnel from his short rifle. A small explosion erupted in midair, and another orb fell to the ground.

"Between Kathera and James, it doesn't seem too bad," said Heather.

"That's because the empire doesn't expect intruders from the tunnels," said Amnor. "Those are maintenance guardians, designed to primarily monitor the tunnels for irregularities. Be assured the absence of two guardians will be investigated, and with more than another maintenance guardian."

Kathera stopped at a small recessed section of wall. She examined a dark patch for a moment and then gave it several quick taps. A small access panel noiselessly swung into a long, narrow room. Four large rectangular displays, two over two, covered the upper part of the right wall. A long strip on the ceiling lit up to illuminate the room the moment she entered, and the displays emitted a soft glow. Various video feeds of the utility tunnels appeared on the screens, with twenty-four views displayed on each large screen. While most images appeared static, a maintenance guardian floated down the tunnel in one view. In another, two maintenance guardians were near a large tube lying on the floor.

"Did Anderik tell you about this?" asked James.

Kathera studied the displays and nodded. "While you were off in the exile city, we were discussing some options. He told me about monitoring stations throughout the complex where maintenance personnel can better identify problems. He thought we might be able to get a view of the outside from one of the stations."

Amnor stepped near the upper right screen. "Allow me," he said, touching the edge and swiping across it several times.

With each swipe new images appeared. In the third set of views, surface images of the military side of the spaceport appeared. Spacecraft sat on most of the landing platforms. In the center of one image a dozen small sentry ships guarded an empty landing pad. Dozens of uniformed soldiers filled the spaces between the ships. One patrol of six marched off to the left while five replacements entered from the right.

Kathera stared at the view of the guarded pad. Her head tilted from one side to the other, as if it would help to see the image better. "Wonder what they're expecting there?"

"That's where Casey parked," said Heather.

Kathera cocked her head at Casey standing next to her. "I don't recall you mentioning the ship is invisible."

Casey studied the display. "It's not. It has something like adaptive camouflage, which it's really good at. Almost like being invisible. But it's still very much there."

Several soldiers started moving in the foreground, waving their hands at something out of view. From the right, a lone soldier ran into view towards the newly arrived patrol, who had walked around and positioned themselves on the opposite side of the landing pad. He altered his path to directly cross the pad. The soldiers waving managed to get his attention enough for him to slow down, but he continued his course. Three steps later his forward pace was abruptly halted, and he fell backwards.

"Looks like he found our ship." James smiled. "Or at least one of the landing struts. I gotta admit that sight never gets old."

On screen the perimeter activity increased. Some soldiers looked amused at the expense of their dazed comrade trying to stand back up. Several new patrols moved into view around the ship.

"Now for the million-dollar question," said James. "How do we get to the ship? 'Cause it looks like they might be expecting us."

"Yeah, it looks like an organized mad house," said Heather.

"Maybe we should just run for the ship," suggested Casey.

Everyone turned to Casey.

"Okay," said James, "I'll take the hundred on the left, Kathera will take the hundred on the right, and the rest of you can divide up those fighter ships and ground vehicles. Oh, and we'll just hope none of the laser turrets on the walls are actually armed, manned, or automated."

"Casey," said Heather, shaking her head, "you have some brilliant ideas, but that isn't one of them."

Casey shrugged. "Anyone have any better ideas?"

"Not yet," said Kathera. "Although it probably won't take much to top that."

"There's gotta be something better," said Heather. "Even if we manage to get into the ship, how are we going to take off with all the sentry ships?"

James turned to Kathera. "Where do we go from here?"

"Anderik told me there are maintenance accesses into all terminal buildings, including the one closest to the landing pad." Kathera swiped the upper left screen a few times. One of the views displayed a different angle of the heavily guarded landing pad. She pointed at a nearby terminal-like building with a three-story-high wall of windows. "That's the building. This tunnel goes under it and there's supposedly access into it. It doesn't look like there's much in the way of security inside."

"Just between the building and our ship," said James.

"I, too, would much rather have a better plan than 'run,'" said Amnor, "but we can at least get to the building and assess things from there. If we take out any sensors or guardians before we're detected, we might make it to the building without our exact location being identified. But we'll need to move quick, before something finds us in here."

They exited the room, and Kathera led them quickly, and cautiously, along the passage. She pointed up at the corner of the next intersection where a small indiscreet box was located. Several small clear bulbs covered the surface. A second later a blast from her handgun left the sensor sparking.

"Won't destroying the sensors just tell them where we are?" asked Heather.

"Probably," said Kathera. "Which is another reason to hurry."

Over the next few minutes three more sensors were taken out. Kathera diverted off the main passage to the bottom of a narrow flight of stairs that climbed up. A door was at the top landing. A palm-sized panel on the right emitted a dim red hue.

Kathera turned to Casey. "Those panels require an authorized user's handprint to unlock. It'll likely set off an alarm if any of us touch it. See if the Night Blade can cut an opening in the door, hopefully without triggering an alarm."

Kathera backed down the stairs, and Casey stepped to the door. He unsheathed and extended the blade, and it pulsed a warm blue. He touched the tip to the door, pushed it gently through, and brought it back out. With the blade held safely to the side, he peered through the hole.

"Looks like there are two guards, not too far away," said Casey. "They don't seem to have heard anything."

"Probably better to take them out before you finish cutting through the door," advised Amnor.

Casey shook his head. "Definitely not very sportsmanlike."

"I don't know what you mean by that," said Kathera, her forehead creased in confusion. "They aren't playing games. None of them will give you the chance to live if they've been told to kill on sight."

Amnor nodded.

Heather's eyebrows rose in concern. "I'm with Casey. We shouldn't kill someone if we can avoid it."

"And what happens," said Casey, "if we miss one, or both, or you just injure one? Then the alarm will certainly be sounded, and we'll have a lot more to deal with."

"Finish cutting through the door," said Kathera. "We'll watch the guards."

"If they come this way, you can take them out," said Casey. "I just don't like the idea of basically shooting someone in the back. Maybe we'll be lucky and they won't hear or see us. Let me know if they're coming or appear to suspect something."

The blue glow increased, and Casey touched the Night Blade to the door once more. It cut quickly and quietly through this one versus the one he'd made in the cement. He smiled at how smoothly the cut moved around the door. Then the corners of his lips dropped when the odor of burning metal drifted into his nose.

"Looking good. Still good," said James as the cutting progressed, watching the guards through the enlarging gap.

"Hold up," he suddenly hissed. "They're looking around. Looks like they're smelling something, probably this melted mess."

Casey retracted the blade from the door, and the plasma glow vanished. "The cut's almost done," he whispered.

"They're moving, but not coming this way," whispered James. "Doesn't look like they've called any backup, yet."

Kathera judged the range through the cut. "It's a difficult shot through the cut. They are walking away from their post, though not towards us. I think James is right, that they're trying to figure out what the smell is from."

"The cut's close enough we can pull it back. Might be quiet enough they won't hear it," said James. "Kathera, Amnor, be ready with your guns while I pull this back. I don't want to push it out, in case it falls and makes noise. On the count of three."

James briefly touched the top edge of the rough-cut oval. Deciding the cut was cooled enough, he grasped the edge, looked at the others, and whispered, "One. Two. Three." He gently pulled, and the door section bent easily back on its remaining few inches.

Casey watched the two guards. One began to turn around. Immediately two bright bursts blew through the opening and plunged into the chests of both guards. The two soldiers collapsed into heaps. "Kath—" he started, and then noticed Amnor was the one who had fired.

Amnor was unapologetic. "The one was turning, and I didn't want to risk us being seen."

Casey attached the blade handle to its disk while the others cautiously stepped through the makeshift door. He followed, stepping into a wide corridor that was over two stories tall. To the right, the hall stretched back deeper inside of the building. On the ground level, dozens of portraits of stoic men dressed in military and royal attire hung inside small recessed sections on both walls. At regular intervals along the wall, red lights flashed.

To the left, the wide hallway extended to a semicircular counter that separated the hall from a large foyer. Eight high-backed armchairs were positioned behind the counter, exactly spaced from each other. Beyond the counter, the hall opened into a spacious room with three-story windows that spanned the entire width of the outside wall. The room was devoid of furnishings, seeming to serve more as a formal reception than waiting area.

Along the bottom of the windowed wall were a half dozen translucent doors that exited to the spaceport's ground level. A single gray armored sentry stood guard outside each door, their attention riveted on the heavily guarded landing platform about two hundred yards away, where dozens of soldiers waited while mini-tanks and air sentries patrolled the vicinity.

James followed Kathera while she cautiously moved along the corridor towards the curved counter. "Yeah, running to the ship isn't a good idea," he said.

Behind James, Amnor's voice was barely above a whisper. "Keep quiet and get close to the wall. Those air sentries are scanning for irregularities in the buildings."

Chapter Forty-Three
Inside Hurdles

A BLINDING FLASH EXPLODED against the inside of the large center window. The impact did little more than blacken the security glass and surprise the guards outside. Kathera and James, who were in the lead, dove for cover behind the chairs at the reception desk.

Casey spun left into a recessed section of the wall, and the heat of a second burst burned the air next to him. Against the opposite wall, Heather and Amnor ducked into a small recessed section. At the reception counter, James and Kathera had pulled the chairs together for shields. Their guns were aimed down the hall from where they had come a minute earlier.

Volleys of plasma fire tore through the hall and burned into the counter or glanced against the windows. Gunfire and plasma bolts were returned down the hall at six soldiers who moved methodically along the recessed sections towards their targets. While projectile rounds deflected off the soldiers' gray armor, they tried to avoid the plasma fire.

The first soldier stumbled backwards when a plasma bolt ripped into his chest armor when he attempted to move closer. Plasma exploded through the side armor of a second soldier when he failed to dodge quick enough. A third fell under the onslaught of several plasma strikes. With half the patrol down, the three remaining soldiers retreated to better cover.

Outside the large glass windows, the guards had recovered from their surprise and positioned themselves near the doors. Behind them, three patrols ran towards the building from the landing pad. Four doors opened simultaneously, releasing the din of the spaceport into the room, and four guards entered. The sudden noise drew the defenders' weapon fire, and three guards failed to cross the thresholds alive. The fourth made it into the room before he collapsed, lifeless. With three doors blocked open by bodies, the outside chaos—shouted orders mixed with the roar of flying and hovering ships—bullied its way inside. A barrage of plasma fire from down the hall ripped into the chairs, walls, and curved desk, and sent James and Kathera ducking again for cover. Amnor shot back at the three soldiers hiding inside alcoves and earned a return volley that punched into the walls beside him.

From his position, Casey could not see the soldiers well enough to get a clean shot. His shoulders tightened again when another barrage of gunfire blasted around them. He exhaled, grateful none of them had been hit. Then a thought struck him. *The soldiers aren't terrible marksmen; they're pinning us down.* His eyes darted around, first glancing at the large windows. The last two guards from the original six were waiting for the three patrols en route from the landing pad. Then a realization hit: he had hardly been shot at. *Do they know where I am? Are they intentionally not shooting at me?* He recalled what Kishon had told Hagon in the underground: they needed him to get the ship and his friends were expendable if they happened to get killed, but the preference was to use them as leverage against him. Casey scoured the windows, and he wondered what was coming.

Movement in the upper periphery of his vision drew Casey's focus to the second-floor railing on the opposite side of the large corridor.

Three black-clad soldiers wearing black helmets with dark faceplates moved stealthily along the second floor towards the reception end. They kept low and back from the railing, but Casey noticed the flash of red stars emblazoned on their lapels. He fired a couple of shots at the soldiers, two dropping back to the wall.

Almost directly across from Casey, a rapid series of plasma bolts pounded the wall next to Amnor and Heather. Heather's face was pale, and her gun quivered in her hand. Next to her, Amnor returned fire down the hall at the soldiers.

From above, the third soldier leaped over the railing, arms spread out like the narrow wings of a bird of prey. Rather than fall, his descent was controlled, almost graceful, and he landed softly next to Kathera behind the counter. Surprised, she started to rise from her kneeling position and swing her handgun around. The soldier's left hand back-knuckled her gun aside, his right fist slamming up into her jaw. She staggered backwards like a drunkard trying to remain vertical.

The soldier snapped a side kick at James's rifle when he turned to engage the surprise attacker. The short rifle violently jerked to James's right, its butt jamming unforgivingly into his chest. A right roundhouse sent the rifle flying and James teetering back. He snatched the metal rod from its straps and parried a quick series of jabs and kicks. James ducked under a kick meant for his face and answered it with a loud *thwack* into his attacker's abdomen, doubling the soldier over. As the black-garbed attacker fell forward, James whipped the rod around like a scorpion's stinger and struck the back of the head, collapsing the soldier to the ground.

Casey started towards the counter area, but plasma bolts chased him back into the recessed section.

The other two black-clad soldiers glided from the second floor and landed near their fallen comrade. James turned, and his jaw met the fist of the nearest soldier. He staggered back, and the second soldier stepped towards Kathera, who was still regaining her focus from the previous assault. James snapped the rod up to deflect another punch from the first soldier and smiled smugly when his attacker stepped back shaking his hand.

"Captain"—Casey jumped at the sound of the female voice—"you have three above you."

Casey's eyes shot to the railing above him. Three dark shapes swooped down like raptors, and he sprang back. A gust of air blew over him, and the three soldiers landed softly on the floor. Two faced him while the third moved towards James at the reception counter. Casey mentally rebuked himself for forgetting about the second floor above him. His gun fired an errant shot at one soldier, who smashed the weapon out of his hands with a roundhouse kick. Casey stepped to the left and drew out the Night Blade. The sword hissed through the air into middle guard. The two attackers jumped back as white-blue flames raced along the blade's edge.

Across the hall, Heather saw the new attacker closing in on James while he circled his current opponent. She sprinted towards the reception area and jumped at the new soldier. The soldier's head turned only to have Heather's jumping side kick smash into his faceplate. His head jerked back with a violent crack, and he dropped to the floor. She faced the soldier circling James.

The black-clad soldier stepped back to assess his new opponent. Heather half-stepped forward with a left jab. The soldier raised his arm to defend against the fist and missed her right roundhouse that collided into his sternum. He folded, and James smashed the rod down across the back of his helmeted head, sending him unresponsive to the floor.

Heather nodded at James and turned her attention on Kathera's attacker. James retrieved his rifle from the floor and aided Amnor in returning fire back down the hall.

The two soldiers facing Casey seemed more amused than intimidated by their opponent and his sword. They shifted back and forward, like they were toying with him. One lunged, and Casey snapped the Night Blade. The man's forearm rose to block, and the blade rang and hissed in shrill disappointment as it deflected off the defense. The sword swept into a thrust, and the forearm circled up and out to block it again.

The second soldier moved towards Casey's left. Casey sliced through the air to ward off the advance, his sword glancing off another forearm block. The sword danced through the air between its opponents in rapid succession, testing for a weakness in their defenses. Down, across, up, diagonal. Nimble in their movement, the soldiers easily deflected the sword's fury. Smoke from the sliced and tattered sleeves of the forearms left trails in the air. Under the shredded shirt sleeves, a dark shield became exposed that covered the entire forearm like a knight's vambrace. Casey backed along the wall and wondered if the soldiers had other armor. The soldiers' hands were bare, and their easy and flowing movement suggested if they had other armor it was limited. In unison, the two soldiers quickly circled their arms out, tucked their hands by their chests, and then thrust their palms out.

"What—" grunted Casey when a wall of wind nearly toppled him backwards. His eyes squinted against the onslaught and infiltrating dust.

He stepped back to maintain space as his opponents eagerly pressed forward. The attacker on the left began moving both hands around his body in a clockwise motion while the second soldier moved his hands counterclockwise.

Better not see what that does, thought Casey, and he feinted a backwards stumble to his right. The soldier on the right jumped in to strike. Casey twisted slightly left, sweeping the Night Blade low and snapping it behind the soldier's left knee. The slice dropped the soldier to the ground screaming, and the left soldier's attention wavered. Casey grounded his left foot, stepped with his right while the left knee lifted to launch his jump. His right smashed under the soldier's left jaw. The head jerked back. A small twist of air wobbled weakly at Casey when the man flailed back. A left side kick slumped the man to the floor unconscious. Shifting right, a left rear roundhouse across the screaming guard's faceplate knocked him silent to the floor.

Looking at the counter area, Casey saw the last soldier crash into a chair. Nearby, Heather stood defiant, her hands held out in a relaxed fighting stance, the corners of her mouth lifted in satisfaction. The gunfire had stopped. James's rifle lowered, and he tenderly rubbed his jaw. Amnor slowly walked to the reception counter and examined the fallen soldiers.

Heather raised her brow at Casey. "It's about time you'd stopped toying with those guys."

"Yeah, well, real fights aren't the same as the dojo."

Casey jumped back defensively when an energy blast tore into the soldier lying on the ground to his left. A second burst ripped into the unconscious soldier on the right. His eyes shot back to the reception area in time to see another shot ensure the soldier in the chair was also dead.

Amnor stood near the chair, his face emotionless while his rifle still pointed at the last soldier. "You need to get your priorities right on who should live," he said grimly. Then he fired into the other three bodies that lay nearby.

"In their defense," said James, "I don't think those guys were much of a threat anymore."

"Well, they aren't now," said Amnor.

James raised his brow at Casey and Heather. "On that cheery note, how're you guys?"

Casey's eyes dropped to the black-clad soldiers on the floor, smoke swirling up from charred uniforms. "Thankfully more alive than them. By the way, Heather, thanks for the warning. I might not have gotten out of the way soon enough."

"What warning? I didn't say anything. I didn't see those guys until they were on the ground."

James raised his hands, one still gripping his short rifle, as if to stop an argument. "Okay, we can sort out who said what when we get to the ship. But first"—he pointed the rifle at the large windows—"we've got to get through that."

Chapter Forty-Four
Outside Hurdles

O
UTSIDE THE TRANSPARENT WALLS, several patrols of soldiers lined up near the doors, waiting, their short assault rifles butted up to their shoulders, ready for action. Three arrowhead ships hovered menacingly in the air.

"What're our options?" asked Heather.

"Back to the tunnels," said Kathera. "There're too many. Maybe we can get some help from the exiles."

Amnor vigorously shook his head. "We need to get to the Rayneiri to warn them of the attack and assassination. There must be another way we can get to the landing platform."

"We don't have time to explore." James raised his eyebrows at Amnor. "Unless you know something?"

Casey studied the show of force outside. "What we need is a big distraction so we can get to the *Fallen Star*."

"That'd be great," said Kathera, "Except—"

A blinding flash of light and a thunderous explosion erupted outside the large foyer windows. The fivesome dove under the reception counter as the windows imploded and showered pieces throughout the foyer and into the corridor. One arrowhead sentry ship erupted into flames, lurched forward, and clipped a second ship, sending them both crashing to the ground. More flashes of energy burst along the remnants of the exterior wall. Shouts and screams clouded the air as soldiers got tossed aside like rag dolls by the explosions. A few survivors on the fringes of the destruction crawled away. The third ship yawed right, turning its attention away from the terminal building.

"Captain, go now!"

Casey's eyebrow rose, and he looked around. It was the same female voice he'd heard earlier, but nobody else acted like they heard it. "Time to go," he shouted. He darted towards one of the missing center doors.

Approaching the remains of the wall, Casey crouched and surveyed the outside. Heat nipped at his skin while it consumed segments of the structure. The others emerged hesitantly from behind the protective counter, uncertain about Casey's course of action. Outside, surrounding the empty-looking landing pad, streaks of plasma flared and dissipated around a large orb of energy. Dust and smoke diffused the explosive flashes while the odor of burning metal and rock floated through the air like an unseen specter. Another arrowhead sentry ship started hovering towards him when flames exploded from its front and the ship careened off out of control. The underside of another ship convulsed when fire erupted and sent it spinning uncontrollably into the ground. Shouts from officers attempted to regain order but failed amid the chaos.

Heather and James ran up behind Casey, followed by Amnor and Kathera a moment later.

Heather's head shook accusingly at Casey. "What are you doing? We don't stand a chance out there!"

Casey gave her a wry smile, his eyes confident in his decision. "Run for the ship! It's the distraction we need." Without waiting for a reply, he dashed outside.

Reluctantly, the others followed.

Shouting rose above the furor when the group was spotted running towards the landing pad. Angry energy blasts and projectiles chased after them. A squad of soldiers clustered near the pad, waiting for the five to get nearer. A ball of energy detonated behind the squad and bowled them aside. Additional arrowhead sentry ships and soldiers lay siege against the landing pad, unleashing a storm of weapon fire against an unseen foe. Plasma, projectiles, and explosions clashed and flared harmlessly against the energy field.

Halfway to the landing pad, Casey watched the *Fallen Star*'s ramp descend. The ramp caught the attention of nearby soldiers, who sprinted towards it. The two fastest soldiers slammed into the unseen perimeter shield and slumped to the ground. The other soldiers slowed and probed the space in front of them. Ripples of energy jolted rifle ends while they prodded for weakness.

James, Amnor, and Kathera fired at the soldiers. Two collapsed before the others realized what had happened. They spun around and returned fire. Behind the soldiers a distortion field expanded towards them like a racecar. The impact sent the patrol tumbling through the air more than fifty feet away. Remnant sparks of energy faded from the space where the enemies had been.

Casey reached the landing pad and felt like he hit a wall of gelatin. For a fraction of a second, his forward momentum slowed. Then he continued in a full sprint to the ramp. James and Heather arrived a couple seconds later.

Between breaths, James pointed to Casey and the ramp. "Get up there and get the ship ready. I'll make sure everyone's in."

Casey raced up the ramp and into the already-lit control room. The walls, floor, and ceiling faded from their neutral tone into clear views of the surrounding chaos outside. Above the center and forward consoles, 3D images of the *Fallen Star*, surrounding buildings, and spacecraft materialized. A surround sound of heavy breathing filled his ears when the others entered the control room and collapsed into the seats.

James dropped into the right seat. "We're all in, and the ramp's up."

Casey nodded while he examined the exterior displays. A faint blue glow extended around the perimeter of the image of the ship on its landing pad. Outside the glow's edge, several more soldiers lay motionless or dazed from their failed attempts to access the ramp. Across the landing zone, a dozen arrowhead sentries rose up from their landing pads and swung towards the *Fallen Star*. Five larger ships were also lifting off.

Heather sat in the seat behind James. "Okay, can somebody tell me what just happened?"

Kathera's eyes were wide in disbelief. "Somehow we made it to your ship. It would seem Casey has a few tricks up his sleeve."

Casey's hands were on the familiar domes; warmth and a rush of adrenaline surged into him. Through the viewscreens the ground dropped quickly, and the blue glow fully encapsulated the 3D ship floating over the center console. His attention shifted from the viewscreens to the consoles. "Time to get out of here."

"Where would you like to go, Captain?"

The voice startled Casey. It was the same voice he'd heard at the spaceport. He looked around and saw the surprised looks of his companions. "You guys heard it that time, right?"

The others nodded.

Satisfied, Casey replied, "Let's start by getting off this planet."

Warmth flowed into Casey's right hand, and the ship rocketed into a vertical climb. Behind him, Kathera's face drained to pale, and white-knuckled hands gripped her chair. Similarly, the faces of Heather, James, and Amnor also blanched.

The underside viewscreens dimmed when six high-energy plasma beams attempted to rupture the shields.

"No shield damage, Captain," the female voice reported. "Those surface-based defenses are no longer a threat. However, there are three battle carriers in orbit. In addition, seven battleships and five destroyers orbit the nearby moon, Agra. As on our arrival, the 256 orbital defense satellites of El'Tagath are still active. I anticipate being targeted in less than one minute."

Casey looked around, suspecting, but not positive of the voice. "Sounds like we better spare them the trouble and find somewhere to jump to. Just in case, James and Heather, get ready with the weapons."

Below and behind them, the planet's curvature appeared. The forward viewscreens revealed the blackness of space, sprinkled with increasing numbers of white specks. Far to the left, a moon emerged from the horizon. The forward 3D display changed to reveal the planet, moon, and locations of the various ships reported.

Casey hesitated for a moment, then asked, "Shaina?"

"Yes, Captain?" replied the female voice.

"Thanks for your help down there."

"Glad to be of service."

"When will it be clear to fold space?"

"As soon as we've completely cleared the outer atmosphere. About one of your minutes. But I need to know the coordinates of where you want to go."

A violent barrage of plasma fire peppered the shielding.

"And that's provided we are still in one piece," continued Shaina.

Chapter Forty-Five
Jump to the Rayneiri

FLOATING ABOVE THE CENTER console, the *Fallen Star* reached the outer atmosphere of El'Tagath. A red object crested the planet's curvature and sped rapidly towards them. The object materialized and revealed a massive battle carrier closing the distance. Brilliant flashes burst from the front of the carrier, and a split second later five immense plasma blasts rocked the shielding. In the differing 3D displays over the consoles, two dozen orbital defense satellites were also red. A second later the satellites released their energy weapons at the *Fallen Star*.

The *Fallen Star*'s voice was measured. "Captain, the battle carrier *Zeda* is less than one minute away. My sensors indicate it will deploy multiple attack craft, and missile launches are imminent."

"Heather, James," directed Casey, "start targeting any satellite you can and be ready for those missiles and attack craft."

The virtual weapons displays surrounded James and Heather, and targeting rings began tracking satellites.

The console display zoomed in on the battle carrier where one hundred tiny images, looking like fleas in comparison to the immense ship, leaped from the sides. A second hundred followed the first. Several zoomed-in images of narrow, trapezoidal spacecraft popped out in the 3D display. Alien symbols floating beside the images coalesced into 'ahati'. Two more bursts of light erupted from the front of the carrier. Casey instinctively rolled the *Fallen Star* left, and the plasma bursts passed harmlessly underneath.

Red lights throbbed around the control room as Shaina reported, "Two hundred vexor missiles are locked on to us. Recommend deploying shadow countermeasures, Captain."

Floating in 3D reality above the console, two hundred small spacecraft raced towards the *Fallen Star*. From behind them, a swarm of smaller objects blasted away from the battle carrier and blazed between the small attack craft.

Casey's voice wavered momentarily. "Um, yes, launch those countermeasures."

Three bright-blue blurs appeared behind the floating images of the *Fallen Star*. The blurs increased in size and intensity as they trailed behind the ship to intercept the incoming missiles.

Shaina's voice floated through the command room. "We've cleared planetary orbit, Captain. Ready for jump coordinates."

"Rayneiri home world," said Casey. His foot pressed down on an imaginary accelerator as he apprehensively watched the leading missiles enter the blur.

"Those are not clear coordinates, Captain. The coordinates of the edge of this system are simple. I recommend we jump there, and then you can give me better instructions."

"Do it!"

Above the console, one trailing blur exploded, and dozens of missiles within the blue perimeter detonated. Behind the explosion the remaining missiles struggled to regain their target lock, and most began veering towards the other blurs. Dozens swerved and weaved into each other.

The 3D display blurred, and Casey felt heavy. The view outside the ship paused, disappeared, and returned with spectacular views of distant stars. Behind them, El'Tagath was two billion miles away.

"Captain, we have about four hours before the main carrier group can reach this part of the system, if they initiate their local system drives immediately."

"That should give us some time to figure out where we're going," said Casey.

"Except," added Shaina, "there is a destroyer-class ship orbiting an outpost on one of the nearby moons of the furthest planet. Additionally, there are reports of another battle carrier near this area, but I have not located it yet. Once either detects us, we will have minutes to act. There is also a local space gate near the farthest planet, where there are likely more ships. The sooner you provide the coordinates of the Rayneiri home world, the sooner we can make the jump."

Casey looked around sheepishly. "Anybody know those coordinates? Amnor? Kathera?"

"Regrettably, no," said Amnor, "I didn't expect a ship like this to not have star charts."

"Sir," replied Shaina, a slight edge to her voice, "I have star maps of much of this galaxy and beyond. The location request needs to be more specific. Either exact coordinates or a location on a star map from which I can calculate the coordinates. I updated my maps when I interfaced with systems on El'Tagath. I want to be sure to go where the captain wants."

Kathera spoke up. "Do you have star charts for the Bygor Cluster?"

"Of course," replied Shaina, and the star maps instantly floated over the middle console.

Kathera stood and walked to the console where she examined the stars. She reached into the 3D image and pulled it around to study it. "There," she said after several seconds, pointing to several closely packed stars. The image zoomed in on a cluster of seven stars. She pointed to a star floating at the right. "That's the Rayneiri system of Natheri. That's where we need to go."

Shaina responded with a bit of reluctance. "Is that our destination, Captain?"

"Wait!" said Heather. "Don't get me wrong, I want to help, but what about us going home? Shaina, do you have star charts back to Earth?"

"It's the planet we found you on," added Casey. "Do you have a record of the planets we've jumped from?"

Shaina's voice sounded cheerful when she answered, "Yes, Captain."

Three planetary images were displayed off to the side. A deep-green-and-brown planet with dark-blue oceans; a dry wasteland moon; a familiar-looking blue-green planet with bits of brown and beige and wisps of white.

"Shaina, would you be able to take us back home now?" asked Casey.

Kathera looked crestfallen.

"Yes, Captain. My sensors just indicated the destroyer detected us and is now on an intercept course. Estimated time to interception is seven minutes, twenty-five seconds."

Red lights throbbed around the room. The center console displayed an image of a large spacecraft shaped like a three-edged arrowhead.

"Captain, my sensors are detecting an anomaly a short distance away. I cannot identify whether it presents a threat or not."

"Shaina," said Casey, "let's make good on our promise. Go to the Natheri System. We can drop Kathera and Amnor off so they can warn the Rayneiri. Then we'll go home."

Kathera exhaled in relief and sat down.

"I am ready when you are," said Shaina.

Casey's left brow rose, and he looked around. "Everyone ready?"

Unsure what to expect, Amnor and Kathera simply nodded.

"Hang on to your seats," said Casey. "Shaina, let's do it."

The familiar light appeared on the controller dome, and Casey pressed it. All motion appeared to stop, and then starlight stretched before them.

Chapter Forty-Six
Another Welcome

T HE *FALLEN STAR* EMERGED from the space fold near the fourth planet of the Natheri System. Above them and to the left, the other six stars of the Bygor Cluster shone brighter than the others in the black velvet of space. In front of the ship, the fourth planet radiated greens in multiple hues. Ribbons of sapphire-blue weaved around the planet and joined with sprawling oceans and seas. Reds and browns striped the center of one continent, giving the planet the look of a giant glass marble. Two moons were visible beyond the planet's horizon.

Floating above the command console, the fourth planet displayed its full color and revealed a third moon on the far side. Scores of red spots, morphing into green, orbited the virtual planet. Around the command center, red-hued lights dimmed and brightened a few times.

Shaina's voice projected through the room. "Captain, the Rayneiri have detected us. Five military cruisers have been directed to intercept. Their defenses are on high alert, and they are attempting communication."

A pop-out image jumped from five red blips that appeared over the center console display. The zoomed-in image revealed the spacecraft to be *W*-shaped, with the command bridge in the center and wings that angled back before sweeping forward. Stubby gun batteries dotted the top, bottom, and sides of the ships.

"Why is it we can't just appear somewhere and not wake everyone up?" said James.

"I do have an anti-detection system," responded Shaina with a bit of a huff. "I just cannot activate it without the captain's authorization."

"Well, that's good to know," said Casey. "We really need to find out what else you can do, 'cause you're full of surprises."

"Captain, the communication is urgent."

"Oh, yeah. Let's hear it."

A forceful voice blared through the command room. "Unidentified starship, you have entered restricted Rayneiri space without known authorization. Transmit your imperial authorization code or we will respond with deadly force. You now have sixty seconds to comply. Any action considered hostile will be dealt with decisively."

"Sounds friendly enough," said James.

"Sounds like the other welcomes we've gotten," replied Heather.

"Kathera?" asked Casey.

Kathera had walked to the center console and now stood between James and Casey. Her hands fidgeted, and her face was pale. She steadied herself with the console. "Shaina, please transmit this: This is Kathera Woodaril, daughter of Brihili Llyr. I am requesting asylum for myself and my cousin, Amnor. We have an urgent message for His Majesty concerning the preservation of the imperial family. We do not have an authorization code, but request permission and an escort to land on Natheri. The *Shaina Ariana* and her crew will depart after Amnor and I are on the planet."

"Your message has been sent and received," said Shaina.

Silence pervaded the control room while seconds ticked on. Casey raised a questioning eyebrow at Kathera, but her focus was somewhere far away. Above the console, the military cruisers floated towards them.

Kathera stared at the emerald planet outside the front viewscreens, lost in memory. Casey exchanged glances with James and wondered if they were about to get caught up again and unable to leave. Behind James, Heather's mouth was slightly opened, as if words were stuck. Amnor sat behind Casey, his calm facade betrayed by a crossroads of anticipation and anxiety in his eyes. The cruisers continued to close the distance to the *Fallen Star* in the 3D space over the console. Around the command center, red lights pulsed their demand for attention.

Shaina's voice was urgent. "Captain, my recommendation is high alert until we know the Rayneiri intentions, not just what we are told. Those cruisers are more heavily armed and armored than they appear. The allotted time is well past, and I am detecting more systems coming online. I cannot help protect you, your friends, or myself without your instruction or authorization."

"Shaina, I appreciate your concern"—Casey's eyes closed, a breath slowly exhaled—"but we have a credible warning that Kathera and Amnor need to deliver, and I promised to take them to the Rayneiri."

"Shall I at least activate the shields?"

"No," said Casey calmly. "But be ready just in case."

Ten more tense seconds passed, and the war cruisers continued their intercept course. In the forward viewscreens, the five distant specks began to take shape. The floating cruiser avatars above the console pulsated an angry red.

"Captain, I am detecting increasing energy signatures within the Rayneiri ships. They are fully armed, and their deflector shields are high. I strongly advise activating our shields."

The war ships were fully visible in the front viewscreens.

"Casey"—James's knuckles turned white, and his hands gripped the chair—"I think Shaina's right on this."

Around the room, the red warning lights throbbed. Casey's breathing rate increased as uncertainty crept in and questioned his lack of action.

"Captain?"

The anxiety in the ship's voice increased Casey's doubt. He breathed in deeply, held the breath for a few seconds, and exhaled slowly. "Shaina, stand down."

At that moment, the pulsing red around the war ships over the console vanished.

"Captain, the Rayneiri have lowered their shields. There is a communication request, audio only."

"Hope it's good news. Let's hear it. Or turn it on, whatever it is we need to do to hear and talk to them."

A deep voice sounded from the front of the command room. "I am Captain Ilnich of the Rayneiri Space Defense. Your petition was forwarded to Rayneiri Command. Emperor Pherez personally extends his welcome to Lady Kathera, daughter of Llyr, along with those who are escorting her. We are tasked to escort you to the palace landing zone. You are directed to follow the lead ship back to Natheri."

Casey cocked his head at Kathera and mouthed, *Lady?* and then acknowledged the communication. "Thank you, Captain Ilnich, for your assistance. We'll follow your lead."

The five war ships slowed to a stop, rotated to face the planet, and formed a wide *V*-formation. Casey maneuvered the *Fallen Star* to a safe distance behind the tip of the *V*. The two cruisers on each end of the *V* dropped back to flank the *Fallen Star*'s right and left sides.

Casey turned to Kathera, who still stood behind the center console. "I'm not going to ask now, but I'm really curious about what just happened, and I'm hoping to get some answers."

Kathera stared ahead and nodded, her hands trembling slightly. "Might be a little hard if you're back on your home world."

Casey's mouth opened briefly and then closed while his eyes stared down at the console. He did not know how to respond and wondered if it was right to leave.

A few seconds later, Heather spoke. "Shaina?"

"How can I help?"

"I've been dying to know. How is it you know English, but didn't talk to us before?"

"When you found me, I didn't know your language. It was very different than the others. When we left Earth, I accessed much of the data being transmitted. From that, I processed multiple languages and matched the language you spoke. However, when I last spoke to someone on Earth nearly a thousand years ago, they ran off afraid. After that I was left alone in that stone prison. I didn't want my new captain to leave, but I was uncertain how you might react to me speaking, so I didn't. When we arrived at El'Tagath, I interfaced with the universal language system, discovered recent language keys, and exchanged data."

"So that's how they learned English," said James.

"Did you talk to me through my ear translator things?" asked Casey. "I kept thinking it was someone talking to me, but nobody else heard it."

"That is correct," replied Shaina. "Soon after you left the spaceport and entered the Mysian palace, my scans were unable to identify your precise location until you returned to my vicinity. I identified your translator beacon and communicated with you."

"But how were you able to hear us?" inquired Heather. "I thought these earpieces were only receivers."

"Although they are primarily receivers, the translators can transmit data, including audio, over a short distance," said Kathera. "Remember, we swapped out the other ones because those beacons were being tracked."

Shaina continued, "I interpreted the captain's stated need for a distraction as a request to activate certain countermeasures. Otherwise, I would have not been able to help."

"Thank you for that," said Casey.

"Captain, there is a transmission from the Rayneiri."

"Open the channel."

Captain Ilnich's voice instructed, "Continue following the lead escort ship into the atmosphere. Two flanking ships will remain at your side. Defense systems will target your ship if you stray from the designated escort."

The communication ended abruptly, and the lead cruiser descended into the atmosphere.

Casey deftly guided the *Fallen Star* to mimic the descent. "Guess they're not much for conversation."

"Maybe it's a test to see if you're listening," suggested James.

Within seconds the clouds of the upper atmosphere wisped by the viewscreens. Large expanses of multi-hued greenery, bordered by a winding continental coastline, were clearly visible through the floor of the command room. As their altitude decreased, a patchwork of cities and agricultural areas, interspersed among the greens, materialized. Below them, jungles swelled with the hills and merged into forests that reached high into the mountain ranges to the left, where the colored canopies hinted at changing seasons.

Increasing numbers of buildings of varied shapes and sizes appeared on the horizon. To the right, the shoreline of a sea lapped the coast while they flew over the outskirts of the cityscape. The lead ship turned sharply left and continued flying over the outer fringes of the city. Below them were large plots of land occupied by agricultural operations. Scattered among fields of greens and browns were massive greenhouse-like structures. Ahead of them, a wide silvery river reflected daylight at the incoming ships while it snaked from mountains on the left, meandering through the city on the right before its delta emptied into the sea. When the lead ship reached the riverbanks, it veered left and continued its flight trajectory up the river. The riverbanks on both sides gently climbed into the surrounding country while large boats traversed the wide waters.

"Kind of reminds me of the lower Columbia River," said Casey.

"Yeah," agreed James, "except I think some of the boats down there might be bigger."

The lead ship rolled left and followed a smaller strip of river towards an expansive plateau. Walls of an ancient fortress guarded the perimeter. Amid the vegetation, edges of weapon batteries blended in with the old architecture. The roofs and spires of various buildings reached above the tall walls.

The lead ship decreased its speed as it flew over the walls of the fortress. Hidden among the buttresses and ramparts, the ends of large cylinders tracked the movement of the *Fallen Star* while it hovered over the walls. Before them, the palace complex on the plateau stretched out for two miles. Most of the taller buildings clustered in the center, surrounded by trees and gardens. Between the perimeter wall and the palace was a large open space covered in luxurious green that looked like a velvet carpet. Smaller ancillary buildings were scattered along the walls, obscured by the foliage.

The green clearing was several football fields in width and stretched back a half mile to the palace buildings. The lead ship slowly crossed to midfield, stopped in a high hover, yawed to face the direction it had come from, and then descended to a landing on the field.

Casey mimicked the landing and gently set the *Fallen Star* down about a hundred feet behind the lead ship. The two flanking ships slowly circled the complex and stopped in a hover over the walls. A contingent of fifty soldiers filed out of a building attached to the nearby wall and lined up in two parallel columns facing the *Fallen Star*.

Casey led the way to the back of the ship, the ramp lowering and letting a cool breeze sift in.

"I hope those guys are friendlier than the last," said James, eyeing the precision lineup outside.

"They're a formality," replied Kathera. "We'll be fine." She nodded gracefully at Casey. "Thank you for bringing us here. May your journey home be uneventful. I hope you enjoy the peace."

Amnor gave Casey, James, and Heather a polite bow. "Yes, thank you for your help. I'm certain things will be much safer for you on your world than if you stay here."

Casey watched Kathera and Amnor walk down the ramp. Next to him, Heather shifted uncomfortably. Casey looked at his friend. The corners of her mouth tried to smile but were too heavy to remain lifted.

"Is this the best decision?" she breathed.

Casey turned to his brother, who shrugged his shoulders. Moisture sparkled in the hazel of Heather's eyes.

Casey's gaze turned down the ramp. "If we get involved," he cautioned, "things could get ugly really quick. You know this side of the galaxy is bordering on war. And I'm not sure when we'll get back to Earth."

"Casey." James's voice was quiet. "If we can help, we should."

Casey felt like a burden was lifted from his shoulders. He nodded, the left corner of his mouth curling into a half-smile.

Heather smiled at Casey and started down the ramp. "Well, let's go see what we can do to help."

James nodded at Casey and then followed after Heather.

Casey grinned and shook his head with a quiet laugh to himself. He looked back into the ship. "Shaina, please take care and lock up. We don't know these people and it'd be best not to let anyone else in."

"I expected as much, Captain. Good luck. Remember they're not expecting you to stay. Be careful not to—what is your saying?—stir up a hornets' nest."

Casey smiled. "We'll try not to."

Chapter Forty-Seven

An Old Friend

KATHERA AND AMNOR WERE at the head of the two columns of soldiers when Casey got to the bottom of the ramp. Kathera turned as Heather and James caught up to her. Casey simply nodded to Kathera when he approached, and the corners of her mouth lifted in acknowledgment. They continued their walk between the two columns of soldiers.

Behind them, the ramp had already retracted into the *Fallen Star*, and, now that he was walking, Casey looked around. The green field they were on was not grass as expected. Smooth-cut stone covered the ground, and a short, furry green lichen-like organism freely grew across the surface. The effect was the impression of tightly cut grass, like a putting green. Over five hundred feet away, shades of grays, browns, and greens covered the perimeter walls of the fortress. A glint halfway up revealed a darkened portal behind which something large moved, slowly tracking the group. Scrutinizing the battlements identified the locations of another dozen carefully disguised defenses. Casey guessed there were more weapons targeted on him and his companions than he had found.

An elongated van-like vehicle emerged from between a couple of buildings in the central complex and hovered noiselessly to the end of the columns of soldiers. The vehicle settled to the ground, and a wide door lifted open, exposing a sand-colored interior. A dark man dressed in a deep-green uniform walked out. Four gold dots glinted off the raised collar of his pressed shirt. In the afternoon light, gray and white flecked his short-cropped black hair. He looked back into the vehicle, gestured something, then turned and waited for his guests.

The man stood at relaxed attention. When the new arrivals got closer, his head tilted slightly while he studied the members of the group. A second later his face brightened in recognition. "Kathera!" he said warmly, "it has been a long time. I may not have recognized you, except I was informed someone claiming to be you had entered Rayneiri space. Emperor Pherez asked me to personally check. His Majesty is currently engaged in a meeting in the Grand Council Room. Your unexpected, and unusual, arrival has intrigued him, and you and your companions are invited to meet with him when the meeting adjourns."

Kathera's head tilted forward gracefully, and her body dipped naturally into a small bow. "Counselor Eldon, it has been a long time. I had come to think I would never be able to return to my mother's homeland again. May I present to you my companions? My cousin Amnor, who has information of great importance for the survival of the imperial family and empire, and my other three companions, who have graciously agreed to help where they can and have requested to remain on Natheri."

Her brows rose, and Casey nodded in response to her questioning glance. "They hail from a world outside of the known planetary systems and civilizations. This is Lady Heather"—Heather blushed at the formal introduction and bowed respectfully—"and her two friends, who have become trusted allies of mine: Casey, captain of the *Shaina Ariana*, and his brother James."

At the mention of the ship's name, Eldon's eyebrows rose. He paused, and his attention seemed split, like he was listening to something. "So," said Eldon in a subdued tone, "the legends and rumors are true. A few days ago, we received a communication that hinted as much." He nodded at Kathera. "Your companions have permission to remain. Now, we should go to the palace. You are all welcome to join me in the carriage. The palace is not far, but it's certainly quicker than walking."

The escort ships hovering over the fortified walls flew off. Eldon turned and walked to the hover vehicle, the others close behind. He stepped to the left side of the open door and politely motioned for Kathera to step inside, followed by Heather, James, and Amnor. When Casey approached, Eldon held up his hand for him to stop. His eyes narrowed, scrutinizing Casey from midsection to head. Casey felt warmth in his cheeks, like he had been called out for making a mistake.

Eldon's voice was hushed, almost reverent. "Captain Casey, may I see your sword?"

Casey nodded and detached the handle from his side. Turning the guard towards himself, he presented the hilt to Eldon.

When Eldon grasped the grip, his index finger deftly touched the switch, and the ebony scales flashed out into their elegant, slightly curved shape. His other hand moved to a two-handed grip, and he held the blade out. He moved it slowly, as if remembering parts of a sword form from a past nearly forgotten—middle guard, thrust, high block, diagonal cut, middle block, horizontal cut. A smile reveled in the reliving of a fond memory. The blade retracted, and he returned the handle to Casey.

"Thank you for your trust," said Eldon. "It has been a very long time since I held a Night Blade. May I ask how you came by it, and whether you have its twin?"

A knot tightened in Casey's throat. "An honorable man named Anderik gave it to me before insisting we leave him. He was too wounded to continue with us and believed he would only hinder our escape. His last act was to slow down those who were pursuing us. I don't know about the sword's twin."

Eldon studied Casey's face, his eyes distracted by something. Then, with a slight nod, he said, "Let us go and see His Majesty, the emperor. He, his wife, and the princess are finishing in the Grand Council Room and will be waiting to meet Kathera, you, and your friends."

Eldon directed Casey towards the back of the stretched hover van. Cushioned seats lined the front and sides of the cabin. Three empty, overstuffed chairs were along the back. With the forward seats occupied, Casey sat across from the door, next to Kathera. Casey took a seat on Kathera's right. Along the back wall were three larger, overstuffed seats, empty of occupants. Eldon entered the vehicle and sat in an empty seat to the left of the door, opposite Casey.

The door closed, and the cabin silenced. The carriage lifted into a hover, the field outside the window dropping lower. A short distance away, the *Fallen Star*'s liquid-silver color shimmered in the daylight, and, like a mirage, the ship disappeared from view. The soldiers' discipline was tested, as most could not stop from trying to see what was no longer visible.

Eldon's hands rested on his lap, and he leaned forward towards Casey. His left eye narrowed slightly, and his brow knit together. "Tell me, is that really the *Shaina Ariana* of legend?"

Casey squirmed in his seat. "Sir, I am not very familiar with the legend. We discovered the ship on our home world and were accidentally transported to this part of the galaxy. The legend was related to us on El'Tagath. From what we've learned, the *Shaina Ariana's* method of travel is unique."

Eldon nodded. "Indeed. How long did it take you to travel here from El'Tagath?"

Casey studied Eldon's sincerity while he carefully considered his response. "I don't know how long it actually took, but it felt like less than a minute."

Eldon's mouth started to open, then froze. His eyes had momentarily widened before he regained his composure and shifted his gaze to Kathera.

Kathera nodded at the unspoken question. "That would be my assessment as well. When we came here by a space jump, or 'space fold,' as Casey called it, the trip seemed nearly instantaneous. Although it seems similar to jump gate travel, no gates are needed, and it seems no time elapses from entry to exit."

"How is that even possible?" asked Eldon. "To have that much power in such a small ship?" He shook his head. "That's never been believed to be possible, which is why the *Ariana* legend is a childhood fable from hundreds of years ago."

"Counselor Eldon," said Kathera, "jump technology has become more efficient over the last hundred years. No doubt you're aware that the Sokari and Mysians have been working on portable gates."

"Yes," said Eldon sullenly. "We have heard reports of those tests. But the power requirement is still enormous, so they are only theoretically possible on the largest of ships. And jumps still require an exit gate for reliability. From the reports I've heard, any jump of more than five light-years, without an exit gate, has a high chance of catastrophic failure." He shook his head lightly. "However, the eventual miniaturization isn't what I was referring to. It's the speed of travel. While jump gate travel is much faster than light, it still takes time from entry to exit. The further the jump, the longer it takes. You're talking about near instantaneous travel without regard to time or distance."

"Which is why," Casey said, "I refer to it as space fold. Like an on-demand wormhole."

Eldon's lips pursed together. "The idea has been purely speculative for centuries. Fanciful thinking without any possible, or probable, way to execute it. The jump gates are the closest to a space fold, but their energy requirements are more than a small ship can store."

"Counselor Eldon," said Casey, "may I ask a question?"

Eldon nodded. "Absolutely."

"Did you know we were coming? And, if so, how?"

Eldon smiled mysteriously. "We intercepted an encoded transmission a few days ago about the likelihood of the *Shaina Ariana* being discovered. We weren't sure about the credibility until we received an independent report from one of our own, who mentioned the same thing. That brings us to the question, what is it that brings you here unexpectedly?"

Casey's right brow rose at Kathera. "I promised to bring Kathera here. Partly to give your emperor warning about an assassination plot we overheard, but also because she is no longer safe on El'Tagath. Amnor has been working as a double agent in the Mysian palace guard and confirmed there is an assassination plot and an invasion planned. His involvement with us has compromised his position."

Eldon's gaze shifted to Amnor. "Is this correct?"

"Sir, what Casey said is correct," confirmed Amnor. "However, this is not the best place to disclose the plans. It would be better if I reveal the details directly to Emperor Pherez so he can assess the truth. But I will say this much, to emphasize the gravity of the situation, the plan is to assassinate the emperor, his wife, and daughter within the next day or two. An invasion is expected within a few weeks, to take advantage of the discord following the assassination."

"Do you know who this assassin is? There has already been suspicion of such a plot, but no details," said Eldon.

Amnor's jaw clenched momentarily. "There are two, but I won't disclose them here. It would be best for the emperor to always have his most trusted guards around him at all times."

Eldon nodded. "I think the sooner we find this out, the better, so we take precautions and expose these assassins. You may tell the emperor what you know in the council chamber. It's as secure as any place in the complex."

The hover transport stopped at the bottom of a granite-like staircase that swept up to ten-foot-high double doors. Ornate stone arched above as a lintel. Two dozen guards fanned down the stairs when the vehicle stopped, lining the walk from the vehicle to the door with their green uniforms. Gold braided cords dropped from red shoulder epaulets and looped under each arm. Each lapel had a red sun outlined in gold. The guards wore an emerald-colored helmet with an extended rear brim and a clear-crystal face shield. Holstered handguns hung on the right side. Each guard held a short-barreled rifle in ready position, fingers poised near the triggers.

After the carriage door opened, Eldon stepped out and walked up the granite steps to the double doors. The rest followed, Amnor bringing up the rear. When Amnor entered the doors, the guards immediately fell into a two-column march behind the group. They walked along a twenty-foot-wide hallway, where light reflected off the green-flecked marble floor and danced on the ceilings and walls. The hall continued deeper into the building with smaller side passages breaking off at regular intervals.

Eldon stopped at a large double door safeguarded on each side by six guards. Each half of the ten-foot-wide door was intricately inlaid with differing shades of browns and greens, and trimmed with emerald-like stones and gold accents. Eldon leaned towards the door, spoke quietly, and waited.

After a pause the two doors split away, each half disappearing into the side walls. A short hallway extended back to another set of equally sized doors. Two palace guards stood at attention on each side of the hallway.

Eldon faced Kathera and her companions. "The council has been dismissed so only us, the emperor, and his family, along with the emperor's guard, should be in the room. It is protocol that, except for the imperial family and guards, no firearms are permitted within the presence of the emperor. If you wish to enter the Grand Council Room, you must leave your guns here with the door guards."

Kathera nodded, removed her guns, and handed them to the nearest guard. Heather and Amnor similarly disarmed and waited by Kathera.

James reluctantly unstrapped the holster and handgun from his side. He slowly handed it to the nearest guard. "I hope we don't regret this."

Casey removed his handgun and began to unstrap the belt with the Night Blade handle when Eldon's hand raised to stop him.

"You are welcome to retain the Night Blade," said Eldon. "It is considered a weapon of honor."

Casey nodded and refastened the belt. He bit his lower lip, feeling a little confused, and looked at his brother, who just shrugged.

Eldon walked through the opened doorway and down the short hall to the second set of doors where he waited. When the others had all entered the hall, the first doors silently slid shut. A couple seconds later the second pair of double doors slid open.

Chapter Forty-Eight
The Council Chamber

T HE DOORS OPENED INTO a vast room. In the center of the room sat a twenty-foot-diameter, raised circular pool. The serene, mirror-smooth water reflected the room and flowed effortlessly over the edges and down the sides, giving it the look of a short cylinder of water standing on its own. Directly above the pool, daylight refracted through a large, circular, blue crystal skylight the same size as the pool. The prismatic edges scattered shards of light into dancing colors across the upper edges of the walls.

A long, black marble table curved in each quadrant of the room. The four quarter-circle tables were set back about fifteen feet from the center pool and spaced twenty feet apart to give the look of a segmented circle surrounding the water. The center-facing sides had black marble fronts that reflected the room in a faint shadow. Six black cushioned chairs sat behind each table.

Along each wall were a half dozen palace guards. They wore the same uniforms as those standing on the steps except for gold shoulder epaulets. The guards stood like statues, seemingly oblivious to the occupants of the room. The guard nearest the newcomers watched while they entered the room.

Two dozen banners hung on the right wall, their emblazoned symbols and crests splashed the room with color.

On the left side, between the two quarter-circle tables, was a three-tiered dais. A man sat in a large comfortable chair on the center tier. Two women sat in chairs next to him. Another woman stood in front of the dais, talking. With her back to the door, her long black hair moved while her hands and arms accentuated her words.

The man had short, dark-brown hair with gray strands revealing themselves along the temples. His pressed green uniform had five gold circles on the raised collar. A dark-red sash crossed from the right shoulder to the left hip and disappeared into a waist sash of identical color. His brown eyes shifted from the woman in front of the dais to study the new arrivals while they entered the room.

On the man's right sat a slender woman, elegantly fitted in a long-sleeved, red-colored dress, embellished with gold embroidered highlights. The complexion of her oval face was darker than the man's, and a weaved gold band delicately intertwined golden-brown hair that touched her shoulders. Several large emeralds draped around her neck on a wisp of silver. Her bright green eyes glanced from the conversation before her to the new arrivals.

On the man's left sat a younger woman wearing a similar green uniform, without the sash. Two silver dots glistened from the collar. Her eyes, face, and complexion were younger versions of the other woman. Light-brown hair was pulled back loosely, a gold band holding it just above the shoulders. Focused on the conversation with the woman in front of her, her eyes only briefly shifted towards the double doors when they opened.

The black-haired woman—her hands fully engaged with the conversation—did not turn to see who had entered. She was dressed in dark-chocolate-colored pants with a matching light jacket and black boots that covered her calves.

Eldon walked between the tables that stood to the left and right of the entrance, circling left towards the dais while the others followed. The ornate doors silently slid closed behind them.

Allowing a respectable distance between himself and the woman talking, Eldon stopped about twenty feet from the dais and gave a small bow. "Your Majesty, Emperor Pherez, forgive the interruption. I was informed to come in immediately."

The black-haired woman turned. Her eyebrows rose, her mouth gaping open. Casey's jaw dropped, and Heather gasped. James's exclamation, "What the—" was cut short by the woman's excited, "Heather!"

Leila ran over and embraced Heather, who responded stiffly. "I'm so glad you guys escaped. My dad wanted me on his ship before anything happened, and he wasn't convinced you guys weren't dangerous. Then—" Her voice cut out. Her gaze dropped as she let go of Heather. "It's good to see you. I hoped maybe you'd found a way home."

"Leila," said Heather, her voice vacillating "is it really you? I mean, how'd you get here? Why are you here?"

Leila was about to respond when Eldon interrupted with a forceful clearing of his throat. "Ahem. My ladies, there will be time later to talk, and a more appropriate place to do so. At this moment there is more pressing business."

Heather's face flushed, and Leila took a step back.

Counselor Eldon bowed towards the dais. "Your Majesties Emperor Pherez and Empress Diantha, and Your Highness Princess Rhyaa, it is my pleasure to present to you Lady Kathera, daughter of Brihili Llyr of the Chahuru House." Kathera gave a modest bow. "Her cousin Amnor"—Amnor bowed towards the dais—"and the crew of the

Shaina Ariana, Lady Heather, Captain Casey, and his brother and first officer, James." Heather stifled a snort.

The emperor brought his chin down in a slow nod towards each person when they were introduced. The empress studied Kathera carefully.

Rhyaa smiled at Kathera, and her eyes sparkled when the *Shaina Ariana* was mentioned. Her mouth started to open, then shut to keep from speaking out of turn.

Turning towards the group, Eldon spoke. "Lady Kathera, Amnor, and crew of the *Shaina Ariana*, it is my great honor to introduce His Majesty, the Emperor Pherez, his wife, the Empress Diantha, and their daughter, the Princess Rhyaa."

Kathera bowed nearly to her waist; Casey and the others followed her cue.

Eldon was about to continue speaking when the emperor stood. Eldon remained silent while Pherez stepped down from the dais and walked towards the group, his eyes assessing each person. After a moment of studying Kathera, his eyes brightened, and his mouth hinted at a smile. The emperor placed his hand on her shoulder and pulled her into a warm embrace. "Welcome home, Lady Kathera. I know it is long past, but I still grieve the loss of your mother." Stepping back from the embrace, Kathera choked on a nod and simply bowed again.

Pherez nodded an acknowledgment towards Amnor, Heather, and James. His gaze then shifted from the sword handle to Casey's face. After a moment, his head bowed in a brief nod to Casey, and he returned to his chair.

Looking at his guests, the emperor's eyes narrowed in seriousness. He leaned forward and said, "There will be time for reunions and casual talk later. Counselor Eldon, it would appear that our guests already know Lady K'reina, though by a different name. However, while you may not remember her, you know her father, and you may recall the report of her being lost to space about ten years ago." Eldon nodded. "Her father brought her here just a short time before your guests arrived."

The emperor raised his right hand to silence any questions. "Before we get into the whys and hows of all of you being here, it is my understanding that Lady Kathera has some vitally important information for me."

Eldon nodded. "That is correct. It confirms some intelligence we received and may provide additional information. However, it would be prudent to first dismiss Lady K'reina."

"Lady K'reina," said Emperor Pherez, "my counselor is correct. I look forward to hearing more of your account." His brows rose as he looked at Heather. "Along with how it is all of you came to know each other and ended up here."

Leila bowed, a thin smile partially restrained on her lips. "It would be a pleasure to share the story with you, Your Majesty." She gave Heather another quick hug. Then she surprised Casey with a brief embrace and whispered in his ear, "Thank you for keeping us safe, and for helping me get back home."

"Um, sure. I'm glad you got home."

Leila's eyes twinkled in amusement at Casey's confusion. He watched her quickly walk between the pool and table and pause at the door while it opened. She took a couple steps into the open doorway and stopped again, uncertain. She rocked back, partially turning, like she might walk back into the room. Then she shook her head, continued through the open doorway, and into the short corridor. Behind her, the double doors silently slid shut.

Eldon's right hand gestured to Kathera. "My lady."

"Yes, sir," said Kathera. Her attention turned to the dais. "Emperor Pherez, without relating the whole story at this time, the sum of it is, when Casey and I were rescuing his companions on El'Tagath, we overheard a conversation about a plot to kill you. We later met up with Amnor, who works as a spy within El'Kanah's imperial guard and who has been providing valuable information to those resisting El'Kanah's rule. Amnor confirmed the plot to assassinate you, the empress, and the princess within the next few days. He insisted that the details of the plot should be shared with as few as possible and asked to tell you personally."

The emperor nodded, his face solemn. "The fewer ears that know a plan, the fewer lips to spoil it. Amnor, this is a safe place. My personal guards assigned to this room are highly trusted. This room is as secure as any place in the palace complex, perhaps even more so since sensitive matters of the empire and diplomacy with allies are conducted here. I assume your friends are welcome to remain if they already know some parts of the plot. If it'd be better for them to leave, we can excuse them."

Amnor's head cocked slightly at his companions. A momentary hesitation twitched his brow when he looked at Kathera; his mouth started to open, then closed. His eyes shifted back to Eldon and Pherez. "Emperor Pherez, Counselor Eldon, you are correct. My companions are welcome to hear what I have to say now, if they choose to stay. It is probably just as well that they are here."

"Very well. If any of you choose to leave, you are free to do so," replied Emperor Pherez.

Casey barely heard the emperor—his mind still juggling that Kathera seemed to be somehow related to royalty and Leila was at Natheri—when he saw a slight movement in the corner of his eye. He turned towards the double doors and saw the guard on the right slowly shifting his hands on his short rifle. The movement stopped almost as quickly as Casey turned. He pretended to look back at the dais—briefly noting Amnor watching him—but kept his peripheral focused on the guard. The guard's right hand continued its slow movement, repositioning itself on the grip and trigger. The left hand held something under the rifle's forestock.

Pivoting to the double doors, Casey shouted, "Stop!"

Chapter Forty-Nine
The Hornet Nest

T HE GUARD SNAPPED HIS hand to the right and sent a small black sphere flying to the back of the room. At the same time, he leveled the rifle barrel at the emperor.

Casey's outburst startled everyone. Pherez shifted back in his chair just as a red bolt of energy tore through the air. The plasma ripped into the emperor's upper left shoulder instead of the heart. Pherez dove forward, rolling to the ground, right before another energy bolt burst into his chair.

At the banner end of the room, an explosion rocked the room with a shock wave. Kathera, Amnor, James, and Heather were sent sprawling forward to the floor. Eldon tumbled face-first, his head bouncing against the marble-like surface. Casey stumbled forward, his hands out, and tucked into a roll.

The empress screamed. Rhyaa yanked her mother's arm and shoved her to the floor, taking cover behind the curved table on their left. A plasma burst seared Diantha's right arm in her stumble and fall behind the council table.

Casey was back on his feet and spun towards the banner wall. The back end of the room was blackened and banners were shredded. The six guards on the wall, along with the two closest guards on each adjacent wall, were down. Near Casey, Amnor jumped up from the floor and sprinted towards the wall opposite the door where the two center guards were dazed from the explosion.

A superheated bolt of energy burned into Rhyaa's right arm when she dove after her mother. Seconds later, a storm of red energy blasts strafed the dais side of the room, killing all six imperial guards.

Kathera, James, and Heather stumbled from the floor and lunged towards the council table on their right for cover. The traitorous guard aimed at the three guards between him and the dais. Casey whipped out the Night Blade—its extended edge lighting with a crisp blue flame—and charged.

The assassin fired the short rifle while he freed and fired his sidearm. Bullets and plasma tore into the imperial guards. Seeing Casey's charge, the assassin turned and fired. Casey dove left and felt the plasma burn past.

A chaotic eruption of energy and projectiles flurried across the room. Burn spots smoldered on walls where plasma bolts missed their mark, and pockmarks erupted across the room's walls.

Casey rolled out from the dive into a kneeling stance and quickly reorientated himself. To his right, James was sprinting towards the assassin. A plasma charge from behind nipped James's left side, and he flailed to the floor. His less-than-graceful roll knocked his head against the inside wall of the marble table. Casey's breath caught when his brother didn't move. Near the dais, energy bolts chased after Heather and Kathera as they jumped, slid across the tabletop, and dropped to cover on the other side where the imperial family was hiding. To Casey's right, on the wall opposite the door, two more guards had fallen and Amnor was aiming a short rifle across the room.

Casey's attention reverted to the assassin. His instinct brought the Night Blade up in a high front block. Bright red plasma dissipated against the shimmering blue sword. Less than twenty feet in front of him, behind the crystalline faceplate, the edges of the assassin's mouth frowned briefly before smiling with deranged certainty. With the blade in front of him, Casey cautiously stepped towards the assassin, expecting more energy blasts. The assassin's eyes narrowed on his smug face while he lowered his firearms and waited.

The imperial guards on the door's wall fired at the assassin. At that moment, from across the room, red-orange bursts erupted around and through the guards. One collapsed into a heap. A second attempted to dive forward, but a plasma bolt blew through his right shoulder. He spun around and released his gun, which slid across the tabletop and fell off the other side into the center of the room. The guard lay crumpled near the table, his gloved hand clutching his upper arm below a smoldering pit in the right shoulder armor. The remaining guard had evaded the energy bolts and crouched behind the quarter-circle table, uncertain of where the new attack had come from.

The assassin's attention diverged from Casey to the palace guards behind him. Eying the crouched guard, the assassin dispatched a double plasma burst. The guard slumped forward, smoke drifting up from his armor.

Seeing an opportunity, Casey sprinted at the assassin. He thrust the Night Blade in an attempt to catch the assassin off guard. With the ease and skill of a master martial artist, the assassin sidestepped the thrust without even turning to face Casey.

Surprised at his opponent's unexpected move, Casey's momentum carried him too far forward. He pivoted to face his opponent when something smashed into his lower right leg. Pain ripped up his body, and a powerful second kick slammed into his chest. He toppled backwards and crashed under the table at the door's right. He rolled weakly to his left side, the Night Blade—its flame extinguished—held loosely. Struggling, Casey lifted his head and, through blurred vision, watched the assassin turn away and casually stroll towards the dais.

Where's the other attacker? Casey wondered while he shifted position and squinted to focus.

Behind the curved council table at the opposite corner of the room, Casey watched three shadows moving slowly. Booted feet between the table and dais slid back behind cover. His fuzzy vision moved right along the wall to the table across from him. Two guards exchanged fire with Amnor, who was crouching defensively behind the table.

Casey's mind felt muddled with confusion. Then his head shook at the realization that Amnor was a traitor and had not only led them into the trap but used them as part of the plan.

A plasma bolt streaked from the opposite side of the room and took down one guard. The side attack distracted the second guard, and he fell under Amnor's plasma burst.

Casey gritted his teeth and pushed himself up to a sitting position. His lower right leg was swollen, hot, and radiated throbs of pain. His blurred vision and brain fog actively opposed his attempts to focus. He tried to stand, but his right leg screamed its refusal to hold even part of his weight. Through the mental fog he saw the assassin slowly walk along the back of the curved table, pause a couple times to shoot a target across the room, and stop by each fallen palace guard to unleash another plasma burst into the body.

Casey's throat tightened. On the pool-side of the table, just below the assassin's line of sight and barely concealed by the tabletop, crouched his brother. Conscious once more, James cautiously retrieved the guard's rifle that had dropped to the floor near him. James aimed at the opposite corner of the room and fired. Amnor ducked behind the table as the energy blast missed him.

The assassin rounded the table that shielded James and zeroed in on the dais. His mouth twisted in evil pleasure, seeming to relish the thought of finishing off the imperial family hidden behind the next table.

Hints of shadows behind the table inched away from the approaching killer.

Heather and Kathera, each holding plasma rifles, bobbed above the tabletop and fired at the approaching assassin. Next to them, Rhyaa appeared holding a narrow, double-barreled handgun. Her eyes squinted through burning pain while she steadied her aim and fired at Amnor. The tiny explosive projectile blew apart the table corner, and Amnor dove under cover to dodge the assailing fragments.

Heather and Kathera's plasma bolts pounded the assassin's chest plate and instantly burned through the armor. The assassin stood unfazed and defiant while smoke snaked up from the holes. He casually fired three plasma bolts. Heather and Kathera barely ducked beneath the marble table when two plasma bursts exploded off the polished surface.

Rhyaa's focus on Amnor blinded her to the assassin's attack, and the third plasma bolt whipped across her back. She shrieked, curled into a ball, and dropped behind the table.

Heather's gun reappeared and hastily retaliated against the assassin. A wicked smile lifted the assassin's mouth while the energy simply washed around him in flashing arcs.

Casey struggled to rise while dizziness threatened to take him back down. His eyesight cleared enough to witness the assassin take three more direct plasma hits like they were no more irritating than a bucket of water splashing on him. Casey blinked and squeezed his eyes shut, inhaled and exhaled slowly, and willed his sight to clear. For an instant, the cacophony was silenced. Opening his eyes, he realized none of the palace guards were left standing.

Forty feet in front of Casey, James crouched in front of the curved table, the butt of the short-barreled rifle snug into his shoulder, his eyes scouring the room. A flash of plasma burst from the rifle and Casey turned right in response to a yelp of pain. Behind the next table Amnor was backing towards the wall, clutching his arm gingerly against his abdomen as a rifle lay smoldering on the floor.

Behind James's table, the assassin stood and waited for something. The once-green palace uniform was now black, tattered, and smoldering. It had the look of the undead with wisps of smoke curling up from the charred clothing. Through the crystalline faceplate, the assassin's expression was amused—like a cat holding the tail of a mouse, waiting for it to make a move—while he toyed with the two women who shot at him. To Casey, he seemed too calm, like he expected something to happen. Casey moved his left leg to take more weight so he could stand, then he noticed his brother.

On the other side of the desk, still hidden from the assassin's line of sight by the marble council table, James shifted his body as if readying to attack. Casey was trying to read his brother's next move when James leaped to his feet and dove headfirst over the table at the assassin. The assassin's dark eyes narrowed, and his mouth stretched into a smug smile, revealing he had expected the attack. James flailed in a complete miss when the assassin skewed back in a right twist. James crashed to the floor when the assassin's short rifle whacked across his back.

He rolled on the floor, sprang to his feet, and threw several punches. Each fist met air as the killer ducked and dodged. The two opponents half-circled, assessing each other.

The assassin held his guns like melee weapons and appeared uninterested in using them for their primary purpose. He swung the rifle. James ducked right and under the makeshift club but failed to avoid the assassin's handgun that smashed across his jaw. A follow-up side kick launched James back across the tabletop, and he fell into the center of the room in a barely moving heap.

The calculating eyes of the assassin scanned the next desk—which concealed the imperial family—and narrowed when Heather's and Kathera's heads ducked out of view. His cold eyes swept back to the center of the room. A chill gripped Casey's spine when the eyes locked on him. Turning around, the assassin walked back behind the previous table and returned to the large doors. He paused between the two tables nearest the doorway and set his guns down. His black eyes glared his intent at Casey: after James, Casey would be next. He no longer wanted quick kills. He wanted those who messed up his plans to suffer a painful death.

In front of the dais, Casey saw movement. Several yards past James, Eldon had rotated to his side and was forcefully pushing himself up to a kneeling position. The assassin's head tilted to assess Eldon's threat, and then he continued towards James, who struggled to rise from the floor.

Chapter Fifty

Final Blows

James turned his head right, in time to see a foot arcing up into his face. He twisted left, and air from the assassin's boot waved his hair. The foot came back down, heel first, into his right shoulder, and he slammed face-first into the floor. James lay motionless.

Panic gripped Casey's chest, and he renewed his attempts to get off the floor. He tried shifting his full weight to the left foot to stand, but the right leg felt like something had bitten into it and would not let go of the floor.

Just beyond James, Eldon stood shakily and faced the assassin. His forceful voice wavered briefly while he steadied himself. "You dare betray your emperor." His hands began to move fluidly across his body like he was beginning a Tai Chi form.

The assassin smirked at Eldon. "He was never my emperor."

Eldon's left hand swept down towards the pool in the center of the room, arced upwards, and then cut straight across his chest in a knife hand towards the assassin. A jet of water rocketed from the pool and slammed the assassin to the floor. He leaped back to his feet and was hit by a fast-flying fist of water across his face shield, sending him reeling to the ground. Eldon's third set of movements froze the water jets into icy shards that lanced across the room and into the assassin while he tried to stand. Most of the icicles smashed harmlessly against the armor, but scarlet trickled under the clear face shield where some icy projectiles had breached.

Eldon began another form when a blinding flash of energy burst from the side and burned into his left arm. A second bolt lanced his left leg, and he collapsed into the puddles of water.

On his far right, Casey saw another assault rifle trembling in Amnor's armored hands. Casey's eyes darted around him, but no firearms were within reach.

Energy bursts flashed towards Amnor. The rifle dropped to the floor when one bolt seared his left arm and sent him scrambling behind the table.

From behind the council table, Heather and Kathera charged the assassin. The killer stood calmly with a mocking smile while the two women circled him. Kathera shifted her grip on the short rifle into a club-like hold. As Heather feinted a couple of jabs, Kathera swung the rifle at him from behind. He read the feints and easily ducked under the rifle. He glared menacingly at Kathera and, without missing a beat, weaved his body to avoid a roundhouse kick from Heather.

Straightening, the assassin's right fist snapped under Kathera's jaw and jerked her head back. His foot then slammed into her abdomen, doubling her over and backwards while she gasped for breath.

Heather launched a double jump kick at the assassin's side. Dodging the first foot, the assassin's face accidentally ducked into the second, cracking the face shield. Stepping back, he rubbed gloved fingers against the broken faceplate while his grim smile returned. Kathera chambered a side kick that caught only air when the assassin pivoted away. The two women released a series of attacks from two sides while their target bobbed left and right, undulating in and out of strikes and kicks like a snake, always seeming to slip out of reach. In between their attacks, the assassin blocked and feinted quick punches, toying with his opponents.

In an explosion of adrenalin, Kathera's left knee pumped up and launched her into a high jump kick. The assassin tilted his head away while his left hand intercepted, caught, and used the kick's momentum to pull Kathera. Twisting to the side, he caught his hand under her thigh and threw the kick's energy away from him. Kathera yelped as she was thrown like a rag doll. Crashing onto the floor, she slid across the puddles and slammed into the ledge of the pool. The water running over the sides began soaking her unmoving body.

Heather took advantage of the throw and exploded a side kick into the assassin's back. He rolled forward and sprung back to his feet, spinning around to face Heather in time for her hammer fist to smash into the side of his neck. The assassin staggered back, his stumble turning into a sprint towards his guns.

Heather was on him when he reached the table. His hand grabbed the short rifle and swung it around at Heather. Her left leg launched upwards in a roundhouse that sent the rifle flying from the assassin's grip and skidding across the center floor. The assassin twisted back. His knuckles smashed across Heather's cheek, and a front kick discharged into her chest. She tumbled, rolled back, and crumpled motionless several feet from James's body.

Casey felt helpless watching the assassin toss his brother and friends around the room. The killer turned and walked back to the table to retrieve his handgun. Casey's grip tightened around the Night Blade, his jaw clenching as his focus narrowed in on the assassin, and he forced himself to stand.

The assassin grabbed the gun's grip and lifted it from the table. Turning right, he took one step forward and pointed the handgun at Heather.

Casey lunged the remaining distance. A blue flame flared along the Night Blade as it silently cut through the air and hissed through the gun. The gun's barrel clanked to the floor and rolled away. Dropping the gun's remnants, the assassin jumped back, his black eyes wide in surprise.

The tip of the Night Blade leveled at the assassin's throat while Casey stole a glance at Heather. She lay twisted on the floor, unmoving except for shallow breaths. His attention returned to the assassin.

Reaching behind his lower back, the assassin's hands withdrew narrow daggers, their foot-long silver blades tinted a sickly green. His eyes narrowed to slits as he cautiously edged towards Casey, daggers angled forward like long teeth.

The right dagger lunged at Casey, and his torso pulled back to dodge the bite. Expecting a secondary attack, his sword blocked up and right where it deflected a left dagger thrust. Blue sparks crackled at the green hues when the two weapons clashed. The first dagger flashed. Casey's head tilted right, and the slender blade hissed by his ear. He lunged and was parried by down-crossed daggers. The crossed short blades slid up the flaming sword, and he jumped back as the daggers sliced at his shirt. His right leg complained angrily at the abuse, and his jaw clenched tighter in response. The Night Blade tapped aside a right-handed thrust and countered with a cut to the assassin's forearm. The sword edge glanced off amid bluish sparks, and a piece of burning uniform sleeve fell away to reveal a forearm shield. He whacked aside an upwards dagger thrust and parried left to block the second dagger.

With his right leg numb and the left wobbling at the extra strain, he slowly stepped backwards towards the center of the room.

A crooked smile complemented the assassin's cracked faceplate, and the fury in his eyes burned. Sensing a change in his foe, the killer pressed on Casey's retreat as they exchanged feints, thrusts, blocks, and cuts to test each other's defenses.

Stepping backwards to dodge another green-tinted cut, Casey's right foot rolled, the ankle twisting on something. Tears flooded his eyes at the pain that tore up his right side. Out of the corner of his eye, the end of a gun barrel rolled away.

Instantly two daggers pounced on him like dragon fangs. He swept the blade up and deflected the right dagger from penetrating his chest. His right side collapsed when the left dagger bit into his shoulder.

The assassin yanked the blade from the wound. Casey jerked with the extraction and buckled to his right knee. The strength from his right side drained, and the Night Blade drooped to the floor. Tears burned his eyes, transforming the killer into a dark blur swirling in watery depths.

Not far away, Casey, through his blurred vision, saw the bodies of his brother, Heather, and Kathera lying still, scattered around the center of the room. *I'm sorry*, he thought, *I failed you*.

The assassin chambered both daggers for a final strike.

Shards of blue crystal exploded in a torrential downpour. Streaks of light and color flashed, reflected, and refracted around the room in a dizzying array. Momentarily disoriented by the sound and brilliance, the assassin hesitated in his lunge.

Seeing the blur's movement, Casey shifted left and up to his good leg. His wrists whipped the sword blade across him in a rising cut. The blade edge struck the assassin's right forearm shield that had dropped low in the failed lunge. The blue-flamed blade slid up the shield and sliced neatly through the right arm below the bicep. The assassin howled and staggered back as his cauterized forearm dropped to the ground.

Casey shifted left again, his right side screaming at every movement and threatening rebellion. He blinked rapidly and squinted through the tears to clear his vision. The assassin had stumbled back several yards and held the stump of his right arm tightly against his abdomen. Heat from a plasma bolt seared the back of Casey's left shoulder. He turned. Amnor stood inside the segmented circle of tables, a plasma rifle delicately supported between his injured limbs.

A shout called from above. "Watch out!"

Casey whipped around to see a glinting object spinning towards him. A shrill *ching* reverberated as he snapped the Night Blade up and deflected the flying dagger. An explosion from somewhere behind him jostled him forward.

Without pause, the assassin stooped to the floor and snapped up the other dagger from his severed arm. With rage-filled eyes the assassin snaked the single dagger forward. Casey skipped the Night Blade into middle guard and readied himself for a final attack.

A small explosion detonated behind the assassin and shoved him forward to the floor. Casey's head tilted down as he braced against the concussive force.

The assassin's single dagger-encumbered hand failed to catch his fall and he fell onto the green-tinted blade. Lying face down, the assassin tried, and failed, to remove his hand from under his chest.

Casey blinked to clear his eyes and stared at the assassin struggling on the floor, the end of the slender blade protruding from between the left shoulder and spine. The body convulsed for a couple seconds.

Then movement ceased. Remembering his other opponent, he spun around quickly. Twenty feet behind him, Amnor lay dazed against the nearest desk, the blackened remains of a small explosion darkening the floor in front of him.

Leila's voice called down from the ceiling, "Casey, you okay?"

Casey looked up. Forty feet above him, Leila peered down through the shattered remains of the crystal skylight. In her hands was a slender long-barreled handgun. Two palace guards stood to her left, each apprehensively pointing the muzzles of their short assault rifles down into the room's chaos.

Leila's gun began to point behind Casey when a half dozen wild plasma bolts strafed the crystalline remains near her. She stumbled back out of sight with an agonized cry. An energy blast blew through the face shield of one guard, and he fell backwards from view. A second bolt clipped the remaining guard's right shoulder, and his rifle fell from his hands, splashing in the pool below. The guard grasped his shoulder and dropped out of sight.

Casey whipped around to see Amnor precariously swivel a plasma rifle at him. Returning the Night Blade to middle guard position, Casey stepped towards Amnor.

Bright flashes of energy shot from the rifle. Casey deftly angled the sword, and blue flames licked across the blade while it absorbed the incoming blast. Amnor's eyes widened. He fired a second shot, and the energy bolt flew harmlessly past its target.

Casey continued towards Amnor. A better-aimed shot was again absorbed by the Night Blade. Amnor attempted to scoot back but was blocked by the marble table. Casey stepped into point-blank range. Amnor squeezed the trigger as the Night Blade sliced through the rifle. The rifle remnants dropped from his injured hands, and Amnor's eyes desperately searched the room for options. Casey lowered the tip of the Night Blade's flame to hover at Amnor's chest while perspiration glistened on his face.

Casey's eyes narrowed at his former ally. Adrenaline urged him forward, but he held his ground. "Why?"

Amnor gritted his teeth in a defiant smile. "It was part of my mission."

"Mission?" Casey's head cocked curiously. "What's the other part?"

"Doesn't matter now. Someone else will finish it."

"I'm sure the Rayneiri can convince you to tell them."

One corner of Amnor's mouth curled. "Not likely. Unless they can speak to the dead."

Amnor clenched his teeth hard and jerked his jaw quickly to the side. His limbs became like gelatin, and his body slumped. His head struggled to lift and turn towards Casey. The cold hardness in his face was gone, and sadness replaced the defiance. He fought to pronounce his words. "Tell Kathera—I never—wanted to hurt—her. That—that—I did this—for—our—family's honor. Tell Amnah—" His eyes glazed over as the last barely audible word escaped his final exhale, his head drooping against his chest, lifeless.

The Night Blade lowered, its tip barely off the floor. The blue flames winked out.

Chapter Fifty-One
Old Horizons

THE OVERSIZED DOUBLE DOORS of the council chamber blew apart. Twenty imperial guards poured in and froze at the unexpected disaster. Burn marks pocked the floors, walls, ceiling, and curved council desks. Smoke smoldered from chairs. A piece of crystal dropped from the shattered skylight and clinked against the floor near the center pool. Scattered around the room lay the crumpled bodies of imperial guards, their uniforms charred, armor burned from plasma blasts.

In the center of the room, several bodies were littered around the pool where puddles of water covered the floor and shards of ice melted. Shallow breathing and small movements indicated most were still holding on to life. Only two were lifeless. One lay face down, clothed in carbonized remains of an imperial guard uniform. The point of a dagger protruded from the upper left back, and a severed forearm lay on the floor nearby. Against the council desk on the opposite side of the room, the other lifeless body looked like it had collapsed in on itself.

Standing near the second body was one of the newcomers, a narrow-bladed, black sword hanging low in his grip. Casey had turned abruptly towards the paralyzed guards when the doors burst open, but his shoulders slumped as his somber face returned to what lay before him on the floor. Slashes of red colored his tan shirt, and the fabric of the left shoulder was seared. Black-and-blue bulges were manifesting themselves on his face and exposed skin while his chest labored in breathing.

The other newcomers were scattered around the pool. Not far from the center, James struggled to push himself up. Bruises colored his face, and he rubbed his jaw tenderly. Nearby, Heather was slowly untwisting herself, closing her eyes and breathing slowly with each move. Next to a council table on the right lay Kathera. Her eyes tightened and relaxed while she gingerly caressed her left side.

Not far away, Counselor Eldon grimaced in pain while he rolled himself over and sat up. A black-blue lump deformed his left cheek and reached its ugly color into his hairline. Blood pooled under his left eye where the swelling increased. Seeing the palace guards, his tension eased.

A junior officer, one with a single silver dot on the lapels of his palace uniform, recovered first. He yelled at Casey to drop the weapon. Exhausted, the sword slid from Casey's tired fingers to the floor, and he struggled to lift his hands above his head. The officer barked orders at two guards to take Casey into custody and commanded eight others to find the emperor. He directed the remaining guards to check everyone in the room and locate anyone needing medical attention. The officer then called on his transmitter for assistance.

The eight guards quickly located the emperor on the floor behind a council desk near the dais. He was trying to stand while his right hand held a crude bandage—made from torn clothing—over his left shoulder. The bandage poorly covered the congealed blood, blackened uniform, and burned skin. His face was bruised. Nearby, the empress was lying unceremoniously on the floor, unconscious but breathing. Princess Rhyaa shakily raised her gun at the soldiers when they rounded the table, but quickly lowered it. She pulled herself up next to her father to convince him to sit back down.

The two guards assigned to Casey cautiously approached him, shifting their focus from him to the bodies around the room. When he did nothing to oppose their advance, they grasped his arms and yanked them down behind his back. His right leg collapsed, dropping him to his knees, and they shoved him to the ground.

"Stop!" called out a strained voice. It deepened into a commanding resonance and repeated, "I said stop."

Everyone's attention shifted towards the emperor. He stood behind a council table, his hands shaking while they pressed against the tabletop. Next to him, Princess Rhyaa equally tried to support herself and her father. Guards stood nearby, uncertain how to help.

"Release him and return his sword." The emperor's voice wavered while his body swayed. "He, and his friends, are the reason we are alive."

The guards released Casey's arms. One guard reached down to retrieve the sword. Casey shifted back from his knees to sit while dizziness rushed him. His face dropped between his upraised knees, his hands covering his head. The guard stood, leaving the sword on the ground, and stepped back, unsure what to do.

Another dozen soldiers rushed into the room along with ten healers and their attendants. The junior officer directed five healers to the emperor and his family, and the rest to the other survivors.

James had crawled over to Heather and was talking quietly to her when two healers and their attendants approached them. Another healer knelt beside Kathera and examined her side and wounds. Eldon wobbled when he tried to stand, and a healer and two guards convinced him to sit.

The healers quickly assessed injuries and directed their attendants in applying different salves and balms from leather-like bags. On or around some injuries, the healers would gently massage or manipulate the wounded tissue, ligaments, or bones. Wraps and bandages were applied to retain the ointments or to immobilize injuries.

The fifth healer, a woman with graying hair, but whose face retained a youthful vibrance, knelt next to Casey with her attendant. Her head tilted to the side curiously while she examined him. The charred remains of the shirt's left shoulder fell away when she moved it aside. Her eyes opened wide, and then her head moved questioningly from side to side while she lifted the burned and torn shirt to examine the skin beneath. She shook her head again. Her trained eyes then scanned his face. She nodded to her attendant, who opened the brown duffel-like bag and pulled out a small jar. Casey watched, exhausted but curious, while the healer applied a creamy tan ointment to the bruising and cuts on his face. The balm numbed his injuries almost as quickly as it was applied, and a citrus-like scent lifted his mood.

An insistent female voice echoed from the small entry hall into the council room. "You've got to let me in. My friends are in there!"

A deeper voice followed, "K'reina, I told you to wait for me. Officer, you can let her in."

A second later Leila rushed into the room followed by a palace guard. She noticed Casey sitting near the pool while a healer treated him. He looked up and smiled weakly, nodding in her direction. Her mouth thinned in a smile, and she nodded in return. Then she saw Heather and James and rushed over to them. Kneeling between the healers, she embraced Heather while James put an arm around her. The healer's attendant, who was helping to treat James and Heather, urged Leila to sit while indicating cuts on her face needed care.

The junior officer walked around the room trying to piece together what had happened. He stopped by Casey while the healer continued applying the salve to his face, then examined the two dead bodies on the floor. He had seen one, the crumpled body, with the group that had arrived with Kathera and wondered, *Was he the cause of this mess?* With the fallen imperial guard face down, and palace uniform and armor severely burned, there was nothing recognizable about the body. Any one of the plasma blasts on the torso could have been the cause of death, but the dagger pointing out his back seemed to be the final stroke. The officer used his boot to turn the dead guard over and stumbled back in surprise.

The face of the palace guard was distorted, like it had lost its normal underlying bone structure. Muscles and small bones had shifted, giving the face a loose, undefined look. The skin color was light gray with an almost translucent hue. The junior officer shook his head in disbelief when he realized what he was seeing. A hushed word came out, barely above a whisper: "Skinwalker."

The healer examined Casey's right shoulder and frowned. Casey noticed the stab wound was frothing around the edges. Not waiting for her attendant, the healer grabbed and opened a black glass jar from her bag. Using a thin metal spatula-like device, she dipped out a red gel and smothered it into the wound. Casey grimaced and felt a coolness soak into his shoulder. While the attendant began wrapping the shoulder, the healer's attention turned to Casey's right leg. She moved the shredded pant leg, and Casey's mouth clenched, his eyes tightening shut when pain ripped up his side. The woman smiled with a nod, and then expertly slit the pant leg with small shears to expose the multi-hued and swollen leg. With Casey's adrenaline exhausted, the woman's slightest brush brought tears to his eyes, and he fought back by clenching his teeth even harder. The healer placed one hand just above the knee and the other below.

Casey closed his eyes tightly, tears squeezing from the eyelids. Focusing on breathing, he became aware of a warmth pulsing into his right leg. Reluctantly, he opened his eyes. He half-expected to see a heating device on his leg, but he saw only the healer focused intently on her hands and his leg. She moved her fingers slowly above, below, and around the knee, and then proceeded up and down the leg. He raised an eyebrow at the woman, but her focus remained on the work of her hands.

While the tears cleared from his eyes, Casey looked around the room and noticed a couple of the other healers also with their hands performing massage or manipulative movements on their patients. The tension in Eldon's face faded and his breathing relaxed when his healer touched his plasma burn.

The rushed sounds of footwear on the floor broke the relative silence of the room, and a woman—wearing a pressed green uniform with two silver dots on her lapels—ran into the council chambers. She stopped and tensed at the unexpected destruction. For a moment she hesitated, her body tilting forward and back, unsure how to proceed.

Across the room, a master healer attended Emperor Pherez while he sat on a chair near the dais. The healer applied a poultice to the emperor's burn and wrapped it. Other healers were attending the empress, princess, Counselor Eldon, and the others in the room. The officer took a few reluctant steps towards the emperor, then paused mid-stride, uncertain, when she realized dead bodies littered the room.

The emperor looked towards her. She immediately bowed. "Your Majesty, forgive the abruptness of this intrusion. We just finishing decrypting the transmission we intercepted a couple days ago." She shifted her weight, trying to compose herself amid the chaos. "And there's a part that requires your urgent and immediate consideration."

Eldon leaned against the inside edge of a council table while a healer finished wrapping his wounds. "Officer Gersemi, can't this wait for us to get things back in order? If your intelligence report is about the invasion, we already know about it, and we should have some time to prepare for it."

The woman shook her head vigorously. "No, sir. This is not about the invasion." Her face reddened. "I didn't know we'd received more intelligence on that. This transmission was sent from the Erlendr Cluster and coded with extreme urgency."

"Astronomy was never my strong point." The emperor grimaced as the healer treated another burn. "I'll admit to not being familiar with that star cluster."

Eldon's eyebrows rose in disbelief. He studied the woman curiously and asked, "Are you certain it's from the Erlendr Cluster? What is the message, and who was it sent to?"

"There is no data indicating who the message was sent to." The woman's feet shifted nervously, and she lifted a small octagonal ring in her palm. A dim light emanated from the center. "It seems to be from the same location as the transmission we intercepted a few years ago. However, this message contains star coordinates and additional information about the planet. It's the only way we were convinced it came from where it seemed to originate. But, sir, the part that is most vital states: 'Heir to Mysian Empire confirmed and temporarily elusive. Waiting to find ship. Termination expected within seven days.' We don't know who the message is from."

She shook her head with a shiver. "Based on the content and old embedded signatures, our analysts suggest it may be from a

Hykosean assassin who disappeared at the time of the Mysian coup. The Hykosean was rumored to be a key part of the coup. At that time, our intelligence suggested—without proof—that the Mysian emperor's son, the mentioned heir, had somehow escaped the coup and assassination. It was postulated that the Hykosean was sent after the heir to finish the job, and make sure nobody could question Emperor El'Kanah's claim to the empire."

Eldon's eyebrows rose as he looked at the emperor, who mirrored his surprise. The counselor's voice was edged with exhaustion as he said, "Emperor Pherez, getting to the Erlendr Cluster might be impossible. But, if the legitimate heir is alive, this could be good news. It could prevent a war and restore peace to the systems."

"If"—Pherez stressed the word—"*if* the heir can be located and protected before he is killed in seven days."

"Your Majesty, that would be about four days from now," corrected the officer. Pink flushed her cheeks as she continued, "That is why I felt it was urgent to let you know."

Kathera brushed off her healer and stood. "Did I hear that right?" She took a few steps towards the officer and stopped by Casey. "That the Mysian heir, the one said to have been killed along with his father and family, but rumored to have escaped, is the one who was found?"

The communications officer cocked her head and studied Kathera while she extended her hand down to Casey.

"Yes, my lady, that is our understanding," said the officer.

Casey looked up at Kathera's outstretched hand. He turned towards the healer kneeling nearby, who returned a gentle smile and single nod at him. He retrieved the Night Blade lying nearby with his left hand while his right grasped Kathera's for assistance. His weight felt uneven on his right leg, but the pain was nearly gone. He touched the blade's switch, and the black scales slipped back into the handle, which he then secured against the sheath disk. Kathera tilted her head in an unspoken question. Casey nodded back. His wobble steadied, and he grinned at the healer, whose smile reminded him of a parent who knew something she was not sharing.

"Thank you. Not sure what you did, but it feels a lot better now." Then Casey looked at Kathera and shook his head. "I'm totally lost."

Kathera's brow rose. "Do you remember the conversation we had in the garden back on El'Tagath?"

Casey nodded.

"The reason El'Kanah is in power is because he somehow coordinated a coup that killed anyone other than himself who could lay claim to the empire. Remember, there was going to be a peace accord between the Mysian and Rayneiri Empires, with an arranged marriage between the oldest son and Princess Rhyaa."

At Kathera's reminder, Casey glanced at Rhyaa, whose face looked like it had tasted a lemon.

"Question," asked James from the floor where he still tenderly rubbed his jaw. "How exactly will finding this heir improve things? I mean, Altor has things pretty much locked up and under his control from what we experienced. How can it even be proved this 'heir' has the right to the empire?"

Kathera shook her head gently with mild exasperation, as if preparing to explain something that should be easily understood. "This heir has a legitimate right to the Mysian Empire, and his lineage can easily be proved by bloodstone. If he has the missing Mysian signet, or amulet, it would further legitimize his claim. Finding him, bringing him back, and exposing the current emperor as illegitimate should undermine El'Kanah's support, especially if we have the backing of the Rayneiri, and some of the other systems."

"I'm certain we will have allies for this," said Emperor Pherez. "El'Kanah is threatening other systems besides ours. The question remains, how are we going to find the heir and protect him in less than seven, I mean four, days?" He nodded at the intelligence officer. "And, hopefully, avert an invasion that will likely start a war?"

"Your Majesty"—Casey gritted his teeth when his right leg complained mildly—"the *Ariana* can take us wherever we need to go to find the heir. I offer my service to assist in this endeavor, although I promised first to return my brother and Heather back to our home planet."

"Casey, are you crazy?" James's tone was serious, but it was quickly betrayed by a grin. He grabbed a nearby tabletop to support his effort to stand. "You're not ditching me that easy."

"Nor me," added Heather. She grabbed James's offered hand to stand. "Although it'd be good to get a little better fixed up first. But we probably can't fix your stubbornness."

Leila stood, her head bowed to the emperor. "And if I can be of service, I offer my assistance as well."

A smile cracked Casey's dirt-and-sweat-encrusted face. "Guess we'll delay our return trip home. Where is it we need to go?"

The intelligence officer eagerly held out the small octagonal ring and moved her hand over it while her head shook in disbelief. "I'm not sure how you could possibly get there in such a short time, unless you know some jump gate shortcuts we're not aware of and take an extremely high-risk jump into dark space. For that matter, we're not entirely sure how the heir got there. However, the message does reference a one-way wormhole near the Mysian frontier that might be a possibility."

A 3D galactic image erupted from the ring, the arms of the spiral galaxy reaching out and hovering a couple feet above the woman's hand. "The message originated from a smaller planet in an outer system of the Erlendr Cluster. We're here"—she pointed at a small prick of light on one side of the galaxy—"and the Erlendr Cluster is over here." She touched a spot in one of the outer arms of the spiral galaxy. The image zoomed in towards a cluster of over fifty stars, continuing until a single star and its planetary system resolved in the air above the ring.

The officer continued, while her finger touched inside the floating image to further zoom in, "From what we know, it's a world with plenty of water and large land masses, and it's the third planet from its local star. As I mentioned, we're not entirely sure how the heir managed to get there. And, except for limited information in the transmission, we don't know much about the star system or planet."

The image zoomed in to a familiar blue-green planet with a single moon.

Casey's eyebrows rose, and he exchanged glances with the surprised faces of his brother, Heather, and Leila. He grinned at Officer Gersemi. "But we do."

End of book 1

Thank You!

Thank you for reading *Hunt for the Fallen Star*. With many other options to choose from, I appreciate your time reading my book.

If you enjoyed my book, please share it with others. A short review helps them discover this book, and it helps me as an author.

 Amazon
Create a Review Page
Hunt for the Fallen Star

Please go to Amazon, or wherever you purchased this book, and leave a review on the book's page.

 Amazon Book Page
Hunt for the Fallen Star
https://www.amazon.com/dp/1733018654

Everyone I know appreciates the recommendation of a trusted friend. Be that friend. Please let your friends know through social media, email, text, in person, or even a phone call.

Hope your day is fantastic, and thank you, again.

Christopher Cox

While I don't post very frequently, I have several social media pages where you can get more information and connect with me.

YOUTUBE

 GOODREADS

INSTAGRAM

 FACEBOOK

THREADS

 WEBSITE

NEWSLETTER SIGN-UP

Acknowledgements

First, I am grateful for my parents who were my fans when I first started writing stories in the second grade. They continue to be great examples to me and are wonderful grandparents to my children.

As the manuscript neared its final version, I am appreciative of Ramy Vance's insights and suggestions that furthered improved the story. He also referred me to his editor, Shavonne Clarke.

Shavonne's editorial staff at Motif Edits did wonders. Specifically, my thanks go to Kat for line editing and Caroline for proofreading.

I am grateful for my children and their enthusiastic support. I've read this book three times to them over the years, each time a little different as I tried to bring things together into the final version. They keep reminding me I need to get the next book finished so I can read it to them.

Finally, as mentioned in the book's dedication, I am most grateful for my dear wife, who continually encourages me in my writing, and is my greatest support. She's my sounding board for ideas, asks questions that make me think, and is my greatest cheerleader and fan. This book would still be "a work in progress" if it wasn't for her love, confidence in my writing, and persuasion to get it done.

About the Author

Prior to working in IT for 16+ years, Christopher instructed at a helicopter flight school, installed security systems, and directed eight seasons of youth high adventure camps.

He has several degrees, including a master's in cybersecurity. His first book, *Everyday Cybersecurity: A practical approach to understanding cybersecurity, security awareness, and protecting your personal information and identity*, was his master's capstone project.

He enjoys being in nature, particularly the mountains. He also likes rock climbing, shooting sports, technology, and spending time with his family.

Besides the United States, where he currently resides in Utah, he's lived in Chile and Australia. He's also visited Canada, Mexico, Argentina, Peru, China, and Mongolia.

He trains in Korean sword (Haidong Gumdo). He also takes classes in traditional taekwondo with his wife and kids.

Somewhere between work, family activities, church responsibilities, and home projects, he squeezes in creative and writing time.

Hunt for the Fallen Star is his first fiction book.

Everyday Cybersecurity: A practical approach to understanding cybersecurity, security awareness, and protecting your personal information and identity

While the title is a mouthful, this was written for non-technical users, normal people who value privacy and security but who aren't IT or technically savvy. Not only does it cover safe computer use, but also being secure online and the importance of physical security.

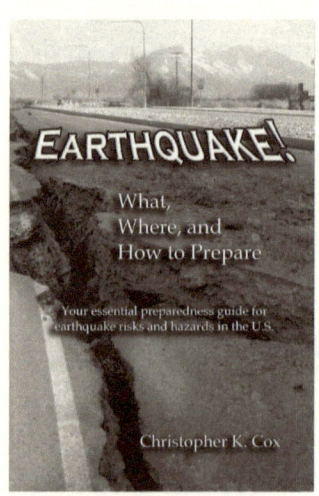

Earthquake! What, Where, and How to Prepare: Your essential preparedness guide for earthquake risks and hazards in the U.S.

Based on several earthquake preparedness presentations, there are three parts in this book. Part 1 covers the "What" about earthquakes, like an Earthquakes 101 section.

Part 2 dives into "Where" the risks and hazards are in the United States. Most of the United States has at least some earthquake risk.

Part 3 goes into the preparedness aspect with information and suggestions for being better prepared at home and work.

www.ingramcontent.com/pod-product-compliance
Lightning Source LLC
Chambersburg PA
CBHW050603170726
48283CB00001B/92